Praise for

'Creepy, clever and unnerving'

'I loved it... A fast-paced and smart thriller'

GILLIAN MCALLISTER

'Hugely enjoyed it'

STEVE CAVANAGH

'What an amazing, roller-coaster ride'

ELLY GRIFFITHS

'Powerful read'

MICK HERRON

'Smart, sassy and totally on point'

SARAH PINBOROUGH

'A fast-paced, unpredictable ride'

KATERINA DIAMOND

Angela Clarke is a best-selling novelist and screenwriter, happily living (and writing) in her 'apartmentini' in London. She's the author of crime thrillers and the humorous memoir Confessions of a Fashionista. Follow Me was named Amazon's Rising Star Debut January 2016, long listed for the Crime Writer's Association Dagger in the Library 2016, and short listed for the Dead Good Page Turner Award 2016. A sufferer of the rare genetic condition Ehlers Danlos Syndrome III, Angela is passionate about bringing disabled talent and stories to all.

Also by Angela Clarke

On My Life
Trust Me
Watch Me
Follow Me
Confessions of a Fashionista

THE ANNIVERSARY PARTY

ANGELA CLARKE

HODDER & STOUGHTON

First published in Great Britain in 2025 by Hodder & Stoughton Limited
An Hachette UK company

This paperback edition published in 2025

The authorised representative in the EEA is Hachette Ireland,
8 Castlecourt Centre, Dublin 15, D15 XTP3, Ireland (email: info@hbgi.ie)

1

Copyright © Angela Clarke 2025

The right of Angela Clarke to be identified as the Author of the
Work has been asserted by them in accordance with the
Copyright, Designs and Patents Act 1988.

All rights reserved. No part of this publication may be reproduced, stored in a retrieval system, or transmitted, in any form or by any means without the prior written permission of the publisher, nor be otherwise circulated in any form of binding or cover other than that in which it is published and without a similar condition being imposed on the subsequent purchaser.

All characters in this publication are fictitious and any resemblance to real persons, living or dead, is purely coincidental.

A CIP catalogue record for this title is available from the British Library

Paperback ISBN 9781473681590
ebook ISBN 9781473681583

Typeset in Sabon MT by Manipal Technologies Limited

Printed and bound in Great Britain by Clays Ltd, Elcograf S.p.A.

Hodder & Stoughton policy is to use papers that are natural, renewable and recyclable products and made from wood grown in sustainable forests. The logging and manufacturing processes are expected to conform to the environmental regulations of the country of origin.

Hodder & Stoughton Limited
Carmelite House
50 Victoria Embankment
London EC4Y 0DZ

www.hodder.co.uk

In memory of Ann Stenhouse, whose encouragement, patience, and droll takedowns underpin my writing career. I wouldn't be here without you, my friend.

'In the gardens of memory, in the palace of dreams, that is where you and I shall meet.'

Through the Looking Glass, and What Alice Found There,
                                              Lewis Carroll, 1871.

BETH

'On behalf of my wife and I,' Danny says with a grin, pausing for the cheer that ripples through fifty of our closest friends and family.

The camera zooms momentarily in on Emma from work (I don't see her anymore), her hair straightened like we all did in 2009. Then it pans back round to focus on Danny. His dark hair freshly cropped into the close style he still favours, his glistening eyes adding genuine emotion to his gawky boy-next-door good looks. You could believe he was young enough to not need to shave back then. If anything he is more handsome now; time has painted a gravitas onto what was a puppyish face, shading in lines and shadows, building an experienced air of old school glamour, like a 1940s movie heart-throb. A man you can trust.

The onscreen Danny shifts in his tailored grey three-piece, the jacket line tracing his broad shoulders, the flash of a diamanté pin holding his single cream rose buttonhole in place. Traces of nerves melt round his eyes, as his own clear joy is reflected back at him by the room. Only I, the bride, my red hair teased into a generic half updo, a forced smile on my over made-up face, look uncomfortable. People probably put it down to wedding nerves. Danny gives a little laugh. 'I'd like to thank you for joining us on this very special day.'

The morning frost had burnt off into the soft blue skies of a late March day, Crauford House's large Georgian windows providing golden light for the videographer's film. The room full of smiling faces, giddy from champagne sipped from cut glass flutes. And less than five miles away, one thousand people had silently lined the streets of Wootton Bassett, as the bodies of soldiers killed in Afghanistan were carried past.

I can still smell the flowers, feel the sharp bones of my bodice dress pressing into my flesh, as the onscreen Danny says the words I now know are coming.

'As you all know, Beth is not one to talk about her feelings,' Danny gives a warm-hearted smile.

My mum's feathery lilac fascinator shivers above her soft pinched face, as her big pale blue eyes scrunch closed and she titters in acknowledgment. Sat at the end of the long top table, in her carefully chosen matching dress and jacket, her slender manicured hand grips the meaty one of my stepdad, John. Mum at least knows the truth, that there was a before and an after. Two different Beths. A secret shared between only three of us in that room. When you burn all bridges to your past you don't get to keep those who might have been important to you before. You don't get that right.

I see the unintended sting of Danny's words hit me. The thick white tablecloth pulls taut under the gilt edged china plate of my half eaten beef fillet, as I twisted my hands into its long draped folds. Trying to hold on.

Our wedding video large on the flat screen next to the log burner.

'Why're you watching this?' If my voice sounds shaky, neither Danny nor Oscar notice. Oscar's already snuggled in his favourite fleecy onesie. His mop of unruly blonde hair shines bright against our cobalt blue lounge. A picture-perfect family.

'For homework,' Oscar says, his grin revealing the proud gap of his first lost milk tooth.

'They have to write about "Something That Happened Before I was Born",' Danny supplies, holding out the edge of the fringed wool blanket we bought on our last trip to Wales, so I can join them for a cuddle. I force a smile on my lips, shake my head at the offer. Danny tucks the wool back under his jeans with strong fingers. He ruffles our son's hair, pulling his little body into his own.

My husband is still fit, strong, a gym-goer four times a week, the body he has now barely different from the one in the video in front of us. His hasn't been swelled, stretched, sucked, and wrung out by giving birth. Not that I would change that. I never thought I could experience such happiness till I held Oscar's tiny unfurling form in my arms. 'This was four years before you were born. Ten years ago,' Danny tells him. I allow myself to bask in how happy he sounds, in how much I love the two people in this room. Until the overwhelming strength of that feeling settles into a sharp-edged weight pressing into my insides: I will do anything to protect them.

'Or it will be,' Danny continues. 'On the fourteenth March, when we have our party.'

'Can I have sausage rolls?' asks Oscar. Important priorities for a six-year-old.

'Definitely,' Danny's laugh is rich and luxuriant. 'A ten-year anniversary should be pastry, don't you think, Mummy?'

I laugh my affirmation. Try to absorb every atom of this moment, the shared giggles, the joy, the light in our cosy front room. Surrounded by photos of our family. The framed print Danny and I bought from the David Hockney exhibition we loved. A squat wooden Buddha from our honeymoon in Thailand, the ice cream swirl of a Cornish seashell found on the beach the weekend my morning sickness told us I was pregnant. A bus rumbles past the bay of our Hackney Victorian terrace, vibrating the floor beneath my feet. A flash of red warning the outside world is still there. Waiting.

'Again,' Oscar cries, as on the video the applause for the end of Danny's speech breaks out. He grabs the remote, his little fingers jabbing.

'Hey,' Danny laughs, as the image on screen gets caught in a loop. Me, on my feet, arm raised to join the toast, the delicate lace on the bodice of my dress wrapping round me like suffocating ivy. Turning towards Danny, and away. Towards Danny and away. As if someone else is moving me, an unseen puppeteer twisting me this way and that. *Which way will you turn? Which path will you take? The one that leads you here? The one that leads you astray?*

I leave them in the lounge. Enid Cat passes me in the narrow hallway, as she jumps up onto the slender console table we dump our keys and post on. I run a hand along her comforting tortoiseshell fur, feel the flex of her strong tail, desperate for something to ground me. But Enid Cat isn't feeling benevolent today, or maybe she can sense my own guilt. With a knowing look, she undulates out from under my palm, and she and I pad on in different directions. My bare feet navigating the carpeted step that slices an unnatural corner into our hallway. A remnant of the building's patched past we always meant to fix, but never got round to. Each item of my overdue to-do list hangs on me like a damaged Christmas bauble. Another broken thing I drag along with me.

Our whitewashed kitchen is cold and dark. The sun, usually visible through the glass of the side door, has given up on the day. The brick wall of next door's extension mud brown from the heavy clouds. A better match for my mood. For what I deserve. *As you know, Beth does not talk about her feelings*. A failure, even after all this time. I tried so hard to be good. To be fixed. To protect those I love from my sharp jagged edges. I took everything about the before Beth and I buried her deep. Far down, in an iron casket, under six feet of concrete, like she was nuclear waste. To shield everyone around me from the truth. But there's a crack in the concrete, a rip into my core, and now the corrosive poison is leaking out.

From my pocket I pull the latest ticking bomb, my fingers shaking as I stare at the scrap of lined paper. Blink back tears to read the words that have decimated everything. Told me my time is up. I read them again, though I know the shape of every letter by heart already.

I know who you are.

Someone else knows what I did.

BETH – TWENTY FOUR DAYS TILL THE PARTY

'No, Rob, I was thinking – as it's already five thirty – I probably wouldn't come back into the office,' I say into my phone. The fence erected along Oxford Street to protect pedestrians from the building work, only serving to funnel hundreds of shoppers into a smaller space. I seem to be the only one trying to go the other way. The bright shopfronts splashes of garish headache-inducing colour in the grey drizzle swallowing the last of the light. Thumping music hurls out of each open door, as people push their way in and out of the city's busiest shopping street. I am still pissed my boss booked me a meeting in Soho at this time of day. I could've easily pitched the potential client – a rather lacklustre pop-up luxe lingerie brand started by the vacant daughter of some ageing rock star – in the morning. Then I would have avoided this scrum. My foot splashes into a puddle. A woman with bleached blonde hair pulls her takeaway coffee out of my way just in time. But I'm not lucky enough to avoid the sharp poke of a black umbrella, wielded by a gormless-looking lad to my right. I scrunch against the cardboard shopping bags of a woman in a shearling-edged jacket who has joined me in the futile attempt to swim upstream towards the Tube. 'Sorry.'

'No need to apologise, Beth,' Rob's voice says in my ear. 'We can do this in the morning.'

'I wasn't talking to you,' I say, but he's already gone. I leave my headphones in my ears, wipe the rain from my phone, and shove it and my hands into the pockets of what is normally my favourite green coat. I like the way the belt cinches in at my waist, how the heavy wool – which is getting heavier as it soaks up water – swings around my legs as I walk. But it doesn't have a hood, and as another drop of rain works its way over the brim of my black felt hat and down the back of my neck I'm hit by the overwhelming exhaustion you get when you just want the day to be done. I want to be home.

Luck does not look like it's going to be on my side. I near the entrance to Oxford Street Tube, the crowd starts to bunch. A sure sign the platform's overcrowded, and they'll hold us out here. Bodies clump and push behind me. The pavement obscured by a mass of legs, feet, the flapping edges of coats, and that familiar feeling of claustrophobia threatening to seep into my skin with the rain. The feeling that if something happened, I wouldn't be able to get out. The backpack of the man in front of me catches me on the face.

'Hey!' I put my fingers to my cheek. Tall, with his bag on two shoulders, he's basically weaponised his rucksack. But he either doesn't hear, or doesn't care. Just another stony face grimly focused on the now closed Tube entrance. I could get an Uber? But I'll sit in traffic for two hours at this time of day. I step to the side of the crush, aiming for a space opening, with flashes of blue painted Tube station hoarding, in front of the *Evening Standard* guy. And that's when it happens.

I thought I was doing that thing where you see faces where they aren't. The guy you wave at manically over the road until you realise, mortified, no, that's not your cousin. The woman walking through the interchange in Bank underground station who looks, just for a second, like your old English teacher. But this time it's not a trick of my imagination. It's not wishful thinking. It's definitely you.

Your hair is longer now, thick curls pushed against your forehead by a black beanie. A slender boxer's face. That dipped chin, looking up with a cheeky grin: ever the bad boy with the heart of gold. It's the eyes I recognise first. Dark blue. Intense. They haven't aged. And it's been ages. Twenty-four years since I lost my virginity to you. I was fifteen. We were so young, but we felt so grown-up. And here you are, now, a visitor from another life. Staring out from the front page of the *Standard*: *Forty-year-old man stabbed to death in Hyde Park mugging.*

I haven't seen you since my mid-twenties. I've done my fair share of internet snooping, of course. A few late nights spent looking at your Facebook page. You don't have high privacy settings. You have a younger girlfriend, all stylised jet black hair, ruby red lips, and pert tits, like a living cartoon character. There are photos of you at gigs, on tour, sweaty from playing, a beer in one hand, your arm slung casually proprietorial over her shoulder. She looks exactly the type to date the drummer in a band. I thought you lived in Liverpool? But it's your eyes, your name in the paper. You that has been killed. Despite the noise of crowds around me, I can suddenly hear my own breathing. Loud. Hard. Fast. I take a copy from the stack on the blue stand, not able to talk to the bellowing, puffa jacket wearing seller. First time I've held a paper in years. I always read the news online. I could've scrolled past you, missed it. But now I have you in my hands. The front page dominated by the threat of a no-deal Brexit. Your photo the human story drawing the reader in for more inside. I flip to page three.

> *Forty-year-old man stabbed to death in Hyde Park. Michael Armsmith, a musician from Liverpool . . .*

I had that right then. Were you here for work? Playing at a pub close enough I could have seen you?

> *. . . was found in Hyde Park in the early hours of this morning, by a female jogger. Police are interested in talking to anyone who may have been in the area from 6 p.m. yesterday.*

The Anniversary Party

What do you do when you discover your first love, your first serious boyfriend, has been murdered, twenty odd years later in a park half an hour from where you live?

You grope for the wall. You sit down. On the wet dirty pavement. Among the stamping, slipping, sweating legs of the passing world. In your favourite coat. And you don't care because you're remembering those blue eyes looking at you when they first told you they loved you.

BETH

'You alright, Miss?' The man asking is young, early twenties, Eastern European, possibly Romanian. His dark hair shaped into a fashionable quiff. For a second I'm flattered he said Miss, like he thinks I might be young. It's probably a language issue. Then I remember I'm sitting on the floor.

'I'm fine, I just . . . ' I try to push against the hoarding behind me, he gets a strong hand under my arm, helps me up, his face a look of concern. People have started to stare now. The Tube gates have opened, and people are shuffling forwards, passing, side-eyeing the lady who just sat down in the rain. Though no one else intervenes. My skin tingles with heat. What was I thinking? 'I'm fine.' I repeat. Because that's what you say, isn't it?

'You're sure? You want water?' The young man says.

I extract my arm from his hand. Start joining the lemmings shuffling towards the Tube steps.

'Thank you. I'm fine. I promise. Thank you. I just need to—' I point towards the station entrance.

His eyebrows meet, and he looks like he's about to protest, but I slot between two men in long black macs, into the slipstream of commuters. I just need to get home.

The Victoria line is a welcome anonymous condensation crush. A telling dark patch of dirty water on the back of my coat, visible as I walk through the interchange at Highbury. That was overly dramatic. But no one gives me a second look. Not when I quickly brush tears from my eyes on the overground either. I can feel my phone buzzing: a call – but I ignore it. Can't talk now.

Enid Cat greets me as my key opens our front door, wrapping round my legs, as if she can sense I need the comfort.

'Hey there. Good girl, good girl.' I stroke my hand through her fur. Thankful someone sees me. I need to lock this all down now. I never talk about the past with Danny. I can't. I've never mentioned Mickey's name. I blink as I remember those intense blue eyes. Mickey above me.

'Hello!' I call, hurrying to get out of my incriminating coat, leaving it draped, dry side up, over the folded *Standard*. Already planning to drop it at the dry cleaners tomorrow. Danny's expected voice doesn't greet me. He's usually back by five. Instead the welcoming open face of Hellie, Oscar's nanny, appears. Her light curly hair, which never seems to suffer from lack of volume, hangs around her pale cheeks. The outdoorsy, vaguely Nordic vibe that first attracted me to hiring her six months after Oscar was born, is added to by the Fair Isle jumper she's wearing.

'Hey!' She smiles. 'You're back early?'

'And you're here late – sorry. No Danny yet?'

She shakes her head.

'Maybe he got caught on the Tube – the Victoria line's screwed.' I try not to glance at my coat as she retrieves her own down jacket from her wall hook.

'It's all good,' she smiles. 'Oscar's had a fish finger roll and peas. I've just sliced him an apple,' she says. I can hear the distinct tones of *Danger Mouse* coming from the lounge.

'You're an angel – thanks.'

'Yeah well I did use normal ketchup – Tesco were out of organic.' She looks sheepish. Before meeting my quizzical eye and cracking up.

'You know the whole organic thing is just middle-class career mum guilt? When I think of the crap I ate as a youngster – the colour of things – they must have been full of additives and God knows what. Do you remember Slush Puppies?'

Hellie looks at me blankly.

'God, to be young and innocent.' I force a laugh. Trying to shake Mickey from my mind. 'They were the height of the eighties – they sold them in the newsagents. Crushed ice drinks. They came in truly alarming colours. Like drinking plastic.'

Hellie grimaces. 'Sounds . . . horrid. Eight tomorrow okay?' She unwraps her rucksack from Oscar's metal scooter.

'Not sure about Danny, but usual for me. You doing anything fun tonight?' I suddenly want to be in my twenties again. Seeing where the night takes me as I head for drinks. Still up at 2 a.m. in a pop-up club under the arches of Waterloo station. Red lights. Sticky cocktails. Flirting outrageously with whoever is nearest. You don't know what you have till it's gone. A flash of Mickey smiling at me, sat on the next swing in the park. His hood up against the drizzle. His hand over mine.

'New series of *Queer Eye*,' Hellie laughs, dragging me back to our hallway. The pile of unopened post on the table. Oscar's wellies at the bottom of the stairs. 'I know how to live.'

I wave her off, closing the door. Feeling my face drop from its false jollity. I didn't even realise I was doing it: projecting, being the best version of me. Hellie could have coped with my tears. She's a friend. She would have hugged me. Put on the kettle. Let me tell her about Mickey. About the first boy I loved. I shake myself. That's not an option for me. I made my choice long ago. No one is allowed that close. No one's allowed to know. Details like that – it's too dangerous.

Oscar's curled on the sofa, in front of the TV. I remove his empty plate from the upholstery, put it on our reclaimed coffee table and sit down next to him. I can't help pulling his warm body against mine, smelling his hair. Johnson's No More Tears, reminding me of the milky sweet baby I'd held in my arms. We'd spent nights awake together in this room while I breastfed him, and watched late night telly. He squirms out of my grasp and folds himself forwards so he's on his stomach, chin on his fists to get closer to the screen. I content myself with a squeeze of his small strong calf.

'What's going on?'

'Penfold thinks this is the big one,' he answers.

Fully enlightened, I stare past the screen and let my thoughts roll back through the past. To Mickey. We didn't meet till we were eleven. Secondary school. I have no recollection of our first encounter. You don't at that age: it's just a sea of faces and hormones. It wasn't until I was fifteen and he sat in front of me in the cold drab Portakabin we had English lessons in, that I became painfully aware of Mickey. The way his blazer stretched over his broad shoulders. The way the right cuff of it was frayed: the black threads turning to fluff his blunt thick fingers snatched away. His hands fascinated me. His nails cut so aggressively low, the skin of his fingers nearly swallowed them. There were blisters and calluses across the pads of his palms from drumming. They weren't pretty hands. I could feel every part of them when they moved over my skin.

I made the first move. I remember the look of shocked confusion, the slight shadow round his eyes adding to their intensity. Perhaps he too had bought into the teen movie narrative – about boys being the needy sexual ones. About girls being mooning wallflowers who gazed from afar. He caught up quick. And I thought it would last forever. That heady rush of sexuality. The power that comes with blossoming tits and hips. Wolf whistles, cat calls, men turning to stare when you walk into shops. Not that I was anything special, I was just young and female. What you don't realise at the time, is that what makes you glisten as a teen, fades fast past thirty, and sods off completely by the time you're my age. Don't get me wrong, I don't like being harangued in the street. Those first few untroubled walks are a blessed relief. But then you realise what it means. When you pass a building site and are greeted with a resounding silence, it's not because you're witnessing a feminist revolution. Today's builders aren't more enlightened, you've just vanished.

Mickey wanted me like an addict wanted a drug. We were studying John Donne in class, and studying each other out of it. *O my America! my new-found-land*. We were sexual adventurers, pioneers. It was intoxicating. Sex got better. I got better. But that first taste of lust was enslaving. To be so desired. *Come, madam, come.*

I jump guiltily when I hear Danny's key in the door. It's just my coat – wet from sitting on the floor. It's just a newspaper – with my now dead first boyfriend on the front. But I don't want him to see either. Or I do? Part of me longs to open up to Danny. To tell him the truth. But that's the danger with the past – you pull one loose thread and the whole lot unravels. (I worry for a second about Zayn. But no, he's my best friend. He's got my back.)

I find Danny pulling his coat off, his usually laidback face, crunching into annoyance. 'Bloody tube.' A shadow of stubble visible across his face. He looks tired.

'Hey,' I say, scooping my coat and the newspaper away from him, resting them on the stairs. Out of reach. Out of sight. 'How was your day?'

'It always screws up at the worst possible time.' He's pulling off his lilac tie.

With everything else, I'd forgotten he was out late last night with a client. It's usually me who's caught up socialising. Danny's work in insurance doesn't usually call for it. But this one – a sports centre that was looking to get underwritten – was different. 'Do you want me to do dinner? Oscar's already eaten.' I should've started already, instead of daydreaming about my old boyfriend. I glance at my coat on the stairs.

'No.' Danny scrubs his hand over his face. A strong hand. Dexterous fingers. Clean, shaped nails. No calluses. 'It's fine. Besides,' he adds with a knowing grin, 'we're having celeriac – do you know how to prepare that?'

The implication that a vegetable is beyond me rankles, but I keep it from my face. The truth is I hate cooking. And it gives Danny something that is wholly his domain. We're a team. I pay the bills, he runs the household. 'Nope,' I grin back.

'Didn't think so,' he laughs, heading towards the kitchen.

'I'll just . . . ' I look round the hall, settle on the unopened post on the side. Grab the pile and wave it in the air, even though he's no longer looking. 'Sort a few things out here.'

It's just a wet coat. It's just a newspaper. I'll put them in the bottom of my wardrobe. My phone vibrates in my pocket, telling me I've received a message. It better not be Rob wanting to talk now. But it's Zayn's name on the screen. My one friend from before. We knew each other at school. We were friendly but not close. Probably because Zayn was dealing with his own identity stuff back then. We vaguely stayed in contact – just the odd random message or email throughout university, and after. He was in Singapore for a couple of years, then Australia. He does something to do with software. We'd all but lost touch when I bumped into him again when we were twenty-five. He was back in London, and back in my life. We've been close ever since. He's the only person, apart from family, that I speak to from before. Zayn's ignorance of what happened when he was away finding himself in the Outback of Australia was a gift. The one remaining strand from before, apart from Mum. Someone who really knows me. I had to give up so much. I close my eyes and briefly picture Carmen's smiling face. I'm only thinking of this – of her – because of Mickey. I open the message:

> *I've been calling you. You okay? Have you seen? Mickey Armsmith has been killed. It's all over Facebook. I'm so sorry, love. Call me if you want to chat.*

I swallow the lump in my throat. Zayn's a good friend. I fire off a quick response telling him I can't talk right now. Receive two kisses and a hug emoji back. Flick through the post. A postcard advertising a sale at an exercise brand I once bought some leggings from. And what looks like a marketing circular. An otherwise blank envelope with my name printed on the front. I'm already walking towards the door of the lounge to drop it in the bin, but professional curiosity makes me open the envelope. I slide out a scrap of lined paper – like the type you used to get in school exercise books, and freeze. It's as if a hand has closed around my throat.

I turn it over. Looking for a brand. Some logo. A signifier that this isn't what I think it is. I tear the envelope apart, but there's nothing else inside. The theme tune to *Danger Mouse* starts up.

'Can I watch another?' Oscar calls.

'Yes. Yes,' I say too quickly. *Just don't come out here.* I can hear Danny chopping in the kitchen. The knife crunching through the celeriac, the snap of the blade as it hits the board. I can't get moisture into my mouth. Can't seem to swallow. I feel like I'm going to choke. Cough. Like I'm going to cry. I stare at the words which have been printed on the lined paper. The same font as my name – her name – on the outside. The same fading black ink. The same thin white line, where presumably the printer head isn't connecting to the nozzle, running through every letter.

I know who you really are.

BETH

I'm concentrating so hard on the note in my hand, Danny makes me jump as he appears in the hallway. His striped chef's apron over his shirt and trousers, the chopping knife in his right hand. Two wires dangle down from the headphones in his ears. 'Did you get a chance to look at the catering email?'

Instinctively I shove the incriminating paper in my pocket. Dammit. The canapés for the party. 'No, sorry – I'll do it tonight.' I'd meant to go through Danny's suggested menu on the way home. Before all this happened.

'What's that?' he indicates the hand that's in my pocket. His eyebrow slightly raised. My heart's hammering.

'Something for our anniversary – don't want to spoil the surprise,' I finish with a warm smile. The lie skipping off my tongue.

'Alright,' he winks. 'I promise I won't go looking for it later.' The thought making me feel sick. He heads back into the kitchen, tapping his headphones back on. Humming along to the song he's listening to.

I grab my coat and the paper with a dead Mickey on the front and hurry upstairs.

The curtains are open in our bedroom. The dark sky outside reflecting a ghostly negative of our floor-to-ceiling white fitted wardrobes and the rectangle of our dove grey duvet. The green enamel of our reclaimed ceiling lamp hovers next to punched-out squares of light from the windows of the identical terraced houses over the road. I pull the curtains closed. I've always hated the feeling someone could be out there, watching in the dark. But someone has been watching. Someone has been here. Someone knows. I take the note from my pocket and stare at it. *I know who you really are.*

For a second I'm back there – *damp between my legs. My unzipped boots flapping round my ankles.* But I slam it down fast. No. I won't think about that. About what happened. Is this real or am I just panicking? Guilt catastrophises the air I'm trying to suck in. Should I have dropped Zayn? My mum? No. It's not like I completely changed who I was. More like blended in the edges, so I was less visible. Now I have Danny's last name, nothing unusual in that. Half my year at school did that. You can find them online now whatever their original name was. I changed my hair colour. Plenty of people do that too. Apart from that, what is there to show any kind of concern? Choosing to use an alias on social media isn't a crime. Nor is deliberately cutting yourself off from your past friends. I haven't done anything wrong. Except that's not true. Beth hasn't done anything wrong. Past me . . . past me did the worst thing. For a second I long to pick up my phone and call Carmen. Hear her gentle voice say, 'You alright, babe?' Except she probably has a different number. And she wouldn't want to speak to me. Not now. It hits me: there will be a funeral for Mickey and I can't go. I reach for the bed behind me, lower myself shakily to sit on the edge.

The note could be a coincidence. It genuinely might be a marketing campaign. *I know who you really are: use the laptop that truly gets you!* Or some weirdo religious sect trying to recruit people. It's probably a Brexit thing: I know you're truly British or some claptrap. It's an innocuous enough set of words. It doesn't have to mean what I've taken it as. I glance at the closed curtains again, as if there might be someone on the other side. I'm being irrational. I'm on the first floor. This mail out – or whatever it is – just landed at the wrong time. It hit during the shock about Mickey. I'm just not thinking straight. Everything is okay. I force myself to stand. To strip off the day's clothes, drop them in the washing basket. Pull on my blue trackies, my grey jumper. Take

The Anniversary Party

my make-up off. Pull my hair back. Pat eye cream onto the fine lines. Massage the skin of my face up, plumping it, remembering how I looked when I was a teenager. When Mickey would put his calloused hands on my smooth skin. *You can't go back, even if you wanted to.*

'Beth,' Danny's voice carries up the stairs. 'Grub's ready!'

'Coming!' I sound cheerful. I feel like I'm watching myself from afar, my socked feet padding down the stairs. Into the kitchen.

Danny holds out a plate for me, a knife and fork balanced on the side. 'In with Oscar? Next episode of *Game of Thrones* when he's gone up?'

I take the plate. Danny has crisped the skin of the chicken breast, sprinkled cracked black pepper and salt over the celeriac mash, got the tenderstem broccoli that perfect shade of *al dente* green. I feel sick.

'You alright?' He takes the plate back from my hands, returns to the kitchen side, and has his arms around me. I curl into his chest, feeling his reassuring bulk, inhaling his bergamot scent from his shirt front. The fabric thin enough for me to feel the muscles of his chest move against my cheek. When I was little we got a new puppy, and Mum wrapped a hot water bottle and a small clock in an old towel for him to sleep on – it was to replicate the heartbeat of his mother, to make him feel safe. I can hear Danny's heartbeat.

'Baby, what is it? Has something happened?' Danny whispers into my hair.

The boy I first kissed is dead. The boy I lost my virginity to is dead. The boy I first loved is dead. And someone – maybe no one – I don't know – has sent me a note. Or a badly timed marketing campaign. And I'm scared. And I feel as if I'm being pulled back. As if someone has taken a swing at the wall I erected to protect us all.

Danny strokes my arm. I squeeze my eyes tighter so nothing can escape. 'Hey,' he soothes. I force myself to straighten. Pull away from his warmth. Stretch a smile over my face. 'Just tired. Long day.'

He stands for a minute, his arms dangling at his sides, unsure, a slight frown in his eyes. 'You know you can tell me anything, right?'

My loving husband, in my beautiful home, with our beautiful son. *I know who you really are.*

'I know.' My smile begins to ache.

Danny's face sags slightly. His gaze drops. My heart pinches in my chest, and I have to swallow the lump in my throat. I want to reach for him. Curl into him again. Tell him everything.

'Okay,' Danny says, almost to himself. Picking up both our plates, the mash already beginning to congeal. Butter from the chicken forming a ridge of fat.

'Honestly,' I find myself saying. Feeling like Danny is miles away, not right next to me. 'I'm absolutely fine. I promise.'

BETH – TWENTY THREE DAYS TILL THE PARTY

'Screw Bradbury Ltd.' Rob is frothing himself like a latte. His overly long hair is just the right side of messy, the teen-style locks lifting attention away from the sagging round his late-forties eyes. Tall, and imposing, he always feels like the illuminated face in a Caravaggio painting, the whites of his eyes glow as they stare right into you.

We did not win the confectionary account we bid for last week. The American-owned company deciding to take their business to mainland Europe rather than gamble on our unknown future trading status. The potential second EU referendum is rocking the boat beneath our feet. Honda announced they're closing their Swindon factory, and a mewling of messages woke me to the growing pressure on our biggest client. I don't have time to think about silly little notes. I let myself get carried away.

Rob wraps one closed fist in his other hand. 'Least we've got Unity!'

That's my cue. As *PR Weekly* noted, as the only female director at Trench PR it was no surprise I was chosen to spearhead the PR campaign for the UK's first AI sex dolls. At least today's crisis meeting appears to be contained to the two of us in here. Rob's wood and chrome private office, like a pocket gentleman's club, is the only place for true privacy in the goldfish bowl open plan space the rest of us share.

'I've spoken to a contact who is keen to write a counter article – reframing the product as socially and sexually progressive, focusing on the fact the models come in all genders, ethnicities, there are non-binary options available,' I say. 'Recasting any criticism as outmoded . . . '

'Woke feminist claptrap,' Rob nods.

'I don't think that's fair – people have some valid concerns.' Myself included. I mean what kind of person – really – is willing to spend upwards of twenty grand on a lifelike sex doll, with a customisable vagina, and the ability to talk back to you? When Mickey and I were teens, our idea of experimentation was watching a grainy porn video recorded off a kid at school's dad's specialist satellite channel.

Rob is frowning, scrolling through his phone. 'She said it was "the pornification of victimhood". I mean, what does that even mean?'

I open my mouth to reply, but he keeps going. His manicured finger jabbing his screen.

'And this bit – this bit here – she says . . . ' He makes exaggerated air quotes. '"Unity has weaponised the objectification of women in hitherto unforeseen ways". Geoff has been monitoring the fallout on Twitter . . . '

I bet he has. He's been gunning for me ever since I got promoted to the board and he didn't.

'We just need to reframe the sex dolls in people's minds.'

'Love dolls,' Rob snaps automatically, and I curse myself for not using the preferred term I myself pitched.

'Here, and in this bit she talks about how some of the love dolls look like teen girls. I mean, come on! They are made from silicon. What does she want, for them to have wrinkles etched into them?'

I wince at the mention of wrinkles, suddenly feeling the lines on my forehead that have appeared over the last few months reflected in the shiny surfaces of the room. Rob continues his rant, and I tune him out. My mind drawn to when I had smooth flawless skin. Fifteen years old, and riding on the back of Mickey's bicycle, racing back to school after a free period. The big vats of dried pasta and jars of tomato sauce we made ourselves for lunch. Barbecues in his dad's garden in summer. Being allowed half a glass of beer. It all feels so innocent now. *I know who you really are.* Before the real world slammed into me. A safe place, and I have to swallow the lump forming in my throat as I realise how incredibly grateful I am to Mickey. So thankful that he gave me that. And I know what I need to do.

'We need to head this off, Beth,' Rob is saying. 'Really deliver. This is a chance for Trench PR to shine.' I've worked with Rob for years and him talking about the firm as a brand is an early warning sign. He really is worked-up. The artful tuck of his T-shirt into his Hermes belt snags as he strides, revealing a glimpse of abs only aggressive gym work could achieve. I think of Mickey's skin. His slender teen waist. The line of hair that tapered down his flat stomach. Men didn't shave then. Danny still waxes his chest and back hair. I gave up on my own gardening before Oscar was born. I like its softness. How it was when Mickey and I were first discovering each other.

Rob pauses, and looks at me expectantly.

'We're going to smash it,' I smile. They're going to buy the creepy things anyway. There's a massive waiting list of people desperate to buy a lifelike replica of a real woman to shag – if real women have the scaled measurements of Barbie.

'That's my girl,' Rob grins.

And my jaw clenches. I force a smile. 'All this is fine – don't worry about the article.' Geoff's just exaggerating. 'I've got it all under control.' I add one more confident smile. 'And just to let you know, I'm going to be out of the office next Wednesday. A personal matter. Is that okay?'

'Course.' Uncertainty tugs at the side of his eyes for a second: Rob is only truly happy when we are all here, safely under lock and key, churning out the big bucks. But he masters it. Gives me a thumbs up worthy of an eighties toothpaste ad.

I've already forgotten about Unity by the time I step through his door, back into the echoing open-plan space. Running through how I'm going to make this work. If I should? But by the time I reach my Ikea desk I already know it's a done deal. I've spent so much of my life denying myself. Keeping everything sealed away in dusty boxes. But I can't let down the innocent fifteen-year-old kids we used to be. Just this once, just this time: I'm going back.

BETH – FIFTEEN DAYS
TILL THE PARTY

'Bloody hell, it's like a school reunion,' I say under my breath. Being this close to Sevenoaks made me sick with nerves. What if someone saw me? 'There must be nearly two hundred people here?'

Zayn doesn't turn to look at the mourners, but keeps his city-smart, eco-conscious Tesla steadily crawling forwards while he looks for a space in the row of parked cars that line the Tunbridge Wells side street. 'You can tell you've never been to a Muslim funeral,' he says. But his voice lacks its usual spark – or sparkling cyanide, as I jokingly refer to his bubbly but deadly quips.

Clumps of people dressed in black have spread across the provincial green lawn that slopes up to the church. A church. With big stained glass windows, and a spire. Mickey would hate this – it must be his mum's doing. The disconcertingly familiar adult faces of those we grew up with, all gathered in their smart, respectful suits and tasteful dresses, making the archetypal English small town setting feel like we've stumbled into a Sunday night ITV murder mystery.

Zayn flicks on the indicator, then rests his tanned hand on the back of my seat, as he turns to reverse the car into a gap on St Mark's Road. His designer stubble scoring his set jaw as he concentrates. His uncharacteristic silence while parking allows all the noise to start up in my head. I should be managing the growing storm over Unity. A young blonde girl has uploaded a clip of her pretending to be an AI sex doll who had two voices. One delivering a Stepford Wives, manic-eyed positive message on why she was a sex-positive feminist. The other, deeper, making her sound almost male, revealing the doll's very existence was the first step of an evil plot to eradicate 'the pesky existence of those who identify as women'. Though I doubted any true misogynist overlord would use such inclusive terminology as 'identify as women', you couldn't fault the impact. The clip had gone viral on TikTok. Others had already started to dress themselves up in lingerie – or worse, school uniform – with make-up applied to make them look like plastic dolls, or ventriloquist dummies, and were lip-syncing to the original audio. And to think we had thought TikTok would be largely based on music clips just a few months ago. Then one day Zayn's flatmate Nate was cooking us the latest viral TikTok recipe and just like that it was mainstream. Figures were coming through that ninety-five per cent of Gen Z and Millennials questioned were using it. And tens of thousands of them were seeing anti-Unity content. As a PR who trained in a pre-social media world, it still took my breath away how these flashing colourful little apps had changed the landscape of our society so fast. It's exhausting. The world is already accelerating away from what Mickey knew. Who knew what platform would be shaping mainstream media and conversation in just a few months? A world Mickey would now never see.

I let my eyes wander up the trees that lined the pretty street. Trees that had been here perhaps a hundred years, who would perhaps still be standing here in a hundred more. When Mickey, I, and anonymous notes would all be long gone. I remembered a term I'd learned at uni studying the Romantic poets, how they viewed the vast continuity of nature as a noumenon, as something that exists independently of our sense of perception. It matched the disassociation I felt now. As if I was existing while things unfolded around me, without truly understanding what was happening. Above me a few brave leaves were budding green. The new beginning of a continual cycle, a fresh start, while here in this moment there was no peace in the transcendental: we were here to mark the violent end of life cut short. There has been no news of arrests following Mickey's murder.

A woman in a black peacoat squeezes in front of the car, jolting my attention back. Was that Helen Parr? She still has the same brutalist slab of white blonde hair and icy stare. The brittle head girl of our year. I bet she's a divorce lawyer, and head of the PTA. I don't want to think about the last time I saw her. What she said. I slink down lower in my seat, even though I know the windows are tinted and there's no way anyone can see in.

Zayn switches the engine off. Turns towards me. The dark grey of his quiff tonally blending into the rest of his black hair. His narrow face serious, the slight kink in his nose making him look more handsome, not less. He's very pulled-together in his black suit and dark green shirt. Men always have it easier at weddings and funerals.

'You're looking good. Did you get your Botox topped up specially?' I ask.

'Are you sure you want to wait in the car, sweetie?' He's not falling for my distraction.

'I'm fine,' I turn to look away. Watch as taxis draw up and drop more people off. Four women are walking towards the church. I recognise them from the year below us at school.

'It's been a long time since . . . ' Zayn says quietly.

My head snaps to look at him. A muscle in his cheek spasms, like he's been slapped. We've never spoken about what happened when he was in Australia. Why I no longer see anyone from uni, from school, from before. Zayn didn't have a great time at Oakwood Secondary. He always said once he was gone and out, it was over and he never wanted to go back. Reinvented himself. I've met friends of his who didn't come out till their twenties, others who have transitioned genders, others still who are gender neutral. Defining who you are for yourself, being reborn – it's a normal part of his world. I thought we shared that. I didn't think he was still in touch with anyone from back here, but there's always Google, always ways of finding out. I feel like the car is moving again, starting to roll backwards. Has he known all this time and not said anything?

Zayn draws in a breath. '... since we graduated.'

I exhale. The car stops moving. It's okay. It's that stupid threatening note. It's this. It's made me believe the past is reaching for me, that Nemesis has me in her sights.

Zayn's dark brown eyes flick away, his lips purse slightly. 'People change, they grow up. Or at least some of them do.' He's watching anxiously out the window now, as two men who look vaguely familiar, in cheap grey suits, with too-long paisley ties, stride towards the church. And I realise this is about him. About what he went through. And I feel like a crap friend. Awful. I squeeze his hand. He seems to shake himself, remember he's no longer the skinny little kid who was picked on because he's different. He gives me a perfect grin. 'You don't want to show them how fabulous we both are?'

My heart twists. I can't do this with him, I can't be there for him. My presence would detract from Mickey's memory. But I can be here. I can be as close as I can get. I can honour him.

'You know me,' I say quietly. 'I want to remember Mickey privately.'

He holds my gaze for a beat, before letting my hand go. 'Okay.' Then opens his door. I turn away from the exposed outside, let my red hair fall over my face. 'There's tissues in the glove compartment,' Zayn says. His smart brogues click onto the road outside. Then he adds, under his breath, almost to himself: 'Right, let's do this.' And the door slams shut behind him, making my ears pop.

A delighted shriek of greeting comes from the crowd of mourners on the grass. This is all wrong. I scan the crowd, scowling, trying to pierce my judgement of that person through my eyes and the tinted glass. And that's when I see him.

His rangy frame, all skinny shoulders and skinny hips, still a jerk of movements, like an unfolding ironing board. An awkwardness

The Anniversary Party

he never grew out of. Kareem Farah. His long thin fingers flit round behind him, tuck a wayward white shirt into his black suit trousers. His belt looks plasticky, and his shoes slightly too shiny, the suit looks dated, as if the whole outfit might be left over from school, or a waiter job a few years ago. We're almost forty, and still in that grace period where there's only a few weddings left, the odd, increasingly unfashionable christening, but the uphill climb of frequent funerals haven't started. Kareem hasn't needed to invest in a regular outfit yet, but it's telling, nonetheless. His once floppy black hair is now cut in a generic office worker style, the vague hint of a side parting.

He chats to a tall chunky man with his hands in his chino pockets. Kareem is still moving in fitful energetic little jumps, a hand adjusting his black tie, his hair, his waistband again. His face has lost the plump veneer of youth, and his cheeks look sunken, dark circles under his eyes – perhaps he's been crying? Was he still close with Mickey? A wave of jealousy, and then guilt washes over me. There'd be an irony in that. That Mickey had stayed friends with the boy I'd cheated on him with, when I haven't spoken to him in years. Mickey's dad still lives in Tunbridge Wells. Did Mickey look up Kareem when he came back to visit? Perhaps pop in for a pint at The Guinea? Maybe Kareem has seen Mickey's band play? I know I'm being irrational. People don't tend to stay in contact with old boyfriends. But Mickey and I were different. What we shared had changed as we'd grown up, but it was built to last. He'd come to visit me at university. Coming to Top Banana with me, though he hated cheesy music. We'd laughed, mildly flirted, he'd told me about his latest girlfriend. The depth of his feeling for me only showing when I was jostled on the dance floor, and his strong hand came out and caught me before I was knocked to the ground. And after, when he was still living at home, I'd come back from London, we'd go to weird dance nights and gigs he'd heard of. Drink cheap sticky drinks from plastic cups. Mickey's curls dark with sweat, plastered against his head, arms in the air, biceps pumped, jumping and dancing and laughing in humid blacked-out rooms above pubs. I'd sleep in his single bed, he'd sleep on the floor. We saw each other in London. We were close. Friends for life. Until it happened. Until I was forced to cut all ties. Did he look for me? Was he angry? Hurt? Did he still see Kareem because it was a link to me?

That was self-indulgent. Look at how many people are here, at how loved Mickey was. He probably never thought of me. He probably didn't notice when I vanished. I hope he didn't know. If he did, a part of me hopes he didn't believe it. That deep down he knew who I really was. I shudder. I've accidentally used the same words as what was printed on that awful note. How many people standing on this lawn know what I did? Why I had to hide?

I look for Mickey's dad, it doesn't take long to find him. Still the same: balding, stocky, but with a strength you could see under the soft layer of fat. Standing at the church door, his soothing face familiar with that gentle welcoming smile, even now. Even when he is commemorating his son. He's wearing a suit, which I don't think I've ever seen before. It's far from his familiar patched jumper and trousers he wore for plumbing. His black tie lolls over his belly, and his jacket sleeves seem to catch as he smiles and pumps the hand of the person he's greeting. Still being the best dad he can, a friendly look, a joke, but as each person enters the church I see his face drop. Behind him, the asymmetric hem of her black dress making it look like she's hanging in midair, must be Mickey's sister Hannah. The same, but different. Older. I can't have seen her since she was thirteen. Her face is sullen, a step back from her father who is doing his best to make this an event. At this age, with all your family and friends gathered, you'd be expecting to celebrate the wedding of your child, not their funeral. A memorial, I remind myself. A celebration of life. Though we all know it's because the police won't release the body straight away as he was murdered. A queasy wave rises again in my stomach. I look away from their pain.

Kareem is still jolting animatedly in front of the tall guy. What was his name? His older brother was studying to be a vet. His mum was the doctor's receptionist. Funny I can remember that, and not his name. Kareem's fingers flutter up to tug at his contained hair, and there's something about the movement that plunges me back there. To that night.

Mickey hadn't come to the house party at Pete's big Sevenoaks house, even though I wanted to go. Pete's parents were away, and his detached house had eight bedrooms, and backed onto a patch of woodland. Everyone was going. Even the cooler kids. Because who could pass up all that unsupervised space at sixteen? But Mickey had opted to stay home and play computer games instead. And I had taken it personally, in that self-absorbed teenage way. As if it meant he didn't love me as much, if he didn't follow my every whim. Or maybe we'd rowed? Kareem's girlfriend Sarah was at her dad's for the weekend. It was natural we hung out together. The two long-term couples in our year, we did everything as a foursome.

But I wasn't used to being with Kareem on my own. The house was dark, and loud, and full of running, screeching people. That pulsating sense of risk that large groups of teenagers create. Someone had set up speakers in the garden, and covered all the lamps inside with scarves. And what did I feel as Kareem and I snorted red wine through a straw for a dare? And sipped throat-burning vodka from mugs? And shared joints on the steps of the terrace? I was bored. Is that why it happened? Did I so long for something – anything – that when we ended up in one of the eight bedrooms on our own I engineered it so we started to kiss? I remember his hands up my T-shirt, squeezing my breasts so hard I wondered if he and Sarah hadn't actually slept together after all. Unbuttoning his jeans. Him hiking up my skirt. Afterwards he had cried. And swore, a lot. He was terrified of what Mickey would do to him. I don't remember any mention of me, or his girlfriend of two years.

That one stupid night smashed apart our childhood gang of four. Kareem begged me not to tell Mickey, but I had come clean anyway. I thought it was the noble thing to do, in that black and white way you do when you are young and life has yet to teach you it is actually a maelstrom of grey. Kareem and I were a couple after that. Born from a stubborn belief that I couldn't have hurt Mickey for anything less than a genuine love. I think we lasted six weeks before we both admitted we had nothing really in common apart from both having hurt the people we really cared about. Sarah never spoke to Kareem again. Whereas me and Mickey remained friends. Until that was taken too.

I wonder what Kareem does now? I look at the neat hair, the shiny shoes. Some kind of nondescript office job? Did he still hero-worship Mickey? His friend who was almost famous, who had a hot young girlfriend, who toured with his band? Did he supplicant himself as his faithful sidekick, always there when Mickey came back, because he felt guilty about what we did? The night of the party was in July. Everything broke apart during the school holidays. How many people here know the truth about what happened back then?

I realise I have wrapped my arms round myself. This is uncomfortable territory. But being here is dragging it all up. It was a silly mistake made by an impetuous sixteen-year-old girl. No one would really judge that. Not unless they knew what happened after. Not unless they thought there was a pattern of behaviour forming. A canker growing in me. But how many people know all the pieces of the puzzle? Mickey did. Kareem does. Has he drawn that line? Made that connection? Seen the ugly truth of me? The rotten, rotting seam that runs right through me and my past? Does he know who I really am?

I inhale sharply, shrink away from the glass. I can't be seen. It's tinted. There's no way he can know I'm here. But at that moment, as if he heard me, Kareem stops talking and turns, definitively, to stare at Zayn's car. His eyes boring through the glass, seeming to look straight at me.

BETH

'You could have stayed longer?' I watch suburbia smear into motorway out the window of Zayn's car.

'I could hardly have left you in the car for the wake as well.' He flicks the lever to squirt water to clear his windscreen. 'Besides, I'd done my bit.' He's already filled me in on everyone he saw. Who got hot, who got rich, who got divorced, and who got his number.

'Do you think they're happy?' I watch a globule of water strain its way down my window, as if it's fighting with everything it has to go the other way. Broken ever smaller until it blurs to nothing on the wet glass.

'Who?' Zayn says.

'All of them?' I say.

He purses his lips before he answers. 'You could have come in and seen for yourself.'

No, I couldn't have. I think of Kareem looking at the car, as if he'd known I was there. Edgar Allan Poe's guilty beating heart in a Tesla.

'I spoke to Mickey's dad.' Zayn sounds softer, though he doesn't take his eyes from the road.

Mickey's dad: ever hopeful that we'd stay together. That we'd get back together. Still years later, when I was living in London, and Mickey was on girlfriend number twenty-seven. I could see it in his eyes. A fondness. A sadness for what could have been. But we'd basically been children when we got together. Fifteen is so unformed I barely recognise that girl in old photos. Look at the different lives we led. Mickey and his band in Liverpool. His remarkably young and sexy girlfriend held up by her friends as she sobbed outside the church. Me in London, with my career. And Oscar. And Danny. My husband. My husband who is so different from Mickey. Mickey had a rawness to him. I almost caught it today on the breeze. His scent. The tang of metal weights and sweat. An addictive smell. His skin cold from where he'd cycled in the rain, the faint hint of car fumes. If I close my eyes, if I will it enough, I can almost conjure it. Danny smells of expensive aftershave.

'How was his dad?' I ask. 'I mean – obviously, given the circumstances and all?'

'Alright,' Zayn answers. 'I met his girlfriend. A nurse. Kind-looking. You would have liked her.'

'That's good,' I say. I want him to have someone to care for him. To look after him.

Zayn nods. Satisfied. 'Italian? I need to carb load after that.'

'I thought you were going to hit the gym with Nate?' I don't want to interrupt Zayn and his flatmate's regular weights fix.

'I don't really fancy it after that,' Zayn says, without taking his eyes from the road.

There's a loose thread on the hem of my dress and I pull at it, still thinking about Kareem. His sudden stillness when he'd looked at the car. Like an animal about to be attacked. Or about to attack.

'I gave him a hug,' Zayn adds. He turns briefly to look at me, his eyebrows asking if he did the right thing. 'Mickey's dad.'

I smile. He's a good friend.

'On your behalf,' he says.

My fingers snap the thread on my hem. 'You didn't say that? I mean you didn't say it was from me did you?' How could Zayn be so stupid? How could he be so hurtful? What on earth would Mickey's dad have thought? Guilt crashes over me again and I feel tears prick my eyes. I would have given anything to have gone into that church. To have honoured Mickey and my love for him like he truly deserved. But I couldn't. There was no world in which it was worth the risk. Just brazenly walking back in.

In plain sight. It would be all over social media in seconds. It would be out. And then how long before someone told Danny? Or Oscar? My stomach lurched. I grip the door handle, try to steady the rising panic.

'No, of course not,' Zayn says, overtaking a white van in front of us.

I force air back into my lungs. I shouldn't have come today. It was selfish. Foolish. Too risky.

'You alright?' Zayn glances at me again.

'Feeling a bit carsick,' I manage. 'I'll be okay. Keep talking. Distract me.' Don't look at me. Don't let me think. Pretend everything is okay by pretending something else is wrong. Distract.

Zayn nods, gives half a hum, taps his fingers on the steering wheel. He's uncomfortable. Does he know I'm lying? That this is all a lie? Or is he just trying to control his own emotions while driving? Though he does it in very different ways to me, I've often thought this is why we are such good friends. The urge to pretend that everything is okay. Zayn is all about the drama, unless it's real. Then he's quiet, sombre, his voice cracks, like it does now. He forces a smile onto his lips, but it won't stick. His nose wrinkles and I see his wet eyes.

'He whispered to me: "Just remember how he was".' I reach for Zayn's knee and give it a squeeze. A tear drops and he swipes it away. 'He's okay,' he adds.

'Yeah,' I reply.

Just remember how he was. And I realise that's what Mickey's dad was doing all those times I saw him over the years, all the times he expressed a hope we might get back together. That's why he was so fond of me and the old times. Because when Mickey and I were together we were still children. And I think of Oscar and my heart breaks for Mickey's dad. Oscar will always be my little boy. And Mickey will always be his. And I know that all the lies are worth it. It's the only way. I will never let anyone take Oscar from me.

HIM

Black isn't her colour, but she still looks good. The dress is tight. I feel a stirring in my groin. I won't show it, but I'm angry at her tears. I understand she has to look sad. I'd expected crocodile tears. But I can see the truth. The tension next to her mouth. That slight pull down when she doesn't realise anyone is watching. It's like a crack into her soul. Into her heart. This has hurt her. And I feel jealous. Rageful. Like I want to obliterate him from her life. I want to obliterate all of them. I want her all to myself. Just the two of us in a room, a tower, like a fairy tale. Like it should be. But I know. I know life is not princes and princesses. I know she is not my Rapunzel, my Cinderella. But she could be. She could be everything I wanted. Everything. But we have to deal with some things first. Some small minor issues.

I think of that tension on her face. And I want to touch it. Smooth it out. The soft skin to the side of her mouth. My finger. My finger in her mouth. And her sucking, sucking and looking at me with those blue eyes. She can do innocent, I've seen it. Sucking my finger and all innocent eyes. The excitement rises in me. I have to control my breathing. Soon. Soon. I keep soothing myself. That's how I cope. I make promises. I have to be patient. I should enjoy the build-up. The anticipation. Savour it. Because when the time comes to bite the fruit it will be sweeter still.

Outside it's getting dark. The rain clouds merging with those of the night. Pulling the covers up. Smothering the day.

Checking I've not been seen, I leave the Italian restaurant.

BETH – TEN DAYS TILL THE PARTY

I'm sorry to have to contact you with bad news. Kareem Farah was killed in a bike accident yesterday on the Lower Sevenoaks Road. His family have asked for privacy at this difficult time, and will be holding a small ceremony for close friends and family only. They have asked for no flowers, but for donations in Kareem's memory to be made to the Child Bereavement Trust. A terrible loss. RIP Kareem.
   Helen Smith-Parr

Kareem is dead. I stare at the screenshot of the Facebook message Zayn forwarded. *But I just saw him?* Brittle head girl Helen, still in charge after all these years. Who breaks news like this via Facebook? The fact she is hyphenating her name with presumably that of her partner's irrationally irritates me. She doesn't strike me as a feminist who wants to keep her own identity, more someone who wants to sound posher than she is. Get angry or cry, that's what my dad always used to say I did. I blink, the image quivers, the words blurring. I steady myself against my desk. Bright sunshine pours absurdly through the office double height windows, casting everything in cheery unflinching tones. There are smears on my phone screen, fingerprints on my laptop screen, croissant crumbs on my keyboard. All the grimy detritus of my life spotlit. I reject the incoming call from Zayn.

There must be a mistake? Kareem was at Mickey's memorial on Friday. Restless, jumpy in his cheap suit, electric with life. I think of the moment he looked directly at the car. Seemed to see through glass and metal to what I was thinking. As if he knew I was thinking about us. And now he's dead. Gone. I could have spoken to him. I could have opened the car door and walked up to him. Asked what he was up to? If he was happy? Except that could never have happened. People like Helen would never have allowed it. I reject another incoming call from Zayn, scrubbing at my face. There is no mention of a wife in the message. Was Kareem seeing Helen? Is that why she's messaged? No, surely not. An absurd pang of jealousy at her being the one to deliver the news twists in my chest.

My desk phone rings, and I jump, automatically answering it.

'Hello, Trench PR, Beth speaking.' Ever the good girl. Ever the star employee. What am I doing? I can't talk to people now. What if it's Matt from Unity sex dolls? My social media spying tells me *This Morning* is being accused of rage-bait for inviting one of the dolls onto the couch with Phil and Holly.

'Beth?' Zayn's voice cuts through my panic. 'I'm so sorry,' he says.

I exhale. Then feel a rise of anger: I rejected Zayn's call. Can't he leave me alone for one minute to try and process this? 'I can't believe it. And after Mickey. That was only last week. I don't understand?' Is this what happens now? Have we reached the age where people we know start to die? And these were both acts committed by others – a violent mugging, an accident. What about illness? My friends and I are heading into our forties. My heart squeezes as I think of anything happening to Zayn, to Danny, to Hellie, to me. To Carmen. A small voice telling me it might have already, and I would never know. 'Oh God.'

'There should be a better way – than a cut-and-paste Facebook message.'

Zayn echoes my own earlier thoughts, making me feel pathetically grateful he did insistently call, and guilty for momentarily wishing he hadn't. 'Yes, but then we probably wouldn't find out until months later, when it's too late to . . . ' I trail off. I couldn't go to Mickey's memorial, not inside, not really be there. This time it isn't even an option. This message mentions a small ceremony for close friends and family only. Is Helen going? I didn't know Kareem anywhere near as well as I did Mickey. Never met his parents. Never kept in touch. Our relationship was over before it started. But still, I had held those thin fingers, felt the press of his jittery skinny body against mine. Two people I've kissed are now dead. Two people I've slept with. A strange giggle burbles out my lips. 'Sorry. I can't believe it.' I'm repeating myself. Is it shock? Can you feel shock over someone you shagged a couple of times two decades ago? Air catches in my throat. In my peripheral vision I sense Geoff's attention. Feel him circling like a vulture in skinny jeans. I shouldn't be upset. I don't have the right.

'There's a piece in the *Sevenoaks Observer*.' Zayn sounds calm. 'Says it was a hit-and-run. He was a cyclist.'

'How awful.' I can see Kareem's lanky body in Lycra, but I didn't know he rode. I didn't know anything about him, apart from that penetrating look. But that wasn't real, that was coincidence, my imagination playing tricks because I was overwrought about Mickey. And now this. Another ex-lover I have never told Danny about. I wince. Another barbed omission I need to keep hidden in my blood-covered hands. 'Does it say anything else about him – what did he do?' I could have spoken to him. He was right there.

'Deputy manager of some care home,' Zayn sighs. And I picture him pulling his hand over his thin face, at his desk in his corporate office. 'He had a fiancée. Thirty-two, recruitment consultant.'

Oh no. Was she at Mickey's memorial? If I'd spoken to Kareem, would we have been introduced? 'Oh God.' I say.

'You alright?' Zayn repeats.

Geoff circles closer. Whispers are starting. The sun a spotlight on me in the wide-open stage of our duplex-height office. 'Yes. Gotta go.' I put the phone down, force myself to stand. My legs shake. Do they remember? Muscle memory of wrapping around Kareem. Belt buckles, and lips. His hand tucking his shirt into his waistband. The twenty metres walk across the office feels never-ending. Everyone knows when you've had bad news, don't they? Even from a master of emotional suppression like me. I'm too well practised to let it show on my face. My protective layers, long ago applied, are thick, impenetrable. I smile brightly at Geoff who pauses in front of me, his squishy face tilted in mock sympathy atop his grey turtleneck. 'You okay?' But I keep on walking. Through the glass door into the echoing concrete reception. Thankfully the new receptionist is away from her desk. I power on into the clinical white marble ladies. Every surface flawless and spotless, and lethal if wet. I walk into a cubicle, closing the toilet seat to sit on. And lock the door, even though the receptionist is the only other female member of staff in today. Finally I let my face and body react. Breathe in the sickly vanilla scent that auto-sprays every fifteen minutes.

I didn't know Kareem. Hardly knew him. I feel myself clench. As if my body is telling me I'm lying. That it remembers. People I know, people my age, have started dying. I call Danny. I need to hear his voice. I need him to tell me it is okay. I can just say it was an old school friend. No one special, but a shock nonetheless. No names. No details. Nothing too risky. The phone rings, four, five, six times, then his voicemail cuts in. I press call again. One, two, three, four, five, six rings. 'Hey, you've reached Danny . . .'

I hang up. Where is he? Is his phone on silent? My need for him is primal, and only escalated by it being withheld. I try again. It goes straight to voicemail. A muted scream of frustration escapes my lips. I slam the top of the stainless steel toilet tissue dispenser

The Anniversary Party

with my palm. The tingle of pain sharpens my senses. I'm alone. The cubicle walls rise up around me, casting dark shadows against the white ceiling, they close in tight, tall and slender, like the walls of a coffin. And I know I couldn't have told Danny anything if he had answered. Not in reality. It would be too much of a risk. And I suddenly feel something in the shadows stalking me, circling me like prey, sweeping over me again. Is it grief? Sorrow for the tragic loss of two lives? Or sorrow that I cannot tell my own husband about them? That I cannot tell him who I really am?

HIM

It has affected her. And that hurts. Jealousy a familiar ache, a well-worked muscle flexed. I have to keep it under control. I have to keep it secret. Not let anyone see I am raging inside. How can she feel sad for a man she used to know? A boy. I kid myself I want to ease her pain, but I don't. I want to scrub it out. Obliterate her feelings for anyone else. I want her to only care for me.

She's changed her plans. Withdrawn. Back to her husband. To him. *Danny.* I want her away from him. I want her all to myself. I imagine stroking her arm, pulling her into me, breathing in her scent, the weight of her body against mine, the feel of her on top of me. I move my newspaper to shield my lap. She usually walks with such purpose, but now she waivers, the events of the last few days making her unsteady on her feet. I could support her. I could make her feel better. But no. All I can do is watch. Observe. Wait.

Just a tiny bit longer. Until I can make her truly, wholly mine.

BETH – SEVEN DAYS TILL THE PARTY

'To Mickey and Kareem!' Zayn says. Sways. My kitchen lights twinkle in the reflection of his glass.

'To Mickey and Kareem,' I raise my own glass in answer to his. Almost make them meet.

'What did happen with you and Kareem back then?' Zayn pours more wine into my glass. There are one . . . two . . . that's three. This is the . . . third bottle.

Sometimes I forget Zayn and I weren't as close back then. But if I think about then – before – he is there, on the periphery. Like he's black and white, and all the other images are in colour. Perhaps if we'd been closer then things would have been different. I wouldn't have made the same mistakes.

'We dated,' I say.

'Dated or *dated* as Nate would say?' Zayn raises an eyebrow mimicking his flatmate's guileless attempts at keeping up with his own more O.T.T. mannerisms. He cackles.

No. It wasn't like that. The sex wasn't good enough, it felt forced, disconnected, alien compared to Mickey. 'Just one of those stupid school things.' We went to his cousin's eighteenth birthday at a Chinese restaurant. After dinner they pushed all the tables back and it became a dance floor. I sat astride Kareem on the chairs round the edge. Desperate to make it mean something. To showcase our great passion. His cousin said something suggestive. Looked at me like he just had to wait his turn. I dumped Kareem the next day. Within a few weeks I was back with Mickey. His dad welcoming me like an old friend. No malice, no upset.

Mickey tried very hard to be as he had before. And we carried on. It wasn't until after Easter that I finally broke up with him.

I loved Mickey with all my heart, and part of me always will. But we'd grown apart. And I at least was too immature to see it. Kareem was part of that. That break-up. A wave of revolted guilt washes over me. I treated Mickey so badly. The pain I must have caused. His wet eyes. And I didn't really get it. I was a stupid child. A few months later we took our exams and school was over. 'You do know?' I look around for Zayn's cigarette packet. I need another one. 'This means the first two guys I screwed are now dead.'

'Christ,' Zayn says. 'We're old.'

'So old,' a noise comes from upstairs. I freeze. The definite creak of the floorboards. 'Shush!' I grip his arm and knock some wine over his shirt. How loud was I talking?

Zayn tries to brush it off, but only smears himself with a bit of hummus he has on his finger. 'Damn it.'

'Shush! Oscar!' I manage. The stairs creak.

Danny appears at the kitchen door, bleary-eyed, his hair spiked from the pillow on one side. What did he hear? Panic sluices through me. I catch, and send spinning an empty bottle.

'Danny!' Zayn flings his arms open in welcome.

'You guys are still going?' Danny says. There's reproach in his voice. He sniffs. He hates cigarettes. He has that exasperated disappointed look. 'It's nearly four a.m.'

'God!' Zayn looks at his Apple Watch, and tips his wine over himself. 'I'll get an Uber.'

Four a.m. I've got to see Unity in the morning. Sex dolls. Love dolls. Deal with Matt. Bloody hell. 'How is it so late?' Did he hear anything? I told him an old friend of Zayn's had died. Not a total lie. Not my worst. I push my fingers through my hair, the washed wooden slats of the kitchen floor tilt. I rest my head in my hands.

When I look up Danny has gone. Zayn has his coat on. A pint of limescale-cloudy water is in front of me on the table.

The Anniversary Party

Zayn pulls me into him, kisses the top of my head. 'I love you,' he says.

'Love you too. I'm not old, am I?' I squeeze him back, want him to stay, want another drink, don't want tomorrow to come.

'We're both spring chickens. Gonna live forever. Light up the world like flames!' Zayn mangles his words as he staggers towards the door.

I sip my water. Through the double doors the dark blue night shifts into green, then grey, then pale white. All colour has been rinsed from the world. I open a private tab on Safari on my phone. Guilt nibbles at my edges. People use private tabs so there's no search history. For porn, for looking for something they shouldn't, for keeping things from their partners. Because it doesn't remember what I've opened before I have to type in all the login details for my secret Facebook account. Not my name, not my email address, not my photo. All fake. Another part of the world cut off from me, another part within which I have to lie about who I really am. Mickey and Kareem's pages have become memorials. Hundreds of people I don't know mourning them. Someone has posted a photo of what looks like a scrap of paper. Writing on it that I can't read. Something tugs at my memory, but no. I don't understand that. It must be an in-joke. These are people who knew them now. Who loved them now. Those who have a far greater claim to be sad.

As streaks of red the colour of cut blood oranges run across the March morning sky, I finally go to bed. Every step on the carpet covered stairs reassuring myself that Danny didn't hear anything. That he doesn't know.

BETH – SEVEN DAYS TILL THE PARTY

I wake with a gasp, as if someone has slapped me. The piece of paper online. I know where I recognised it from. It looked the same as the paper the anonymous note was sent on. Our grey sheets are wrapped around my body, tight, wet. I reach out for comfort, but Danny is gone. His side of the bed cold. I roll off the mattress, kick the half-drunk pint of water I obviously left on the floor last night. The glass tips, and water soaks a dark patch into the carpet. Drops glistening on the soft weave. Dammit. Where's my phone? Panic grips at me. Flashes of last night. Zayn singing. Danny's disappointed face. I said I had screwed Mickey and Kareem – did Danny hear? I look at my watch. Bloody hell, Oscar will have left with Hellie already. Crap. And I've got to stop at the office before I meet Unity. Bugger. Why didn't Danny wake me? I think of his look last night. Irritated. I swallow the fear. He would have said. He would have.

The threatening note is still in my handbag. The letters printed so hard into the paper you can feel the indentations. *I know who you really are.* That faded retro feel to the lined paper – as if it's been torn from the cheap mass-produced notebook the corner shop used to sell. It does look familiar. Wasn't there writing on the one I saw last night? Was it the same as this? I blink, images shuffling in front of my eyes, my sluggish brain trying to order them. It looked like the same retro paper as the one posted on Facebook. But why would someone have posted a photo of that on Kareem's memorial page? Is my mind playing tricks? I can't shake the feeling that I recognised that image.

I find my phone downstairs where I left it. The battery flat. I swallow my frustration. Bloody Apple. All these updates and the blasted thing can't last more than a few hours. I glance at my laptop but it's too risky. Oscar uses it sometimes to watch videos. Danny might pick it up. It's harder to avoid them stumbling on something. Harder to control. I have to wait. I shove a charger into my phone, and shove my body into the shower. I turn off the extractor fan, crank up the hot water and focus on trying to sweat out the alcohol. I don't feel too bad. That's not a good sign. That means my hangover hasn't hit yet. I'm probably still drunk.

After I feel my pores have given up some of the wine, and that I'm thirsty enough to drink the shower water, I turn it cold. One quick hard blast and it's like a squeegee clearing the misted screen of my mind. Deeply unpleasant but necessary. Everything comes back into focus. There was a photo of lined paper posted online. I'm sure of it. I have fifteen minutes before I'm late, and I pull on skinny jeans, a navy slash neck jumper. Peel the dry cleaning plastic from my green wool coat.

Waiting for the phone to power up feels interminable. It takes two seconds to order an Uber, and I stay next to the hallway plug so my phone can get maximum charge. I open a private tab again, tap in my login details, open up Facebook. I scroll down through Kareem's site. No sign of a photo of the scrap of paper. I check to make sure it's showing all comments and not just most recent. Nothing. Maybe it was on Mickey's? But there's nothing there either. Lots of heartbroken emojis and RIPs. That's it. Did I imagine it? My mind twisting the truth, riffing off my anxiety around the note? As if I could be outed. Perhaps it's a remnant of a dream, and my drunken mind mixed the two memories up? But it still niggles at me like kale caught between my teeth.

This is what you get for two hours sleep and a hangover at my age. I'm going mad. I'm jumpy. It's probably my poor system trying to get rid of all these stimulants. I ignore the empty bottles, and the congealing hummus on the kitchen table and get my cab.

'I'm delighted you finally made it out here,' Matt Jacobs, the illustrious owner of Unity love dolls, gives me a sideways glance. I've been avoiding this since we took them on in January. The warehouse is out along the A13, towards Rainham. Where the houses and flats thin into industrial parks, sprouting like utilitarian mushrooms against the edge of the marshes, the green stretching into where the Thames bends like a snake. No one lives here. They just drive in to perform their tasks in these cold shacks of buildings, fleeing as soon as they can. I don't blame them. There were no other cars in the gravel car park when my Uber pulled up outside. I half-expected some protestors stationed outside, but, so far, people's reactions have been restricted to hot takes and think pieces. Probably perpetuating the reach of the sex dolls. Increasing sales. There was no one else in the Portakabin-style office I walked through to reach this warehouse out back. It feels like Matt and I are entirely alone, and I want to step outside to glimpse the anchoring peaks of Canary Wharf in the distance. Remind myself it's not too far to home.

'And we get to share the arrival of Treasure together,' Matt is saying. He's making it sound like we're expectant parents to the cutesy monikered AI sex doll. The wispy beard he petulantly perseveres with stretches to reveal glimpses of his weak chin. God, I feel sick. Can I tell a client not to smile? We don't want him to appear weird. This is already a potential image disaster, I need him not to look like every stereotype of a sex predator there is. He clearly works out, his arms muscular, and the top half of his face is attractive, but it all goes wrong near his mouth. And he stands too close. Apparently he has a wife, though the suggestion that we involve her in the press was mooted by him, and I've never met her. He has the unfortunate air of someone who doesn't spend much time with other human beings. I guess that's what you get for working alone with fake vulvas.

I step back. Force a smile onto my face, my skin tight and dehydrated, strains with the challenge. 'A breakthrough of undoubted significance. In . . . err . . . this industry.'

A flicker of annoyance flashes across his usually over-eager puppy face, as if he caught my insincerity.

I move quickly. 'Could you show me the latest designs? It may be important for the next press release. For context,' I add.

His face visibly relaxes. I forgot the golden rule there: don't make the weirdos feel weird. I need more sleep, water, eye drops, perhaps a bacon sandwich. And I'd been toying with going vegan. What an idiot. I need to look after myself more. I need to get up earlier, start meditating, maybe doing that thing from *The Artist's Way* where you journal three pages of free flow stream of consciousness each morning. It's supposed to be like therapy. I could go to the gym with Zayn and Nate. Look up that Adriene who does the YouTube yoga videos. Stop imagining I'm seeing anonymous threatening notes everywhere. Stop feeling like the shark can smell blood.

Mickey is dead anyway.

Kareem is dead anyway.

I could die anyway.

Matt witters on as I follow him into the warehouse. 'Once we've escorted the dolls through customs, we reassemble things in here,' he says. 'They're delivered straight to the back entrance.' He indicates the huge wooden gates that can be pulled open, the smaller human-sized door punched in them, a very poor cousin to the entrances to Oxford and Cambridge colleges. But there are no quads of green manicured grass on the other side. I picture a truck reversing, its back open, eager to spill its load into this dark damp place.

Air snags my dry throat and my stomach lurches. Suspended from the ceiling are twenty naked women. Because that's what they look like at first glance: real women hanging from hooks.

'Magnificent, aren't they?' Matt beams. 'The heads and hair arrive from China detached, but our clients prefer the girls to be constructed when they reach them.'

My mind grapples with what it's seeing, and comes back with Rocky in the meat market, surrounded by carcasses. 'They're so lifelike,' I manage.

Matt looks pleased. He turns the nearest doll towards us, her long blonde hair swaying as she does. Close up I can see she is a cartoonish approximation of sexy. Her face reminds me of Manga drawings. 'This is my Treasure,' he says. 'Though she is just the base prototype. The finished possession will be able to blink and talk. Respond to questions. Make suitable sounds. For us to use.'

He looks up suddenly, his eyes locking onto mine. Lines from the anti-doll articles run through my head. *Unity have weaponised the objectification of women.* I involuntarily rock back on the heels of my ankle boots. Grip the thick hem of my coat to ground myself. Feel my neck grow flushed.

Matt returns his loving gaze to his Treasure. 'We can take her on *This Morning*.'

Stale wine roils inside me. Treasure has smaller, perter boobs than some of the well-endowed models around us, and wide hips. Her genitals are hair-free. I'm surrounded by naked women, or rather giant life-size sex toys. 'She will have to be . . . clothed.' I gesture. This is going to look awful: it's going to make great television.

Matt doesn't seem to notice my discomfort. 'She's based on one of our most popular girls. You can order her with whatever hair colour and style you like and we send her out with three different outfits.'

'It's good to have options,' I stare at Treasure's feet. The toes are long, slightly twisted on her right foot, like mine are from years of walking in work shoes. They are unnervingly realistic dangling there.

'We can fully customise your love doll in any way you wish. 3D mapping is available – from a full body scan. With an appointment,' he gives a little laugh, as if it's funny. 'Our customers appreciate that we can create a truly unique companion doll.'

A companion doll? I'm using that in a press release. I nod for him to continue. It's like driving past a car crash, it's horrific, but you can't look away.

Box fresh. Untouched. Totally yours. And I realise he's made the perfect woman: a pornstar, that no one else has slept with.

'For example, this lady is modelled on the wife of one of our clients who sadly passed away a few years ago,' Matt strides between the hanging bodies and turns one towards me. Her blank Manga face young, her body, though more apple in shape, still rendered absurdly nubile by the flawless plastic. I wonder how old the woman was when she passed away? How old her widow is now? Is this a reliving of youth? Rendering her virginal again? 'You get to experience the first time all over again.' Is it romantic or terrifying? Regardless, I know it's a great angle for a publicity article: Grieving Man Has Sex Doll Modelled on Dead Wife.

A flash of Mickey above me comes into my mind, and I drop my gaze in case Matt sees me blush. I turn and touch the nearest doll, distracting myself. 'Cold,' I say. Mickey and Kareem will be cold now. A shudder runs through me.

'That's why we sell the USB attachments,' Matt beams. 'It allows you to warm parts of your love doll to a more realistic thirty-seven degrees.'

Jesus Christ. 'So, they can be modelled on anyone?'

'We have a minimum height limit of 150 centimetres,' he says, stroking the back of one of the dolls nearest him.

Oh God. So they don't look like children. I won't put that in the press pack. I stare at the intricate vulva of the doll next to me. The skin is texturised: a realistic colour, with stubble detail.

'Go ahead and touch her if you want,' Matt says, business-like.

I look up sharply. He's not being inappropriate, is he? No. This is just a product, like any other. I try not to wrinkle my nose. Just keep going. Keep asking questions. 'So, you can do different-coloured hair and err . . . ' Think of something else – don't make this weirder than it already is. I look around. Against the wall are some boxes, yet to be unpacked, with Chinese characters penned in Sharpie on the outside. 'What about things like tattoos?'

He fixes me with his dark eyes. 'Do you have a tattoo? I can't say it's ever appealed to me.' His voice is completely matter-of-fact, as if we're discussing which wine we like. This is his world, after all. His passion. I keep my voice light, professional.

'Yes – just a silly teenage thing.' I blink and I'm back in that Brighton tattoo parlour with Jessica. Both screaming drunk. Daring each other on. Her flirting with the tattooist so he wouldn't ask for ID. I never tell anyone about my tattoo. Even in truth and dare games. It's embarrassing. Bloody hangover, it's made me sloppy.

'And what is it of?' Matt asks.

It's like he's feeding off my discomfort. Forcing me towards an edge I don't want to meet. No. It's me. I only feel uncomfortable because I'm hungover. Because I overshared with a client. Oh God, Rob is going to kill me.

'The design can affect our plan of action,' he says. 'Theoretically. Some of the more intricate ones are difficult to recreate – they can be done, but they cost more,' he peers at me. Expectant. A leg of one of the dolls bumps against my back, as if prodding me to answer.

'Angel wings,' I say. Heat seeps up my neck.

'Oh well that's easy.' He turns back to the doll. 'We'd just have an artist go ahead and paint that right on.' He indicates her top arm.

Mickey's thumb gently stroking over my shaved bikini line, tracing the edge of the fresh tattoo. Fly me straight to heaven.

Matt glances back at me, frowning slightly as if he can read my thoughts. He runs his fingers down the doll's arm, across her lower back, over her hip, as if he's trying to sense where the correct spot is.

I clear my throat. I want to be out of this room. Away from the hanging swinging naked bodies. I might be sick.

My hand scrabbles in my pocket for my phone. 'Sorry,' I say, 'I've got to take this.'

He looks surprised. Lets go of the doll, and she swings away from him.

Hair from another brushes against my arm as I leave. Human hair. I know that's what they use. Only the finest quality. Ethical temple hair, that's donated as part of a religious ceremony and payment used to benefit the community. It should be reassuring. But as the hair dyed a perfect shade of someone's fantasy touches me, I feel nothing but nausea. Images flash through my mind. Mickey taking me from behind, my ponytail wrapped round his hand, copying the porn we'd watched. Droplets of white wine push out of my skin. Dirty beads of shame. Matt is looking lovingly at the doll again, his hand cupping her elbow. The other dolls swing gently on their hooks, their heads forwards, a field of swaying human hair.

I grab my handbag from the empty desk in the front, summon an Uber and call my excuses to Matt. He's perfectly happy with his fembots. I'll work from home for the rest of the day. I'm too jumpy for the office. The impact of Mickey and Kareem's passing has hit me harder than I thought. And the Pinot didn't help. I watch as the tiny car emblem excruciatingly crawls closer on the map on my screen. The wind is cold, with nothing to cushion it from whipping round the serrated edges of the squat buildings. But it's better: I can't be inside the warehouse, with those pre-packaged pick 'n' mix male gaze eroticised approximations of women, a moment longer. Seven minutes outside is preferable to that windowless room, the suffocating smell of silicon, Matt murmuring, 'my Treasure'. Are these the natural next steps to all women smoothing and shaping themselves with Botox, fillers, butt workouts, into ever-identical versions of beauty recognisable from the reality TV screens to the local bar? Removing all differences, charm, humanity? I don't need the nagging question to take hold: just how many men are there like Matt, who would prefer the curated, silent, compliant companions to the messy reality? Thank God I never succumbed to men who preferred their own projected ideals over me.

Finally the Uber arrives. I collapse into the salvation of the back of the thankfully uncommunicative driver's car. My fingers stinging from the hot dry air of the Prius's heating. The industrial units rotate, like Tetris blocks, into the more familiar office towers of central London. I just need some sleep. And water.

I reach into my bag for my bottle, my hand brushing against paper. It's an envelope. I thought I left The Note at home? Carefully hidden between the pages of a book in the pile next to my bed. The hairs rise to attention on the back of my neck. I pull it out. Turn it over. On the front, printed in capitals, like before, is my first name. But this is new. Where did this come from? Through the door at home? Did Danny or Oscar put it in my bag for me? But I didn't notice it this morning. Then again, I was hurrying, panicked, worrying about what I thought I saw online, and not paying attention to what was happening in front of me. I force my hands to stop shaking, and slide a finger under the flap. It's as if the brittle wind has blown through the closed car door as I slide out another small scrap of lined paper.

BETH

Only two letters are written on the note. A 'd' and an 'e'. The lined paper cut immediately after – like it's been snipped partway through a word. It's a nonsense. A nothing.

'This alright for you?' the Uber driver says from the front.

I slide the paper back into the envelope as if it's his child's photo I've just been caught with. 'Great. Perfect. Thank you.'

'Can't stop long – the cameras,' he says gruffly.

I push the envelope back into my bag, breathe as I watch my boots connect with the ground, as if everything is normal. 'Thanks,' I say. I slam the door and pelt away from the car, even though I read that article that said passengers were marked down on Uber for forcefully closing vehicle doors. I pull my bag onto my shoulder, the envelope jabbing at the soft skin under my arm. My breath comes quickly as I fumble my keys in the door.

'Oh Beth!' Cat from next door's voice makes me jump. My heart pinballing round my chest before it collapses into my stomach. *Not now*. Cat pulls the black painted door of her own terrace to, but instead of going down her front path to the road, she comes towards the low-level wall that divides our two properties. Her pointed face, reminiscent of a Jack Russell that has cornered a rat to play with. Her tailored puffa jacket making her resemble a tight roll of black bin bags with a head. I can't be doing with recycling issues, or slightly malicious updates about other parents at Oscar's school, or whatever this is.

'Cat! Hey!' I smile, trying to get my key into the door anyway. *Take the hint*. But though she's wearing the smart slacks and carrying her leather laptop bag I recognise as her meeting-in-town attire, she doesn't seem to be in any hurry.

'I'm glad I caught you. You've been busy, hey?' she says. I wish Cathy was the one who worked from home – I've always preferred her of the two. Despite seeming to crave human interaction during the day while her wife and daughter are out, Cat can't help making spiteful little digs about my ineffectuality. None of my usual deflections seem to work with her. 'I wanted to check that your friend got hold of you?'

'My friend?' I rest the key tip against the lock. What friend? Only Zayn comes over regularly – and she's nosy enough to know him.

'I'd not seen him before,' she says. *There we go.* 'I came out when I saw him outside. He was sort of walking up and down, like he was nervous,' she laughed.

A man? I think of the note in my handbag. Could it be from him? My hand drops down, and the edge of the key scratches against the wood door.

'I mean, you can never be too careful these days, can you?' She says. 'I thought he might be lost. But he said he'd come to see you in person. So unusual nowadays, isn't it – for people to just drop by? He didn't catch you then?'

'I don't think so. It depends who it was,' I forced a laugh. Zayn isn't a strange man. There's Rob, the guys at work – but they would've just called me if they needed me. They wouldn't come to my house. Suddenly the cool appraising way Matt looked at me pops into my head. That thin wispy smile. But he couldn't know where I live? Cat is staring at me, waiting for her titbit. I keep my voice bright. 'Did he leave a name?'

'Said you were friends when you were younger. I always think it's interesting who people grew up with, don't you? Very revealing,' she gives me a knowing look. I bite down my irritation. 'Said he used to call you Lily!' Ice cold fear pins me to the spot. Cat gives her faux nasal laugh. 'Said his name was Mickey.

I remember cause I thought you'd never seen a man less like a mouse. That's why I'd come outside . . . '

But I no longer hear what Cat's saying. What if Danny had been in? Or Hellie? Mickey came here. How did he find me? That shouldn't have been possible. 'When was this?' The edges of my vision seem to quiver, as if someone has shaken the very foundations of my life. My very perfect lie.

'Monday, three weeks back.' Her chagrin at the interruption soon expedited in her obvious delight in knowing something I don't. Something I need. 'It must have been, because it was last general waste day and I noticed they'd put their cardboard in again,' she nods her head towards our other neighbour.

Three week's ago. On the Monday. The day he died. Mickey came here, fifteen years after I saw him last, and then within hours he was dead. 'What time? Can you remember?' My voice sounds admirably calm. This is what years of putting on a good show has done. Inside something dark and slippery turns over in my stomach.

Cat frowns. 'Well, I was back from dropping Amelia at school, but they hadn't collected the rubbish yet. I thought that might be who it was to begin with – the lad who comes down and empties the food waste into the one big wheelie bin, before the truck comes down. But it wasn't.'

'So that would mean?' I prompt her.

'Oh, I always forget you don't really work from home,' she flicks her eyes up and down me, as if I might be an apparition. 'I see Danny all the time. And that pretty young au pair girl,' she laughs. I feel the sharp tip of a dig: *you don't work from home* is shorthand for *I spend more time with my child than you do*. I swallow the retort that Hellie is actually a trained nanny. And pretty much part of the family. 'The truck always comes round at eleven-ish. Unless it's a bank holiday, obviously.' And she gives that smug little inane laugh again.

Behind me a black cab rattles down the road between the parallel lines of cars, and over a speed bump. The wind whines through the tops of the trees that push stubbornly through the pavement, as if the very breeze is fed-up of this exchange. 'So, between nine and eleven?' I say. I feel like I'm cross-examining a witness, but this is important. Why did Mickey come here? Could he have left the first note? But no, because he can't have left this one. I tighten my grip on my handbag.

Cat nods, her smile smug against her pointy nose and chin.

'And he didn't say anything else? Or leave a note or anything?' She's looking at me questioningly now. I need to reign this in. Everything is fine, and I am in control. Everything is perfect.

'No,' she places a hand on the dividing wall. 'He didn't get you then?'

'No, but don't worry, I'll give him a buzz,' I slot the key into the lock. As if I'm going to tell her he was killed mere hours later, she'd explode with excitement. 'Thanks Cat!' I trill, and slip inside before she can add another word.

I catch my breath in the hallway. If I'd been here . . . If he'd come later . . . If he'd left a message. Oh God, Mickey. I think of his dad at the memorial. He always insisted Mickey was fond of me, even years after we split. Might he have mentioned something to his dad before he came? But this isn't some romcom movie: your ex-boyfriends don't just show up after fifteen years to declare their undying love. And if they did, you'd probably advise they got help. What we had was decades ago, we were different people. But then you never forget your first. Had something happened to make Mickey remember me? To make him come here? I pull the note from my bag again. But these are two separate events? They must be. Except what if I did see that photo of the same scrap of lined paper on Kareem's Facebook? Maybe whoever posted it deleted it. Or whoever is looking after the account took it down, thinking it wasn't important. But is it important? What does it mean? On the edge of the scrap of lined paper, as if it was torn through the last word written on the page, are two letters. Both lowercase. Not scoured in black biro, but in blue ballpoint pen. A message. It has to be.

I call Danny. His phone goes straight to voicemail. I hang up and send him a text:

Hey Love, Did you put an envelope in my bag? xx

That must be it. Danny did it. Or Oscar. But why? I was fifteen minutes in the office on the way to Unity Sex Dolls. I just grabbed the paperwork I needed. And went to the loo. I left my bag on my desk. Someone could have put it in then? I think of Matt alone in his building with his freaky life-size dolls. I left my bag on the desk there too. Why didn't I keep it with me? Any of them could have done this. The words from the last note replay in my mind. *I know who you really are.* It's happening, isn't it? What I've always feared. The past is coming for me. Mickey found me. Who else could? I grope behind me and sit on the bottom stairs.

There has to be a rational explanation. I'm wired from my hangover. Freaked out by Mickey and Kareem, and the bloody creepy sex dolls. I'm seeing things that aren't there. Conflating events in my mind. There's some simple explanation. This is just a bit of paper. Yes, I don't know how it got in my bag but that's easily explained. Someone must have put it there. Perhaps by accident. Perhaps I picked it up in the office with my notes for Unity. *The Perfect Partner.* Perhaps the first note really was a direct marketing mailout that we ran from work? Therefore, I would have seen it before: a prototype, or similar. Someone else's project. There are a million logical explanations. I force myself to look at the paper. It grows taut and crackles under the grip of my fingers. I stare at it, and it's as if it is coming into sharp focus.

I now know for sure this is no trick of my mind. No marketing campaign.

It can't be.

The letters 'de'. The way the 'd' loops up and down. The way the end of the 'e' slightly flicks up.

It's my handwriting.

BETH

The rattle of the wind against the house windows snaps me out of my reverie. Another storm coming – we've had so many this year. Deluge upon deluge. Parts of the country disappearing under sluices of muddy water as rivers burst their banks. The roads slick with grimy liquid with nowhere to go. The ground beneath too full to stomach it. Climate change making its presence known. I've always been susceptible to the pressure change of incoming storms. That's what explains this throbbing between my eyebrows. Pressing down on the thorns of my hangover. I've been staring at this scrap of paper as if it's a hypnotist's watch.

I shove the note into the green recycling bag before I climb the stairs to my room, the weight of the last few hours catching up with me. I'm overwrought. Stressed. In need of a break. Enid Cat is curled up waiting, a warm tortoiseshell pebble on our cold grey linen sheets. I'll take a nap. A reset. Oscar has after-school club later, and then football. Hellie won't bring him home for hours. I kick off my shoes, undo the top button of my jeans, and slide under the duvet. Enid Cat's head pops up, accusatory for disturbing her.

'Hello girl, you tired too?'

I run a hand over her comforting warmth. Close my eyes.

Mickey is above me. His mouth on my neck. His hands holding me down. Between my legs. I arch up into him, feel him hard against my thigh.

I awake to a sour taste in my mouth. Guilty at sleeping in the middle of the work day. About dreaming of another man. Enid Cat has gone. There are no missed calls on my phone. I grind my palms into my eyes, clammy and jumpy from my dream. All my nerve endings singing. The last dregs of alcohol burning out of me, no doubt.

The last week has been a strain. I shudder as I remember Matt looking at me as his hand cupped his Treasure's elbow. Remember Mickey gripping me there at a party. His fingers tightening until it hurt. I need to bring order back to my existence. I get up. Let the shower in our en suite run till it's hot over our freestanding bath. Think about how Danny and I renovated this place together. We'd found the bath at a reclamation yard, persuaded a taxi driver to let us put it in the back of the cab to get it home. It was so heavy it took us nearly an hour to get it into the hallway before we'd collapsed in fits of giggles. I'd straddled him there on the hallway floor, as we pulled fast at each other's clothes, desperate to feel skin on skin. My bare knees cold on the tiles, Danny's hands on my hips, holding my gaze until the moment he came. Afterwards we'd sat in the bath in the hallway drinking champagne from a bottle. I'd never felt a connection like that with anyone before Danny. Then a few years later, we'd bathed Oscar in this tub when he was a baby. I'd cradle him in one hand, and cup water with the other to rinse his tiny fluff of hair. Careful not to get any soap in his eyes. Danny standing by with the softest towel we could find. I get into the bath, the enamel cold under my bare feet. Step under the spray, closing my eyes, pushing my hands back through my hair. As if I can wash it all away in the middle of a Thursday afternoon. As if it could be that simple.

Afterwards I strip the bedding, pull on new, identical grey linen sheets. Rinse the wine bottles in the echoing kitchen, and put them in the designated yellow recycling bag. I pause in our utility to push the note deeper into the bin, pull a pile of newspapers over it.

My hopes of finding Enid Cat curled against the radiator in the bland box room on the front of the house that forms my study are fruitless. Never mind. I'll have to make do with the blue polka dot ceramic mug of ginger tea I brought up for cheer. Ruched clouds the colour of gravestones stretch above the rooftops outside, pebbles of granite and concrete stacked against the incoming tide of rain. It's not quite dark enough to pull the short brown curtains closed. I curse again that I still haven't got round to replacing them. Oscar will be playing football inside the school hall this afternoon. I plug in my laptop, and the external monitor bathes the room in frigid blue light. I should repaint the walls in here too. The rest of the house is done, warm, welcoming, but I never seem to get round to tackling the only space in the house that is all mine. I am aware I am keeping myself busy. Active. Focused. Don't look down.

I open my Unity files. Click through my notes. Think about how to spin the growing anger at the arrival of the lifelike dolls. Their pleading glazed eyes. Cold skin. The way you can manipulate them into any position you want. I stare at the blank page. I've done this before, I coax myself. Many times. I just have to find the positive. Distract from the truth. I'm a master of that. I've been doing it my whole life – it is my life. Just start. It's the starting that's hard. Once it's down you can fix it. My nap has made me feel worse. I take a scalding sip of tea. I don't want to sell questionable sex dolls. I want to stop running. I want to stop lying. I want to be safe.

Before I know it, I'm back on Facebook. There is no sign of the photo I thought I saw yesterday. I'm not here for that, of course. I just want to see what people are saying. Something to make me feel better. Normal again. It's odd trying to relive the past on a forum that didn't exist back then. What would our life have been like if we'd come of age online? I quickly squash the traitorous thought: *you wouldn't have got away with it*.

I rub my fingers roughly against the fabric of the chair, as if I can wipe off the contamination from The Note. Right now social media gives me the ability to consensually snoop. I can see the last things Mickey and Kareem posted. Mickey on a night out with his girlfriend. Photos of them holding up bottles of beer at a barbecue. A young girl turns cartwheels in the background. She seems to be the daughter of his girlfriend. They look like a little family. Kareem's last post was made a month ago – about *The Apprentice*. Crushingly banal. But both their pages are filling with memories posted by friends. Some make me tear up, but others are more dubious. One on Kareem's page is from a girl who said she went to university with him. But there's something in her chosen reminiscences, of her heartbreak for his fiancée (whose name she has misspelt), that reeks.

> I am so crushed by this news. I'll always remember when I was struggling with my finals and prepping for my first City job, and Kareem made me smile by saying he believed I could do anything. I will remember his smile forever.

I wonder if she's even seen him since they graduated? But how is her self-absorption different from mine? Am I not making this all about me? A wave of disgust comes over me and I close the window. I glance at the clock. Twenty minutes till Oscar is back. An early night tonight and I'll feel better. This is just booze blues.

My treacherous fingers open the site back up. Like Icarus to the sun. I need to feed my pain, share it, learn new things about Mickey and Kareem. Make them whole again. Bring them back. At least online.

I've got to stop this.

My memory tumbles through the sheets with Mickey and Kareem. It was that dream. It's made it flesh and bone again. The heat. The smell. The gasped air. The tingling skin. I think of Mickey's protectiveness, the way he would listen rapt no matter what I had to talk about. The time we talked through the night about John Donne. Kareem's shy taking of my hand in the street.

His determination to stand by me. Danny and I haven't slept together for five months now.

I need to disentangle myself from these flashbacks. Get on with normal life. I pause to watch the rain for a moment. Punishing myself by not closing the brown curtains. Forcing me to see the ghostly reflection of my face. You can't tell my hair is red, it looks paler this way, almost blonde. Like before. My fingers are typing before I really acknowledge what they're doing: *Carmen Vassell*. Seeing her almost takes my breath away. The dip-dyed braids are gone, and she wears her hair in two Afro space-buns nowadays. Bright purple lipstick framing her big smile. Two sleek drop pendant earrings swinging above her khaki cashmere jumper. I wish I could talk to her about all this. She would have had something to say about Unity's Matt and his creepy sex dolls. She would have been horrified by the anonymous notes. Devastated for me over the death of Mickey. They met a few times, when he came to visit me at uni. And after, there was a time in a bar on Portland Place. All fresh-faced young professionals, making our way in the world. Me and Carmen in our office clothes, him in his baggy jeans, and tattoos on show. I don't remember what we talked about, but I remember the light and laughter: and how we sat in the golden setting sun until it got cold, and huddled in our coats till we staggered to the Tube. This is not the first time I've visited Carmen's page. Ever the smart cookie, her privacy settings are too high to see anything other than her beaming profile photo. She looks happy, and I like to think she is. I wonder if she ever misses me? Or if it's too painful to think of the past, and she lies, pretending she never knew such a monster.

Before I close the laptop lid, I add a new password to my computer. Making sure Danny and Oscar are locked out. I can't let them use this anymore. It's too risky. Then, I return to the kitchen, turning on the light. I hear Enid Cat's cat flap click, she pads past. Not deigning to stop. I play BBC Radio 6 Music out loud on my phone. But the wry jollity grates against the cold empty room, the floorboards grumbling at my very presence. I switch the radio off. Danny is usually home by now. But he hasn't messaged me. I call him, but it rings out. 'It's me. Just checking you're okay?'

A text appears almost straight away:

Still stuck at work. Be back late. Don't wait up x

That's twice in one week he's worked late. Unusual for him. Is he punishing me for getting drunk last night? Or did he hear the truth? The thought comes unbidden and vicious into my mind. No, that's my own guilt, my own tiredness getting to me. But I can't stop playing with the frayed edges of the idea. I hate letting Danny down. Everything I do is to protect us. I force myself to move round the kitchen again. It won't be long till Hellie and Oscar are back. Till the house comes alive again. I dry and put away the crockery on the draining board. Open the fridge to sort through that, but pause before I attempt to throw away a deflating cauliflower. I can't bear Danny's annoyance if he was going to turn it into soup or something. Instead I start sifting through my handbag, sorting through receipts: those for the bin, those for expenses. I chuck out two used tissues, and retrieve a new small pack from the utility cupboard. I pause. I last all of ten seconds, then I shift the newspapers in the recycling bag, and retrieve the note. Slide it back into my sweatpant's pocket. The paper crackling as I return to my study. Leaving all the lights on as I go, not wanting to be alone in the dark. *I know who you really are.* And now this note: cut from my own handwriting. It feels violating. Has someone really rifled through my personal possessions, taken a page of my writing, cut it up, and sent it back to me? And why? It makes no sense. Literally. The note just reads: *de*. I must be reading more into it, probably because whatever this is, is happening at the same time that two of my ex-boyfriends have died. I say it out loud, rearranging the words to see if they'll fit the hole inside me. 'My first two boyfriends are dead. My first two boyfriends have been killed.' The words flatten against the hallway walls, glance off the framed studio photos of me, Danny, and Oscar. The perfect happy family. But even I can't make myself believe the words.

I close myself into my study again. As Enid Cat won't oblige, I pull the blanket from the back of my chair over my knees. Flick on the little oil radiator I keep in here.

Two of my ex-boyfriends have been killed. Verbalising it makes it real. Makes me realise how unusual it must be. An uneasy feeling blooms under my skin.

I check my watch. Zayn might still be at the office. I open FaceTime on my laptop. Press call.

'Babes,' Zayn's voice says, as a rectangle of his chin and shoulder appear on screen. I can see his flatmate Nate behind him in their open-plan kitchen. Home then. 'I'm dying,' he groans and angles the camera so the grinning, fresh-eyed, clean-skinned, good-looking Nate disappears and his full face appears on the screen.

'Shouldn't have drunk on an empty stomach!' Nate calls laughingly in the background.

'Hi Nate – that might have been my fault!' I'm surprised at how jolly I sound. Normal. If a little like I smoked fifty fags last night. When in reality I only smoked one. Three at the most. But I can't talk to Zayn properly if Nate's there.

Nate's face appears smirking over Zayn's shoulder. The hood of his black jumper framing his head like a neck pillow. The shaped, shaved edges of his hair once again reminding me of the detachable Lego version. 'Not you too?' He gives a white teeth grin.

''Fraid so,' I can't help but smile back. He really is very good-looking. I check the small rectangle that shows the camera image of me. My red hair fluffy as I haven't run my ghds through it yet. And I forgot I wasn't wearing any make-up. What am I doing? Zayn will think I'm cracking up. This was a bad idea. I'm just being stupid. I'm overtired because of last night.

'Urgh, don't look at me,' Zayn's hand obscures the camera, and I can't help but laugh at the synchronicity of our thoughts. He turns to address Nate: 'Go away with your working liver and your bouncy collagen cells.'

'Can't a man get himself some dinner?' Nate says jokingly. 'I was thinking of cooking some nice fresh fish – maybe a bouillabaisse, mussels, clams – or what about a nice greasy curry?'

'Oh God – if you even think about cooking, I will evict you!' Zayn cries.

Nate cracks up, thumps Zayn on the back. 'Don't worry bruv, I'm going to the gym. I'll get something there. Bye Beth!' He waves at the camera.

'Bye Nate,' I say.

Zayn pauses while Nate moves around in the background. There's the sound of the hall cupboard being opened, and coat hangers being shuffled. Then a distant yell and a bang of a door being pulled to. 'Oh, thank God – he's gone.' He slumps onto his arm, so the camera is right up against his face.

'Poor Nate,' I say. 'You did basically just force him to go out for dinner.'

'It's my flat,' Zayn says.

'Yes, darling, but he does pay you to live there,' I reply. Though I'm relieved. Least I can talk to Zayn privately now. Maybe. I open my mouth, but I don't know how to say it. It is crazy. It is in my head, I'm sure. I clear my throat. 'Do you need me to bring over some Diet Coke?'

But Zayn knows me too well. 'What's wrong?' He says. 'Not Danny again?'

'No, no, everything's fine with Danny.' I think of the disappointment in his voice last night, the way he looked at me, the empty bed this morning. I glance towards the door, as if I can hear footfall on the stairs. As if he has chosen this moment to come home. But it's nothing.

'Then spill,' says Zayn.

'Do you think it's odd . . . that my first two boyfriends have both died within a fortnight of each other?' I stare at the wall beyond my own laptop. I can't quite bring myself to look at Zayn.

'Well I wouldn't want to be your third boyfriend!' he quips, taking a swig from his reusable water bottle.

I look at the wall again.

Zayn puts the bottle down. 'You're serious?'

I think of the notes. The one I found in my bag. 'It's just – it doesn't feel right. They were both alive three weeks ago. And now they're not, and . . . I found this note in my bag.'

'What note?' Zayn sounds concerned now. 'From who? From one of them?'

No, and it's in my handwriting. I can't say that. And I can't tell him about the first. *I know who you really are.* Because he will ask what it means. And that can't happen. He can't know. No one can know. 'No, not from one of them. It's just apparently Mickey tried to come see me the day he was killed.'

'Christ,' says Zayn.

'After fifteen years. And then Kareem dies too. And this note – I don't know who it's from.' Because it's in my writing.

'What does it say?'

'Nothing – nonsense. It's probably nothing, but I just can't help thinking something is up.'

'Go to the police,' Zayn says definitely.

I stare at him. I can't breathe. Can't speak. Of course he would suggest that. What was I thinking? *I feel the cold concrete bench beneath my legs. The walls damp, dark, the smell of bleach and piss. The metallic clang of the cell door closing, the lock turning shut. No way out.* Under my desk my hands start to shake. How could I be so stupid? I have to get Zayn to forget this. What if he pushes? He could go to the police himself. He could blow it all wide open. Oscar. Danny. My heart contracts in my chest. That can't happen. 'Beth?' Zayn says. 'You still there?'

'Connection froze,' I manage. Act normal. Be normal. Edge slowly away from the danger. 'I'm sure it's nothing,' I say. 'I'm just overthinking because of shock or something.'

'Yeah, maybe, but you're obviously anxious. And that isn't like you, Beth. Nothing gets to you, babes. If you think something is wrong you should go to the police.'

I hear the scratch of the key in the lock before the door is flung open and bangs against the wall downstairs.

'Enid Cat!' Oscar's voice shouts in delight. And there's a canter of feet against the wood floor. My baby. My family.

'Careful,' calls Hellie. 'Take your coat off – it's drenched. Don't just drop it on the floor!' She says in exasperation. Oscar's burst of laughter bounces up the stairs. He sounds so carefree, so joyful. And I suddenly feel completely alone.

'I've got to go,' I say to Zayn. 'Oscar's back.'

Zayn's face looks concerned, like he might be about to say something else, but I cut the video.

Zayn's right: I am anxious. And it's made me reckless. How could I bring up The Note? Of course he would suggest going to the police. My mind moves quickly through the options to lead him away from this line of thought. But the answer is easy: I know what to do. But I feel no comfort. Because even if I resolve this with Zayn, I can't ignore the spines of the idea that have sunk into my skin. Within three weeks, my first two boyfriends have been killed in suspicious circumstances. And I see it. There is a link: me. And I can't risk getting help.

The cacophony of Oscar recedes into the kitchen. I hear Hellie push the front door to. The vacuum from the wind outside rattles the study window, and I shiver. It's like something bad is trying to get in.

HIM

She changed her plans, and this inconveniences me.

I hate alterations to my routine. To hers. I like to know where she is at all times. Events of the last few days have impacted on her. More names from the past rearing up to taunt me. I despise anyone who has her time. Anyone who takes her away. By rights she should be mine. We could enjoy dinners together, drinks, hotel rooms, baths. I always plan candles. I want her to shower me with her laughter. To drink in the sweet smell of her perfume without guilt. Marc Jacobs Daisy during the day. Tom Ford Velvet Orchid when she goes out at night. I keep a bottle by my bed. I spray it on my pillow, close my eyes, imagine she is here. With me. All night. Every night. I want to keep her to myself. Possess her in a way I've not known before.

I'd dressed for her today. Carefully, in a way I thought she might like. Took extra time over my shaving, my hair. Anointed myself. I wanted her to smell me. I wanted her to notice. I wanted her to see me.

Instead I go to the gym and run. Run and run and run on the treadmill till I'm sweating only her. Wringing out her every move. The way she rolls her shoulders when she's tired. The way her hair sweeps down one side of her face. That jade green dress she wore to her Christmas party. The black panties she wears. Silk with a lace scalloped edge. A matching bra, criss-crossed so her erect nipples would poke through. Calling to a finger, a tongue. Is she wearing them now? Is she wearing them with him? I touch myself in the shower. I can't help it. Water running over me,

I think of her in the shower. Water running over her breasts, the swoop of her hips.

I've watched her so many times, it's like I can almost reach out and touch.

BETH – SIX DAYS TILL THE PARTY

The bed quivers as Danny rolls over. Barely opening my eyes I can see sunlight is making the white curtains glow like orange warning lights. The alarm hasn't gone off – it can't be six thirty yet? I groan, turn away from the light, pull the duvet up round me like a shield.

'Morning, sunshine.' The heat of Danny's solid body rolls into me. His bare chest against the skin above my vest. The soft towelling cotton of his pyjama legs wrap round my legs. For a second we could once more be the couple who shagged on the hall floor, who spent whole days lying in each other's arms talking. 'Almost the weekend,' Danny whispers. A dry-lipped kiss on my temple. Wisps of my hair catch on his scratchy dark stubble. I breathe him in, all sleep, and citrus notes from yesterday's aftershave.

'What time did you get in last night?' I mumble. I'd eaten cereal for dinner, and fell into bed around 9 p.m. I'd been meaning to read but my mind wouldn't focus. I must have dropped off. The memory of the new note punches into sharp focus. I feel myself stiffen.

'You alright?' Danny's hand freezes on my hip.

Two of my ex-boyfriends are dead. Someone is trying to contact me, scare me even. And Zayn wants me to go to the police.

'Yeah, fine,' I adjust my legs, curling them up and away. As if the truth may seep out of my skin.

'Okay,' Danny sighs.

I want to reach for him. I want to roll into his arms. I want to tell him everything. But I can't. He would never forgive me. He can never know.

The mattress dips again as Danny turns over, a blast of frigid air passing over me as he folds the duvet back to sit up. I hear the squeaky scratch of rubber against the wooden floorboards as his feet search out his slippers. 'Just after eleven, I think,' he yawns. 'Client was a talker. Going through a divorce.' He scrubs his hand over his face, up, over his eyes. 'We need to run through the final list for the party, check there's no one else you want to invite?' Danny is already on to the next thing.

The morning sun pressing in from the outside is no longer ignorable, neither is the weight of last night's conversation with Zayn. 'What time is it?'

Danny adjusts his watch strap, freeing the dark hairs on his arm that have got caught overnight in the chain links. 'Almost . . . '

He's interrupted by my phone starting to play its morning alarm. A split second later his joins in, a disharmonious stereo version of the same piano keys.

Danny silences his, as I grab at the charger lead that snakes across the floor to yank mine towards me.

'Coffee?' he says. 'I gotta get going – early client this morning.'

At the mention of clients I feel guilty about Unity's Matt. With everything else, I didn't finish the press release yesterday. 'I'll get one on the way to the office,' I say. Seeing the banner alerting me to a text from Zayn.

> *Report the note to the police – even if it's just to reassure you, babes. xx*

I swipe the message away swiftly. 'You go in the bathroom first, love,' I say.

Danny's sleep-wrinkled face is suddenly warm, and close to mine again, a smile, the delicious scratch of his stubble, as his lips press against me. I want to swallow him in. I want to be safe. I close my eyes and wrap my arms around him. Feel the muscles move under his skin. But he pulls gently away.

'Thanks, beautiful,' he says.

'Go,' I grin. 'Before I change my mind and keep you here.'

On his way out, he grabs the shirt hanging ready on a hanger on the outside of the wardrobe.

I keep the smile on my face until I hear the shower start up. Then I delete the message from Zayn from my phone.

The sun is trying to come out as I walk with the flow of coat-huddled workers from Liverpool Street towards Finsbury Square and the office. The dark chunky fabrics of winter are starting to be shed, and there's the odd flash of a beige mac or a bright scarf, a splatter of white blossom and exploratory yellow daffodils that dot the journey and the park. Spring hasn't got a firm hold yet, but it's coming. Bringing all the hope of new birth, new life, new beginnings. And I am mourning two untimely deaths. Watching with trepidation as anonymous notes swirl around like blossom rotted by the frost.

I check my phone again: nearly ten o'clock. That must be enough time now. I drafted the sex dolls press release before I left. Told Hellie I was about to follow her and Oscar out. No one would know any different. I should just check what time police stations open. I pause before I reach the square, tucking myself down a side street and against the black mirrored glass front of an office block. A building hoarding smothers half the road, and pushes itself right up against the plum painted Flying Horse pub. The builder's signs warning of the necessity of hardhats at the same height as the posters advertising a darts tournament. Cars can't fit down here. And despite the hoarding, there's no signs of actual builders. I google the nearest police station. Bishopsgate Police Station, open from 7.00 a.m. to 7.00 p.m. every day. Surely Zayn won't double check what I'm saying? Why would he? It's only me who doesn't trust anyone else. Only me who has had their fingers burned so badly I obliterated my own fingerprints from my life. Better to be safe than sorry. I tap out the message, reading the words back twice before I press send: *Police said it's nothing. Note just some freaky coincidence. xx*

I can see the three dots indicating that Zayn is typing. I glance up to check there's no one I know walking past, but it's just the usual comforting anonymous strangers of London. My phone beeps with his response: *Good. No need to worry then xx*

I exhale, and put my phone back in my pocket.

The new twenty-something receptionist – I think her name's Chloe – is coming out of the striped frosted glass office doors as I reach them. Rob had them put in when we moved in and the place was converted into the paint-by-numbers quirky cool you'd expect from a top PR firm. It always reminds me of a giant barcode. And we're products as we beep our way past.

We stand awkwardly on the street.

'Hey Beth!' Chloe smiles in that eager way which makes me want to take her out for a whiskey and tell her what to do when some of my male colleagues try to put their hands inside her size six Topshop jumpsuit. She's an ethereal little thing, all pale skin and long wavy, blonde hair, like a water nymph from a pre-Raphaelite painting. Her soft otherworldly beauty pleasingly incongruous with the utilitarian clothes and ankle boots she favours.

I don't feel like small talk today. 'Hey, I was just working at home this morning on the sex dolls – I mean the Unity project.'

Chloe looks momentarily taken aback, and I realise I'm a senior partner, and I don't need to explain myself. If she had more than a few hours of real-life experience she'd spot something was up. Luckily, she doesn't. It's a reminder: I'm letting things slide. It's a manifestation of anxiety. I need to listen to my mindfulness app. Get a handle on it. Now is not the time for small telling mistakes.

Chloe is still talking. 'I'm about to get coffee. Geoff fancies a Danish,' she adds, as if they are best buddies and she's not just his regular source of snacks. 'Can I get you anything?'

It suddenly feels too bright out here. The stream of workers buzzing past us like bluebottles. 'No thanks, err, Chloe.' That is right, isn't it? 'I had breakfast at home.'

'No worries,' she says and skips – skips, for God's sake – away from the building. Why am I being so mean? It's not her fault she loves her job. It's not her fault I really don't love mine right now. Maybe that's what this is? People I grew up with, people I was younger with, people I had idealistic hopes and dreams with, have gone. Mickey dreamed of being in a band. Least he followed his dream. Though he hardly made it – at least that's what I deduced from the small venue gig photos on Facebook. Kareem wanted to go into films. But he ended up working in a care home. My mind runs through the differences between the creative Mickey and Kareem. And then there was Phil Brown from my Saturday job, I think with a smile. All he wanted to do was be an accountant. He was born for it. Steady and reliable at nineteen. The opposite of what I wanted to be. Spreadsheets, numbers, analysing things . . . and now that's how everything is run. The whole world chugging along on algorithms. Spreadsheets decide how much and what type of milk is in the supermarkets. Spreadsheets decide what is available to watch on the telly. And they decide how and who we target for PR campaigns. We're all number crunchers now. A wave of tiredness hits me as I remember Danny pulling away from me this morning, the notes, lying to Zayn, lying to everyone. I want to be skipping down the road to buy breakfast for people. For that to be the simple summation of my goals.

The swoosh of the glass doors releases the reassuring canned freshness of climate-controlled air, and I take a lungful as I pass Chloe's desk, round another geometrically frosted panel so visitors can't see us working, and into the exposed brick open-plan space. It's almost empty. Rob is presumably in his office. Only Geoff and Christoph are at their desks, the back of Geoff's purple turtleneck and Christoph's retro red checked cowboy shirt to me. Neither turn or look up, the bulbous, expensive noise-cancelling headphones beloved by the whole office doing their job: keeping them in their bubble. It's eerily reminiscent of that scene in *The Matrix*, when you realise all humans are plugged into the simulators in tanks, oblivious to the reality around them. The kid in me can't resist sticking my tongue out and waggling my fingers at the back of their heads. Nothing. I laugh. What a world we live in!

Then I see it.

An envelope in the middle of my desk. My heart slows. It's as if I'm wearing those same headphones, I can only hear the aching thud of my own drum heart. Everything else has faded out. It's the same as before. My name printed in block capitals on the front. The same as the one I found after visiting the sex dolls warehouse. The same as was delivered to the house. Now here too. I squeeze my handbag under my arm, as if I can feel the outline of the matching envelope in the inside pocket. I knew there *would* be more. I knew this *wasn't* the end. I think of the brown-edged decomposing blossom petals already swirling through the London air. Here. Whoever is sending them has been here. Instinctively I look around. But nothing has changed: the back of Geoff and Christoph's heads haven't moved; their fingers still tap at their keyboards.

A lump forms in my throat, like a wad of processed white bread caught, pressing on my windpipe. My hands shake as I pick up the envelope. It's not sealed. I open it like a purse, knowing what I'll find before I do.

A small scrap of lined paper. Handwriting – mine, spells out: *ad man walking*.

What? It's definitely my writing, but a different pen this time: black, it looks like a fountain pen. But I haven't used one of those for years? Ad man walking? What does that even mean? Why has someone sent this? What's going on?

Oh God. The idea forms in my mind. No. That can't be. My fingers scrabble at my handbag, my nails catching against the soft grain of the designer leather. The other envelope is still there – still in my inside pocket. I take it out, the paper shaking, crinkling, rusting in my fingers guiltily. I look up. Still no one has noticed I'm here. And I lay the other scrap of lined paper next to this one. It's the same paper, but a different pen. It's the same writing – my writing, but I can't remember writing this? Ever writing this? But together the words work, the blue ballpoint fitting against the black cartridge ink. I stare at the words on the paper in front of me. And no mindfulness app is going to fix this. I'm not imagining this. The words spelled out in front of me are very real:

De ad man walking.

BETH

Dead man walking. It isn't a coincidence someone started sending me anonymous notes at the same time my two first boyfriends died. The notes aren't just about me, about my past, about what I did, they're about what is happening now. Mickey, Kareem. Two accidental deaths. Except what if they weren't? Mickey was stabbed by an unknown assailant in a presumed bungled mugging. Kareem was killed by an unknown assailant in a hit-and-run. What if it isn't a tragic twist of fate? This reads like a threat. What if this note is saying it's only a matter of time until another man dies? Another man linked to me? *What if they come for Danny? No – don't think that.* Who sent it?

Before I know what I'm doing I've tapped Christoph on the back. He jumps, his ski-tanned startled face turns as his hands fly away from his keys, in a move that starts like surrender and ends with him pulling his headphones off his thin grey hair.

'What?' Euro house beats leak from his headphones.

My face must say it all. I must look crazy. I feel crazy. 'Did you put this on my desk?' I wave the piece of paper in front of him. His green eyes dart after it like they would follow an agitated butterfly. His long chin drawing eights in the air as he does.

'What? No. Why?' I'm aware he's shrinking back from me. I know I'm making myself look bad: crazy, emotional, hysterical. All the elements I've spent my adult life carefully sloughing off like dead skin cells. But I can't stop. Geoff has looked up now, the movement enough to penetrate the artificial concentration bubble of his black headphones. He pushes them up so they look like Mickey Mouse ears against his bald head.

'What's going on?' he says.

'Did either of you put this on my desk?' I wave the envelope at them.

'No,' Christoph says, sounding almost frightened. Geoff's face twists into a smirk, and I catch his furtive look at the Unity client name on the wall. You don't need to be Freud to work out his desire.

'Why, what is it?' he reaches for the envelope. 'Rob's not given you your marching orders has he?'

'Of course not,' I snap and pull the envelope out of reach. I don't want either of them to see it. I don't want anyone to see it. It's evidence. It's proof – I was right, the building dread, the doubt: someone is targeting my ex-boyfriends. And this is a message to confirm it. A threat of more to come. 'Neither of you saw anyone deliver this?'

Christoph shakes his head.

'Compromising love letter?' Geoff's fleshy face smooshes into a lewd leer.

'Don't be ridiculous.' I feel raw, exposed. I'm being hunted. But they're not hurting me. They're hurting my ex-boyfriends. They're hurting people I've cared about.

'Oooh,' Geoff calls cattily, giving Christoph a knowing look. I'm giving him what he wants: I've become the hysterical woman screaming in the office. 'Hit a nerve, did I?'

'I'm happily married,' I say.

'What the hell is going on here?' Rob has appeared from his office, looming like a shadow in his tailored black suit and tight T-shirt. The whites of his eyes livid as they move from annoyed to amused and back again.

I feel heat crawl up my neck. Geoff and Christoph look like naughty schoolchildren.

I'm too fired up to stop. 'Did you see who put this note on my desk?'

'What note?' he strides towards us, the heels of his brogues emitting clipped pings on the poured concrete flooring, his voice indignant. 'What's this about?'

'Beth's got a secret admirer,' Geoff says.

'Shut up, Geoff,' I hiss. 'I don't – I haven't.' What can I say? Someone is sending me unnerving notes? Notes that are made from my own handwriting, but that I have no recollection of writing? Notes that have started to appear at the same time as my ex-boyfriends have started to be bumped off? It's mad. This can't be happening. 'Did you?' I hold the envelope out.

A look of disgust wrinkles over Rob's manscaped face. 'Why would I leave an envelope on your desk?'

'Someone must have? Someone must have seen something?' I say, desperate for answers. Someone put it there. Someone left it for me.

All three men are staring at me. Rob's face has morphed into disquiet, Christoph anxious, and Geoff can't help but smile, his teeth artificially white against the yellow undertones of his skin. This is his dream come true. His main rival at work, the one who landed the prestigious Unity Sex Dolls account, appears to be having a breakdown. I'm coming across as unwell. Whoever is sending these notes wants me to know they can get to me at home, and they can get to me at work. They want to unmoor me.

'Are you feeling alright, Beth?' Geoff is all faux-concern. 'If you're not feeling well you should go home. I can cover her accounts, Rob. Easily.' He gives an ingratiating smile in Rob's direction.

Rob is watching me with concern in his Caravaggio eyes.

Tell them. Tell the police. This person has to be found, stopped. You have to stop this. But then I'd have to tell them why, why this is happening. Who I really am. They'd cast me out. There would be no way of keeping it from Danny. And the police – I feel my throat tighten – the police would know it all. There's no way they wouldn't think I was involved. I'd be a suspect. Again. I'd lose my job, Danny, Oscar. The thing inside of me writhes, rises up, and I know it's my monster. The one that can never get out. 'I'm fine,'

I hear myself saying. 'I just . . . ' I look at the three men who are now staring at me, expectant.

'Seriously, darling,' Geoff says. 'If it's the time of the month . . . ?'

Anger explodes inside me. No one gets to say that except me. How dare he? I force a smile onto my face and it takes hold. 'I was just winding the boys up,' I wink at Rob. 'They looked so funny sat there – like Autobots, plugged into their headphones.' I laugh, and slip the envelope into my pocket. 'You know me, I like to shake things up every now and then. Keep you all on your toes!'

Rob's shoulders physically relax, and a smile spreads across his face. Geoff pouts.

Then I remember Chloe. If someone delivered this, she would have seen them. They would have had to pass her desk. She will know who this is from. 'I'm gonna pop out. For coffee,' I say.

Rob's face falters. He glances towards the clock on the wall, as if to say *you've only just arrived?*

'You all sorted? Great. I'll just be a minute,' I answer, and head to the door before they can stop me. I'm the picture of calm efficiency. In control, upbeat: me.

As soon as I reach reception I start to run. Chloe is not back yet. I dash out onto Finsbury Square – wham! Something, someone, slams into my shoulder, knocking me forwards. A dark coat, a man. The blank windows of the buildings around me spin and jitter, a zoetrope of the glassy dead eyes of the sex dolls.

'Watch where you're going!' The man turns, scowling at me. A phone glued to his ear. 'Nah, I'm fine – just some stupid cow . . . ' He vanishes into the slipstream of workers out to run errands.

I rub at my shoulder. 'Screw you,' I mutter. Frustration, anger, and fear all hissing out of me like pressure-cooker steam. The person doing this could be anywhere. The trees in the park I picnic under in summer, rise like dark winged birds of prey. The hotel bar we use for after-work drinks leers at the end of the street, its tinted glass the perfect observation spot to hide behind. *They could be here now.*

Another suited man, grey wool coat billowing, strides towards me, confident I will move from his trajectory. I do, heart hammering, eyes skittering. Someone has been watching me. Someone is sending me threats. *Dead man walking.* Someone is killing my ex-boyfriends. Find Chloe. Find out who.

I look up and down the street. Which way? She said Geoff fancied a Danish – Pret. I jog, weaving past a guy with a man bun, and a black rucksack worn two straps over his maroon bomber jacket. There are so many men. A young dark-haired woman in a sleek black leather jacket, her bag dangling from the crook of her arm. These people are out, carefree, getting on with their lives, oblivious to the menace of carnage I carry with me.

Floor-to-ceiling glass windows showcase the familiar clutch of passive aggressive customers around the food shelves in Pret, vying for the last hot porridge pot or egg and tomato roll. I can't see Chloe, but it's hard to distinguish anyone from the uniform office attire of grey and black. I push open the glass heavy door and the smell of soup and coffee hits me, my stomach descending down a rollercoaster.

A petite girl in a jumpsuit is bending down to pick up a green smoothie from the shelves. I dash forward, tap her arm.

'Hey?' I say.

An unknown woman turns to face me, a look mixed of apprehension and aggression on her snub-nosed face.

'Oh. Sorry, I thought you were someone else.' My voice falters. A few people turn to look, stepping back. Every unexpected urban encounter is a tinderbox situation. Every person primed to get out of the way, then gawp, absorbing every unflinching moment of conflict so they can relive it in vivid technicolour back at their desks with their colleagues. I can sense people working out if it's worth turning their phone cameras on for. 'Sorry,' I repeat, and move on, as the mob closes once more around the shelves.

Where is Chloe? Did I pass her? I want to speak to her alone. Away from Geoff, Christoph, Rob. Prying ears. My face tingles at the memory of the way the guys in the office looked at me. The man on the street. I have let the deaths get to me, upset me, damage my carefully curated facade. The truth gets out through the cracks. I can't have that. I need to regain control.

Perhaps Chloe went somewhere else? Costa? Nero? Starbucks? The stupefying number of chains scroll through my mind. I dash towards Nero, which straddles the corner. But faceless diners line the stools by the window, obscuring the view. If I go in I could miss her. I can't – won't – have this conversation overheard. An uncomfortable thought squirms inside of me, but I force it down like swallowed bile. It's better to wait outside our office – that way I can catch her before she goes back in.

Then I see her. On the City Road side, Airbuds in, walking swiftly in those chunky boots past the closed red painted Chinese takeaway, and the shuttered green of the small Italian family restaurant. Her golden hair streaming back like she's Ophelia suspended in water.

I check left, right, but the traffic is sluggish, so it's easy to weave between the cars.

'Hey!' I wave. But she doesn't look up. 'Hey! Chloe!' I try again, as I near her.

She obviously catches the movement in her side vision, tapping her headphones to stop them, smiling and waiting while I scoot round the last glaring car driver.

'Fancy seeing you here,' she says. Her pale cheeks tinted pink by the cold wind.

I've no time for jokes. 'I tried to find you in Pret.'

Her smooth face barely wrinkles in confusion. 'Did you change your mind? I can go get you something?'

'No, no.' I look back towards the office, and then sweep her towards the closed green frontage of Giovanni's. There might be people inside, preparing for the lunch service, but the kitchen is out back, no one should be able to hear. 'I want to ask you something.' I pull the note from my bag. 'This was on my desk. Do you know who put it there?'

'I did,' she says, looking surprised.

The pavement shudders under my feet. What?! 'You wrote this note?'

She laughs. 'No – I just put it there. It was on my desk when I got back – and it had your name on it, so I left it for you.'

Behind us an angry explosion of beeping breaks out among passing cars. I stare at her.

Her pert face moving from upbeat to doubtful. 'I was just trying to be helpful. Have I done something wrong?'

'You didn't see who put this on your desk?' I thrust the note towards her. She must have. She must know.

'No. I—'

'Where were you?'

Her face crumples more, her bottom lip protruding, reminding me of Oscar, and I think for a terrible second she might cry.

'Sorry,' I say. 'I didn't mean to snap. It's just—' I force brightness into my voice. 'I think Angela is playing a bit of a practical joke on me.' I wink. 'And I was hoping to catch them at it.'

'I don't know who it's from,' she says looking at the envelope in my hand. I pull it away. I don't want her to see the cut-out letters inside. 'Rob sent me for his dry cleaning.'

That's why she wasn't at her desk. Why she missed who delivered this. Or maybe they deliberately waited till she was out the way. 'Cool. No worries.' I'm playing my most upbeat. 'No problem – just, if another one comes – let me know as soon as possible, yeah?'

'Course,' she nods. Then turns one ankle boot towards the other, gripping her bag, unsure what to do now.

'Right.' I take a step towards the road, then remember I told Rob I was getting coffee. 'I just need to—' I signal over my shoulder in the general direction of the cafes. 'I'll see you back at the office.'

She smiles. Nods. 'Sure.'

What am I going to do? How am I going to find out who delivered this? Who is doing this? 'Oh,' I stop, as I reach the kerb. 'One more thing – can we keep this,' I signal between me and her. 'Just between us.'

Her pencilled eyebrows raise.

'Like I said – prank, trying to catch them at it,' I smile.

Her naive face looks reassured. I should take her for that drink. I can't think about when I was her age. Before everything went wrong. When I was still happy. I turn as a lump solidifies in my stomach. I run the envelope through my fingers, the edge catching at my skin in a tiny paper cut. Then thrust it and my hands into the pockets of my green coat, and walk quickly in the other direction.

Dead man walking. It's a threat. Someone is killing my ex-boyfriends. One by one.

And I know who is next on the list.

HIM

I have to make sure no one sees me watching, as she puts the envelope into her pocket. She smooths the crinkled paper with her fingers, straightening out the kinks. I imagine I am the paper, and she is stroking me. Straightening my kinks. Smoothing me. Comforting me. Treating me with such care.

The rage rises like my erection. The fire of lust exploding into anger. I have never seen her like that before. So worked up, so vibrant. She was fizzing with energy. Drawing all eyes to her. And I am jealous of that note. Jealous that it did that to her. That it brought her blazingly alive. This is what I have been brought to – feeling envious of an inanimate scrap of paper. But the sensation burns bright inside me anyway. Because it's not just the note, it's not just her stupid partner, it is all of this. It is all keeping her from me. The universe is conspiring to turn her away. To keep her looking in the wrong direction. And that is an error I need to correct.

My breathing stills and I think of that: of everything and everyone else disappearing. Of having her all to myself. Of keeping her just for me.

BETH – SIX DAYS TILL THE PARTY

Returning to the office, the late March sun shines a bisected slash of light onto my desk like a crime scene spotlight. Christoph glances up warily as I pass his chair. Geoff can't keep the smug look from his face. He'd show no mercy if he knew the truth. And I wouldn't blame him. The monster inside me slithers up against my skin, trying to find a way out, trying to reach the sun. That cannot happen. Thankfully there's no sign of Rob. Now is not the time for one of his spontaneous stroll patrols round the company. I don't stop at my glowing desk, but head for one of our small glass meeting rooms, where I can talk in private. The wall panels are artfully tinted, so you can never be sure what time of day or night it is outside. Not for the first time I'm reminded of casinos, but the image takes on a twisted significance now I feel like I'm rolling the dice myself. I can't risk going to the police. My hands shake as I slant the blinds shut to the rest of the office. I have to do this myself. I have to warn Phil. But it's been years since I saw him.

I start on Facebook, but he's managed to keep himself away from the algorithm. Perhaps it would work better if my account was really me, with people I know or knew in the past, but it's not. All Facebook can do is show me countless wrong Phil and Phillip Browns. How do you find someone with such a common name online?

My computer flashes up a notification that I've received an email from Matt at Unity Dolls. Crap, I'll get back to him after this. After I've found Phil. After I've warned him. Doubt is creeping in. What if I'm wrong? What if the notes aren't linked? What if I'm letting fear take over my reasoning? But I can't do nothing, in case . . . in case this is really happening.

What was the name of the road Phil lived on? I disappear down the rabbit hole of Google Earth, trying to work out by process-of-elimination the name of the street I visited over twenty years ago. Even when I think I possibly have it narrowed to Chipstead or Barnfield Road, the addition of his name turns nothing up. Well of course it doesn't. The idea that he lives in the same house as he did when he was nineteen is clearly madness. I live in a whole other city, I'm married to a man he's never met, I hang out with people who I'd never met then. I do a job I didn't even know was a thing when I was that age. Phil could be in Australia. Or Russia. Or in the next street down, and I'd never know. He's just a person. Someone I used to know. That I shared a few weeks of flirting with when I was a teenager. We only slept together a couple of times. We clearly didn't really have anything in common or we would have stayed in touch.

My mobile rings: Matt from Unity is calling. Crap. I still haven't picked up his email.

'Hi, Matt,' I smile into my phone. 'I've just got out of a meeting.' I surreptitiously glance over the office, but both Christoph and Geoff are absorbed in their own screens.

'Beth, hey,' he says.

There's a pause. What does he want? 'Hey!' I say upbeat. He really is one of those clients that needs helicopter parenting.

'Did you see what the *Guardian* said about Treasure?' he sounds genuinely hurt.

Damn. No, I didn't. I haven't even looked at the papers today, and that's a pretty basic cornerstone of my job. I make a sympathetic noncommittal sound.

'I was thinking if you'd perhaps like to come back to the warehouse next week, we can brainstorm a new strategy . . . ' He tails off. 'If that's what you think we should do to tackle it – it is pretty bad, isn't it? They called me "unethical".'

I think of the swinging naked figures. The way he talked to Treasure like she was a real woman. The note I found in my bag when I got back from there. He could have put it there... What if it's him? I shake myself. I'm letting panic take over.

'They can't do that, it's slander – unless they were quoting someone else,' I say, trying to focus on what he's saying. On screen I'm clicking onto the *Guardian*. Oh God – the article is number two in their most-read. 'Try not to panic,' I say, and I'm not sure if I'm talking to him or myself.

'I don't know how they can say that?' Matt's voice moves from upset to angry. 'Treasure would never hurt anyone.'

He's talking about the freaking doll. 'No,' I soothe. 'Of course not.'

'I don't know what I've done to deserve this?' He sounds pitiful, but the words hit me like a shower of stones from a passing car. *What I've done to deserve this*. I do know what I did. It was unforgivable. The monster inside me flexes, wriggles, reminding me of what I'm really capable of. But Mickey, Kareem? They didn't deserve this at all.

'I just really think,' Matt is still speaking in my ear. 'That we need to get in the same room and come up with a plan to tackle this head-on, you know?'

I need to get off this call. 'That's a really positive idea, but let me put some finishing touches to what I've been working on, and then get back to you.' I minimise the *Guardian*. Phil's name covers my screen. I click through onto my calendar. I need to get Matt to go away. I need time. I try to focus on the blocks of colour on my screen. Try to make my brain understand what they mean, but every time I blink Phil's name appears like a floater in the darkness. 'I can update you with where we are – it's going to be okay. And... Err... I don't want to eat into your day, so how about I give you a call Wednesday at 3 p.m. instead?'

There's an infinitesimal pause, while Matt obviously tries to work out if this is a brush-off, or if he's really getting his money's worth.

'I've got something that will fix this,' I add confidently. 'No one will pay any more attention to all this.' I just need to get him off the phone. I can come up with something later.

'3 p.m. Wednesday. Skype?' he says.

'Perfect!' I chime. Bugger, I'll have to do my hair and make-up, and book the meeting room with the good light. For a moment my work brain almost wins the internal struggle for focus. Then Christoph passes by on his way to the kitchen and the brief shadow he casts over the meeting room causes me to physically jump like I've just missed a swerving car.

'I can't wait, Beth,' Matt says. And I can imagine him smiling at one of his dolls.

As soon as I'm off the phone I'm back on Google. It takes me a couple of clicks to remember the name of the school Phil went to. Beauford Boys – apparently rebranded as a mixed Academy of Science a few years ago. But with that I finally get lucky. The school have archived their alumni newsletters as online PDFs. And apparently, in 2018 Phil Brown (Class of '97) went back to give a talk on careers day about accounting. Lucky students. Lucky me – because it mentions the name of the firm Phil now works for in Brighton. He really did become an accountant then. I open his hyperlinked company website. A smiling photo of Phil Brown on their About Us page. His hair is grey, darker on top, lighter and thinning on the sides, running into pale skin. He gives a cream-coloured smile, one side of his mouth slightly higher than the other. It's like time has washed the colour out of him. He's angled away, wearing a navy suit, white shirt, navy tie, and if it wasn't for the thick black-rimmed glasses he wears, his face would lack all definition. I realise he is old. Older. A man. I would have walked past him in the street. This man whose futon I once shared. He looks like his dad. It's gone 1 p.m. now. He could be out at lunch?

My hand hovers over the phone. What if I'm wrong? I could be overreacting? I could be making links where there are none? Have I just let my fear override my rational thought processes?

I've taken various psychology courses as part of my PR training over the years – it's helpful to know how and why your audience respond to certain things. I know that when we feel anxious, fearful, or angry, our amygdala floods our system with cortisol, norepinephrine and adrenaline, our stress hormones, preparing us for fight or flight. And my palms still feel sweaty, my muscles are tense. But am I being hypervigilant? Too responsive and alert to danger? Is this my brain trying to spot a threat that isn't actually there? Possibly, but if there is even the slimmest chance this thing is real, I have to try. If someone – and the monster shifts restlessly inside me, as if it knows the truth – if someone is killing my ex-boyfriends, I have to warn Phil.

The phone is answered before I've even thought about what I'm going to say.

'Pritchard and Simms Accountancy, how can I help?' sing-songs a female voice. She sounds barely older than I would have been when Phil and I were a thing. And for a second I think of the army of young women who are still answering the phones up and down the country. Perhaps she is one of those who is writing scathing tweets about Unity? Angry at what looks like yet another facet of gender oppression? Is it her job to answer the phones, or do her male colleagues just never bother?

'Err, hi!' I falter. What if Geoff or Christoph look up? What if Chloe comes in? Our very own keen young woman trying to make a good impression. What if Rob pounces on one of his patrols now? I make sure the door is shut and angle the blue wingback away from the rest of the office. I wouldn't put it past Geoff to have learned how to lip-read.

'How can I help?' Repeats the woman on the other end, a slight annoyance tainting the end of her sentence. As if she's giving a very false smile.

'Hi,' I repeat. I wish I'd brought my water bottle in with me. 'Can I speak to Phil?' Does he still call himself that? It said Phillip on the website. 'To Phillip Brown? Please?' What am I going to say to him? He would have read the papers back then, seen the news. He will know the truth about me. Will he take my call? The handset creaks and slips in my sweaty fingers. How am I going to explain? What if he asks? This is risky – if he makes the connection between the past and present, someone else will know. Someone who could tell Danny, Oscar – who could unravel everything. I almost slam the phone down. But he could be in genuine danger?

'Who's calling?'

I feel as if another wave of cortisol is washing through me, telling me to run. Phil doesn't know Beth. Beth didn't exist back then. My old name, the old me, forms on the tip of my tongue. I can't. I can't say it: it'll be like summoning the monster. 'Erm – my name is Beth. I'm calling from Trench PR.' Crap. I shouldn't have given the company name – what if she makes a note of it? It's a trace, an identifier. This was a mistake. You can't reach back into the past without disturbing things.

'Please hold,' says the young woman. And the dramatic dah-dah-dah-duh of Beethoven's fifth symphony cracks to life as hold music. I read once that Beethoven described those opening chords as the knock of fate at the door. And I'm almost sick.

Right. Okay. This is it. *Hi Phil – we used to know each other back in the day.*

Dah-dah-dah-duh!

No – that won't work. *Phillip, hi, we used to work together at WHSmith in Sevenoaks. Bit of a bolt from the blue I know, but I think someone might try to kill you—*

Dah-dah-dah-duh!

My heartbeat feels like it's matching the music. I hold the phone away from my ear. Is there any way to do this without telling him? If I just focus on now, just straight up ask him if he's noticed anyone suspicious hanging round recently perhaps we can leave the past alone? I'll just level with him. Tell him what's happened. About Mickey, and then Kareem, and the notes – and he can make his own mind up.

The strings of Beethoven cut, and I hear a male voice coming from the phone: 'Hello.'

I press it against my ear. My heart in my throat. 'Hello, Phil? I don't know if you remember—'

'This is Phillip Brown. I'm afraid I can't get to the phone right now—'

Voicemail. I almost laugh. She put me through to voicemail? I stare at my phone screen while the tinny voice of Phil's message continues to play. But I haven't been through years of cold calling press contacts to let that stop me. I redial.

'Pritchard and Simms Accountancy?' Answers the same female voice.

'Hi, I called a second ago to speak to Phillip Brown. But it went through to his voicemail. Is he in the office today?' My own voice has taken on that pally tone I use when trying to get through to journalists. I push my hair off my forehead, and my palm comes away clammy. I am literally sweating this out.

'I'm afraid I'm not in the same building as Mr Brown,' she says. Crap. It's a virtual receptionist. She's probably never even met Phil. She's probably not even in Brighton. 'I can take a message and email him?'

What message would I leave? What would make him call me back? I'm too used to being ignored by editors to trust that. 'Is there anyone else in his office you could try?' If I get through to someone else, they can pass me over. I need to speak to someone actually in the same building.

'I could try Lisa Drummonds?' she says.

'Please,' I say. Whoever Lisa is, she can tell me if he's actually there. She can probably put me straight through.

But after another burst of Beethoven, another voicemail starts up. I redial. The same woman answers. 'Hi, me again,' I say. I'm trying to make it sound like she's in on the joke with me, but I can feel my panic rising. What if I can't get hold of him? 'Lisa wasn't picking up either. Is there anyone else to try?'

'I can try the main line?' she says.

There were only three photos on the firm's website. They might all be on the phone. They might be out of the office. They might all have their phones on divert. I flick between screens on my phone. There's no mobile contact listed for Phil. No email. 'Sure, let's try that,' I force a smile. People can hear it in your voice.

The phone line rings. And rings. And rings.

And then reconnects to the same woman. 'Pritchard and Simms Accountancy,' she says.

I stifle an exhalation of frustration. 'Hey,' I smile. 'Still me!'

'I'm sorry,' she says. 'I've tried all the contacts. Would you like me to email Mr Brown?'

And say what? I can't dictate a message about Phil possibly being in danger, and I'd have to give my real name for it to mean anything to Phil. And then it would be in black and white, written down. An ankle chain bolting me to the past. Too trackable. 'No, it's okay – if I could try his line one more time?' He might have come free.

She connects me. Beethoven starts up. Dah-dah-dah-duh! I cross my fingers.

The line clicks and it rings. Once. Twice. Three times. Last time it only rang once. I lean forwards in my chair. Swallow. This is it.

Click.

'Hello. This is Phillip Brown. I'm afraid I can't get to the phone right now.'

I close my eyes and breathe. He's obviously there. He was obviously on the phone before, and now he's put it down. If I can just get him to pick up.

The beep sounds.

'Hi. Phil. Here's a voice I bet you thought you'd never hear again! Look, I don't know if you'll remember, but we used to know each other.' I try to embalm my words with meaning. 'Years ago – at WHSmith in Sevenoaks? And, well – look – can you just give me a quick call? It's a matter of life and death.' I laugh as if it's a joke. Then leave my number and hang up. My heartbeat still sounding in my ears. My breath still coming fast. Call me back, Phil. Call me back.

But my phone screen stays resolutely blank.

BETH

Returning home I expect to find the house changed from this morning. But the last ribbons of the golden sunset play across the twilight sky framing our normal-looking terrace in an Insta-worthy backdrop. I let myself in the front door and get hit with the reassuring scent of expensive fig candles, with undertones of warmed crispy breadcrumbs – Oscar must have had chicken bites for his tea. Enid Cat pads down the stairs, her tortoiseshell tail high, as if indignantly daring me to reprimand her for being there. She wraps herself around my ankles, while I run my fingers over her. The feel of her fur, her muscles, her warmth grounds me.

'Naughty cat,' I whisper, but she just purrs, and sidles off towards the kitchen. As I close the door on the rest of the world, I have to blink away tears. This is my haven, this is where I feel safe. I won't let anything threaten it.

It feels like years have passed since I left this morning. I have travelled back across time to try to speak to Phil. The ground shifting dangerously under my feet. The late nineties, the past, swirling around me. The note on my desk a stake through the heart of my day. It looks the same, feels the same here, but everything has been displaced. I'm playing a very dangerous game, and I know I still haven't really turned to face what is pursuing me. I haven't looked into its jaws. Not yet. Just a little while longer. Mickey and Kareem could genuinely be a tragic twist of fate, I reassure myself.

I'm surprised to see Hellie's down jacket still on the end of the banister.

'Hiya?' I call, following the sound of *Scooby Doo* that's coming from the closed lounge door.

'Hey – good day?' Hellie jumps up from where she was curled up on the blue sofa with Oscar. Her light hair springy round her face, her oatmeal jumper offsetting her skin. Oscar's already in his soft flannel jammies, the scent of his honey bubble bath in the air.

I ruffle Oscar's soft hair, 'Hello there, you. Your dad not back yet?' But his attention is firmly on the screen.

'No,' Hellie smiles. 'Not yet.'

'God, sorry love. We seem to be keeping you late a lot recently.' I add an apologetic laugh, aware I don't want her to leave. I don't want to be alone with my thoughts. My longing to see Carmen hits me like a sucker punch to the gut. I've been spending too much time in the past, opening boxes that should have been kept closed. I love Zayn, I really do, but it's not the same. And now I've thought about Carmen, about how much I truly miss having that close female friend, it hurts. 'Glass of wine before you go?'

Hellie bites her lip, her even white teeth small, sharp. 'Ah, I would if I could – bad day?'

She's a young, single woman in her twenties, living in London. Of course she has plans. Of course she has her own Carmen to get drinks with, and catch cheap theatre shows with, and to spill her darkest secrets over cocktails with. I have to quell the sudden urge to close the lounge door, to keep her here, to tell her what's happening. Instead I say: 'Just the usual, you know. But don't let me keep you any longer – you got anything fun on this weekend? Tell me – let me live vicariously through your social life, now I'm old and boring and don't go out.'

'You're not old, Mummy,' Oscar suddenly pitches in. Turning his bright little face up towards me.

'Thank you, sweetie,' I smile.

'Old people wear glasses,' he adds definitively, and returns his gaze to the screen.

'Okay then,' I grin at Hellie, who suppresses a giggle as she heads into the hall to grab her coat. I follow her.

'He's had chicken bites, mash and beans. Some juice, no milk.'

I nod. Frown at the blank screen on my phone – nothing from Danny, and nothing from Phil. My stomach sloshes. 'Has Danny texted you?'

Hellie doesn't look up from zipping her coat over her slim frame. Looping her hair out from under her collar. 'No. But it's fine.'

'Probably has another client do, and I forgot. It's probably my mistake.' It's not parents' evening, is it? 'You know what it's like – busy, busy at work.' I think of the damning *Guardian* article about the sex dolls. Phil's voice on his answerphone.

'I'm sorry I can't stay for a drink.' She gives my arm a squeeze. 'Another time, yeah?'

Great, now she's pitying me. 'I'm fine, go on. Get going.' I open the door and hold it for her.

'Same time Monday?'

'Please, thanks,' I smile. Unless I've forgotten something else. 'And have fun tonight – don't do anything I wouldn't do!'

She laughs as she heads into the street, as the words turn to ash in my mouth. *Don't do anything I wouldn't do*. Because if she knew, if Danny knew . . . I instinctively glance at my handbag, within which the notes are buried like landmines. If they knew what I was capable of . . . I close the door fast, but it doesn't stop the encroaching darkness.

I fire off a text to Danny, but there's no reply. A small well of panic springs up – what if something has happened to him? What if someone has spoken to him? But then I reassure myself this will be about me getting drunk with Zayn. He's evening the balance. The stress of it all keeps pressing down on me. So I decide to wrap myself in the push and pull, the laughter, and the snuggles of getting Oscar upstairs for story time and bed. 'Come on little man,' I grin, round the corner. '*Harry Potter*?'

His eyes dart delightedly towards me and I want to drown in this feeling of being someone's whole world, of being loved, of being and keeping him safe. I blink hard again as I chase him squealing up the stairs, his soft pink little toes sinking into the thick striped carpet.

It's gone half nine when I finally hear the key in the door. I put my cereal bowl down on the coffee table, wiping a spill of coconut milk from the worn wood. Pause the Netflix documentary I have barely absorbed. I jump as a log spits and hisses behind the glass of the stove. An angry wall of flame flares behind the glass, rather than the comforting glow it had been a minute ago. I meet Danny in the hall.

'Hey – you're late?' I say.

He has his dark grey shell jacket zipped up tight, his black gym rucksack on his shoulder, his dark hair damp. 'I went for a run – that okay?' He glances at me from under his brows. And I feel guilty for pushing him away this morning. I have been so busy thinking about how to protect him from what feels like a growing threat to our future, I haven't been listening to him in the here and now.

'You alright?' I step towards him to give him a kiss and a cuddle, but he turns at that moment, dropping his bag, not meeting my eye.

'Yeah,' he says, unzipping his jacket, and shrugging himself out of it. I'm surprised to see he has on a navy jumper and jeans underneath, and not the suit he left in this morning. They must be in his gym bag.

'How did your client meeting go? Want a cup of tea?' I signal towards the kitchen.

Danny is giving off a closed vibe, like something has happened, and he doesn't want to say. Like he's erected a wall. Everything that's happened today rushes through my head: Mickey, Kareem, Phil, the notes. The unreality of it all feels jarring. As if I've been bingeing on a boxset for hours, only to look up and expect the characters and world to be real around me. I want him to ask if I'm okay. I want him to hold me and tell me it's all going to be okay. I want to tell him I'm scared. I want to feel a connection.

'Meeting was alright – fifty-fifty they'll sign. Don't worry about tea, I've got to batch that veg.' His eyes are fixed on the kitchen, like he's avoiding looking at me. He picks his gym bag back up, gripped tight in his other hand.

'It's Friday night, that can wait.' I reach out and grab his arm, feel the muscle flex under the soft wool. 'You sure you're alright?'

He stops, turns his dark eyes on me. He looks tired, the soft lines on his face darker in the shadows of the hall. 'Yeah, I'm fine,' he says. He's lying. 'I just want to get everything done ahead of next week.'

He pulls away, glancing at my tell-tale bowl on the coffee table. 'Made yourself a nutritious dinner, I see?' I almost believe the jokey tone he's trying to put into his voice. 'I thought you might be out for dinner tonight?'

'No,' I say surprised. Is this all just a silly diary miscommunication? We could have been curled up on the sofa together with a bottle of wine all evening. Instead of it being just me and my terrifying thoughts. My phone screen is still blank. No news from Phil. He's not going to call is he?

I follow Danny into the kitchen. The window a rectangle of black, like someone's punched a hole in the wall. The bifold doors at the end of the kitchen, like the gaping dark mouth of a tunnel. I feel myself shiver. It must be the draught in here. Perhaps we should get blinds. Danny's in the utility. I hear the washing machine beep on. He comes back out – blinks as if he didn't expect me to be there – and drops his empty gym bag by the door. 'You want a sleepy tea?' he asks, flicking on the chrome kettle.

'No thanks.' I need to get rid of this stilted feeling. Things are usually so easy between me and Danny. He pushes the sleeves of his jumper up his striated forearms, and begins to take carrots, potatoes, and a swede, out of the veg drawer in the fridge. The fear someone has spoken to him rears up again. I long to curl my fingers around his arm, feel the warmth of his skin, but it's like an invisible forcefield has closed between us.

'Why don't we run through the catering choices for the anniversary party?' I say, forcing a smile.

He pauses, butternut squash in one hand, and looks at me with the first real flicker of emotion all evening. His head tilted in question. 'The ones I had to get back to the caterers days ago?'

Ah. Another ball I've dropped. 'Sorry – work, things, I didn't realise the date,' I grin, but a shadow passes across his face, and he turns away.

'Yeah, I know you've been *busy*,' he says, a hunch in his shoulders, his solid back a wall, as he takes a knife from the block and slices forcefully down through the squash with a crack. 'Always on your phone, or laptop,' he adds as if he can't keep the words in.

I've been so distracted by the notes, the deaths, and even work, with it all kicking off with Unity, The Perfect Partner. I haven't been paying enough attention to Danny. The irony that he is who I am doing all this for tastes bitter on my tongue. But I've got to make amends, fix this. Danny, Oscar, they are everything to me. 'Okay,' I say, waving my phone at him before I slide it out of sight in my back pocket. The screen is still blank – no missed calls. 'New rule: no laptops and phones on weekends?' He raises an eyebrow at me – it's not enough. 'Or in the evening after 8 p.m. Give us proper quality time, right?'

He huffs gently as if to say: I'll believe it when I see it. And I have to bite back the urge to say: everything I do is for you. It's my wage that pays the mortgage. I have built my whole life around you.

The doorbell rings. I jump.

'It's late – who's that?' Danny tilts his head up, his old-school Hollywood looks making him a pastiche of a catalogue model staring into the distance.

He's right – it's gone nine. Who would be at the door now? If Cat or Cathy next door need anything they always WhatsApp first. My mind races with awful possibilities. Another note? Is this it? Have they finally come to confront me for what I did all those years ago? 'I'll go!' I splutter, and race down the hallway before Danny can. Enid Cat has appeared at the bottom of the stairs. Her fur standing on end as she glares at the door. 'You sense it too, hey?' I mutter, trying to soothe her with a quick stroke. It's probably just Amazon, I try to tell myself, but my hand still shakes as I put the chain across and open the latch.

A young black guy in dark jeans and a padded gilet stands on the step, holding a huge bunch of flowers: white roses, lilies, sculptural sprigs of greenery giving it structure. Double-parked on the street, hazards flashing, is a van with a florist's name emblazoned down the side. The terraces opposite all look warm and cosy with their curtains pulled, lights on. 'Ms Beth Taylor?'

'That's me – hang on.' I push the door to, slide off the chain. Open the door wide to the chilly night air. I can hear the hum of traffic from the main road in the distance. There's a smell of wood smoke that could be coming from us, or several of the local houses. All is normal. 'Sorry,' I say instinctively, feeling foolish for overreacting. I want to explain: I'm not always like this.

'Sign here.' He thrusts his electronic pad towards me. Then passes over the flowers, heavy with a bulb of water in the bottom of the cellophane. A cloud of heady scent hits me. I'll have to remove the stamens.

From Danny? Maybe these were supposed to arrive earlier – and he was miffed I hadn't thanked him? Maybe that's what this is all about? Just a silly misunderstanding. I smile. Thank and say goodnight to the florist, and close the door. A cosy glow comes from the lounge. Danny has flicked Radio 4 on quietly in the kitchen. It's going to be okay. I stand the bouquet on the hallway table and find the card among the velvet soft petals. They're beautiful. I slide open the little white envelope and take out the stiff white card:

The Anniversary Party

Dear Beth,
Thank you for all your hard work on my Treasure.
Matt x

These are from Unity's Matt?

'Who are those from?' Danny is wiping his hands on a tea towel in the kitchen door. He sounds petulant, like Oscar.

'My client,' I say. 'I've no idea why he's sent them.'

'Of course they are,' Danny says. The venom in his voice startles me.

'What does that mean?' I snap. 'Who else would they be from?'

'I don't know, why don't you tell me?' Danny lobs the question like a grenade.

What is this about? Why is he in such a bad mood? 'You can see the card, if you want?' I offer it to him.

'I've got the stock on,' he snaps, turning and heading back into the kitchen. His words sting. I want to run after him. Why did Matt send these? I thought he was pissed off at me? It's so OTT. And look what he's done, he's upset Danny. No, Danny is overreacting. Taking whatever anger he has from his bad day, or whatever, out on me, on us. When I am doing everything I can to protect us. My trainers squeak aggressively on the kitchen floor, as I stomp in and retrieve a glass vase from the utility, the washing machine sloshing away with far too much fabric softener. Danny doesn't look up as I reach across him to take the scissors from the block. The solid warmth of him almost makes me falter, but no: he's behaving like a child. I return to the hall, Enid Cat pacing in circles like she's guarding the entrance, and I start cutting into the cellophane. The smell of garlic wafts from the kitchen, mixing sickeningly with the scent of the blooms. I am here with my husband, my child is asleep upstairs in his bed, and yet I feel so completely and utterly alone.

It's only after I have transferred the flowers to the vase, and I'm arranging them on the hallway table where visitors will see them straight away, that a thought occurs to me. How does Matt know where I live? Perhaps Chloe, still new at the office naively handed over my address? I will have to speak to her. Assure myself it's because of GDPR compliance. Distracted, a sharp thorn from one of the stems jabs into my finger. I snatch it away.

A drop of blood falls from my finger, a splash of forbidding red on the pure white petals.

BETH – THREE DAYS
TILL THE PARTY

The rain against the window wakes me before my alarm does. It's nearly eight thirty. Danny's side of the bed is empty and cold. He's the early riser of the two of us. It's Danny who deals with Oscar, the lunches, and Hellie, all before I get out of bed. There's no mug of tea waiting for me this morning, and I have no memory of him giving me a hug before he left. A sure sign he's still angry. The weekend was exhausting. We took Oscar swimming, went to the farmers' market, had a roast at the local pub. All the perfect family activities. Guilt over my lies meant I poured love into Danny, tried to make him laugh, smile, feel supported. I was present throughout, I didn't dare look at my phone or laptop after our conversation on Friday. And I actually found myself having a wonderful time. I didn't realise how much I missed the sense of belonging. There were moments, when Danny and Oscar and I were laughing over something, where I felt happy again. But it was fleeting. Oscar was a delight, but the more I tried to connect with Danny, the more he pulled away. He didn't even want to talk about the party. It might have been okay if it wasn't for the bouquet of flowers.

Why did Matt send them here? Even if it was a misguided act of kindness, I don't like it. It feels as if a boundary has been crossed. Could he be sending the notes? But why would he do that? If he knew who I really was he wouldn't be working with me, let alone sending me roses. I've obviously been neglecting Danny. My mind has been too focused on Mickey, Kareem, the notes, the terrifying idea that my past is sneaking up behind me.

Not for the first time over the last few weeks I feel like I'm being squeezed out of my life. Sliced out like a splinter and crushed into a new shape. Or an old one. One I don't want to be again.

There're still no messages from Phil on my phone. I toy with calling Zayn, but I lied to him that I'd spoken to the police, and that they'd said everything was fine. And perhaps it is? I'm almost certain I'm being irrational. If I could just speak to Phil, just reassure myself that everything is okay. That there's been no one dodgy hanging around, or anything like that. That the notes and what happened to Mickey and Kareem aren't linked. Just cruel karmic justice for what I did. I close my eyes again on my pillow, and think back to the night it started with Phil. He was a year older, which at eighteen feels much more significant. He'd already been at university for a year, had that knowing air of being cracked open, exposed to the wider world beyond Sevenoaks. His hair was thick, and dark red. And I remember him always raising his eyebrows. He was funny, and when he told jokes he did it like he was delivering a stand-up routine with exaggerated hand gestures and body movements. I guess some might call it cheesy, but it made me laugh, and broke the monotony of that summer selling bibles for christenings, the latest Mills and Boon to the older ladies who pre-ordered them like clockwork, and restocking the video chart at Smiths. Boys wearing their hair in curtains was still a thing, and Phil's flopped in front of his face in the moments when he wasn't putting on an act, the quieter moments where he was more vulnerable – more true to who he really was, I guess. His skin pale against the blue of our Aertex uniform tops. He had quite a few angry spots, and was clearly very conscious of them. But – and this was a big deal where we lived – he had a car. Which meant freedom. He took a group of us to Alton Towers for the day, me and another girl to a packed Bournemouth beach. I feel quite fond of my younger self's genuine excitement at stopping in a service station without my mum or a teacher for the first time in my life. I was naive. It was before everything changed.

Phil would drive us all to the nightclub just out of town. And as my mum's house was the furthest out, I was always the last to be dropped home. One August weekend, Mum was away with her friends from the grief group she'd been going to since Dad passed away and I had the house to myself. Phil gave me a shy, nervous smile when I invited him in for coffee. It's not like it is now with the kids drinking Starbucks and Nero from the age of fifteen – even with him seeming so cosmopolitan having gone away to university, I don't think either of us drank coffee. It's just what adults said in movies. I remember the intensity with which he looked at me after we paused kissing. His shaking hands on my body. Was I his first? Surely he'll remember that? He'll remember me. He'll call back. I'll give him till lunchtime and then try again.

I arrive at the office with relief. Shaking my hair out and down from the baker boy style cap I wear in the rain and wiping drops from my green coat.

'Urgh, it's awful out,' I say.

Chloe, her blonde hair extra voluminous from where she too was presumably caught in the rain, grimaces from behind reception. 'You want a hot drink?'

'No, I'm fine. Had one on the way,' I say, even though I'd paused outside my usual small blue-fronted Italian cafe, but not been able to face the thought of liquid sloshing inside me. I couldn't stomach food either. A scab has formed where I pricked my thumb on the roses from sex dolls' Matt, and I haven't sent him a thank you message yet. The flowers feel less like gratitude, and more like a decorative way of holding me to account on the growing mess that is the Unity doll release. The story made *The Sunday Times* yesterday.

I pass Christoph, his grey hair banded by his headphones, a beige and mint green checked shirt on today. The rest of the office is quiet. Either the rain deterring people from hurrying in, or they're all out at meetings. I don't see Rob, his blinds are down, but there's a fire exit door in his office which he uses to come and go.

He likes to give everyone the idea he could be there all the time. Before I crack on with Matt and the sex dolls, I decide to have a quick look at Mickey and Kareem online. Maybe there is a link between them — apart from going to the same school — that I've missed? I've been mooning over their pages, but not taking a very scientific approach. There could be something, some thread that ties all this together? Or there'll be news about their killers. If they arrest some teen gang member in London, and a housewife driver in Sevenoaks — that would be proof there is no link. That this really is all a horrid fluke of the universe. The monster shifts its weight inside me, as if to imply it knows I'm lying to myself. I have to do something, I can't just sit here and wait.

But googling Mickey and Kareem soon turns into a full-on nostalgia fest. There's no news about Mickey and Kareem's deaths. Nothing more I can find on their local news sites. The world has moved on. It's only me that's firmly staying in the past. I'm soon flicking through hundreds of photos. Everything they've posted, been tagged in, or commented on for years. Each time a photo appears that is an old one that has been scanned, or re-taken of an actual printed photo, my heart catches in my mouth. I'm in some of them. I instantly comb the comments underneath, fearful someone will recognise me, call for the picture to be taken down, burned, me scratched out. If they knew, if they put two and two together, they wouldn't want to be seen with me would they? Unless it was in lurid curiosity, like those who went to school with people who went on to become serial killers popping up to share wholesome photos from back in the day. Before the horror unfolded. Before they knew the grinning fifteen-year-old with the frizzy hair and the purple Adidas top sat cross-legged on their single bed was capable of unleashing hell.

There's Mickey and me both sat on the swings in the park. Mickey in baggy dark blue jeans, a chain looped down his leg, a dark hoodie, me in a blue fleece open over a white and silky scrappy dress with sparse large blue flowers on it. I loved that dress. My undyed blonde hair, a badly-cut version of Rachel on *Friends'* famous do. My face grinning, pale, freckled, bare apart from clumpy Revlon mascara. Kareem, and Mickey's good friend Jessica, each have one hand on the frame of the swings and are leaning dramatically away, making a frame for the shot. Kareem in his striped grandad shirt, Jessica in her trademark black mini dress, thick tights and DMs, her brown shoulder-length hair with a streak of red in it. Her face almost pretty, but her eyes always seeming to be slightly too small, and slightly cruel. But maybe that's me just feeling her intellectual snobbery through the past. I'm sure she grew out of it. We were all capable of casual cruelty at that age. And I now know I'm capable of much, much worse. Slightly behind me, looking awkward and unsure, his hands in his skinny black jeans, a black leather jacket, his hair in long black curtains almost obscuring his face, is Jessica's older boyfriend Jonny, giving off strong Brandon Lee in *The Crow* vibes. I'd forgotten about him. Tall and wiry, he had a car, could legally drink and took Jessica to the pub regularly. They were in a band together, and had already been dating for what must have been two years by this point. Mickey used to talk guitars with him. We used to think he was so cool, but he was actually very sweet and polite. I always felt Jessica was a little too friendly with Mickey, and I wasn't overly surprised when shortly after I ruined our relationship Jessica broke it off with Jonny and got together with him instead. Though it didn't last long. We were all friendly afterwards – I went for a drink with her before I left for uni – but I haven't seen her since. And now all chance of reconnecting is gone. I wonder if she posted this photo? We look so young, though we thought we were terribly mature, of course. There's none of the poise today's teenagers seem to exude, though we didn't have the digital pictures to delete and learn from. There was no taking it again. This is one laughing glowing bright moment in the park behind the pub near school. We look so unpolished, so unshaped by what was to come. Two of the people in this photo are now dead. I wonder what happened to Jessica and Jonny? It was only a few short years after this that my life spun horrifically out of control, and that freckled, smiling, happy blonde girl disappeared forever.

Rain drizzles against the huge windows, muting the anti-glare one tint further, so the hunched passersby become charcoal smudges on an ashen pavement. Black cabs and delivery vans swallow more of the light as they crawl past. Even the park and trees opposite seem deadened by the weather, all a bowed, dark, dripping green, as if the trees too are trying to curl into themselves, and hide from the wind and rain. The office remains empty. The tinny beat coming from Christoph's headphones the only sound echoing through the double-height room. I look at the office clock. It's nearly twelve. I've been completely lost in my own thoughts. And I realise with a dropping sensation, Phil has not returned my call. I'm going to have to try again.

Thinking about the past, about before, has heightened my internal warning system, as if every cell is screaming not to pick up the phone. That reaching back is too dangerous. But no one has written anything under the photos posted to Facebook alluding to me. No one has called for them to be taken down. Perhaps it's okay? Perhaps people have forgotten? It's as if my handbag at my feet pulses. A guilty quickening heartbeat. *I know who you really are.* They haven't forgotten. And they have finally hunted me down.

I glance at Rob's office, but there's still no movement behind the closed blinds. Maybe he's working at home today. Maybe there's a big meeting, or an off-site training day I've forgotten about, I think with a quick sharp stab of panic. But no, colourful blocks on the shared office diary just confirm that people are elsewhere: one or two have holiday booked, long weekends, the rest are with their clients. I guiltily think of Matt – I still haven't thanked him for the flowers, nor tackled any of the increasingly pressing Unity mess. I'll do it after this.

Picking up the phone I scroll back through to Phil's office's number. Just one more call and then I can put this all to bed. Stop obsessing over the past.

It rings.

'Pritchard and Simms Accountancy?' Answers the same female voice from last week.

'Hi, can I speak to Phil Brown please?'

There is an infinitesimal pause. A slight swallow on the other end of the line. The sound of Christoph's tapping keyboard keys echo like the quick, clipped steps of invading soldiers. 'I'm afraid we're not putting through calls to the office today. If I can take your name and number—'

'Why?' Am I imagining the strain in her voice?

She takes a deep breath. 'The office is closed for today. If I can just take your number?'

'Why is the office closed? I rang on Friday and you didn't say it would be closed.' The plastic handset creaks in my grip. I can hear the panic in my voice. Something is wrong.

There is a moment's hesitation on the other end. Another breath is taken. 'I'm afraid there has been some bad news,' she says quietly, confidentially. 'There will be an official statement from the firm, but for the time being we are being asked to hold all calls. But . . . ' Her voice is kind, sad. 'I'm afraid Mr Phillip Brown died last week'.

BETH

I hang up without saying anything. It's happening. It's really happening. My fingers fly over the keys: Phillip Brown, Pritchard & Simms Accountancy, Brighton. And there it is on the *Brighton Reporter: Breaking News: Police name man stabbed to death in town centre as local accountant Phillip Brown*. A photo of a body covered by tarpaulin on the wet road. People in forensic suits. Police. Phil's body is under there. The man I once kissed, held, danced with, covered in plastic on the wet cold ground, while strangers move around him, analysing, collecting samples. Oh God. *Dead man walking*. It's all true. This is really happening.

When? I scan the article. *Police are appealing for witnesses who were in the area shortly after 6 p.m. Friday night*. Friday. I called Phil just hours before that. The room feels like it tilts. Mickey, then Kareem, then Phil. And it's definitely him. There's a photo. A different one than on his work site. Captured, beer in hand, sat back laughing in a chair outside in a small fenced garden. A short sleeved checked shirt, unbuttoned at the collar revealing the beginning of white chest hair. His stomach gently bulging into his khaki shorts. Lines crinkled round his eyes, visible round his tinted prescription glasses. It looks like it was taken at a family or friends' barbecue. Just a family man enjoying his time off in the sunshine, laughing at the joke someone's just told. Compared to the posed professional shot on his website, he looks so alive. Real. And now he's gone. My mind flicks through faces like a game of Guess Who?. Mickey. Kareem. Phil. All dead. Within a few weeks. Saliva pools in my mouth. I can't ask for more time off. I can't tell Rob it'd be my second funeral. It'd sound like a lie.

He wouldn't believe three people I know have been killed in one month. No one would. Let alone that – the thought floats free from the weeds of my shock – let alone that the first three boys I slept with have been killed. All of them. All three of them. This is really happening. If they keep going – if whoever is doing this kills more - they'll reach Danny. The thought skitters across my body like a deadly viper. No, that can't happen. I slam the lid on the fear. Panic won't help. I need to focus on what I know. I repeat the words in my head, to try and fasten onto something. *Dead man walking.*

I have to start thinking about this logically. Rationally. Plan. I have to stop it. Find them. Who knew about Kareem? It happened mostly over the summer holidays. We tried to keep it quiet. I didn't want to hurt Mickey more. Kareem was embarrassed to be with me. I flinch at the memory. And Phil? There were the others at the store we worked at. But it was decades ago. I can't remember half their names. I was just ringing him to reassure myself everything is fine. That it was in my head. A panicked overreaction to the strange notes. Mickey was stabbed in London. Kareem was killed in a hit-and-run in Sevenoaks. Phil was stabbed in Brighton. There is no link. Except there is. There's me. *I know who you really are.*

I stand up. My water glass tips, sloshes liquid over the white expanse of my desk. I scrabble to right it. Ignore the spreading mess. I can't. Christoph's head darts up like a meerkat as I stalk past. I catch my thigh against Geoff's empty desk. 'Dammit!' The pain sharp, real, here. I deserve it. I deserve it all. But not them.

The automatic striped glass doors slide open as I stumble into the reception.

'Hey – you okay?' Chloe, her face concerned above her pastel lilac jumper, starts to stand up from behind her curved reception desk. Rain is still slamming against the office front. I try to say something to make Chloe go away, but my mouth feels slack, gaping, so I just keep going.

The doors glide open. Rain, cold, freezing, strikes my face like ice shavings. I gasp. Trying to get air. Trying to breathe. Must get away. I'm running, moving, dodging between parked cars. There's a loud beep from a black cab, but I don't even turn. Streaks of shapes as people pass, and then I'm on the other side of the road, running, running for the park.

I have my phone to my ear. Breathe. Move. Get away.

'You have reached the voicemail . . . ' Danny's voicemail kicks in.

I cut the phone off. Let out a muted scream of frustration.

A group of American tourists are walking through the park. Waterproof jackets over jeans. One of them is looking at her phone. 'It says we can walk to the Jack the Ripper tour . . .'

I know who you really are. You can't run forever. You can't hide forever. Time's up. I know I deserve to be punished for what I did. But this? Mickey, Kareem, Phil? Someone is trying to take everyone I have ever cared for away. A shudder runs through me. *Someone.* Sooner or later the bill has to be paid. But Mickey, Kareem, and Phil had nothing to do with what I did. They're innocent. *But so were others who lost everything.* And the pain that caused, the knock-on, the ripples have reached me, irrigated hate, anger, vengeance. Seeds planted long ago have burst forth with venomous spikes. Someone is killing my ex-lovers. I swerve onto the grass, pitch towards the flower bed. And vomit.

I can see Chloe hovering nervously as I come back inside. Wringing her small delicate hands in front of her stonewashed mum jeans. 'Are you alright?'

My hair is sodden from the rain, and I push a dripping strand of red away from my face. Hope there's no sick in it. It sounds like someone else talking as I answer: 'Something I ate.' But then it is someone else talking. I'm not really who I say I am. I'm not really me.

I go straight into the bathroom. Open one of the mirrored cupboards and take out one of the spare toothbrushes we keep for meeting prep. The grinning illustration of a glamorous woman smiles at me from a can of hairspray. Spray deodorant and tampons look like objects from an alien world. The past, when everything was okay. Mascara has run under my eyes. Phil is dead. Kareem is dead. Mickey is dead.

I rinse the tips of my hair under the tap. Wipe the mess from under my eyes. My hands shake as I wash them. And I hold them under the water as it grows hotter. Wanting it to burn off the blood. Incinerate the past.

Chloe is hovering, her eyes creased in concern, when I come out. She presses a glass of water into my hands. And she feels so warm, so reassuring I want to tell her the awful truth.

'Here, drink this,' she says.

I lift the glass to my lips. They feel dry, sore, as if all the moisture has drained out of me in the last ten minutes. The glass shakes against my teeth. The water tastes cold, metallic. Is that a symptom of shock? 'I want to go home,' I say. I want to run, hide. For a moment I think about throwing things into a bag, getting Oscar, Danny and just driving in the car. Away, away to where this can't hurt us. 'Can you get me a cab?'

'Of course, straight away.' Chloe gives a weak reassuring smile. Squeezes my arm, then hurries back to her desk. Lifts the receiver to her ear. 'Do you want me to call someone?'

Who? The police? Danny? I think of the anger in his eyes on Friday. This has already driven a wedge between us. And what would I say? If I told him – if I could tell him – he would never speak to me again. I have lied to him. He would take Oscar away. I would lose everything. I shouldn't have called him. If I speak to the police they will know, they will blame me, because of who I am. Because of what I did before. I manage to shake my head.

Chloe is talking into the phone. 'They'll be here in two,' she says.

Chloe fetches my green coat. Holds it open like Hellie does for Oscar, so I can slide my arms in. She hands me my bag, and

I can feel from the weight she's put my laptop inside. What was on my screen? Was the window about Phil's murder still open? Did she see? But she doesn't look at me with anything other than timid concern, still gripping her hands, as if she is having to hold her own fingers back from reaching out to hug me. I don't give off warmth. I can't. I've had to keep everyone at a distance.

Because I knew, deep down, that this day would come.

BETH

The rain has stopped by the time the car drops me outside our terraced house. The sun weakly showing from behind the clouds. But I still cling tightly to my green coat, holding it like it's an otherwise open dressing gown, as if it might reveal everything. I walk fast, head down to our front door. I don't want to see Cat or Cathy. I don't want to see anyone. The door is double-locked, and I exhale. That means Danny's still onsite. No one is here. I hurriedly lock it behind me, putting the chain across as if it might keep the truth out. I pace our lounge, the low heels of my boots clicking on the wooden floor, then deadened by the rug, clicking on the wooden floor, then deadened by the rug.

I can't go to the police, that option is out. So far, I only know that at least one person has identified me. And they haven't gone public with it. They haven't told Danny, or Rob, or Zayn, thank God. Not yet. No, they seem to be content taunting me, keeping me on edge, telling me that they are responsible for these deaths. But without spelling it out – the notes aren't confessional. They're seemingly harmless words. Surely no one would take them seriously? And if I go to the police what would I say? There's no obvious link between these three men – they all live in different areas of the country. Both Mickey and Phil were stabbed, but one in a reported failed robbery, and one following an alleged altercation. Kareem was killed in a hit and run. The only real link I'm aware of is me. And I can't tell the police that without revealing who I really am. Who I was back then. And that's out of the question. The moment they know that, the moment they realise, it's over: my life, everything I care about is lost too. And they won't look elsewhere once they know I am standing in front of them. They will assume this is me. I sink onto the soft sofa as my legs shake as I realise no one else can help. I have no choice, no options. I have to tackle this myself. I have to approach this like I would a pitch for work. Find the story. Find the link. Who, what, when, where and why? The familiarity of the task gives pitons for me to thread my nerves to.

I start with 'who?'. Mickey, Kareem, and Phil. I've spent a lot of time online combing through Mickey and Kareem's lives over the last week. If I can find out more about Phil, I can cross-reference what I have. I know the three men are linked to me. But perhaps there is another link that I'm not aware of? Something that explains all this. Perhaps they worked together? Phil could have been the accountant for Mickey's band, and Kareem's care home. Something that ties them together. A taxi rumbles past outside, shuddering the windows and me. They're out there: they're coming.

Phil's common name has hampered my googling of him to date, but now this has happened, I can find out more. The image of the plastic covered body on the ground flares in front of my eyes. The awful finality of it. And my mind tries to return to another time, another body lying crumpled on the ground. *No. Don't think about that.* Focus on Phil, the laughing family man in the photo. My heart twists, thinking of his wife, his children. If that were to happen to Danny, to Oscar. The thought scalds and I pull away from it. Try to detach. But then I can only think of elements. How the once smiling, breathing man that was Phil is now mere oxygen, carbon, hydrogen, nitrogen, calcium, phosphorus. Something to be processed in the street in an investigation.

I need to go back to the beginning. Work on all the names properly. I get my laptop out and start googling news reports on Phil's stabbing. The local newspaper, competing with the twenty-four seven news mentality, has already expanded the earlier article. And I find what I'm looking for, the words scratching at my sadness. Phillip Brown leaves behind a wife, Robyn D'Beauvoir and two children. Two children. Those poor kids. His poor wife. But, thank God, she has a distinctive name. It takes me two minutes to find her on Facebook, her page already full of RIP messages, which I scroll past. Clicking through, it lists her as married to Phil Brown. He was there on Facebook. His name so common, he was lost in a sea of Phil Browns. No wonder his wife kept her distinctive moniker.

I print out Mickey's, Kareem's, and Phil's friend lists and set about comparing them. Facebook helpfully makes them alphabetical, but with Mickey having over three thousand it's a long task. And it turns up nothing. There are shared names between Mickey and Kareem, as you would expect from two people who went to school together. But no overlap with Phil. His Facebook page is partially private, so I can't see much from his online feed, but he doesn't seem to have been very active on it anyway. The last post appears to be from 2014. I find him on LinkedIn, where there is a distinct lack of RIP messages. I guess it's not that kind of forum. Before he was at his Brighton firm he worked for an accountant in the City. I can find no mention of Kareem's care home, or Mickey's band in either of their listed clients. I'm grasping at straws. But I make notes on everything I can about each of them anyway. Age, marital status, job, where they lived. How long I was with them. Which is where it makes no sense.

If someone is targeting people I dated, how would they know that I saw Phil? It was a matter of a couple of weeks. I would never have called him my boyfriend. He would never have described me as his girlfriend. More flirty friends with benefits? He might have hoped for more, but there was uni to go to. So it's people I slept with who are being targeted? But how would someone know that? Ice slithers down my spine. It doesn't make sense, but I add what details I can to my notes. Persevere.

Then I turn to 'when?'. I add when and where each of them was killed. I keep thinking of the voicemail I left for Phil. Did it play out loud in his office? Did he hear it and decide to call me back later? If he'd have picked up, if I'd have spoken to him, could I have stopped this? Would he still be alive?

Where? In order to try to make sense of this all, in order to find proof that I am the link, proof that will get the police to take this seriously, I need to cover every angle. I print out a series of Google maps. I mark Hyde Park on one, add Mickey's name, the date and time (as close as I can ascertain it from the press coverage) at which he was killed. I do the same for the Sevenoaks road Kareem died on, and now the street in Brighton in which Phil was attacked. And then I do the same on another map, more pulled-out, that allows me to see all three spots. You could drive between Hyde Park and Sevenoaks in under two hours. You could drive from Hyde Park to Brighton in two hours. Or you could take the train. London, Kent, East Sussex. These are all London, and around. Does that mean whoever is doing this is based somewhere in this area? None of the crime scenes are a million miles apart. But they also contain two places I have lived: Sevenoaks and London. It's where I and millions of others work because there are more jobs in the South East. But it's good to see it in black and white. It means I can picture it more. Analyse it.

Why? It's the question I haven't wanted to ask. The rotten core of the horrific situation. Why is this happening? Why these three men? My pen hovers over the page, but I can't write it down. Just the thought of putting it in black and white makes me feel sick. For a second I remember writing out another report, a time when I had to. How my hand shook, tears dropped onto my notes, but police biros don't smudge. The page buckled as if straining under the weight of my confession. But the words were sharp, visible, and on permanent record. Seared into my memory.

The sound of the key in the front door. Followed by the thud of it being pushed back, the scamper of Oscar. Hellie's laughter.

I scrabble to gather up my notes, my laptop, the names, the details, the fear, and stuff them into my handbag. I have to keep them with me at all times. No one must see. I plaster a smile on my face, as Oscar careens into the room and jumps up at me, blonde curls bouncing, eyes fixed on the prize. He's in his school uniform, cold from being outside. Cheeks pink.

'Mummy!' I pull him into me and ruffle his hair to dislodge a dried leaf that has clung onto it. I want to hold him forever. It's started, and I don't know how far it will go. Am I in danger? Is Danny? Is Oscar?

'Oww, you're squeezing me too tight, Mummy.' Oscar pulls away from me and my desperate fingers have to bury themselves in the folds of my jumper not to drag him right back.

'Sorry,' I say. The grey trousers covering his little legs stretched tight over the knees as he bounces, impossibly flexible, from kneeling to standing on the sofa. I can't let him know anything is wrong. 'You been to the park?'

Hellie's smiling face appears at the door, turning the arms of Oscar's discarded blue coat the right way out. 'It was still busy,' she says. 'Despite the weather.' She pulls her own knitted bobble hat off, her hair static sticking to it on the way up.

I have to get it together. I have to be here for my child. I have to make everything alright. 'No fair-weather park-goers round here.' I cup and breathe onto Oscar's fingers. 'Hackney is made of hardy stuff. Good day?' The last words twist in my throat, the mundanity catching like lies on my tongue.

'Great,' Hellie takes his coat back out to the hall. 'We ate all our carrots at lunchtime, and painted Mummy a lovely picture to cheer her up.'

Cheer me up? Has it been obvious that the last few weeks have been distressing? I thought I'd kept it hidden from home. I think of the printed sheets in my bag. Danny's anger. I wish I could put them all outside. I don't want any of this in the house. Contaminating it.

'YouTube time!' Oscar proclaims, pushing his hand into my stomach and his knee into my thigh to lever himself up and off the sofa.

'Oof,' I laugh. 'Careful! Mummy's not as young as she used to be.'

But he's already focused on turning on the television.

'I'll get going, if that's okay with you,' Hellie asks.

'Sure. Course.' I stand, pretend to pick a bit of fluff from the back of Oscar's jumper. I don't want her to see any more. 'Thanks. As ever.'

'No worries, bye!' She calls to Oscar. 'See you tomorrow!'

'Say goodbye to Hellie,' I automatically prod.

'Goodbye to Hellie,' Oscar says, without looking up from the screen. Hellie laughs and I hear the door close.

I grab my handbag and go to the kitchen in case he notices. Exhaling. Panting. I'm shaking. How can this be happening? Because I see it now. Someone knows who I slept with? How? I close my eyes. Force myself to think. To remember. Just what lies I have told.

BETH – THE FIRST NIGHT WITH DANNY

The pub belched sweaty chip air and 'Bohemian Rhapsody' behind us. I hugged Emma from work close.

'Let me know you get home alright?'

'Course,' she says, swaying only ever so slightly. 'See ya at the coalface tomorrow.'

'Coalface?' says Zayn. 'I knew a drag queen by that name once,' he grins wickedly.

'I'm pretty sure that's not an okay thing to say,' I give him a look. He's been eyeing Danny's work colleague a little too appreciatively, since we found out they were also out and joined them on the Thames.

'Oh darling, I've worked it plenty of times in some dark, dirty, and downright dangerous situations. How about you, Danny? Ever been tempted to go underground?'

'Right, you, taxi,' I say, pushing Zayn towards the road before he could start pawing the poor bloke. 'Time for bed.'

'Too right,' he says, waving his phone and grinning. I couldn't read the message that was on the screen but I could guess what it said. 'It just won't be mine.'

I sometimes wished sex was as easy to come by as it seems in Zayn's world. He was always hooking up with someone for one night of pleasure, and never seemed to feel any consequences. Just human touch. I look at Danny. How nice that would be. But in reality I know you always got entangled. Other people hurt you. You hurt others if you let them close. I know that better than most. Zayn had been really cut up when after two years Ben had insisted they have an open relationship. Zayn said he'd been too busy at work to start screwing others on top of Ben, but I thought it was more that he didn't want to. He just let Ben get on with it. They limped on for another year after that, but ultimately they broke apart. And that was only just after Christmas. This was all part of the facade. 'You will be alright, won't you?' I hug Zayn close as we said goodbye.

His voice was full of wry laughter, but he gave me an affectionate squeeze back. A reassuring hand on the arm. 'His name's Javier, he's ripped, and he's a yoga teacher. I shall be more than alright, sweets.'

I giggle. Grateful again that I had managed to keep Zayn. The one bright spot in my life. I waved him off as his cab drew up outside the National Theatre. Then there were two. I was uncomfortably aware of it being just me and Danny. He did have that certain something. He was slender, but his shoulders looked broader in his shirt, his jacket tucked under his arm. The sleeves rolled-up to reveal the moving muscles of his forearms. I've always found men's forearms to be sexy. Which makes me think of Victorians getting a flash of an ankle. I giggle. Then caught his eye and blushed. I probably shouldn't have had that last glass of Pinot. I'm usually much more careful how much I drink these days.

'Which way you going?' Danny asks, as the pub hiccupped out another couple, worse the wear than us.

Dressed like they worked in the City, the woman was encumbered by her clicking heels and pencil skirt. Laughing, and speaking the language only the drunk understand, she slammed into her tall gentleman friend and they both lurched towards us.

Instinctively I leapt back, as Danny's hand came up to steady me. I cursed myself for wearing a long sleeve cardi. I would have liked to feel his skin on mine. Anyone's touch. And then I realised how drunk I was. What am I doing? I can't have this. I stepped away from him, so his warm hand was no longer on my back.

'Alright?' He looks genuinely concerned, as the couple started to make ground away from the pub.

'Yeah.' Getting the words out fast like ripping off a plaster. 'I've gotta go.' I start down the side of the sixties concrete theatre towards the Thames, and suddenly realised how clear the sky is. The London skyline a perfect line drawing. As if everything has sharpened up. I've let my guard down. I'd let him get too close. I feel the pull in my stomach of what could have been, what was no longer an option.

'Hey? Hold on?' Danny catches up with me. Drawing alongside as I tuck my hands deep into my pockets, hugging the sides of my thick black cardigan close. I can't look at him. I can't see his hurt expression, those lovely kind eyes, confused. I've been cruel. 'Are you sure you're okay?' he says.

'Sure. I just don't want to miss my train.'

'Okay, which station you going to?' He's keeping pace next to me, as we round onto the South Bank. The river a sparkling ink black. A smattering of tourists and the post-supper theatre crowd weaving huddles through the shaped concrete benches, and waiting at the silver airstream van for sugary-sweet doughnuts and coffee. A couple pass, her arm tightly through the denim jacketed arm of his, her head bent forwards in a laugh, a wave of ginger hair cascading over her velveteen duster coat. The open-eyed awe with which he was looking at her was like a snapshot of pure love. And it hurts. I speed up.

'Blackfriars. You don't have to walk with me, I'll see you later, yeah.' I don't look up.

'Hey, Beth, wait a sec.' Danny's hand is warm, gentle through my own arm, just the fingertips asking me to stop, to turn.

And I do, keeping my face turned away, eyes closed briefly against the pain.

'Beth?' Danny's voice is soft, and I can smell his woody, citrus aftershave. His fingertips retreat from my arm. 'Are you always running away?'

All the air sucks out of me. The South Bank vibrates for a moment, a soap bubble of alarm before it pops.

'I'm not.' I try to laugh, tuck my own hair behind my ear as the breeze tugs it, welcoming the chance to do anything that means I don't have to look at Danny.

'Have I done something wrong?' He sounded plaintive.

I turn to look at his face. He looks young, vulnerable, and I can't have that. 'No. Of course not. You've done nothing – you're kind, and supportive, and you make me laugh.' And when did I reach out and touch him? When did my hand grip his arm, like it had always been there?

'Well now I know you're lying,' he says with a soft laugh, looking up at me from under his lashes. 'You . . . You do like me then?' *Oh God. I can't do this.*

Danny fills the silence. 'I mean, I'm not imagining it – it's not wishful thinking – there is something between us,' he indicates with a brief movement of his head. I wondered if his lips feel as soft as they look. 'I like you Beth, I really like you. But every time I think something might happen – and I would never rush you, ever – but you always pull away?'

A flurry of wind whips round the side of the concrete ITV studios behind us, watering my eyes. 'I'm sorry,' I whisper.

'Don't apologise,' Danny steps closer, his hand gently sliding round my waist. And I can't fight it anymore, I can't keep running, I want him too much. He tilts my chin up. His eyes searching mine for permission, asking silently if this is okay? I close my eyes and kiss him. His lips *are* soft. Then they are electric. Like a charge zinging through me. I run my hands up into his hair. Press close against him, feel him sharply inhale. *Desire.*

We reach my flat, still wrapped in each other's arms and lips. I fumble for my keys, give the door its customary kick. The wood, swollen and warped, always sticks against the pungent carpet lining the communal hallway.

'My flatmates will be out, or in bed,' I say as he kisses down my neck. The two girls I share with aren't what you'd call friends, but I'm friendly enough to know Ines will be in bed with her earplugs in, and Aiko would still be drinking with her Chelsea office colleagues.

Danny stops. Pulls back. Did he think I should live on my own? Maybe we should've gone to his? There was no discussion, we just sort of ended up here. It feels unstoppable now, inevitable, I've repressed this side for so long. I want it. I want him. His back feels strong, muscular under his cotton shirt. I want to see.

'I need to . . . I should have . . . ' He trails off, glancing at the door.

Please don't leave.

'Do you want a drink? I've got red wine?' We were both more likely to get what we wanted if we had a bit of Dutch courage. Maybe this was now moving too fast for him? Of course he was confused, I've been pulling away for months, ever since we met through a friend of Zayn's. They're all part of the same charity group training to cycle from London to Brighton together. And we've kept circling back to each other, me like a moth to the flame, aware I was likely to get burned. Or worse, burn him. 'Look if you don't want to . . . we can just have coffee?' I trail off. Have I come on too strong? Maybe he isn't that into me?

'No, it's not that,' he catches hold of my hand, fixing me with his eyes. 'It's just . . . I've just come out of a long-term relationship.' He indicates the two of us. 'I haven't done *this* for a long time.'

'Me too,' I say, before I think about what I'm saying.

His face relaxes. 'Then you know this is . . . it feels weird.'

And I really don't want him to leave. I tamp down the questioning voice inside. I want this. I want him. I could be everything he's ever wanted. I could be good. I could protect us both. 'Good weird, though, right?' I smile.

He grins. Steps closer, strokes my hair away from my face. 'Definitely good weird. It's just . . . ' he blushes, drops eye contact.

'I haven't ever done this before,' he says. He looked adorably stricken, as if he is offending my honour. 'Met someone and instantly clicked,' he adds.

He felt it too. That first time: something sparking as we made eye contact. The pull wasn't just me. We haven't been able to stay away from each other. It's natural. It's meant to be. *But not for the likes of you*. No, I can make myself worthy. 'Me neither,' I whisper. *A lie*.

'I . . . ' He coughs awkwardly. 'I . . . I've only been with my girlfriend. With my ex-girlfriend.'

Bless. His inexperience makes me feel sexy, empowered. I could teach him things. Be the dream lover. *You don't deserve to have this*. But this isn't about me, it's about what Danny needs. I can give him everything. If I happen to be more experienced than him in bed, it must seem like divine providence, not hard-won know-how. Past lovers flash through my mind. They are no longer real. That person is gone. This is a fresh start, a new beginning, what happened before won't happen again: I am a different person. 'I've only had two relationships before.' I settle into the lie like a warm bath. Beth is whoever I want her to be. Beth has only had two relationships before. 'I've only slept with them.'

I feel him relax slightly. I gave the right answer. I gave the right response. I can do this. I can have this. And happiness flares as a possibility, bright, vibrant like a flame in front of me. And I know I'm going to walk calmly into the fire.

BETH – THE NIGHT OF MY HEN DO

'I don't need these,' I laugh, holding the two L-plates either side of my head like Minnie Mouse ears and pouting for the camera.

Emma from work, in her finest Karen Millen red satin wiggle dress, shrieks. 'More bubbles!'

'I'll go.' I stagger up, my stilettos sinking into the thick carpet of the rental apartment. The threads wrapping round the spikes of my heels like Velcro.

'Like a good little wifey!' cackles Emma, scrunching her snub-nose up in consternation as her Malbec sloshes dangerously close to her ghd poker-straight hair.

I could do without forfeiting our deposit. I shouldn't think about that. This is my hen do. Raucous is a success. I'll remember this forever. *Carmen should be here.* The thought slips traitorously through my Prosecco-weakened defences. I shouldn't be getting married. I shouldn't be doing any of this. I don't deserve it. But I can't let Danny go. I'm too greedy for him. I love nothing more than lying in his arms, kissing, biting, chatting, more. I want to give him everything he wants. If I hadn't let myself fall in love it might have been easier, but it's too late now. Now I can't see a life without him. I try to reason with the monster inside. I gave up so much. My previous life, Carmen. I paid penance. And I will be good now: I will be the perfect wife for Danny. But guilt still fizzes through me like swallowed bubbles. I know, deep down, that what I am doing is selfish. That I am putting Danny at risk. And all without consent. He doesn't really know who he is marrying.

My foot slips as I pass onto the ceramic floor of the kitchen, and I bat the stupid L-plates away, puffing at the synthetic veil someone's clamped over my blow dry. I hate all this tacky stuff. That's the problem with not having real friends at your hen do. Emma and the other girls from the office are nice enough, but they don't know me. Carmen would never have said that bullshit 'little wifey' comment.

'You okay, honey?' Zayn makes me jump. He's leaning against the Formica kitchen counter, nursing a pint of water to his tight black shirt.

My hand clutches at my chest, my diamond engagement ring getting snagged in the veil. 'Christ – I didn't see you there.' I try to disentangle my hand.

'Hiding in plain sight – you know me, darling. What would all those straight boys at work think if they could see me at a fag hag do?'

'That's a gross phrase,' I snap. Then immediately feel guilty. I give him a wink. 'And I bet they'd be simply shocked.'

'So shocked, darling,' he says, his voice mimicking arch camp, mirroring my hand-to-chest movement but without the inelegant tangle with a polyester veil.

I laugh, despite myself.

Zayn leans over the sink to refill his glass, his voice returned to its normal timbre. 'You sure you're alright? Is Emo Emma getting to you?'

I smile at his nickname for Emma. 'My hairdresser was telling me that her wedding made her really reassess who her true friends were and who weren't. Like it brought it into sharp focus.' I think of Carmen again. Of how she, Zayn, and I could have gone out to a fancy restaurant, drunk fifteen-pound cocktails in a banquette booth. Laughed over decadent French butter spread on warm, fresh bread. Eaten steak tartare, and venison meatballs with buttered neeps. Decent food, rather than drinking burning vodka through dick straws, and being forced to play passive-aggressive party games that all feel like they're designed to humiliate me. Zayn would have loved Carmen. Carmen would have loved Zayn. I know who my real friends are. I just can't have them. My hairdresser didn't realise how spot-on she was. 'She said that afterwards it was all clear – she just stopped seeing certain people. That by putting all her eggs in her husband's basket . . .'

'Eggs in her husband's basket? You have had too much to drink. Here – have this,' Zayn hands his water to me. I take a big gulp, washing some of the sickly sweet afterburn of sambuca from my mouth.

'I mean, that by making herself a new family with her husband, by saying that's who she was now, she didn't need them anymore.' I could see the logic so clearly. A certain amount of relief washing over me that after next month I wouldn't have to keep up pretences anymore. I would have completed my transformation: a new life. Beth 2.0. I could understandably ease off the socialising with Emma, and the others. I could stop risking slip-ups every time they suggested a bottle of Pinot after work. Fearing that they might guess, that they might know, that everything I'd constructed would suddenly be burned to the ground. I can't lose Danny, I can't lose Zayn. I have got this far, I have made it work, I can keep these final precious things. *Oh Carmen, I'm sorry.*

'Beth?' Zayn is frowning at me.

'Yeah?'

'You didn't hear a word of that, did you?' he says.

'Sorry,' I say. 'I just . . . ' And suddenly tears are pricking my eyes.

'Sweetie.' Zayn wraps me in his arms, the scent of his oud perfume and the faint whiff of cigarette smoke telling me he hadn't quite given up social smoking despite his protestations. 'It's okay. You don't have to go through with this, if you don't want to – we'll make it work.'

Not go through with it? 'No, no, it's not that.' And I want to tell Zayn, tell him what he really missed when he was away in Australia all those years. The real reason I don't see anyone from my past. Why I go by Beth now, why I've even changed my name by deed poll so all my official documents match. How I lied when I said it was a work thing – a more manageable name for my first big Japanese client that stuck. How it could all crumble if I don't keep being very careful. 'It's just . . . I told Danny a lie,' I say into Zayn's shoulder, my breath catching in a sob.

'A lie? What kind of lie?' he asks.

And of course I can't say. Not the whole truth. Because then Zayn would know too. He would leave too. And I have been lying to him for longer. 'I told him I'd only slept with two people.' The heat runs up my face to meet my tears.

'Two? And he believed you?'

I laugh despite myself. 'Yes. He'd only slept with his ex before me.'

'So he says,' smirks Zayn, holding my shoulders away so he can look at me, eyebrows raised.

'So he says?'

'Everyone lies about the number of exes they have,' he says.

'They do?' Could Danny have lied too? I'd never considered that.

'Sweetheart, last week I told this guy I met in Heaven I was a straight-up virgin. Never slept with a man before. At thirty-years-old. And he totally bought it.'

'You didn't?'

'Course I did – and I told him I was twenty-five.'

I laughed.

Zayn gave me a wink. 'He loved it. Don't worry about it. So, your numbers are nearer . . . ?'

'Four,' I say, quickly. I can't say the real number because he will ask who they are. And I can't tell him that. I can't tell him about the last one, the one that changed everything. The one that destroyed my life.

Something flickers in Zayn's face, but he doesn't slow down. 'You just nipped and tucked your figures. You added a filter. No biggie. Danny's happy. You're happy. You'll both live happily ever after.'

'But I'm marrying him under false pretences,' I say.

Zayn laughs.

I glare at him.

'I'm sorry sweetie,' he sparkles. 'But false pretences? This isn't the eighteenth century. He's not about to sue you for breach of promise, is he?'

'No, but . . . ' It's so much bigger than that. He doesn't know who he is really about to marry. He doesn't know how dangerous his new wife is. Neither does Zayn.

Zayn is still looking at me, searching my face, and not for the first time I wonder if he does know? There's no way he knows. He wouldn't be able to touch me, to be near me, to be my friend. Sure he's all about living in the moment, being who you are in the here and now. And he can be a little self-obsessed – we all can be. But did he really never question my different name? Never bump into someone from school – just bring me up in conversation? See their reaction? Of course he wouldn't talk about me. It's not all about me.

'Look,' Zayn says. 'Danny's not stupid. He probably guessed you fiddled the numbers slightly – I mean, who hasn't? And he doesn't care. He need never know about the other five people you twilight tangoed with.'

'Four,' I lie automatically. 'Danny was the fifth. Anyway, let's stop talking about this. It's a party after all? Let's do this!' I hoist the next bottle of Prosecco into the air.

'Honey.' Zayn's hand gently rests on my arm. I can see Emma grinding against the floor lamp in the lounge like it's a pole in a club.

'He's happy with the truth you told him.' Zayn speaks so quietly no one else can have heard. I snap back to look at him, but he's already heading past me towards the others, face wide in mock delight, hands up, ready to join the party. And I'm left with nothing but the sensation of goosebumps running up my bare arms, causing me to shiver.

Just who was Zayn just talking about?

BETH – THREE DAYS TILL THE PARTY

I reheat a selection of Oscar's favourite veggies from those Danny already prepped in the fridge. Add in two fish fingers. Let him eat it on the sofa, mixing his peas and sweet potato into his ketchup. He doesn't look up from the screen. I watch the colours reflected in his flawless eyes. He's kicked his socks off – one's on the sofa arm, the other a rumpled snake on the coffee table. His tiny toes soft, unblemished against the blue pile of the sofa cushions. My baby. I must protect him. I close the lounge door after me. Head to the kitchen.

Dust motes float in the shaft of sun that streams from the back doors. I take out a piece of paper and I start to write The List. Everyone has one. All their exes. All the people they've slept with.

Mickey.

Kareem.

Phil.

I don't know how whoever is doing this knows, but I know I can't gamble with failing to include people. Maybe someone has spoken to other people? Tallied it up somehow? Who would actually know that I slept with Phil? Did I ever outright tell anyone? My brain crackles through long-ignored images, faces, snapshots from my past. *Before*. Before when there were drunken nights, many people, piles of friends. I was so open with everyone I met. Going back to strangers' houses and drinking and smoking on their couches, pouring out all my secrets like I couldn't catch hold of them. *After*. After it's easier. So many people deleted from my life, or rather me from theirs. I'm very cautious now. I learned the hard way: you have to be careful who you tell, and what. I close my eyes. Picture Phil's bobbing face. His slightly cheesy smile. The red of his hair. The blue polyester of the uniforms. The freshly-delivered newspapers bound together with plastic cords so sharp they'd cut your fingers. The smell of the damp, musty shop, stacked high with specialist magazines, and lurid confectionery, and paperbacks still with some pages uncut from the printers. Phil carrying the deliveries in. Cracking jokes as we emptied the plastic delivery bins, sharing shy smiles as we wiped the warehouse dust from our hands.

Other members of staff – people I would have called friends back then – probably guessed we were together. Gossiped at least. Those small groups are built on tittle-tattle. Could someone have spoken to the people I worked with? Would they remember mine and Phil's names? I can remember a Karen, and Hannah, and was it Leo or Liam whose mum worked in the same store on weekdays? But then none of those had their faces in printed newspapers. A journalist would have found me. It's coming up to the anniversary. It would be a huge thing. A podcast. I know what the audience want.

Someone could be investigating what happened. The old me. The one before the monster. Showing a growing pattern. But though they might try to talk to my exes – people who knew me – surely they wouldn't hurt them?

Someone did find out about Phil, and they found him. I can't leave anyone off the list, on the assumption no one knew about us. I didn't think anyone knew about Phil. I tried to warn him, but I was too late. That can't happen again.

If someone spoke to my old university flatmates they might come up with Wade's name, even though it was only a one-night thing. Oscar laughs in the lounge, and I feel my stomach contract. I have to keep all this away from him, from my family.

Wade.
Tobi.
Iain.

My pen rests next to Iain's name. Breathing in and out. Flickers of the past. Flashes of rooms. Ceilings. Windows. Single beds. Doubles. The feel of stubble rash. The feeling of being sore. Alive. Desired.

Danny.

My husband. Father of my child. My longest relationship. My one great love. The one I was meant to be with. My Danny, who doesn't know half these people exist. My Danny who I lied to.

I hear his key in the lock. Quickly I gather the papers back into my bag with my laptop. He can't see any of this. I can't raise his suspicions in any way. I tuck my bag into the utility room, out of sight. I turn my phone over in my hand. I could keep googling this?

I listen to Danny talking to Oscar. 'Hello mate. You still up? It's nearly eight. Where's Mum?'

New rule: no laptops and phones in the evening. Why did I say that? Because I can feel it – I can feel him pulling away. I can't lose him. I slide the phone into my bag. I'll leave early for work in the morning. If I set myself up in one of the quiet pods in the office I can keep working on this there. Where no one can see.

'Hiya!' I call. 'Just putting the kettle on – want one?'

He appears in the doorway, loosening his tie. 'Builders, please,' he smiles. 'Good day?' The softness in his eyes telling me our argument is over. A ceasefire.

'Oh, you know,' I say. 'The usual.' Phil's voice on his answerphone. Phil's dead body under tarpaulin. The rain washing his blood into the street. That name on the page. That name that started it all.

'You eaten?' Danny takes out a tub from the fridge.

'Yeah, I'm good. Thanks.' I turn away while I fiddle with the kettle, in case he can see it on my face. In case he can hear what is screaming from my every pore.

I lied to you. I lied to everyone. And someone knows.

LILY

The familiar warmth of Iain's sunshine-bathed flat welcomes me in. I inhale the lingering tones of his apple and ginger aftershave, the hint of beeswax and aerosol polish that reminds me of my mum cleaning on a Saturday morning, always making me feel like I'm home.

'Shall I dish up?' Iain calls, slinging his keys onto the white console unit in the hallway, the takeaway box in his other hand as he opens the MDF door into the small open plan living space.

'Do you think it'll keep warm?' I follow him in, grab his arse, squeeze it laughingly with two hands.

He raised his pale eyebrows at me. 'Well aren't you hungry?' His voice drops into a comic sexy growl, his blue eyes dancing.

'More like thirsty,' I try to say in the sexiest femme fatale voice I can muster. 'Catch me if you can!' And I race into the bedroom, collapsing in a heap of giggles onto the sage green duvet, as his arms catch me. Our lips meet. His hand in my hair, mine round his waist, pulling him into me, feeling his want.

'So beautiful,' he breathes between snatched kisses, pulling back to look at me like he can't believe I'm here. His hands stroke in something close to reverence. The thin wool of his jumper is slippery between my fingers, and then everything speeds up as the wisps of hair on his chest tickle my face. I kiss down his body. And then we are together, hard, fast, wet gold heat and pure burning joy.

The scream shatters everything.

'What the—' Iain scrambles off me, taking in the woman standing incongruously in the door.

I pull the bedding to cover me, taking in her navy trench, long legs clad in denim, the sleek black hair pulled into a half ponytail. The porcelain skin of the hand, nails jade green, a neat platinum band of diamonds on her ring finger, covering her face, telling my brain – no, not a cleaner. 'Who are you? What is . . . ?'

Iain's blue eyes are bulged wide in what I realise is panic. Ping-ponging between me and the undeniably pretty woman standing in his bedroom.

'Iain?' She clutches a tan leather handbag to her front, the large engagement diamond glinting on her ring finger. She sounds like a child, desperate for answers, for someone to make sense of the world.

Ice water washes through my veins, vanishing all traces of the golden light that had been there just moments before. Taking with it everything of which I'd felt certain.

Iain is pulling his trousers back up, the dark hair on the tops of his feet a blur as he hops, stumbling off the bed towards her. 'Anna – I can explain!'

He knows her. He knows her name. He is apologising to her. Thoughts fly through my head as I scramble blindly for my own shirt. And flashes of Tobi, of what he did, what he was doing, explode like bright fireworks in front of my eyes. She's me. I'm her. I'm aware I'm shaking, as I pull on my tan jumper, yank at my jeans. The denim rough against the cold wet between my legs. Shame spreads into the fabric. I have to . . . to what? Get away? The realisation. Pressure pushes a mass against my chest, my throat burns. The room tips, and I'm reminded of being seasick on a ferry to France. Feeling the stinging pulse of everything around me, knowing I'm violently off kilter with it.

Iain pleads, his movements startle the woman – her, Anna, and she jerks away too. Mirroring my own desire to run.

'Anna!' Iain runs after her. His feet bare.

Everything that has happened over the last few months shifts in my mind's eye, resettles into an ugly rendering I don't recognise. 'You bastard!' I scream. But I know – I saw it – the pain in her face. The sour pre-burn of vomit puffs into my throat. He used me. Lied. Lied to her. I have to tell her. Have to make her understand. Have to help. My boots take seconds to slide on, and before I know what I'm doing, I'm running after them, through the open flat door.

The woman – Anna's trench coat is flying out around her, the loose belt whipping against the glass front door as she yanks it open.

'Anna!' Iain makes a grab at her arm, and my stomach lurches. 'Please, wait.'

'Don't touch me,' she spits, her dark shaped brows scrunched, a row of perfectly straight white teeth revealed in an animalistic sneer. Raw pain driving her primal reaction, she evades his grasp and launches into the slanting grey rain of Tooley Street. I have to let her know – I have to tell her. I didn't know. I didn't do this deliberately.

Iain follows her, swearing, and slowing as his bare feet hit the soaked pavement. To his left a stack of wooden planks torn from yet another renovation next door, have blown flecks of yellow wood like sand across the ground. A man in a red jacket veers away from his skinny mate, as I dash out between them onto the street. The damp of my jeans cold in the air.

'Sorry,' I manage, passing Iain who is picking grit from his foot. A group of young Japanese students giggle at him. A woman in a black puffa jacket, pulling a wheelie case takes in the unfolding scene. A courier cyclist's head tilts to watch our tawdry drama play out on the busy London street. Shame washes over me again. To be seen. To be this person. I have to tell her – Anna – that I didn't know. That I would never . . . That I'm sorry.

She's still walking, her dark hair having loosened its ponytail is streaming behind her, the machine gun click of her ankle boots hard against the floor.

Ignoring Iain, I run with the undone flaps of my own boots slapping against my ankles. 'Please. Wait. I didn't . . .'

She turns, scared, startled, as I reach for her shoulder. 'Get away,' she yells.

'No, you don't understand.' I try to step towards her.

But her eyes wild, her hair blown free by the wind, suspended in tendrils around her, she moves instinctively away. Back, her foot catches on the kerb, unbalances her. The tap of her heels scrape against the tarmac of the road. Her arms flail, the diamond flashing, as she tries to stabilise herself. There's a sense of movement around me. The woman in the black puffa drops her case handle. The men shout. A horn is hammered. The strain of screeching air from hydraulic brakes. A groaning slide. My hand is out reaching for her. And Anna's eyes, which I now see are a beautiful hazel, lock onto mine in the half the second before the bus hits her. Behind me Iain screams.

BETH – ONE DAY TILL THE PARTY

I've barely slept the last two nights. I've been on autopilot, my body, my face smiling through my job, nodding and agreeing with Danny as he showed me party decorations and playlists I've failed to absorb, tucking Oscar into bed. Robotic, compliant, like an AI doll, but inside I've been howling. The notes, my laptop, my phone; the past has arrived in the here and now, a rip in time through which the monster has climbed to destroy me. Lily has risen.

I'd never have got away with it now. There's too much documentation, electronic trails. I was lucky. It was in that sweet spot where there wasn't much online about Lily, but I could utilise those same tools to build Beth. The greatest grassroots PR campaign I ever constructed. I made a fake person. A few well-placed mentions, a few quotes on old forums, a couple of 'I just found these old photos' uploaded. Does anyone remember the bike sheds at Reading Juniors? Cheesy chips from the van that used to wait outside the Nottingham campus? Add my jokey comments to communities I was never part of, and redhead Beth T or PR Beth (my own in-joke) now looks like she grew up in Reading, went to Nottingham Uni. A fake paper trail that will last forever online. And all a good fifty miles away from where Lily grew up and lived.

I can't remember the last time I focused solely on what I was doing. My brain is so hooked on being stimulated all the time. But last night felt slower, real, not the usual blur. My phone is a time swallower. As Danny laughed at the latest sitcom we're watching on Netflix, I leafed through my mental memories of Phil, Kareem, Mickey. I tried to stay away from the tarpaulin. Blood in the rain. Tried to stay in the safety of the past, when I knew how things would end. They felt turbulent at the time, but they have a childish golden quality now. Before I went to university, before the cotton wool was ripped away and I truly felt the pain of adulthood. Is there an answer back then – something I didn't notice at the time – that makes sense of what is happening now? Who would want to kill my ex-boyfriends? Another boyfriend? But why? And why now?

Despite trying to numb it all with several glasses of wine, I couldn't get sleep to come. By the early hours my defences were down. Danny was snoring beside me, the wind drumming its nails against the windows, and distant sirens wended their way through the death and destruction of the capital. And they came. Thoughts, feelings. About Tobi. Tobi laughing. Tobi surrounded by others. Tobi winking at me from under his lashes. Tobi taking my hand. Tobi on top of the girl with the sharp nose from the Students' Union. The sound that came out of me. Her screaming at me to get out. Even though she was the one in my fiancé's room, shagging him. And Tobi. Tobi's awful, awkward laugh following me down the corridor. As if he was nothing more than a kid caught with candy he shouldn't have. And then the pain. We were *the* couple. A power couple, before that was even a concept I understood. Everyone knew Tobi. And everyone knew he cheated on me. And those final dead months of university. Tears, and sleeping, and then tears and drinking. Staying out all night. Strangers' flats. Anyone with drink or drugs. Anyone who could help stub a hole in it all. Still working, still wanting my grades, wanting to prove I was enough for him. And job interviews. And smiling and saying how great everything was. And trying desperately to claw something from the wreckage of our plans. And Tobi still smiling, still being Student Union President. Still on top. On top of the girl with the sharp nose.

And the day I made it through, the day I survived, I got my degree. And overhearing Katie telling my friends I didn't deserve the 2:1. That I'd just been out partying the whole time. Like I'd been having fun.

And before it all Wade. Seeing the destructive link between it all now. The lit touchpaper. Was it just a slow burn till the explosion? Is what happened with Wade what caused what happened with Tobi? Did I allow myself to be duped? Did I think it was all I deserved? Because I was damaged goods?

For years I have not thought of this. Not turned it over to find the creepy crawlies scurrying underneath for the comfort of the invisible dark.

Phil lying on the wet ground under the tarpaulin. Kareem being flung from his bike. Mickey clutching his stomach. Mickey coming to see me after all this time.

I'd texted Mickey. That night, after Wade. After I went back to my room. Something simple like *Hey.* He replied straight away. Asked if I was alright. It must have been the early hours of the morning. I replied that I just felt like I needed a hug. And even though he was miles away, and he couldn't physically do it, he said he was giving me a hug. And I closed my eyes and imagined I was safe in his arms again.

There's movement across the office. Rob letting himself in, carrying a Nero coffee. His favourite. He smiles as he sees me in the pod. Waves. I barely remember the commute. Time has fractured as the past has rushed into the present.

I signal at my earphones, wave my phone in the air. Mouth: 'On the phone.'

He gives a wry disappointed smile, heads for his office. I can't talk to him now.

I stare at the screen of my laptop. It took me minutes to find Wade this morning. He's still friends with Katie on Facebook, though his account page is set to Friends Only. Not that it matters.

Wade Ellison isn't a common name in the UK. And he is still here. I reread his company's webpage as if it might change anything. Ten minutes away in a cab. Thirty on foot. Just the other side of the City. I might have passed him multiple times. I could go now. I could speak to him in person now.

Other people start arriving at the office. Turning on their computers. Putting down takeaway drinks. Geoff is clutching a fresh juice. Christoph a takeaway bagel. Coats are hung on the backs of chairs. Headphones put on. Handsets picked up. Chloe distributes the morning press for clippings. Everything is normal.

Behind my glass wall I watch them all. None of them know. None of them know any of this. I close the tab about Wade. Open a new one. Type in: Tobias (Tobi) Weinstrasse.

BETH

There are pages and pages about Tobi online. What's difficult is to sort it into some order. He really was legendary at our university. Someone's even written a blog that has a short story that features him as a character. Not fan fiction, but not far off. People are weird. Then I remember why I'm looking: someone is hunting my exes. The world is a crazy place. Is that how they know I dated these guys – from the internet? But no, there were no links between me and accountant Phil online. Besides, that was Lily: Lily slept with Phil. And Lily doesn't exist anymore. I'm not foolish enough to have created links to any of these guys from Beth's carefully curated online presence. I don't follow any of them online. I don't, I can't, look back. With some it was easier than others. I wanted Tobi out of my life when I was done with him. Ours was an overly romantic relationship: like something out of a film. It had the intensity of something that could never last. Tobi was so charming, you would forgive him anything. Did I know before that fateful day in my last year? At the time I thought not. The shock of discovering he was cheating on me was like being torn from one world and being dropped into another. Iain a knee-jerk rebound I may not have fallen for if my heart hadn't been broken. If I wasn't so desperate to be cherished again.

Tobi may not have pushed me, but he definitely put me on the downward path to hell. Nothing in the world was as I had believed it. He came to find me after, to officially break it off. I made him drive me home to my parents. I wanted to be safe. Mum was disappointed. She had thought him very eligible. She had asked if there was any chance I could fix it. I remember lying in the bath crying, tears popping the bubbles. My mother, on the other side of the locked door, told me I had to pull myself together. That I had to put on a brave face and go back to university. That I had to show the world that everything was fine. While my sweet stepdad cleared all the things Tobi had ever given me into a bin bag.

The spring sun, still low in the sky, even at noon, makes a valiant effort to warm the office as it glimmers through the windows. I watch as Chloe bustles round, a Post-it note in hand, taking lunch orders. Geoff dictates his to her – taking the pad from her to check what she's written. She gives him a tight smile, pushing her wavy hair behind her ear. She's wearing an androgynous oversized blazer today. Is she trying to assert professionalism for just these moments? I remember that: so desperately wanting to leave behind the 'tea girl' stage.

Chloe turns towards me, catching my eye through the pod glass. She raises the pad and her chin – do I want anything? I give her a quick smile and shake my head. I have no appetite, I still feel sick. I look at my phone. I think about calling Mum. Telling her about this. Putting it into words. What would she say? My mum, who has aged so much since the incident. My stepdad, frail, using a frame to get to the kitchen to microwave them both tea. The kettle too heavy to pour. I can't bring destruction into their world, not again. Not after before. But I need to talk to someone. Someone is killing my exes. But they are also forcing me back into places I don't want to go.

As if sensing my indecision, my phone jumps to life. Ringing and dancing across the office pod's desk. Matt (Unity) calling. Not now. I decline the call. Return to my self-mutilating search. Chloe comes and goes. Geoff eats at his desk, bits of sweetcorn from his salad dropping to the floor. Christoph leaves – comes back glowing, freshly showered from the gym. It's as if I'm stuck by contrast, pinned in place by the gruesome reality of what's happening. This glass pod a bell jar. The shadows of the day lengthen across the office, reaching for me like dark knowing fingers.

I google Beth Taylor and Tobi Weinstrasse. Nothing. We aren't mentioned in the same place anywhere. But I couldn't expect there to be anything – that wasn't my name then. A small feeling of sadness prickles inside. That part of my life erased. At least online, but someone knows. Or do they? Because there were no links online between me and accountant Phil, maybe that means that his death was nothing to do with Mickey and Kareem's. His really could be a tragic coincidence. I'm clutching at straws. Building them into a defence that could be destroyed with the merest breeze. I don't want to think about Tobi. Or Wade. Or Iain. I don't want to think about any of this. But it's happening whether I want it to or not. *Dead man walking*. Someone has set this monster in motion and only I can save these men. The reality trickles like liquid metal down my throat. If someone is targeting them, then only I know. Only I can warn them.

I sort the Tobi results by date. The recent ones congregate in Germany. He's listed on the board of an environmental tech start-up in Berlin. Because of course he is. Does he live there full-time? His Instagram account – not private – shows a still handsome Tobi. Incredible how Phil aged so much, and Tobi just looks better. Do I look better? Or older? Or worse? Of course I look different from how I did at university. As well as changing my hair colour, I get my eyebrows dyed, tint my lashes, have extensions: I looked different the day I had to leave Lily behind. I also changed my wardrobe. Beth T is much more put together, much chicer than Lily ever was. The ultimate glow up. Giving Beth T the illusion of a woman in control. The perfect PR, the perfect wife, the perfect mother. A makeover fashioned from survival instinct. All the little tweaks I carried out to protect myself did initially feel like a fun form of dress up: cosplaying the ideal woman where Lily had so monstrously failed.

But now the treatments, the clothes, the upkeep are a continuous conveyor belt I feel I'm running the wrong direction on, just to try and stay in the same position. I'm nearly forty. I don't have the figure, the skin, or the natural scaffolding of a nineteen-year-old. I click through photos of Tobi mountain biking, swimming in rivers, and skiing with other healthy looking people. In one he has his arm round a tanned girl with long hair, her yellow triangle bikini top bright against the blue sky, as they stand laughing on top of a green mountain. She must be at least fifteen years younger. I pull my handbag over my tummy, and rest my laptop on top of it.

Clicking back on his work website, I look for an email address. No, that won't do. I can't drop him an email and tell him to watch his back. What am I going to tell him? Panic swells. Phil didn't call me back. I didn't make the danger clear in the voicemail. What am I going to say? How can I explain this? I have to find a way. I type the phone number from the website into my phone.

Then a shadow falls across me. Knuckles rap on the glass door of the quiet pod, making me jump. And I look up to see the silhouette of a man. It takes a second for my brain to process it, the goosebumps on my arms getting there first.

Matt from the sex dolls company is standing on the other side of the door, staring at me.

BETH

'I was in the area, so I thought we could have our chat in person after all?' Matt is saying.

Christ, it's nearly 3 p.m. I haven't even topped up my water. My morning coffee sits cold on the desk. One hand on the glass door, I close my laptop lid with the other. I can't have Matt see my screen.

'Matt!' Rob appears out of his office.

Crap. It will be worse, much worse, if Rob sees what I've been doing. He will know for sure it's not work.

Rob has his bright, 'we're bro-mates' voice on, holding out a tan hand as he approaches us. 'Beth didn't tell me you were coming in today,' he gives me a playful admonishing look. Matt turns to greet him, and I turn my written notes over, and step out of the pod, closing the door behind me. I haven't even done my make-up.

'Oh, well, in the area, thought I would . . . we had a call planned,' Matt's awkwardness sets my teeth on edge.

'Oh, good plan, great plan. Always pleased to see one of our favourite clients,' Rob has a hand on Matt's shoulders and is leading him away from the pod, thank God.

'Is Meeting Room One free?' I need to get them both away from the incriminating evidence. I haven't prepped for this meeting.

'Yes, yes,' says Rob. 'And I can join you, I know Beth's got some incredibly exciting things planned for Unity.'

'Oh, I,' Matt stops, stares at me, his eyes strangely penetrating. I want to look away. I want to step back. I force a smile.

'I mean if that's okay?' Rob laughs, giving me a quick side-eye.

I haven't prepped anything. I haven't thought about Unity at all. Crap.

'Yeah,' says Matt.

'Great,' Rob claps him on the back again. 'Now where's Chloe – Chloe! You like coffee, Matt? I've got these incredible beans, import them specially from Sumatra. Grind them here. They're earthy, but they've got that real undertone of caramel, you know?'

'I'll just get my notes,' I say.

Matt tries to turn to look at me, but Rob keeps steering him towards the meeting room. Does he know I'm not prepared? Is he buying me time? Matt is our biggest client. This is a game-changing contract for the firm. For me. How could I just stop working? *Because it's not life or death.*

Back in the pod I scoop all the incriminating notes into a folder, tuck them securely in my bag. Close all my tabs on my computer. Tobi's handsome faces disappear one by one from the screen. Then only Wade's is left. I close it quickly. I feel sick. I'm so far from where I should be, I barely recognise what's in front of me. I barely recognise myself.

'Do you want a coffee, Beth?' Chloe appears at the door.

I clutch my hammering heart. 'God!'

'Sorry,' she says. 'Didn't mean to scare you. You feeling ill again?'

'No, it's fine. I'm fine. I just – yes, a coffee would be good.' I push my laptop into my bag. Feel her watching me as if she might guess something is up. As if she can see it. 'And do we have any of those flapjacks?'

'I think so,' she says. 'I didn't know we were having clients in today.'

'No, neither did I.' And as I look over, I meet Matt's intense stare from across the room. Rob is still talking to him, but it's as if he, and everyone else, isn't here. I shiver and rub at my forearms as the tiny hairs stand up. 'I'll come help,' I say to Chloe, following her towards the kitchen.

All the while I feel Matt's eyes on me.

BETH

Stuck at work. Be home late. Eat without me xx

I press send as I hurry down The Strand, dodging the evening theatre goers. Not ideal the night before our big anniversary party, but I've got to talk about this or I'll go crazy. I know I lied about seeing the police, but I can't do this alone. I promised I'd be home early to help, but Danny will have to wait. Or manage himself. I ignore the incident, and what it means if I talk to Zayn. The whoosh of a passing double decker bus makes me shudder. Turning onto Zayn's street things instantly quieten, in the way only stepping from one street to another in London can. A small cul-de-sac in the centre of town, the main traffic is restricted to turning taxis. I press the buzzer for Zayn's door.

'Yup,' comes Zayn's voice through the intercom.

'It's me.' He buzzes me in. I take the industrial concrete steps two at a time. Squeezed into a converted warehouse, offices down below, the second storey of the building was adapted into two high end designer flats by an entrepreneurial developer. It's quiet, private. You'd never know anyone lived here from the street, but it is literal spitting distance to the delights of central London. I head down the corridor to Zayn's end, and knock on the door.

'Yo!' he says opening the door, his mobile in his hand. 'I'm getting sushi – you want in?'

'Please,' I hang my coat up in the hallway cupboard, and follow Zayn into the polished wooden open-plan lounge and kitchen. I keep my bag on my arm. I don't want to put it down. I don't want to let it out of my sight.

I head straight to Zayn's wine fridge. 'Can I?' I take a Riesling out.

'Course. You want wasabi?' He barely looks up from his phone.

I unscrew the bottle. 'No. Thanks. Nate not about?' I sound normal. Casual. As if everything is fine. But my hand shakes as I pour the wine.

'Nah. Away. Work.' Zayn says. I don't really know what Nate does, something similar to Zayn, something with computers. I'm sure it was a work contact that introduced them when Zayn moved in here. 'It'll be twenty.' Zayn picks up an open bottle of beer from the reclaimed wooden table, hurdles the back of the corner sofa, and lands with his legs stretched out along it. 'There's olives in the fridge, if you're desperate.'

I can't eat anything. Why did I say yes to sushi? The thought of raw fish. 'You want some?' I open the fridge, bottle of wine in hand, ready to slide it into the door.

'Nah,' Zayn says. 'Don't want the garlic, might have a date later.'

I decide to keep the wine with me. 'Thanks for fitting me in,' I say. I mean it as a joke, but it comes out whiney.

Zayn watches me sit down. 'You okay, hun?' He raises an eyebrow.

This prompts a genuine wry smile from me. 'Trouble at t'mill,' I say. *Tell him. Tell him about Mickey, and Kareem, and Phil. And about Wade and Tobi. Tell him about how you lied. How someone knows. How someone is killing your exes and you are terrified.*

'With Rob?' Zayn lets his feet slide to the floor, leans forward.

'No,' I say, too quickly.

Another flick of the eyebrows from Zayn. 'Okay.'

Tell him. Tell him. 'It's fine, really.' I take a gulp of wine. The heavy taste pleasingly acidic against my tongue.

'Okay,' Zayn repeats, his brown eyes holding my gaze.

I blink. Look away. Now I'm here I don't know how to start. I lied to Zayn about going to the police when I hadn't. I lied to him about the number of people I've slept with. I lied when I didn't tell him I was arrested when he was in Australia. I lied when I never told him Lily was deadly. *I lied, I lied, I lied.* 'Just client trouble,' I say. *I can't do it.*

Zayn sits back, takes a swig. 'What do they want you to spin now? Clothes from a death factory? Mobile phones made by four-year-olds?'

I can't help but laugh. 'No. It was me – my fault. I completely forgot about a call I had with the sex dolls client I told you about. And he just showed up in the office.'

'Ewww!' cries Zayn. 'Actually, in person?'

'Yeah.'

'As if having to speak to people on the phone wasn't bad enough,' Zayn purses his lips in disgust.

'And I was completely unprepared,' I say, taking another gulp of wine. 'I ended up pitching him a fashion shoot using the dolls.'

Zayn spits his beer out. 'No way?'

I laugh now, the release of it shaking through my tense muscles. Matt and Rob's faces. 'And he went for it. We're gonna go high-end. One of the arty mags. Proper designer clothes, the lot.' The laughter seems to have taken over my body. Tears roll out of my eyes.

'Oh God!' Zayn rocks back and mimics a ridiculous pouty model pose. 'I have to see this.'

I take a big breath. I don't feel happy any more. I feel out of control. Panicked. Like I might never stop laughing. I got through the meeting by luck. Fear driving me on. But I can't outrun this. I lied to Zayn. 'Gotta pee,' I jump up, my bag strap tight in my hand. Practically running to the bathroom.

Zayn cackles behind me. 'You really need to work on that pelvic floor, love!'

The Anniversary Party

I lock the door. Brace my hands against the sink. Dip my head and try to breathe. Try to get oxygen. Try to stop the world spinning.

It takes a couple of minutes. Then I slide down onto the floor, and look at my phone. Tobi and Wade. I can't tell Zayn, but I have to tell them. I have to warn them. I have to speak to them again. Bile rises in my throat. I swallow the acid down like I did the wine. It was a mistake to come here. I can't involve Zayn, like I can't involve Danny. I have to face this alone.

I press call on the number for Tobi's office, hold the phone against my ear with my shaking hand.

The international dial tone, and then the sound of a German speaking voicemail. '*Guten tag . . .* '

They're an hour ahead there. They'll be closed. I hang up. I've just got to keep it together. The thought of all those people in my house tomorrow at the party, all that smiling and small talk – oh, I wish I'd never suggested it in the first place. I have to try again. I think of Phil, of missing him. Of what I should have said. Could have said. Can I go to Berlin? There's no time. I rub my palms into my eyes. The acid in my throat going down, blooming across my stomach. I feel it burning through my insides like the truth. I have been too frightened to tell the truth in the past, and so now I must pay. Now I must be brave.

I pick up my bag, let myself out of the bathroom. 'Darling,' I call. 'Really sorry – but Oscar's not well – I gotta go!'

'What about California rolls?' Zayn shouts from the sofa.

'Save them for your date.' I grab my coat from the cupboard. I can hear him coming towards the hallway. I don't want Zayn to see me. He will know something is wrong. I can't tell him. And I can't keep lying to him.

I fling myself out his front door as he catches up with me. I call behind me, waving, blowing kisses, not letting him see. 'Bye, darling, mwah, mwah!'

I clatter down the stairs, holding off the tears until I make it outside. The March night air whipping them off my cheeks.

I know Wade's office is only ten minutes from mine. I don't know where he lives or a number but I know that. Tomorrow I'll try calling Tobi again. I'll wait outside Wade's office if I have to. No one else can die.

BETH – THE DAY OF THE PARTY

I'm not sure I'm going to recognise him. I pace outside the narrow building, a single door in a glass front, next to the wooden facade of a proper olde world pub on High Holborn. Commuters stream past on their way to the Tube, and the odd colourfully dressed student from The London College of Fashion over the road picks their way towards Leon. Today has been torturous. I promised Danny I'd be home early to help the final preparations, but after I didn't see Wade arrive at the office this morning, I knew I had to come back. I told Danny I was stuck at work, and I told work I had to be at home for the party. I have to warn Wade. I tried Tobi again, but he didn't answer. If only I'd been able to get hold of him first. Don't think about Phil, don't think about it being too late. You've emailed as well. Three times. He'll know it's important. He'll get back to you. Besides, he's in a different country. He'll be fine. He'll be safe.

I turn and walk past the entrance to the office again. Someone is going to clock me soon. I put the hood of my orange coat up, despite it being lighter later, we still have plenty of rain to contend with. What if I don't recognise him? It's been twenty years, and we didn't really ever spend much time together. I can barely picture his face. Just a look. *Him taller, stronger, looking down at me. Not contempt, or amusement, but something close to apathy. He's holding a pint in the uni club. Laughing with the other lads at a house party. And then his fat fingers are trying to unlace my top. And the room is cold.*

I close my eyes. I can't do this. I can't see him. I can't relive this. But when I open them, there he is. Just coming out the door. His hair greyer, thinner, stooping like he's walking into the wind, turning up his plaid coat collar. He looks bulkier, squarer. But I'd know him anywhere. And I feel sick.

I have to talk to him – I have to.

I force myself to walk after Wade, down the street. Even though every cell in my body is screaming to run away. I know now. Know with certainty that what happened back then was not okay. That there was no consent. But it was a different time. I was a different person. I thought feminism was something we studied in English class, something from the past, not relevant. I actually believed sexism was something we had eradicated. The war between the sexes was over. That the marches, and the angry women of the seventies had put in the work for us. That everyone was treated equal. I didn't notice there were homophobic jokes on *Friends* every week. That the only non-white character in *Ally McBeal* was a fetishised ideal of an Asian sexbot. That being grabbed on a night out by strangers as you walked past them in the club meant you looked good. We got drunk. We staggered around in tiny skirts and unstable cheap heels. Connecting to the internet on my ancient (and rare) laptop was a slow process of dial-up. Black pages full of green code. There were no smartphones. There was no social media. There was no online galvanisation of social rights. There were no growing collective voices of disquiet. Me Too wasn't conceived yet, though we now know it was happening all around us. We were isolated in our own experiences, in our own spheres of judgment. It was new and exciting to call or text each other from the phones we got for free when we joined Barclays bank. Phones which we kept switched off in a drawer if we went abroad. A small window in time where the possible hadn't quite been realised. Before everything exploded and sped up. Before we all woke up.

Wade and I had normal messy drunken sex. Except it wasn't, was it? And my body doesn't need fifteen years of online feminism to tell me that. Like a basic survival instinct – even after all this time – it is telling me to run away from the predator.

But he still doesn't deserve to die.

'Wade?' I call out 'Wade Ellison?'

He turns and looks at me. His blank disinterested look, morphing into a slight eyebrow raise of question. 'Yes?' he says. He doesn't look me up and down, though I'm certain he would if I was the age of Chloe. His voice doesn't sound as I remember it. I thought it was deep, sonorous, to match his bulk, but it sounds dry, thin. Like he's smoked one too many cigarettes. The kind of man who starts coughing when he's laughing too hard. The kind of man who laughs at his own jokes.

'I thought it was you!' I say.

He waits, that one annoying eyebrow raised. Shifts slightly, as if ready to turn away.

He doesn't recognise me. He doesn't know who I am. After what he did. My cheeks sting like they've been slapped, as the blush rises up my neck and cheeks.

'It's Lily.' I say, the name strange and bitter in my mouth.

Nothing. It's like staring at a stranger. He really has forgotten. I fight the urge to turn around and walk away.

'From university – remember, I was friends with Katie. We . . .' The words catch in my throat and I half-swallow, half-cough.

'Oh, hey Lily,' he says, finally taking in my figure. But it's as if he's looking for something to grab hold of, because I can see in his face that this body, my figure that I thought was good for my age, doesn't ring any bells for him. I try to reassure myself it's the red hair. *You struggled to undo my top. You had sex with me while I was semi-conscious.* 'Good to see you.' He gives me a perfunctory smile. And turns to go.

That's it? I try to rationalise that at least he can't know about what Lily did. That's a good thing in the circumstances. 'Wait!'

He turns, that one silvery eyebrow arched in genuine surprise this time.

I can't let him leave. I can't let him die. 'I need to talk to you actually. I found you – I mean I found out where you worked.'

He looks alarmed.

'I know that sounds weird – but we need to talk.' I repeat. Willing him to see the urgency in my face.

He gives an awkward laugh.

I try to catch his arm, to hold on to him, but my own hand won't obey. It won't touch him. 'Because . . . ' *You raped me.* 'Because we slept together,' I say.

A woman walking past gives a smirk. Oh eff off. This is not how I meant this to go.

'Because we . . . ?' He shakes his head. 'That was like ten years ago.'

More like twenty, buddy.

'I'm engaged,' he says.

Does he really think I'm trying to get together with him? After what he did? What did he think happened between us? That he gave me such a good time that night that I'm still obsessed with him twenty years later?

'I don't want to – look, it's nothing like that.' A man in a trench coat stares at us as he navigates around. 'Can we go somewhere a bit more private?'

'There's not something wrong with you is there – like AIDS or something?' Genuine alarm sounds in his voice.

I almost laugh at the absurdity of it all. This grown man panicking on the street because he had non-consensual sex with someone he's completely forgotten about for the last twenty years, and it might finally have had repercussions. But no, it's a very different death sentence. 'Or – Christ – you didn't have a baby, did you?' He sounds as if that's worse than HIV.

'No, look, can we just?' I look about for a suitable cafe. There's nothing but a Starbucks on the corner. That'll have to do. 'Can we just go there?'

The thought of AIDS, or, God forbid, an unwanted child, seem to have rendered him compliant. *Because they might impact him.* He walks alongside me to the cafe. His arm brushes against mine and I suppress the urge to lash out. He forgot about it. About how he viewed me as an object to have sex with. Did he do it to others? Forget about them too? Did his actions alter my own sense of who I was, what I was worth? I think of the people I slept with after. What he did changed my trajectory, made me go in different, more self-destructive directions. If I could go back in time, I would kick and punch this man. I would tell Lily to stay away from toxic men she thinks are friends, but are actually only waiting for the opportunity to screw her. I'd report him. I'd do something. Anything other than just get up and go to the other empty cold bed all alone, and never mention it to anyone. And for a second I think about forgetting all this. Screw him. Let him get what he deserves.

But I can't. Because my younger self still wouldn't want him to die.

BETH

The queue in Starbucks is long, but the seats are mostly empty. It's right in the heart of the City and I guess people just want to get their drink and go. The street outside is still a steady catwalk of people, heads bent against the weather and the reality of the rat race. Perhaps we would have been better out there? More discrete. Most people in the queue are plugged into headphones, or staring at their phone screens, but they are all silent. Only the orders being taken, and the repeated gritty whir of the coffee grinder can be heard above the background music.

Wade has taken a seat, thankfully, far away from the counter. He's picked one of the oversized wingbacks that face each other over a squat dark wood table. He's leaning forward, resting his elbows on his knees, hands clasped. He's not distracting himself with his phone, in fact he looks all too present, glancing up nervously every thirty seconds or so, as if I might have produced a child from my handbag. I hate him. I'm not sure I've hated anyone before. Or, rather I've not felt hate for someone I didn't also love. There are those moments of pure rage when I could throw something at Danny. But just as quickly he can obliterate my defences, and I'll find myself unable to stop giggling at his jokey reaction. I can't help but smile when I think of Danny mimicking Oscar's terrible twos tantrums: the grown man stamping his feet, clutching his fists, screwing his face up, until he too dissolves into laughter. That razor-sharp line between two extremes of emotion when you love someone. I think of my anger when Oscar was little and he ran out between two parked cars into the street. I was so furious he could have been killed I smacked him hard, then cried too when he burst into tears. And I think of Mum and Dad, and what they did to each other before the cancer. The rows, the passive-aggression. While all the time, to the outside world, they were the perfect couple, dealing with it all effortlessly. Perhaps they were. I think of Danny and me. Danny and Beth. Beth a fake person, a cipher for any good left in me. Just another version of me who took the bad and buried it. Perhaps all couples are like that.

Wade glances up again and I feel the destructive revulsion in me. I never loved Wade. I'm not sure I even liked him. He was just sort of there in the background, until he forced his way into my consciousness. I don't remember seeing him much after we successfully avoided each other for the remaining three years of uni. Was he embarrassed by what he'd done? Or was it a 'smash and dash'? 'One and done'? He only saw me for my parts – like Matt sees Treasure. It wasn't long after that I got together with Tobi. That whole period of my life a shaken box of biscuits.

I carry our two drinks over. Thump his excessive bucket of sugared caffeine down, so the liquid slops onto the table.

He takes it and sucks at the top. The sound of the liquid being hoovered over his lips makes my stomach roil.

I wait for a thank you.

'So, what did you want?' He puts the coffee down. 'I'm quite busy.'

He means important. In his try-hard fashionable coat, glancing at his knock-off designer watch to indicate he has better things to do than be here with some middle-aged woman. Was he always like this? Entitled? Is that why he just took what he wanted? Christ, I just brought the guy who raped me a bloody skinny caramel macchiato. I forget about easing in, like he forgot about consent.

'There is a chance someone may try to hurt you.' I tug at the sleeve of my orange raincoat.

'What?' He looks at me as if I'm mad. 'Who?'

'I don't know for sure, but it looks like someone has been killing the people I have slept with, over the last few weeks.' It feels absurd to say it out loud.

Wade snorts.

I don't respond.

'Wait – you're serious?' He wipes nervously at his chin, missing the dribble of foam there.

'Unfortunately, yes. It might be a coincidence, but the three men . . . '

'Three? Three have been killed in the last few weeks?' he interrupts.

'Yes. In the last month.' I'm astounded by how calm I sound. But the emotion is too raw to show in my words. It's been squashed down inside, and all that is left are the facts. 'The first three men I slept with.' He wrinkles his nose. And I want to throw my drink in his face. 'Before – before our encounter. They have all died.'

'What – how?'

'Stabbed during a presumed mugging, hit-and-run, and then stabbed in an altercation outside a pub,' I say.

'Holy shit.' He leans closer, squinting at me as if I'm a specimen. I feel the muscles in my face tense. 'You're not joking?'

'No,' I shake my head. 'I'm not.'

I fill him in on the bare details. How I found out about the first three. How I've been receiving anonymous notes cut from my own handwriting. 'I had to tell you what I suspect, because if I'm right you may well be in danger. You're the next person I . . . ' I can't finish the words.

'Jesus,' he says, and instinctively takes his phone out, turning it over so his screensaver lights up. It's a photo of a pretty brunette, and a smiling little girl. His fiancée and daughter, presumably. The woman looks friendly, happy. It flickers through my mind that I should tell her what this man did to me.

Wade catches me staring at the image. 'Jane. My girlfriend.' He turns it to face me, his whole face changing as he smiles. 'And

Abbey.' He keeps talking, agitation seeming to drive him on. 'She's a great kid. I met Jane when she was eight months gone. Her previous boyfriend—' His mouth twists at the mention of this man. 'He did a bunk when he found out she was expecting. Cleared his flat out, the lot. She's never really got over it – she's very wary of other women. That's why I was a bit . . . ' He looks uncomfortable. 'When you came up to me outside work. It's taken a long time to get her to trust me properly, to agree to marry me. I've been with them both since the beginning. And now I'm gonna adopt Abbey and everything. A proper family.' He smiles down at the photo.

I stare at Wade. Wade who has taken on another man's baby. He's raised her as his own. He clearly loves his girlfriend. And for a second I think I've made a mistake. This man isn't a monster. He can't be. He seems normal. Almost nice.

He seems to remember himself. 'And whoever is doing this – how do they know? That you slept with me? You must have told them. Or is it like – someone hacked the STD clinic, or something?'

'I haven't – no, that isn't what's happened.' It can't be, can it? I did go to a clinic, years ago, but it's not like they write down the names and addresses of all your partners, is it? Could it be a tech thing, though? Could someone have hacked some database, and worked all this out? Maybe there's a record online of all those with the same strand of chlamydia. A bit like those AncestryDNA tests that can link you up with long-lost cousins and siblings. I can't see it. I think of Danny, of Zayn, of the lies I've told.

'Then how?' Wade says.

'I don't know.' I really don't.

He picks up a sugar sachet from the table, twirling it in his fingers. Pulling the paper taut. Bending it, turning it. I want to snatch it out of his hands.

'So, what do the police say to do?'

'They don't believe me,' I say. The lie is out before I can stop it. Wade is clearly oblivious to what Lily did. Introduce that now and any credibility I have will be lost. I'll be the scarlet woman again. A two dimensional femme fatale.

The sugar sachet splits in his fingers, the granules showering onto the sticky tabletop like stars on a dirty black sky. His body stiffens, just a fraction. He thinks I'm crazy.

I should've seen that coming. Another trope: the hysterical woman bringing the drama. I modulate my voice lower; men are more likely to listen to women who mirror their deeper tones. 'I know it sounds bad.'

It's not enough. He's up, bumping his legs against the table in haste, the big fat coffee tipping, gushing towards me. I jump up too. Faces turn behind us.

'I've got to go,' he says, holding his hands up as if he's surrendering.

'Look.' I grab my notes from my pockets. 'I wrote the names down for you. Just look them up. You'll see. And here's copies of photos of me with them.' I hold the papers out for him. 'I'm not making this up.'

'Just – leave me alone, yeah?'

'Wade, please, you've got to listen!' I reach for him as he hurries towards the door, but as my fingers brush the edge of his jacket sleeve the memories of that night rush towards me. His weight on me. My arms pinned under his torso. I clutch my hand to my mouth. And he's gone.

I hear whispering behind me, and turn to see people in the queue staring. I grab my bag and go. I have to get away from here. I can't see Wade outside, and I don't want to. I'm too claustrophobic for the Tube. I walk fast until I hit St Paul's station, then turn onto the Thames, taking big gulps of air as the sky opens up above the river. And then I know where I'm going. I know where I'm running to. The tears stinging my cheeks.

BETH

Nate arrives home after I've been trying Zayn's street buzzer for a few minutes. The walk along the Thames passed in a flash – is this shock? P.T.S.D.? I can feel the weight of Wade on me. Every time I blink I'm back there. It's like I'm being dragged under water. I can't breathe.

'Beth, good to see you,' Nate's voice sounds like he's talking from the other end of a tunnel. He takes his headphones out, his laptop bag over his shoulder. The memory of Zayn screening prospective flatmates pops into my mind: aesthetics was definitely on the list. Zayn has a type: tanned, muscly, and dark hair. Nate's never mentioned a girlfriend, and we're both pretty convinced he's gay too. Which means I usually enjoy a bit of harmless flirting, but not today. Today I just want to hide.

'Good work trip?' I hear myself ask. I'm sure Zayn said he'd been away.

He blinks, looks perplexed. 'Zayn's not here.'

'Mind if I wait inside?' I stand back so he can unlock. I'm aware there's something pulling at me. Stretching me between now and that cold dark university bedroom.

'Of course, hang on,' Nate quickly checks their pigeonhole, and the few piled up Amazon packages, where their neighbours put their post. There isn't any for them.

I stand aside, as the heavy glass entry door closes off the outside world with a climate-controlled airlock. I'm shivering. I just need to be somewhere safe. Words spill out of me, a sure sign I'm rattled. 'I tried ringing him – Zayn. He's not picking up?'

'Right,' says Nate, his brow furrowing.

I think back to that text message I sent to Mickey the night Wade raped me. *I want a hug now.* I need someone to hold me, to make me feel safe. Wade knew what he did to me. Maybe he thought I was up for it. Maybe he just assumed I was a slag. His face when I said three men. I still feel shame, judged. That was my sole worth to him: a forgotten shag. A handy receptacle, like Treasure. And just as void of humanity. The way he jumped away from me. From me! And the feel of his skin, even through his coat. I grip the metal banister, as I follow Nate up the stairs.

Nate walks quickly, and I have to hurry to keep up. He obviously did not envisage his evening containing his flatmate's best friend who's acting strange. He fumbles with his key to their apartment door, holds it open. 'Err – you want a wine or something?'

Just being in Zayn's hallway makes me feel better. The smell. The painting on the wall we bought together in Battersea. I feel the spinning world slow a little. 'No, thanks.'

'Erm,' Nate stands awkwardly. 'It's just I thought he was out tonight?'

Nate's looking at me like I know this. I nod, try to process what's happening to me. The thought of going back outside makes me feel sick. The folder of my info, including the anonymous notes that have been sent to me throb in my bag. Like they might ignite through the leather and burn everything to the ground.

Nate makes a movement towards the door, as if I might, please, just go back out of it. I must look crazy. I feel crazy. I just spoke to the man who raped me, because I think someone might try to kill him. And he thought I was delusional.

'Right, yes. No.' I can't keep this all in my head. I just need some time somewhere safe to process it. I just need an excuse. 'Can I use your internet?'

Nate shrugs. 'Yeah, sure – you've got the password, right?'

'Yup,' I head to the open-plan lounge diner before pausing. 'Actually, I can do this in Zayn's room. Stop interrupting your evening,' I feel my face smile.

'No, it's no bother,' Nate says. 'I was going to make food – you eaten?'

The thought of putting food in my mouth makes me feel nauseous. 'No, thanks. I don't need anything. Don't worry – I'll just go in here.' I take a step towards Zayn's room. Nate looks bemused. I can't deal with talking to him right now, having to pretend everything's normal. 'It's just a work thing. Client confidentiality, you know? I'll just—' I don't give him a chance to get a word in, before I open Zayn's bedroom door, and close it firmly behind me.

I exhale straight away. I'm safe here, surrounded by Zayn's things. It's as if he's here with me. His bed is neatly made. There's a glass of water on the bedside table, and the resistance band he uses for physio every morning lying across the bed. As if he's only just stepped out. I pick up his scent from the dresser and sniff the rich, woody smell of oud. I breathe slowly, deeply. It's okay. I'm okay.

I sit on the edge of the bed and hug one of Zayn's scatter cushions.

I just need to stay focused. Stick to the plan. Things with Wade didn't go great, but I can try again. Perhaps I could deliver a letter to his office? If he could see all the names, the photos that I have – then he'd see I'm not making this up. And I still need to keep trying Tobi. Now I've vocalised it, now I've said Lily, there's no going back. Instead there's a sense everything is hurtling forward, outstripping me. Is there any way to save Danny from the truth? Save him from me? An image of Danny reaching for me blinks through my consciousness.

What I had with Tobi, it may have ended messily, but it was a real relationship. He knows me. He will listen to me. I take my phone back out.

Crap. Two missed calls from Zayn. But before I can act my phone springs to life in my hand: Danny calling.

Danny. Oscar. What happens if whoever is doing this has gone after him too early? What if they've changed the order? The phone is at my ear. 'Danny?' My words are clipped. Panicked.

'Beth – are you alright?'

'What's happened?'

'Nothing – where are you?' Danny's voice sounds strained. Stressed, like he's trying to be quiet.

I sit bolt upright, the cushion bounces onto the floor. Oh God. Of course Zayn's not here. That's why he's called me! I scramble to explain my absence. 'At work. Got stuck . . . '

'It's our anniversary party – there are fifty people arriving, and you didn't think to ring?' Danny's voice sounds dangerously close to exploding. But I can hear music in the background. Laughter. Voices. Oh God, I completely forgot. This day has been so long, so frightening. It just went out of my mind.

'I'm on my way now,' I pull my shoes back on, smooth Zayn's bedding. I'll have to ask him to cover for me.

'You wanted this party,' Danny hisses.

'All our friends and family – it's going to be great! No one will notice if I'm a few minutes late,' I grab my bag from the side, catching Zayn's neat pile of work books.

Danny makes a contemptuous noise. Zayn's books thud to the floor.

I try not to swear as I pick them back up. Everything is okay. Everything is fine. 'I'm worth waiting for!' I say.

But Danny is gone.

And my hand freezes over the fluttering pages of a notebook.

My mobile drops to the floor, bounces with a dull thud on the carpet. I stare at the splayed pad at my feet. Horrifyingly familiar. *The notes*. The stiff card cover's bent back, and the jagged edge where pages of the lined paper have been torn out, stick up like sharp incisor teeth.

HIM

He is standing by the rows of Ikea glasses in the kitchen. So suburban. So beneath her. I would lift her out of this. Literally – into my place. Never mind this tat, she is a queen. She deserves more than this chump. She deserves me. And still he has a hold over her.

'Hey!' he says, his face full of dumb, ignorant delight. I release the fists my hands have made so I can shake his, but I can't resist squeezing hard. 'Thanks for coming,' Danny says.

I have. Multiple times. Over your wife. I'd give her what you can't forever. 'Wouldn't miss it,' I answer.

He's wearing a tweed waistcoat buttoned over a shirt. Like a cheap Toad from Toad Hall Halloween costume from Amazon. How on earth does he do it?

'What can I get you?' he asks. 'Red, white, rosé, beer?' He signals at the array of mixed bottles in front of him. Clearly using the gifts people have just come with. There's no organisation, no pride. I have to squeeze down the wave of anger that threatens to overwhelm me. This excuse for a man is no match for me. He should be no competition. If I hadn't let her go. 'Any chance of a Malbec?'

His brows furrow. 'Let's take a look.' He reaches out towards a Cabernet Sauvignon. Then behind him the kitchen door opens. For a heart stopping moment I think it's her, but it's another woman. The nanny. I recognise her curly mane of hair, her pleasing arse. She's wearing denim dungarees, like it's not a celebration.

The bottle wobbles under Danny's touch, and I realise he is staring at her. No, not staring, they are making eye contact, they are communicating silently. Danny's head moves almost imperceptibly. The nanny gives a faint smile, lowers her lashes.

'Right, let's get you some of this, bossman.' Danny plucks the Cabernet from the forest of bottles on the side, the spell broken. The nanny smiles a faceless hello at me, before passing into the garden.

Danny passes me a glass of the wrong wine. 'Thanks,' I say. No, really, thank you. Thank you very much. He has just revealed something very useful. Danny and the nanny are shagging.

BETH – THE PARTY

'We thought we were late!' Cat and Cathy from next door are standing on the doorstep when my taxi pulls up.

'Problems on the Tube,' Cathy smiles apologetically.

I've been gripping my phone so tight my hand aches. 'You know what it's like – we've got this huge client launch about to take place. Real game-changing stuff. And time flies when you're having fun!' I sound manic.

'You don't tend to get that feeling in dentistry,' Cathy says.

The page from Zayn's pad crackles in my handbag. Pressed up against the scraps that were sent to me it looks horribly similar. But it's Zayn. My best friend. Zayn who I've known since I was eleven. The only one from before. 'I'm so lucky to have a job I love.' I smile at Cat and Cathy. I need to get them inside; I need to get inside. Danny's Ibiza Chill Out album is playing loudly from the lounge. I can hear tiny feet pound round the hallways and the louder alcohol-raised adult voices. Oscar and his cousin are clearly racing about having a riot. My heart contracts. My baby. Whoever is doing this is dangerously unwell. What if they try to hurt me? I have to be there for Oscar when he grows up. And his dad. What if they try to hurt Danny? My stomach falls away. What if they threaten Oscar?

'. . . It's low-cal salad cream. So much nicer than mayonnaise,' Cat is saying.

'It's bloody delicious,' Cathy says.

And I realise they are holding up a clingfilmed bowl of a gelatinous yellow substance I think is potato salad. 'You shouldn't have.' I shove my key aggressively into the lock and let us in.

'Beth!' my sister-in-law chimes. A blur of faces turns towards me expectantly. A small cheer goes up.

'Bethy-woo!' Zayn rushes over to hug me, his oud scent swaddling me in familiarity. Tears prick my eyes. 'And I thought I was late. Central line was down. Bloody nightmare.'

'Yeah, I heard.' And I was in your flat, in your room, and I found a notebook like the one that threatening notes have been sent to me on. I feel wooden in his arms. Brittle, like I might snap.

'You okay?' Zayn sounds concerned.

The bag on my shoulder burns. The tell-tale viciousness within. Could it be some kind of joke? An innocent explanation: Zayn has been gathering up samples of my handwriting and sending them to me on that paper for a wind-up? That it's nothing to do with the murders? But I told him about them. He recommended I go to the police. He knows they frightened me. It can't be him. I think of the notepad, its ripped edge. I should ask him outright.

Zayn pushes me back so he can see my face. 'Beth?'

I stare at him. Tell the truth. 'Everything's fine – I was just thinking we should have invited Nate. Total error on my part.' Zayn makes a pacifying noise. 'Let me just . . . ' I say. I pull away. Tuck my bag behind our large vase on the hallway table. Notice Danny has found time to throw out the flowers Matt sent before anyone else saw them. Zayn gives me a squeeze on my shoulder, which I ignore. I turn to my guests. 'It's party time!' I laugh, indicating my work clothes. 'Time for the glad rags!'

I disentangle myself from the hugs and back pats as I head for the stairs, the faces as distinct as the gloop under Cathy's clingfilmed dish. If only I'd been able to get through to Tobi. If he – if anyone had picked up when I rang his office. Why don't they list their mobiles? I need to speak to him, to warn him. 'Be right back!' I call as I take the stairs two at a time. I hear Oscar's laughter somewhere in our backyard. My heart contracts. What am I going to do?

I open our bedroom door. Hellie jumps away from Danny, her face red. Hellie – in our bedroom. My mind struggles to process. They were . . . close. Touching. In our bedroom.

'I need to . . .' Hellie tails off. 'Excuse me.' She brushes past me.

Danny's face is sombre, and suddenly he looks older. 'We need to talk,' he says.

Not my Danny. I can pretend I never saw anything. One more lie to rebalance my karma.

I walk past him to my green linen dress that's hanging ready on the outside of the wardrobe door. 'Did Oscar have a proper tea earlier? Though he'd probably be delighted with crisps or whatever is out,' I laugh.

'Beth?' Danny says, reaching for my wrist.

'This won't take me a sec,' I say, lifting my arms away so I can pull my top off. 'Just let me zhuzh my hair, whack on a bit of lippy and we can enter together. Like starting the night over.'

'Did you not hear what I said?' Danny says. 'We need to talk.'

'Don't make a fuss.' I wrap the dress around me, pulling the waist ties tight. I could tell him. Tell him someone is killing my ex-boyfriends. The same ex-boyfriends' existence I neglected to mention before. That I'm not who he thinks I am. That I should have told him a long time ago that he married a monster. That I deserve this and more for what I did. That he deserves more. That I can't go to the police. That I don't know what to do. That . . .

'I'm not making a fuss,' he snaps. 'It's normal to talk. That's what normal couples do.' He kicks at the bed like a child.

I need to be the adult one. I need to repair this. Make it all better. 'We have a house full of guests, Danny,' I say. 'Most people would be happy to be surrounded by those that they love,' I hoist my breasts up so they sit proudly in my bra. 'Now is not the time for one of your negative moments.'

'Where were you?' he says, his voice angry. Bitter. I'm trying so hard to keep us both up.

'I told you – work.' I slide tasselled earrings into my lobes.

'You'd rather be at work than at our anniversary party?' He's starting to whine. He sounds like Oscar, like a child.

Now is not the time. We need to be strong. I need to be strong. I need to protect Danny, me, Oscar. 'Yes, work which pays for all this,' I say. 'Most people would be grateful not to have to worry about who pays for all this. Most people would kill for this.'

I realise what I've said. Kill for? Oh my God. Is that what is happening? Is this about money? Surely most crimes are about money, aren't they?

Danny looks like he's been kicked. He can't know, can he? No. There's no way. But I need him to man up. He can't know why, but it's vital for us, for our family. I can't think about Oscar's face if anything happened to his daddy. Oh God. We're under attack. I'm under attack. I need a new strategy. 'I just need you to be happy.' I stare at him. 'I can't be positive for the two of us. I can't carry us both. I can't do it all,' I say. But I have to. That's my role, the charming efficient peacekeeper, smoothing any rough edges over. I don't deserve Danny after what I did, but Beth does. Beth is the wife he deserves, here to make it right.

'You never want to talk.' He shakes his head. 'You can never accept something is wrong. It's all about how everything – how you – look. Perfect Bloody Beth. Well, you're not perfect.' His words sting. He's not supposed to see the act. Everything I do is for him and Oscar.

Panic rises in me. Something squirming underneath. I need to lock this down. I need to get through this. 'I'm not the one who is getting cross at our anniversary party.'

He looks abashed. Turns away. I exhale. He just needs to give me a minute to think. How do I protect them? How do I protect Oscar and Danny? Of course.

'Maybe you need a break,' I say.

He turns, his eyebrows raised in surprise. 'You . . . you want to take a break?'

I swallow the uncomfortable pressure in my throat. 'No, of course not. I can't take time off from work right before the big sex doll release.'

Confusion crowds Danny's face. He sits down on the edge of the bed. I push on.

'But you've been working so hard getting everything ready for the party and everything, and I do appreciate it. Everything you do,' I say. My words are quick. I need to get them out, before he can interrupt. 'Why don't you take Oscar up to the Black Mountains? It's almost half-term. I could get you that cottage we had before – you always liked it there? Have a proper break away from it all.'

'You want me to go without you?' Danny's voice is small.

Something twists inside my heart. I have to get them to safety. 'You can rest for a couple of weeks, then when this is over . . .' Over? How is it going to be over? What am I going to do?

'Beth,' Danny says quietly.

I smile. Step forwards. Squeeze his hand. 'When this job is over, I can come join you, have the last week together.'

'I'm not sure now is the right time to go away,' he says.

'I'll pay for it all – obviously,' I say. 'Don't worry about that.' I need him to do this. I need him to take Oscar somewhere far away from here. To make him safe.

'I think we should . . .'

I pull him into me, tears pricking my eyes. 'You can take Hellie with you.' I feel him flinch, just momentarily. I'm offering her, sacrificing myself for him. For them. You can't outrun the darkness inside. *Please, God, don't let Danny see it yet – the monster he married. I just need a little more time.* The knife twists in my heart. 'You're right – it'll be too much for you on your own. This way you can have a proper break.' I lean back to smile into his face. 'How's that?'

There's a knock at the door.

'Helloooo?' Zayn calls.

'Muuuum!' Oscar's voice calls, and the door springs open, and he barrels in, and into us.

'Hello, darling,' I say ruffling his hair.

'Sorry,' Zayn nods at Danny. 'I didn't mean to interrupt you love birds, but there are a few people waiting for you downstairs.'

I feel my face form a rictus grin. Could Zayn really be doing this?

'You had something to eat, mate?' Danny says to Oscar.

'We'll be right out,' I flap a hand towards Zayn. My voice sounds unnaturally high, does he know I suspect him? My best friend. Zayn's eyebrows edge towards a frown, but he does step back out of our bedroom, pulling the door closed behind him. I let out the breath I was holding.

I crouch down next to my gorgeous boy, lower my voice so we can't be overheard. 'We've just been talking about a big adventure for you.' I have to get Danny and Oscar to safety. 'How would you like to go back to that house on the big hill we stayed in before?' I say to Oscar. 'The one with the wild horses outside.'

'The ponies?' Oscar's eyes open in delight.

'That's right, you and Daddy and Hellie.'

Danny lets go of me. 'We need to get downstairs,' he says.

'And Mummy?' Oscar says.

'Mummy's got to work, but I'll join you soon. I promise. How's that?'

'Beth,' Danny says, the edge back in his voice.

I make mine bright to compensate. 'Come on then,' I grab Oscar with one hand, and Danny by the other. His palm is warm, soft, and my hand feels small inside his. He tries to pull away, I grip tighter. 'Let's do this!' And I sweep them both out of the room. Hand in hand we walk down the stairs. As our friends and family see us a cheer goes up. I hold Danny's hand tight, not wanting to let him go.

'Finally!' yells my sister-in-law.

I raise my voice. 'Ladies and gentleman, on behalf of my wonderful, loving husband and I.' I pause as another cheer goes up. It reminds me of our wedding day. Except it was Danny giving the speech then. 'We would like to thank you for joining us to celebrate the best decision I ever made.' I grin at Danny. Willing him to meet my eye. *Don't let me do this on my own.*

'Ahhhhh,' coos our family and friends. Zayn, leaning against the front door, gives a slightly sad smile. I think of the torn notepad in my bag, the three dead exes.

'I don't want anyone to vom,' I say. People laugh and cheer. I lift Danny's hand and press it to my cheek. 'But I don't think I could possibly be happier. Thank you, my darling Danny,' and I kiss his fingers.

The room erupts in cheers and claps and laughter. Oscar jumps, giggling at my feet. Zayn steps forward to hug us both.

Over his shoulder, I see Hellie, her face like granite, slip out the front door. Beside me, Danny watches her go.

BETH – THE PARTY

The sound of music and laughter surround me, but I feel like I'm watching it all through glass. My friends, my family, the faces I know so well feel alien. As if they are actors who have stepped into a role for the evening. Or I have. But then I've been playing a role ever since the incident. Beth, my entire life, is a construct. I'm just not as skilled a magician as I thought. But parties are blessedly easy to hide in. You just flit from person to person. A greeting here. An exclamation there. An apology that you really must just go and say goodbye to X, or get Y a drink. A sleight of hand to keep the painful awkward interactions at arm's length. It gives me time to breathe. To settle into this new version of me. Like a software upgrade to the sex dolls. Beth, the understanding wife. It's adult, grown-up, possibly French, though I think that's a cliché. Acid burns in my throat. But each canapé I eat just tastes of ash. You think when the worst happens you'll scream, shout, break things. But I just feel an awful sense of inevitability. This is just another thing I've broken. Another good thing – Danny and me – that I've destroyed.

International Number Calling flashes on my mobile. It could be Tobi. 'Hello?' I answer. Danny gives me an incredulous look, but I ignore him, turn and head down the hallway, past people. Smiling, shrugging, mouthing 'work' and grimacing. In case it's him. Oh God, please let it be him.

The irony of my screaming hysterical contrast to when I discovered Tobi cheating on me isn't lost. I've played this role from both sides, and it destroyed Lily. Cast her into the flames of judgement. *Harlot. Slut. Killer.* That spiralled my life out of control

The Anniversary Party

– unleashed the monster within. And this time? Now I'm different. I don't recognise that silly girl who behaved the way she did.

I duck past Cat and Zayn looking curiously at me in the kitchen, and out the back door, pulling it closed behind me. I teeter to the decking at the back. I'm shaking. I don't know if it's from the cold. 'Hello?' I repeat.

As soon as I hear his confident voice, I can picture him: leant casually back in his chair, a slightly amused, slightly mocking stance. 'Lily Burnell, what a blast from the past. *The Scarlet Woman*,' he drawls. He definitely knows what happened. I feel a flicker of anger – did he ever question his own behaviour? If I hadn't have experienced the horror of walking in on him with another woman, I might never have fled after Anna. Things might have been different.

'Tobi – thank you for calling me back,' I try to stop my teeth chattering. How do I put this?

'A total surprise. A very pleasant one, I might say. What can I help you with, young lady?'

Young lady? He's a year older than me, and we're not teenagers anymore. 'I . . . it's a bit awkward,' I say.

'Oh yes?' His voice rich like honey. 'Not ringing to say I've got a secret lovechild, are you?'

Just like Wade asked? Do all men fear this? Secret unknown progeny showing up and asking for university fees? More mewling daughters, women who want things from them. It feels a rather long-term game compared to the constant relief I felt at the arrival of my period each month during my twenties. Perhaps men spend all their forties holding their breath for the dreaded moment. The warm edge in Tobi's voice is different from Wade's panicked response. More like: here we go again. Always a player. And I am ringing after twenty years of silence – what else could it be for? A friendly chat – a Friends Reunited move to try and reconnect another way? A wave of inadequacy washes over me. 'It's – it's a bit difficult, actually.'

'Oh God, you've not got the clap, have you?' he says. 'Don't worry – I've been treated.' He laughs.

Doesn't that mean he should have called me if he did have it? 'Err, no, I. So, you're in Germany now?'

'Yes, Berlin. Great city. Great bike access,' and I think of the eco-warrior he used to be, and the photo on his company's website of him sat behind a corporate-style desk. An environmental start-up, with serious money behind it. After all he said, he now works for The Man. But then I've long suspected Tobi never really believed in any cause other than himself.

'So, you live out there – all the time?' Desperation sounds in my voice. What on earth do I say? Hey, nice to talk to you after a decade, someone may be trying to kill you because you slept with me?

'Why, you wanna stop by? I still remember that red dress you had. Legs like a gazelle,' he says, his voice full-blown sleazy now.

I feel old. Fat. My body changed by Oscar, time, stress. I want to preserve his memory of me as a nineteen-year-old. Not that I knew how great my figure was then. That's one of the cruellest parts of getting older. All the wasted opportunities. 'I'm married,' I say. 'Very happily married.' *Hellie pulling away from Danny. We need to talk.*

A burst of noise escapes from the house as someone opens the kitchen door, illuminating the dark corners of the garden. It closes and I'm alone again. I take a deep breath. 'Look, Tobi, there's no easy way for me to say this so I'm just going to come out with it. Some odd things – terrible things – have been happening to people I know.' I swallow, turn away from the house, shielding the phone and my words. 'To men I used to know.' A scraped rustle sounds from over the garden wall. A cat slinks past the bins. 'To men I used to go out with.' I keep licking my lips to stave off the dryness that seems to be spreading down my throat. I should've brought my drink with me. There is silence on the other end. 'I know you live in Berlin, and hopefully that means you're safe. But you need to know that there's – other men I went out with – well . . . ' The dry skin on my throat catches and I cough. 'Sorry. I, well. They are dead. Three of them are dead.'

There is silence on the other end.

'Tobi? Can you hear me?'

'Oh yes,' he says. 'I heard you.'

He sounds infuriatingly calm. I thought he'd be shocked. Ask questions. Deny it. 'Don't you have anything to say?'

'Oh Lily,' he sighs. 'I really hoped you'd got over this. After all these years.'

A tingling sweeps up my neck and across my face. 'What are—'

'If you'd just wanted to have some fun, I would have been up for that,' he said. 'A shag for old time's sake. You were always so eager to please.'

His words sting like a slap. 'That is not what I meant.'

'But this emotional drama thing – I hoped you would have grown out of that,' he says. 'It's just like what you did when I tried to gentlemanly extract myself . . . '

'I walked in on you shagging that girl from the SU!' Shame bursts over my skin like cold water. 'And that's not what I'm doing. This isn't the same thing. Look, you've got to . . . '

'Isn't it? Oh Lily-Lily-Lou,' I picture him shaking his head sadly. 'You really do need to get a handle on your emotions.'

'Piss off, Tobi. I'm trying to help you – save you,' I snap.

'Save me?' He laughs. 'Oh, this is good. This is taking me right back there. You're making me feel young again,' he says. 'But really, dear, you need to calm down.'

'Don't talk to me like that.' I force my voice down an octave. The smug bastard. 'Look, Tobi, you need to listen to me. I'm serious. Your life may be in danger.'

His laugh is pure scorn. The sound rips away in seconds the layers of self-esteem it's taken me years to build up. 'No, Lily, I don't need to listen to you. The poor sod you suckered into marriage has to do that – I escaped. And I'm not about to insert myself into whatever crazy-assed drama you have made to get yourself out of that. If you want to get divorced . . . '

What the hell? 'I don't want to get divorced.' I glance at the house but there's no movement from inside, no sign anyone heard that. 'This isn't about that—'

'Sure, you're just calling me with some cock-and-bull excuse to drag me back into your drama for LOLs. Well, sorry, but I'm not interested.'

'It's not about that!' I hate myself for sounding agitated. 'The sex wasn't even that good! We were basically children.'

Tobi's voice flicks to threatening in an instant. 'If you call me again, if you try to contact me in any way – I will do you for harassment. I could trace this phone in seconds. Find out where you live. I will make your life a misery, you crazy bitch. Now fuck off!' The phone clicks off.

My legs shake, and I steady myself against the damp wall. Breathing in the air so cold it hurts. Staring at the phone shaking in my hands.

HIM

The house throbs with vibrancy, like the pulse in her wrist. Life, music, laughter. His anniversary party. Not hers. I know he made her. She never wanted this. To celebrate this sham. This facade. He cannot – does not – make her happy. Not like I can.

I thought I could cope with it. That I would just take a peek. Because no one would notice among the noise and bodies of the party. But I can't bear it. Can't be in his domain. The false king. The false god. I pour the cheap wine he gave me over his bike saddle. Only just resist the urge to hurl the glass. I imagine smashing it in his smug face. He has her trapped, caught in the venal web of children and family. Toys with her. Toys with me. It's all wrong. She is mine. Should be mine. I want her to myself. I can't see her debase herself in this fake celebration. This house of lies. I stalk across the road, slowing my breathing as I pace into and out of the circle of light cast from the lamp post. The street smells of sweaty onions and sour piss.

How can she have said those things? The best decision she ever made? Bullshit. It's humiliating. And she had her arm over that idiot. Kissed his bloody cheek. That should have been me. He is nothing compared to me. He has nothing I don't have. Except her. Nothing matters except me getting her. Getting rid of the lying cheating bastard.

And I've always been a man of action.

I take out my phone, and type:

I'm outside. I'm going to tell Danny.

LILY

Three rows of dirty orange tiles split the wall of beige in two like a thin-lipped smile. The stain of decades of dirt mocks their wipe clean surfaces. This must have last been renovated in the seventies. The smell of bleach is overpowering, and I can't think about what body fluids it tried to wash away. A rectangular window of warped thick glass bricks was probably supposed to be softer than bars, or maybe just cheaper, but the effect of not being able to see the sky outside makes panic rise in my chest. A cell. This can't be happening. It can't.

'In you go, love,' the duty officer behind me says, the affectionate term softening his clipped formality. He's well over six foot, his belly pushing against the white of his uniform shirt, meaty arms hang away from his body. His eyes look tired, and crinkle into lines that sag into his cheeks. What time is it? How long have I been here? There is still light coming through the glass cubes but it's cold and blue. It must be after eight. They're keeping me here all night. A thin blue plastic mattress on top of a concrete slab makes a bed. It reminds me of the old gym mats we used to have at school. I want to cry but I don't think I have any tears left.

'Come on now,' the duty officer repeats.

I hug my arms, the alien sweatshirt they've given me rubs against my bare skin underneath. They took my bra. I feel exposed, raw. This sweatshirt that others have probably worn, against my breasts. My nipples. I let go, hold my arms away, as if I can stop it touching me. I don't want it touching me. I don't want to touch the bed. I don't want to touch the walls. Oh God, the exposed metal toilet, no seat. My stomach churns.

'I'm sorry,' I say. My lips are dry, cracked. My skin feels sticky from crying. My head aches, a pressure radiating out from between my eyes. How has everything in my life changed so much in one day? 'I'm so, so sorry,' I say. 'I didn't mean for this to happen. I didn't . . . I'm not this kind of person.' I think of the gasp Anna made. Her eyes going wide. The shock. The realisation. Then her scream. The screech of wheels. The crunching thud of metal and glass striking a body. *Oh my God, what have I done?*

Behind me the duty officer swings the heavy door shut. The bolt clunks across. I can't do this. I can't stay here. I can't be locked in.

'Please,' dry sobs wrack my body, my chest tightens. 'I don't like enclosed spaces.'

There's a grind of metal against metal, and a creak as he opens a flap in the door. 'I'll leave this open,' he sounds pitying, his eyes droopy in his face. 'Someone will check on you periodically.'

That last bit sounds like a threat. *Do they think I'm going to hurt myself?* As the sound of his rubber soled shoes retreats, other noises replace it. Other people locked in other cells. A drunk man singing. Another crying. All men. How many are there down here? Locked up next to me. Then there's a metallic thud that makes my whole body jump, the back of my legs bash against the bed. The thin mattress squeaks against the wall.

Clang! There it is again. My heart drums a warning, as a gruff voice starts up.

'Oi! Let me out! Oi! You filthy fecking pigs!'

Clang! Clang! Clang! Whoever the man is, he's slamming himself against his cell door. Every instinct in me screams to run. To get away. My jaw locks. My hands curl into fists. But there's nowhere to go. There's no way out.

'Shut it!' Yells the duty officer from down the hall. Then I hear that door shut too.

The man keeps screaming, hurling himself at the door. 'Let. Me. Out!' Clang! 'Let. Me. Out!' Clang!

I press my palms over my ears. Squeeze my eyes shut. Try to block it all out. Try to make it all stop. But when I close my eyes all I see is the body on the ground. Chunks of fractured glass all around her like stars, and everyone screaming. Screaming. Screaming at me.

Because I'm the killer.

BETH – THE PARTY

My heart is hammering in my chest as I clutch my phone tight and run down the side passage, past the recycling bins. Tobi's threats still poison in my ears. That name: he said it over and over. He knew, he knew what I did. What Lily did. I blink and red dripping letters assault my memory: *Slut. Killer. Liar.* Can I smell faeces? I'm imagining it. And now this. Not now. Not here. Not like this.

He's standing on the other side of the street, just outside a pool of streetlight.

I glance over my shoulder. The front door is still closed, the curtains drawn, the sound of the party booming away behind me. What if Tobi calls me back? What if he's tracing my phone already? He was always smart – *he could do that*. He could be calling the police now? Or, he knows where I live already. The way Tobi switched from laughing to threats. Could he be the one doing this? I shiver.

'Bethy, sweetheart,' he says, stepping towards me into the light. He's changed since earlier. He's wearing a different T-shirt, fresh jeans.

I bat his hands away. I don't need this now. 'What are you doing here? You can't be . . . You're not going to – look let's talk about this.' Danny could come out any minute, someone else might arrive, Oscar could see.

'Whoa, slow down.' He sounds infuriatingly calm.

'Are you messing with me?' Is this some terrible wind-up?

'Bethy,' he says, stilling my flapping hands. 'My lovely Bethy, it's okay.'

The scent of him wraps round me like a duvet, I squeeze his fingers back. After what Tobi said, I want to be held. Comforted. I want all this to stop. 'Robbie, you can't be here.'

He gives a soft chuckle. 'Robbie? You haven't called me that for years.'

For years. All my pasts are rushing back to me. Tobi on top of that girl from the SU. Rob walking back into the hotel. 'You frightened me, Rob – that message. You wouldn't?' He smiles down at me, lifts my chin. A shrill laugh breaks from my house behind us, pulling me back to reality. I drop his hands, step back. He frowns, looks hurt.

'You can't just turn up like this,' I say.

'I'm invited. You invited me,' he says.

'Yes, as my boss, but you know you shouldn't be here. Oscar, Danny,' I cross my arms and look back at the house. How have I got myself into this mess? This was never supposed to happen.

'Bloody Danny,' Rob says. 'I'd like to . . . '

'Rob. Danny is my husband. Oscar's dad. I didn't mean for this to happen.'

'*This?*' Rob says. 'Don't talk about what we have as if it's nothing.'

But it is nothing, it was just a stupid kiss. I wanted to feel desired, giddy with the power of attraction once more. But that night as Rob's palms ran up the back of my silk work shirt, and he pulled me onto his lap, I knew it was wrong. I didn't want Rob to want me, I wanted Danny to want me. I stopped. Laughed it off. Made my excuses, left. I thought it was done with, both keeping our distance, reasserting our professional boundaries, a silly mistake we were both happy to forget. But then the notes started coming, and people started dying, and Rob is now here looking at me like he's a lovesick teenager. How did I not see it? Guilt crawls up my legs like ants. 'Look, I don't want to hurt you,' I say.

His snort cuts me off. His face twists in anger, an ugly gargoyle instead of the man I know. I blink. Tobi's threats colouring my view. Making me see hatred everywhere. *You were always so eager to please*. Is that what I'm still doing? Is that how I got here? Since the incident, I'm hypervigilant, always attuned to everyone's emotions in case there's a chance they have caught sight of the threat underneath. I bend myself, Beth, into what I feel everyone else wants. And I'm good at it. I have to be. It's a survival technique; it's got me this far. *But now someone is killing my exes*. I lost sight of what I want, the day I replaced Lily. It's ingrained in me to give others what they want, so they stay happy, so I stay safe. Is that what I did here: did I pick up on Rob's desire and simply give him what he wanted, right when I felt Danny didn't want me? It should never have happened. It should never have got this out of control.

'Rob, listen to me,' I take his hands in mine, will him to understand. 'I'm sorry if I gave you the wrong impression,' I say.

'What?' the disbelief in his face is horrific. 'Are you – no, you can't. I'm Rob Trenchard—'

'Please,' I fight to keep my voice calm. For the third time in the last hour, I feel like I'm willing a man to listen to me. To actually *hear* what I'm saying, not what he wants to hear. 'I shouldn't have acted the way I did. I got carried away. You know I care for you, as a friend.' I think of the notes, the threats, my three dead ex-boyfriends. Were they Tobi? 'But I have to do what is right for my family. For me. I can't have you coming here threatening to tell Danny things.'

I should have looked for another job after that night. I thought it meant nothing to Rob too. If he fires me now – I'll lose the house. It was months ago – why now?

'I'm sorry,' he says, his voice is quiet. 'But I think I'm falling for you, Bethy.'

'It was just a stupid kiss,' I can't keep the exasperation from my voice. I feel him shudder.

Is he really upset? We'd kissed before – years ago at a marketing conference, before I met Danny. Rob was the hot industry bad boy, I was newly single Beth. It was a drunken, sticky, hot moment. I remember greedily leaning into him outside the hotel. And then the memory of Iain blooming like tender bruises on my body, as Rob's hands roamed over me. I'd stopped; I wasn't ready. But that's all in the past. Neither of us even mentioned it when Rob poached me for Trench PR years later. Has he been carrying a torch for me all this time? My ego fluffs at the thought, but no: it's clear what's happened. I've turned myself into a tease, the one that got away. Twice. If we'd actually had sex he'd be long over it. I'd just be another forgotten notch on the bed post. 'My fault,' I appeal to his vanity. 'Just another moonstruck girl swooning over Rob Trenchard.'

Rob seems to pull himself together at those words. Clears his throat, pulls his hands away. 'Course,' he says. I feel the cold of the night suddenly whip around me. 'Just a kiss. As you say: nothing.'

'Exactly,' I force a smile. I reach to give his arm a squeeze, needing to feel his touch again. *We're still friends?*

'Shouldn't have had that brandy after work,' the twinkle is back in his eye.

'So, we're – we're okay?' I ask.

'Course,' he repeats. 'I mean you're a bit older than my usual type anyway.'

Ouch. 'Okay. Well, I'll see you at work tomorrow then?'

'I might be away with clients tomorrow, and next week. So, we'll see,' he says.

God, it's going to be awkward. I think of Oscar, the house, the bills, Danny. If I can just get through the next few weeks, make the sex dolls launch a success, I can then start looking at other agencies. Yellow Boat has always said I (and my accounts) would be welcome there. 'Great,' I say.

He smiles wryly.

'Thanks, Rob,' I say, and reach for his hand again, this time catching his fingers between mine. He half squeezes back, our fingers not quite matching up, they twist awkwardly away from each other.

He gives me a wry smile. 'Back to your party then.'

For a second I want to hold on to him. I'd been so swift to dismiss the kiss a few weeks back as merely an awkward moment – it's like I'm viewing this from a new perspective. What might have been in a different life if it had gone further at that conference? If I'd never got together with Danny? If I hadn't destroyed everything. Then I let go and both our hands drop away.

I'm back over the road before a dark thought twists up inside: maybe it's not Tobi who's orchestrating all this. He is in Berlin, after all – how would he get notes into my bag? But Rob . . . He knows where I live. I work for him. He could easily have put a note in my bag without anyone else noticing. I spin back, but the opposite side of the street is empty. Rob has vanished into the night.

For a moment I don't know what to do. The dark thought spreads like ink blots within me, slowly obliterating the light. No, I have to wrest control back. I try to inhale the upbeat music, the laughter, the warm yellow light that emanates from within my beautiful family home. Sluice off the darkness. I tell my face to relax, smile. I'm ready. Beth walks towards the door. Beth can do this.

BETH – ONE DAY AFTER THE PARTY

'Have you got Oscar's swimmers?' I say, clicking the dishwasher door shut and on. That's the third and final load after last night. I've been up since five, I couldn't sleep.

Danny finishes swiffing the kitchen floor, pulls off the e-cloth mop attachment, and drops it onto the pile of cleaning cloths in front of the washing machine. 'Yes. I am the one who does this stuff every day,' his voice is tight, he looks tired too. I reach for his shoulder as he passes, but he turns away.

'Of course,' I say as brightly as I can. 'Just trying to be helpful. The school emailed to say they'll send over some work for him, by the way.'

'I'm still not happy about lying,' Danny says.

I cut in quick. 'It's not a big deal. He could genuinely have chicken pox. And he's six – he won't miss anything important.'

Danny makes an uncertain murmur.

I need to keep him and Oscar safe. 'Besides, I still think it's best if you guys get away right now. For us. As a family.' I wipe the already clean countertop.

Danny gives me a thin smile, picks his coffee up out of the way. 'Well he knows he's going to see the ponies now, so there's no cancelling without making me the bad guy.'

'It's not like that.' I catch hold of his arm this time, squeeze his bicep. But he pulls away, putting his mug down with a porcelain crunch against the marble. I blink so he doesn't see the tears forming in my eyes.

Then I follow him into the hallway, as he calls, 'Ready, buddy?'

Our son is already at the door, his rucksack on over his pjs, gripping his teddy. I want to pull him close, keep him by my side forever. But I have to let them go. Whatever is going on, I need to focus on that. And I need them to be safe. To be far away from here. To be far away from me. All this is my fault. I have never let Danny see the real me or know the truth. I can't. Couldn't. He would have left. There would be no us, no Oscar – but I was just kidding myself. Tobi knew all about what happened with Lily. The poison within has soaked out, soaked into us. I pushed Danny away, and now I'm forcing him to leave again.

It's for his own good.

Danny turns to say goodbye, and I pull him into me, inhaling his scent. 'I love you. You do know that, don't you?'

He looks surprised, but his face softens. He gently pushes my hair back from my face. 'Of course.'

'Gross!' yells Oscar.

'Right, that's it!' I yell, and lunge towards Oscar. 'The kissy monster is coming!'

Oscar screams and giggles, making it halfway down the hallway before I grab him and smother his head, face, skin with kisses. 'The kissy monster's got you – woo ha ha!' I bellow.

Oscar shrieks with pure delight.

'Right.' I stop kissing him, but don't let go. Not yet. 'You're going to be a good boy for Daddy and Hellie aren't you?'

He nods his head.

'And I'll FaceTime you every night,' I look as Danny opens the door to load the suitcase into the car. I'm glad they're picking up Hellie on the way. That I don't have to see her this morning. That she doesn't see this.

'Come on, mate,' Danny says.

And I pull Oscar into me once more, as if I can hold on to every molecule of him. Before he runs off and clambers into the back of the car. I follow them out.

'I'll text you when we get there,' Danny gets in the front. Clipping in his belt. I hold onto the door, not wanting them to go. He looks at his watch, it's just gone half past seven. A couple of early commuters have appeared further down the street, striding out into the mild morning light. 'Hopefully we'll clear London before the worst of rush hour,' Danny says. 'But I think it'll take four or five hours anyway.'

'Least you'll be together. I wish I was coming,' I glance at Oscar who is staring at his iPad in the back, his little feet dangling over his car seat. Danny gives me a funny look. I smile. 'You're going to have an amazing time! What a treat.'

Danny starts the engine.

'I love you,' I say as I shut the car door. Oscar starts waving. And I do too, keeping going till they pull out, and away, and around the corner into the next street.

I stand for a minute watching the space where my family were. It's only when the car is long out of sight that I realise Danny never said it back. He didn't tell me he loved me. I shake the feeling off. As every second ticks by, Oscar and Danny are getting further away from here. They're safe. That's all that matters. I'm doing the right thing.

Then I hurry back inside, pull on my green coat. Drop my phone and keys into my pocket, and pull the door closed behind me as I head straight out again. I think of the notebook I stole from Zayn's. Compared to the notes this morning it's obviously not a match. It's just a standard lined-paper notebook with some pages torn out. I can't believe I stole from my best friend. The way Nate looked at me as I rambled on in their flat – surely he'll tell Zayn I stopped by? I'll have to have a feasible reason ready. An explanation. I've let my paranoia get the better of me, all the time ignoring the glaring threat I didn't want to acknowledge.

The wind's cold, as I belt my coat tight with shaking fingers. Willing myself into the foyer of Hackney Central, through the barrier, down the concrete stairs. There are more people collected here. In coats, jackets, clutching laptop bags, and wheelie cases ahead of the weekend, staring into their phones, or at the approaching train. Never at each other. I have always loved the anonymity of London, that you can exist unseen among so many people. Even before I sought solace in it after Lily. The rough and tumble of thousands of lives carrying on around you, carrying you, smoothing any sharp edges, making even the ugliest debris a beautiful bead of glass turned in the waves and sand of the ocean floor. Till you are no longer recognisable. But someone did recognise me. *The Scarlet Woman.* Tobi's words were a clarion call to the raging monster inside. It's time I stop running and turn to face it. Iain's name is on my list of exes. The terrible moment my life broke in two. Lily and Beth. Dark and light. I have not hidden it as well as I thought. It's out there. Which means there could be someone else who knows who I really am. What I am capable of.

I'm too tense to sit on the train, my leg muscles feel tight, primed to run. My chest tightens as we pull into Highbury and Islington. Time seems to have sped up. I bite off a skin tag next to my thumbnail as I follow the map on my phone down tree-lined residential streets. More people pass me now, but I can't take in any detail of their faces. My body is screaming at me to turn back, to run.

But this is it. Number eighty-two Corsica Crescent. I stop at the edge of the short-tiled path to the black panelled door of the neat Georgian terrace. There's still a light on inside. I can do this. I breathe deep. I can do this. I wrap the brass knocker swiftly on the door. The noise reverberating through my body. Wait. Swallow. I hear someone approaching. The click of an internal handle. I try to smile, but my face merely stretches and pulls uncomfortably. The door opens. I swallow again. Adjust my gaze down, to take in the woman in the wheelchair.

LILY

Anna's hazel eyes shift in a face my mind had memorised from fifteen years ago, settling into the softened reality before me. No longer the sharp gouged cheekbones of a twenty-something woman, but the softer lines of a still beautiful forty-year-old. Her open smile falters, did she think it was the postman? Her eyebrows knit with recognition. 'You?' Her voice huskier than the high scream I remember.

She's not asking – how did you find me? Presumably because she knows just how easy it is to track people down. Especially if they were careless like me, like every one of my exes. I've known for years she was here. Twenty minutes from my house. It's why I never come to this part of London. 'Please don't shut the door,' I push my foot in the way, though she's made no move externally.

She sighs. 'You better come in.' Anna rolls her chair back. Her rich dark hair has retained its colour, but it's shorter, hanging just above her shoulders now, a new soft fringe feathered over her forehead. The hand at the end of her simple tan knitwear holds the door open. Her other hand rests in her lap, on the thigh of her jeans. I realise with a jolt she's wearing the exact same colourway I was wearing all those years ago. Yet again I think of how she mirrored me discovering Tobi in the arms of another woman. Of how with a twist of fate's wrist it could have been me using a wheelchair now. How that makes it all the worse.

I press my keys into my palm as I step into the vanilla scented hallway, as if the feel of the cool serrated metal in my pocket might keep me tethered here. Before I arrived I was scared, but now I feel nothing but shame. I'm dripping with it. There's a pain at the back of my throat. Each time I blink I see the bus, the rain, Anna's widening eyes. It causes a schism with the serene Georgian house we're in now. As if I can't be both here and in my nightmares of that day.

'Lounge is on the left,' Anna says, closing the front door behind.

There's no turning back now. The empty stairlift, its belt dangling, gapes at me accusingly. And I feel the soft worn curve of a hundred years of feet on the sanded floorboards. It's as if I'm approaching the gallows as the sound of Anna's wheels follow me into the front room.

'Take a seat,' Anna indicates a brown three-seater sofa facing a small iron fireplace. Hung on the chimney breast is a shimmering painting of autumnal silver birches, its metallic acrylic bouncing the morning light over the inlaid shelves of paperbacks that flank the chimney. A small flat screen TV feels like an afterthought, making me feel Anna and I might have been friends under other circumstances.

I lose my coat's belt, lower myself onto the sofa. Feel the soft material with my hands. My eyes flick around the room: the artfully arranged logs in the fireplace grate, a heavy glass paperweight on the coffee table, kindling, matches. Anna knows the truth. Anna knows what Lily did. Could she be the source of what's happening? Of all the deaths of my exes? I have to stop it now. The thickening in my throat is unbearable.

'I'm sorry,' I say. The words ripping back the veil. *The Scarlet Woman.*

She looks taken aback, her neatly shaped eyebrows lift. I don't know what she thinks I'm doing here, but that obviously wasn't it. 'Because of what happened?' she sits back in her chair appraising me. Is she sitting in judgment?

I can only manage a nod. A tear spills down my cheek, drops onto my jeans. I swipe at my weak eyes: I don't have the right to be sad here, in this woman's home. Not after what I did to her.

Anna rolls forward, leans her elbows on her knees and takes my hands in hers. Her fingers cold and smooth. Her scent of orange blossom envelopes me. It's such a gentle nurturing touch, and I realise how long it is I've gone without comfort. How I had to let go of Oscar this morning, despite wanting to hold him tight. I've retreated from Danny, forced him away. Built walls around myself, defences, barricades, but it hasn't protected me. All the death, the pain, the grief. If what is happening is because of what Lily did I have to stop it. 'I'm sorry,' I snivel again.

'Lily, listen,' Anna's tone is explanatory, her eyes clear, her face open. 'It wasn't your fault.'

Half a laugh hiccups out of me – for so long I've dreaded hearing my name from her lips. 'I'm not – that's not my name anymore. I changed it, after what happened.' *Slut. Killer. Liar.* 'After what I did to you.'

Anna keeps hold of my hands, a light pressure tying us together, but she leans back, to better take me in. I am an unexpected specimen from the past to her, like she is to me. 'Why?' she says, sounding genuinely curious.

I can't hold it in anymore. Her kindness has loosed the lid. I can't keep pretending. 'Someone is hurting people I care about,' the accusation comes out in a rush.

'Who?' she wraps my fingers in hers. A silver drop earring rocks at the edges of her hair. *The bus. The rain. Anna's broken body on the ground.*

'I have a husband, a son, I love them so much,' I heave, fear shaking its way out my body. I can't help but cling to her hands. 'I have to – have to apologise, had to see you, in case, in case it was revenge?'

Anna blinks. A car rumbles past outside. I can hear my own ragged breathes. 'You changed your name?' she repeats, as if trying to make sense of this fragmented conversation.

I nod, the stopper out. Me talking at speed to her gradual comprehension. 'Everything, my life. I didn't want to be that person anymore. After what I did to you . . . ' *The scream. The ambulance. The police. Someone said I pushed her.* She was in a coma. They didn't know if she would make it. Returning to my mum's trembling in the police car. The neighbours seeing. The rumours starting. All while Anna was hooked up to a slow beeping ventilator.

Photos of both Anna and me – young, pretty women – were pasted on the front page of the *Evening Standard*. A salacious hint at what was the possible story behind a tragic incident. In Sevenoaks the local papers ran alleged quotes from people in the know. I was the girl who'd got involved with an engaged man. A femme fatale who'd tried to kill her competition. I'd pushed her in front of a bus. They all knew it. Whispers followed me everywhere. Someone put dogshit through Mum's letterbox. Spray painted the front of the house with words: *Slut. Killer. Liar.* The police advised me against speaking to Iain, not that he tried. My whole life had been ripped open, dumped out on the dirty floor. I was shocked, grieving, terrified Anna would die. What would happen to me? It was my fault: how had I believed Iain? I must have known. *I must have known.* I stopped going out after someone threw eggs at me. Mum didn't want to go to the police about the graffiti, about the people who shouted slag as they passed the house. Better to hide.

Anna is passing me tissues from a box on the side now. They're sodden, twisted in seconds. 'Mum had to move,' I shred one in my hand. I'm back there, young, frightened, small. No comeback to what people said I was. 'I destroyed everything.'

'No – I didn't know,' Anna's voice shakes softly. 'You poor thing.'

'How can you say that?' My words are uncontrolled, desperate. For years I've kept this locked down. 'After what I did? After I made you have to use . . . that.' I can't bring myself to say wheelchair, disabled, paralysed.

'It was an accident – I wasn't looking. I was upset,' Anna's voice is calm, factual. She's still holding both my hands in hers, gently rubbing my fingers, soothing. 'What happened wasn't your fault.'

'But you can't . . . ' I can't put the horror into words.

Anna tilts her head, gives a soft smile I recognise as the same move I make when Oscar's said something silly. 'Lily, or . . . ?'

'Beth,' I wipe my nose with one of the tissues. Though I don't feel like carefully curated PR Beth, a thirty-nine-year-old capable woman. I feel lost, hollowed out.

'Beth, nice. It suits you,' Anna rolls her chair backwards to grab a wicker wastepaper bin tucked under a side table. She holds it out. 'Here.' I drop the soggy tissues in. Keeping two back. Anna continues: 'When I first woke up in hospital after the accident, I did think my life was over.'

My spine feels like it's sluiced with ice water, but she keeps going. Her voice moderate, informative – I feel this story is well worn on her tongue. She's been asked this before. *The how. The when.*

'I didn't expect to find myself disabled at twenty-nine, but I didn't expect to find out my fiancé was cheating on me either,' her inflection is arch.

I flinch at that.

Anna returns the bin under the side table. Straightens a mosaic coaster on the top. 'But I put that hurt, that anger into my physio. Getting stronger, getting used to my chair. I was learning not just to be independent from him, but independent for myself, in a new way.'

I can't meet her eyes. I'm ashamed. 'But I did this . . . '

'Have you ever heard about the hedonic adaptation?' Anna says, keeps going as I shake my head. 'It's the principle that people tend to return to a stable level of happiness and personality traits after major life events, positive or negative. They've run research on lottery winners. And those of us who have had life changing accidents. We all end up pretty much back where we began.'

I stare at her. For so long I have pictured this woman as a wrecked being, a guilt-ridden manifestation of every bad act or thought I've ever made. A spectre that ran my mum and me out the house we shared with my dad. A ghoul built from destructive energy. I could only imagine she rued the day she ever saw me, that she wanted her vengeance. I've tried to outrun it, but since the notes started to arrive, and people started to die, Lily has been screaming that it's payback for Anna. It's only what I deserve.

'I don't understand.' I feel foolish sat in this nice middle-class woman's nice middle-class lounge, like there are two worlds and I've been living in the wrong one.

'What happened that day,' Anna says. 'The accident, being a wheelchair user, it doesn't define me.' She indicates the room: framed laughing photos, well-thumbed books, house plants brimming from bright pots. 'I'm a sociology lecturer, I'm a wife – though my husband is currently off being a research fellow at Stanford. I'm mum to a hyperactive nine-year-old, and I take pottery classes on the weekend. Being disabled is pretty far down the list,' she smiles at me sympathetically.

I feel the blush creep across my cheeks. The Anna I built up in my mind is an illusion, a fable I used to berate myself. It has nothing to do with this woman in front of me now. I may have been the lesser wronged, but did I let what happened that day define me? I let it destroy Lily. The implications flood me, rocking everything I believed. Could I have stayed as Lily? The thought is too big, too overwhelming. I have to get out. I can't bring my death and destruction to this woman's life. 'I'm sorry, I shouldn't have disturbed you,' I pull at my coat, trying to tighten the cord back round my waist.

'It's fine,' she says. 'Do you want a cup of tea? There's obviously some things going on?'

How can she be so benevolent? I don't deserve it. 'No, really,' I stand. She moves back. 'I shouldn't have bothered you.'

'I wish you'd come before,' she's still leaning forward, peering at me. It's concern: she's concerned about me, after everything. 'If you've been carrying all this, all this time?'

I can only shake my head in dissent. What if I had come earlier? What if I had faced my fear and come to see Anna, this woman I projected my own self-loathing on, when I was still Lily? Things could've been different. People might not have died. Someone might not have been killing my exes.

'Iain and I kept in touch,' Anna turns to open the whitewashed door into the hallway. 'Even after everything.'

I stare at her back. 'You have?' He's on the list.

'Oh,' she catches my tone. Her lips purse together, drop. 'You didn't know. I'm sorry. He passed away a few years ago.'

I try to absorb the words, everything she's told me. A slew of new truths to replace the old. Bits of my core shunted off the cliff like lemmings.

'How old's your son?' Anna holds the door, as my feet carry me towards it. We could be chit-chatting in the local cafe queue. Waiting for the helter-skelter at the Hackney Carnival.

'Six. Oscar's six,' I say.

'Lovely age,' she grins. 'Sweet name.'

I make it out of the house, down the street, and round the corner before the tears come. But I no longer know who I am crying for. Anna, Iain, my mum, Danny, Oscar, Lily. All of them. Me. I have made a terrible mistake. I have been living a lie. And everything, all the pain, all the dread, all the lies have turned the inside of me rotten. I let what happened define me. Other people's view of me became reality. Newspapers, neighbours, former friends, gossips decided Lily was bad, so she became bad. Even I no longer saw her as innocent. I tried to erase her, paper over her darkness, start again, but she wasn't dead. She was entombed, crushed under layers of bitterness and rage, and digging her out is causing seismic shifts in my identity. I can't deal with this, with Anna, Mickey, Kareem, Phil. Guilt is cracking my last semblance of self apart. I take a deep steadying breath: *I can choose if I let this define me. I can choose to fight*. If I can just keep it together to face this. I have to stop the killer. No one else can get hurt. Lily hid, but I have to act. But is it too late?

BETH

I'm back home by nine, discombobulated from my interaction with Anna. *I can't think about that now. Can't entertain what it means.* I need to keep focused on my action plan. Change my top, grab my laptop, go to the office and talk to Rob. Tell him I need time off. Family emergency, whatever. He'll understand. I think about the look in his eyes last night. He'll let me take the time. Then I can dedicate myself to solving this. It's not going to be like it was before, the police will listen this time but I need to find out who's doing this. If I can prove someone is targeting me, I can tie the deaths together, prove a link. I just need to work out who knows who I've slept with. Danny? Zayn? *Danny didn't say he loved me.* I feel sick thinking about it. There's no way it could be either Danny or Zayn doing this. *But then I completely misread Anna, I've been mistaken before.* Don't dwell on that.

I fetch myself a glass of water. The kitchen feels cold, empty, sterile without Danny and Oscar. I swallow. Check over my shoulder as if I might see a face at the window. I've got to get a grip. I pour myself another glass of water. My throat still tight. The thought of the lies I told Danny and Zayn fill my mouth with ash. I force down another gulp of water. I put the glass down. Double-check the back door is locked. The absurd feeling someone is still here. Watching. Still out there, brushing past the bins like next door's cat.

I collect my handbag from where I left it tucked behind the vase on the hallway table. And then I see it. The envelope. Like the others. There. Just sitting on top of my bag. My bag. Bile rises in my throat. No. Not again.

The envelope has my name printed in capitals on the front, like before. My breathing audible as I open it. Inside is a slip of lined paper, letters stuck on. Letters in my handwriting. Blue ink. Green. Red. Where are they all coming from? They spring around in front of my eyes, refuse to make words. Make different words. Half is a sentence: *Only those with angel wings can fly*. What does that mean? My stomach falls away. *Dead man walking*. And *only those with angel wings can fly*. Are they linked? Do I have to put them together? Does it mean something? Then a long line of gobbledygook. W *w w* . . . Oh God, it's a web address. It's an instruction. A point in the right direction. The paper shakes in my hand. I mustn't knock the letters off. Even though I want nothing more than to scream and tear it all up.

I pull my laptop from my bag. Open it. Reach for the bottom stair, lower myself, shaking. Hurry up. Load. Password in. A screensaver of me and Oscar. Load, goddammit.

I stare at the tiny cut-out letters, fluttering as my hand shakes, like pinned butterflies waiting to die. I met a lepidopterist once, as part of a campaign we were running. He showed me cases of stunning iridescent blue butterflies kept in glass drawers. He told me they palpitate the bodies between thumb and forefinger to kill them. One quick pulse and their heart stops. Like a power button being depressed. A band constricts round my chest.

Finally, my screen rolls into life. I type the web address. One for Metro.co.uk. A news site. Whoever is doing this is ahead of me.

The cut-out forward slash looks small. Wrong to me, like a minus at an angle. Does that mean something? I should be able to read more from these letters. Like crossword clues. Or Runes. An illumination into what's happening. Where are they coming from? Has someone copied my handwriting perfectly – is that possible? The newspaper's banner appears. An advert for a new Mercedes convertible plays along the top. The majority of the page still blank. Come on!

The Anniversary Party

And then it loads. Words hover off the screen, as if I can't quite grab hold of them.

Tube train.
Accident.
Man.
Platform.
Dead.

The laptop tilts in my hand. I'm gripping it too tight. This can't be happening. It can't.

Shocking video shows the moment a man was pushed to his death in front of a tube train from a packed commuter platform.

My eyes won't focus. Won't hold onto the words.

A 41-year-old man was pushed to his death from a packed underground platform at rush hour last night. Shocking video shows the man being propelled forwards, as the train can be seen pulling into the station in the background. Police are interested in speaking to anyone who was in or around Chancery Lane station from 17.45 yesterday . . .

Oh God. Chancery Lane. Holborn. *Problems on the Tube.* I scroll down trying to get the sentences to make sense.

Police report the name of the commuter killed is . . .

I let out a cry. My hand flies to my face. The laptop drops and bounces off the floor. Oh my God. How could anyone know? How is this happening? I need to lie down. I'm going to pass out. Shakily I lower my face onto the rough carpet, the smell of dust, dirt, our washing powder catch in my throat. Breathe. Keep breathing. I loosen my shirt. Pull it off, back, try to get air in. Breathe. Slowly, as the blurred edges of my view come back into focus. As my breathing slows, I realise I'm staring into the laptop screen, now on its side, like a book propped open. My eyes fix on the name.

The man has been identified as Wade Ellison.
Only those with angel wings can fly.

BETH

The smiling woman in the photo: Jane, and her daughter Abbey who's always called Wade Daddy. The thought of losing Danny, of what that would do to Oscar, to me. It's like being punched in the stomach. A moan escapes my lips. I double over. I saw him. I saw him minutes before it happened. And it's my fault. It happened because of me. Maybe the killer didn't know about Wade till I went to see him? Maybe I led him straight to him? He must have been there, watching. It happened minutes after we spoke. Wade was alive, drinking coffee, smiling about adopting his little girl. Talking about the wedding, and then minutes later he was dead. And in such a horrific way. I can smell the sulphur, feel the drag of the air as a tube train approaches. The mice on the tracks. Everyone watching. He must have known. He must have known what was coming. Jesus. I failed him. I failed his fiancée; I failed his daughter.

The footage is grainy. A mass of people gathers on the platform edge. Looking at phones, looking down, along, up. Anywhere but at each other. And then there's a sudden movement. A man – Wade – flies forwards. His stomach first. Arms bananaed back. His shoulder bag flies off. His arms windmill forwards, but they can't slow him. He drops onto the tracks like a beanbag. The lights of the Tube train shine horribly vivid. The video cuts.

The Metro logo appears. A play symbol, the counter scrolling down before the site automatically plays the next video. Taylor Swift leaving a party. Just another bit of news to replace this. People will watch this on their phones, at their desks, sip their coffee and then find out about Taylor Swift's outfit. That's it.

A man's life reduced into seconds of a shocking online video. Something people will forget by the time their next email arrives. Unless they know him. Knew him. Like me.

I press replay. This time I watch behind the fuzzy man I now know is Wade. The man who has no idea he is about to die. I must be able to see something. Something of the person who did this. There's movement, and Wade flies forwards again. The crowd swarm into the gap. Arms reach futilely towards the tracks. I rewind the clip.

Wade flies.

There's a movement. A surge forwards. No one looks behind. There's no one that's visible. It's just a mass. I rewind the clip.

Wade flies.

A clump of people. It's impossible to discern how many, let alone faces, shapes, gender. Surely the police will have better footage? But no, this is the CCTV. This is it. This isn't some American FBI drama, there is no zooming in, no sharpening of pixels. There's just Wade flying through the air to his death. *Only those with angel wings can fly.* The police have appealed for witnesses. Surely that means they don't know who did this? But I do.

I have to go to the police. I stand. But this changes nothing. The note is made from letters of my own handwriting. Found in my handbag. In my house. They will assume I wrote this: constructed it in some desperate bid for attention. Someone who was tying random deaths together, making them about her. Anna may not think Lily was to blame for what happened before, but that didn't stop everyone else thinking she was. *Killer. Liar.* The police will see Lily's darkness. What she did. Dangerous. Guilty. But these deaths aren't random. These are all men I've slept with. Oh God, Wade, I'm so sorry. Only people with angel wings.

Angel wings.

I can almost see the feathers floating in front of my eyes. Fluttering to obscure the answer. I blink. My tattoo. I have angel wings. I slide down the wall. My legs weak. How is this happening? Why is this happening? Who is doing this? What have they done – Mickey, Kareem, Phil and now Wade? All dead. All murdered because of me.

My chest constricts. My ribs close over my lungs, forcing the air out. This can't be real. *Only people with angel wings.* Someone is obliterating everyone from my – from Lily's past. And they know. The notes are now addressed to Beth. But Beth didn't sleep with those men . . .

How could anyone know? No, wrong question. My head aches, my eyes sting, as they force me to look again. To see what is happening. Four men are dead. Four people's loved ones have had their lives torn apart. I have to fight. I have to stop this. I have to try.

Who knows the truth?

BETH

I stare at the notes that have been sent to me – all of them, laid out on the kitchen table. My own handwriting diced into threats. Where is it coming from? Shopping lists? Work notes? I type so much nowadays . . .

The rest of the kitchen seems normal. Glasses drying after last night. A carton of orange juice left on the side by Oscar. It should be homely. Safe. But everything has changed. I let my eyelids close for a welcome second of darkness. Stay calm. Don't panic. Panicking isn't helping. You've faced the storm before, you know how to tolerate its rage.

The notes are still lying on the table. The first one: *I know who you really are*. Then the 'de' one I found on my way back from the sex dolls warehouse. Then the 'ad man walking' one that completed the jeopardy. And now this one. I didn't think anyone knew the full truth. All the people I've slept with. Why would I share it? Some of these encounters I'd rather forget. But I don't wish them dead. And yet someone has found out. How? A doctor? I think again about what Wade said. The thought of him living, breathing opposite me. And then gone. I should have stopped him from leaving. I should have insisted. I've been to the sexual health clinic a few times – years ago, before I was married. Perhaps I should go again since Hellie? *Don't think about that*. I can't even remember who I saw. I have the vague impression of a nurse. A faceless woman. But I went more than once, and even if I said how many sexual partners I really truly had had, it's not like I handed over a list of names. Do they even ask you the number? Or do I just have that in my mind from old *Sex and the*

City episodes? Oh haha, let's all laugh at Samantha sleeping with countless men! How dare someone judge me like this. How dare someone do this. I grip the edge of the table to stop myself screwing the notes up and hurling them across the room. They are all I have to try and stop this. These are innocent men who have been killed. And what about my tattoo? I move the latest note to the front. Stare at it. There must be an answer here.

It was on top of my handbag. The bag I slid behind the vase last night. Zayn was next to me. I'd been trying to hide the evidence I'd been in his flat. It was someone who was here. Lots of people moved through there last night. There were coats and bags everywhere. And this morning, with Oscar and Danny packing up. The thought of Danny. I close my eyes again, try to picture precisely where everything was. People leaving, waving goodbye last night. Coats. Hugs. Kisses at the door. The final relief when they had all gone. The silence of Danny, already in bed, his eyes closed, pretending to be asleep. It can't be him; I won't even think it. He's not capable of this. Only one person in this relationship is capable of pathological dishonesty. I ignore the thought that Danny lied about Hellie. He's not like Tobi. He's not like Iain. He's not like me.

I think about the suitcases piled up by the door. No one else has been in. Not this morning. It has to be someone who was here last night.

I take the calendar off the fridge, flip it over, and start writing. All the names of everyone who was at the party. All our friends, family, and loved ones. One of them did this. One of them had the opportunity. One of them knows all my secrets.

BETH

There are over fifty people on the list. And I keep remembering more. I sent multiple reminders to Danny over the last two weeks. *Don't forget to invite Cat and Cathy from next door – we don't want any noise complaints!* But he had the master list. He sent the invites out. I could call him and just ask him to forward his sent emails over to me, but he's driving. And I'd have to come up with a decent reason I want it. Sending a thank you email? But he will already have done that. He sends the thank you cards from Oscar after Christmas and his birthday. He knows the names of his best friends at school. The names of their mums. Who has a nut allergy. Who is gluten-intolerant. He knows what to say at coffee mornings, at the Strawberry Fayre, at parents' evening. He knows how to make me feel guilty. Even though I'm the main breadwinner who's been financially carrying three people for six years. The one who, two months ago, found one of our nanny's bright pink thongs stuffed down the seat in the car I paid for. Who reasoned my way out of it at the time. Told myself Hellie had borrowed the car for her tryst. That it had been someone else – not my Danny – with her. But I'm the one who got drunk and revenge kissed my boss. I didn't want to face up to what those knickers meant. That my lies had driven my husband into the arms of another woman. But I couldn't ignore last night. Danny and Hellie in our bedroom – close in the way those who are intimate are. There was no stuffing the knickers back, pretending I hadn't seen them this time. Pretending they weren't real like I pretended Lily wasn't. I put the phone down before I even dial. Hellie might answer. I can no longer keep pretending everything is fine.

I stare at the cut-out letters again. They are my handwriting. But where have they come from? Several look like they were written in fountain pen. The letters fatter, as the ink swelled away from my pressure. But I don't use a fountain pen. Has someone copied my writing? Is this a trick? Computer-replicated? Or am I imagining that it is my writing? I keep returning to that thought – that somehow, I am fabricating all this in my mind. That the pressure I've put myself under – living a different life, lying every day – has made me crack. Constant hyper-vigilance making me create my own threat? Making me see things that aren't there. But it's not made up, it's not imagined. I shift the notes round on the table, turning them by ninety degrees. Looking for a clue. Where they've used whole words, or part of words you can clearly see it's my writing. Though some of the g's are excessively curly, like I used to do them when ...

Oh my God.

Like I used to write when I was at school.

They are written with a fountain pen – because we used to use them. We were made to. Or certainly encouraged. I remember the cartridges, small blue cylinders with that tiny ball in the top. The stains on my fingers. On the cuffs of my shirt. I remember the scratch and flick of the nib under pressure, the tension in that awful scratching sound. I never had the beautiful calligraphy down; it was a fight between me and those pens. I remember the hard pressure of plastic against my fingers. Now I use cushioned rollerballs. University was a time of freebie ballpoints handed out at Freshers' Week and typed essays. But that means this writing – my writing – is old. It's twenty, no, twenty-five years old, maybe older. Where has it come from? A letter? I used to have a pen pal. A German girl. Could it be her? Could she be doing this? Tobi works in Berlin. Could she know him? He has a starring role in most stories. That weird blog was written about him at uni. Could he have influenced her in some way? I can't even remember her name. Why would she remember me? And even if she did, how would she know about Mickey, Kareem, Phil and Wade? And why would she care? I read an article in the Sunday papers once about personality disorders. How a perceived slight from decades ago could consume people. But I can't really suspect the nameless twelve-year-old I used to write to about my holidays.

Where else could someone get a sample of my old handwriting? I doubt the school keeps copies of coursework from twenty years ago. I threw all that stuff out when Beth was spawned. I'm a strict fan of keeping our home a minimalist Marie Kondo approved space. Painfully aware that darkness may gather and hide in the detritus of life.

Oh my God.

How could I have been so stupid? I grab for my phone, flick to Instagram, scroll frantically through the photos. The ones of Danny and my clasped hands for our anniversary last year, the ones I posted for Oscar's birthday, the one of the three of us at the park. My feed is populated with other people, other magical moments. If I do appear, I'm always turned away from the lens, curling into Danny, holding Oscar up in front of me, my red hair a curtain obscuring half my face, an arty crop of half my smile. It's easy to say you don't like photos of yourself when you're a woman. And all in case of the slight chance someone googled my image, recognised it from before. Lily stood full in the bright lights of scrutiny, but Beth was born in the shadows. But I grew complacent. The more distance that grew between me and Lily, the less I thought anyone would spy the truth. I was wrong. Someone was watching all this time. And there it is. January, when I was still doing new year, new me.

I've got my Marie-Kondo on – feels great to clear out all the junk.

The photo of a box of brightly coloured papers to be recycled, artfully arranged next to one of the trees that grow through squares cut in the pavement outside: a contrast with a little spot of nature (no identifying signs of our house or street). In the boxes are the old papers I'd stashed in Mum's loft when Danny and I had moved in together. A forgotten timebomb of Lily's life. When I was creating Beth, I had ditched all the old university notes, anything with Lily's name on it. But a few sentimental things had survived. Things I must have felt were important after the incident. I remember wanting to hold on to something that suggested I was once good, once worthy of love. I needed that. The lyrics of a song Mickey had written for me. The cinema stub from mine and Tobi's first official date.

Mum found the box when she'd been retrieving the Christmas decorations, and discretely handed it to me. In case there was anything I still wanted to keep. But the echoes of any emotion these precious artefacts had once held, had been obliterated by the strength of love I felt for Danny and Oscar. They were my entire heart now. After I'd leafed through a version of me I no longer recognised, I cleared it all out. Including . . . It's like the train ploughing towards me hits, and I too am flying through the air. Including my old journal. I'd even put it at the top – feeling the red cover played nicely against the tiny green shrubs round the tree.

My journal. I remember being in my room at my parents' house, reading about the practice in the pages of a magazine, probably *More* or *Just Seventeen*. An overblown romanticised suggestion to faithfully record the details of my love affairs. And I'd done it. Returning to the same journal throughout my teen years, through my twenties, into my thirties. Right up until I met Danny. My book of love. Then I'd barely read it before I put it out with the rest of the junk. I felt divorced from the idealised young woman who had tried to reframe every rough fingering, every lack of orgasm, every emotional sleight, to make her life sound like the movies. Reacquainting myself with her thoughts just showed me how she'd re-cast herself through the male gaze. Self-objectifying, turning herself into the adored, glittering prize that the leading man – Mickey, Kareem, Phil, even Wade – won as the end credits rolled. Long before Beth was conceived in blood and screams, I'd been trained to rewrite myself to fit others' narratives. To fit others' ideals. Even in a space that was supposed to be all mine.

My journal was supposed to be discovered by my grandchildren, so they could read what a wonderful life I'd lived. What adventures I had had. The irony never struck me that I only ever recorded my interactions with men, as if I only existed through my relationships with them. Even after the incident, I had still returned to the well-trodden path of male validation. Desperate to make me feel whole. It wasn't until I, Beth, looked at it this year, that I saw so clearly the record I'd kept was just another false version of me I'd created to survive. From the safety of the mundanity of being a parent, a mother, a wife, I knew I didn't need it anymore. Or I thought I didn't.

I pull one of the scraps of paper towards me. Those lines. It could be. But why? Who would take that?

I press to call Danny before I know what I'm doing. Fury and panic swirling in me. It rings. And rings again. They will still be on the road. Why hasn't he got his handsfree on? Why hasn't he got the sound turned on? Or is he ignoring me: he, and Hellie and Oscar, playing at happy families. My happy family. His voicemail message cuts in, the sound of him so calm, so normal, making me feel worse. 'Hey, just calling about that stuff I cleared out earlier this year – remember? When we took those bags to the charity shop? There was a box of papers, we put them out with the recycling? Do you remember – did you take any of it anywhere else? I need to know. Call me. As soon as you get this.' And I ring off. Battling with the blood that is rushing through my eardrums, through my veins, carrying anxiety and fear and stress and anger in every direction within me. I took the old clothes to the charity store, shared that to my Stories. Danny carried the box of papers out with the recycling. I took the photo of it next to the snowdrops round the base of the tree. And included the tag: *#SpringCleaning.* Cute. I was pleased with the Instagram post. Then forgot about it. I put the notebook on the top. We left it outside where anyone could pick it up. And someone did. Someone took my journal.

I stare at my Instagram, an uncomfortable prickle tracing over my skin. I have over two thousand followers. That tiny thrill breaking through, even now. That buzz of knowing these strangers are interested in what I'm doing. I click onto the list, scrolling through. Some names and faces I know, but many, hundreds, I don't. The profile pictures smaller than on Facebook, the ability to follow anyone regardless of whether they follow you, Instagram is less about friends, and more about people. My people. But I don't know them. Even those with names I recognise could be imposters, stand-ins, fakes. I look over my shoulder. As if someone could be here now, watching. It's insanity. I'm alone. And yet . . . And yet notes kept showing up in my handbag, notes cut from my handwriting, written in a pen I haven't used for twenty years.

I pinch the image on Instagram, and the box zooms in, expands, like a funhouse mirror, so the red notebook fills the screen. The word journal clear on the top. *Idiot.* After everything I had done to hide my former life, to hide myself, one stupid box from my mum's loft exposed me. The past always catches up with you, yes. But I brought it here. I carried the danger. I pulled it to the top of the pile. I advertised its existence online. Danny could've looked at it. Anyone could have. My next post after that? A close up of Danny and my hands clasped, I'd written it was going to be our tenth wedding anniversary this year. In truth, I'd posted it after we'd rowed about money. Wanting to assure myself, and the world, that we were still the perfectly happy married couple. I still tell myself I need Instagram, some social media presence, for work. That it's part of the BethT brand. But it's as much for my own validation as anything. *Pride goeth before destruction, and a haughty spirit before a fall.* This all started after that post. The first Note arrived that week. Someone took my journal and they've weaponised my own false words against me. They've killed people, and it's all my fault.

BETH

I need to think about this calmly. My journal? Lily's journal. If I hadn't got rid of it. If I hadn't put it online. Don't spiral. Start from the beginning. I need to write down everything I know. I have to narrow down that list from the party. I fetch a lined pad from my study, a proper pen. Force myself to sit at the kitchen table and think.

1. Whoever is doing this knows where I live.

I'm registered to vote, but I opted out of the open register. We're also ex-directory. My Instagram account is BethT. Tightly controlled, so there are no front on images of me. Though age is working for me as the years tick by, further erasing Lily from my face. I search 'Beth Taylor in Hackney' online, and can't find myself. Only someone with the same name, listed on 192.com people search who has an age guide of 60-64. Creepily, it only takes registering and purchasing some credits to see the woman's full address and telephone number. But, not mine. I'm not there. There's no way some random stranger could just find my home address (I made sure of that when I realised how easy it was to keep track of Anna years ago). Someone would have to know where I lived, which narrows the options.

Similarly, if someone picked up the journal by chance outside and formed some kind of fixation on me . . . I swallow the rising acid in my throat. Well they wouldn't be able to find out who lived here that easily. Unless they went through our rubbish? But Danny shreds all our correspondence. Danny could have read the journal, I just left it outside – the thought rises and threatens to drown me. I push Lily down, down, down.

2. Whoever is doing this knows where I work.

This information is much easier to find out. A quick google of my name and PR, and you find Trench PR. There's my photo, alongside those of my colleagues. And though the company has an online contact form, and doesn't list the office address on our website, it takes less than a minute to find on Google. Which means anyone could find me via work. They could have followed me from there, back here. There have been points over the last few weeks where I felt like someone was watching me. Just a prickling sensation. I'd dismissed it as paranoia, but what if I was right? I shudder.

3. Whoever is doing this knows I have a tattoo of angel wings.

I'm pretty sure I never wrote about my tattoo in my love journal. Why would I? I've always been embarrassed about it. The guy who did it wasn't very good, and it's so cheesy. Once I got into a relationship with Danny, I was relieved to let my pubic hair grow over it. Not to have to cringe each time I got out the shower and caught sight of it in the mirror. That didn't fit my rose-tinted reframing of my love life. The actress who played me on the big screen would not have a tacky tattoo.

I unzip my jeans, pull my knickers aside and search through the hair. I turn on my iPhone torch and shine it at myself. It takes time to find the faded black whispery lines underneath my pubes. Even a nurse doing my smear test wouldn't see it. So, it has to be someone who has got up close and personal with me. Which narrows those who know about the tattoo to:

Jessica Meadows (she got the same tattoo at the same time).
Mickey – dead.
Kareem – dead.
Phil – dead.
Wade (if he was sober enough to notice) – dead.
Tobi.
Iain – dead too.
Danny.
Zayn.

Zayn hasn't seen my tattoo, but aside from Danny, he's the closest to me. He knows everything. *Four – Danny was the fifth*. Okay, maybe not everything. But he knows a lot. I stare at my mobile. I want to call him. To hear his voice. His laugh. To hear him say this is batshit. A smile plays on my lips – I realise I've been frowning till now. But I can't speak to him. Not until I know who is doing this. I can't let him hear doubt in my voice, or worse: see it in my face. He'd know straight away that something was wrong. I told him about Mickey and Kareem, and lied about going to the police. And then I told him everything was fine – there was nothing to worry about. I lied. Again. But it won't seriously be him. It can't be. It's just unfortunate that he's on this list. It's unfortunate that any of them are. The jagged notepad page I found in his room is a coincidence.

A few years back I had to fill out an insurance form for a work trip with Rob. We had to list any identifying marks that were on our bodies. I remember me saying about the tattoo, when he joked about having a third nipple. I smile as I think of him paraphrasing the Friends' joke, calling it a 'nubbin', before I realise this means Rob should be on the list too. Just one more time the boundaries between Rob and me were blurred. I shouldn't have told someone I work for about something which feels like a dirty secret to me. And then I remember. Oh no. The morning after I heard about Kareem, when I was hungover. I met Matt at Unity. I told him about my tattoo. How could I have been so stupid? I still don't know why I did it. He just sort of expected it, and I couldn't let a client down. Christ. And he knows where I live. He sent those flowers. I still don't know how he got my address. I've just proved it's difficult to find online. Did he follow me? Images of a shadowy figure with his face emerging from a dark alleyway flash through my mind. Matt on a crowded tube platform staring at the back of Wade. He's always made me feel uncomfortable. There's something not right about him. There's something not right about anybody who sells AI sex dolls.

I blink as images of hanging naked women flash before my eyes. It could be him.

Before I know what I'm doing I'm calling Matt's number. I want to confront him. Ask him if he's doing this. But the phone clicks straight through to voicemail.

'Hi! You've reached Matt at Unity, I'm afraid I'm away for a couple of days due to a family emergency. If you need anything please contact my office, or my publicist on—'

I hang up. I look over my shoulder, as if he'll be standing in the doorway behind me. His message says he's away. What would I have said if he'd picked up? Oh hey, just wondering how you got my address, and if you'd killed any of my ex-boyfriends recently? Blood is smashing about my ears, unbalancing me. He'll know I called him. But I'm safe. I double locked everything. All the windows. All the doors. I triple checked. Unless someone is inside already. Okay. *Stop*. I'm just torturing myself now. There is no one in the house. Not now anyway. The fine hairs on my forearms rise.

I slide the list away from me, as if I might gain a new perspective with distance. Clear the phlegm that's forming in the back of my throat. What if it's not Matt? He could just be an innocent oddball with a penchant for life-like sex dolls. Could it be Tobi? I can't see how he would know where I lived? Or why he would care after the way he spoke to me. Unless he got my address the same way as Matt did? A way I haven't worked out yet. But he's in Germany. He made it pretty clear he's still a self-obsessed arse on the phone. Why and how could he be doing this? He can't be in two countries at once. He made it apparent he doesn't give a fig about me. I score through his name.

What about Jessica? Why would she be doing this? It doesn't feel right. We lost contact pretty much as soon as we headed off for university. It was a right time, right place friendship. Nothing more. We didn't ever really have much in common except Mickey. Now I think about it, I'm surprised she wasn't at the memorial. But then she was going to join the RAF. They were paying her uni fees. Presumably she's stationed in another country. Or they lost touch too.

I tap her name into Google. We used to tease her when we were younger that it sounded like a porn star name. Not that I think she cared. That clever brain of hers always had her believing she was above everyone else. I remember when I'd just started going out with Mickey and she asked if I watched *The Day Today*? It wasn't the kind of thing my parents, neither of whom went to university, watched. So, I hadn't seen it. God knows if in my teenage angst I made a flippant reply in the negative, but I can still hear her retort: *You do have to be intelligent to find satire funny*. I never left myself open to be called stupid again. I guess I should thank her, really. She taught me a formative lesson. How to keep up appearances. The building blocks of people-pleasing that engineered Beth.

I add in Sevenoaks and RAF to the search bar and press return. The first few results are of people with similar names, but clearly not her. An accountant in their fifties. A woman, again of the wrong age, who was recorded speaking at a county council meeting. And then a link to the *Kent Advertiser*. An archive article, presumably uploaded when they digitised their back catalogue.

Oh no. How sad.

20th June 1999. Trainee Officer Killed in Sevenoaks Crash. Local student, Jessica Meadows, 19, was killed and a further passenger injured in a road traffic accident on the Tonbridge Road on Tuesday night. Police were called at 11.47 p.m. Tuesday to an incident involving a silver Peugeot 206. An ambulance and a rapid response vehicle were also sent to the scene. Despite their best efforts, Jessica Meadows, a talented local student, was pronounced dead at the scene. A 22-year-old male passenger was taken to hospital and treated for non-life-threatening injuries.

Less than a year after I must have last seen her. When I was in my first year at uni. And I never knew. All these years... This was before Facebook. Mickey and I had gone our separate ways, so that web of digital connections that meant I heard about Kareem within hours just wasn't there. Poor Jessica. She was so young. I always imagined she went to be something important in the RAF, slightly looking down on those beneath her. If I thought of her at all. I rest my palm on my tattoo. Think of laughter lighting her gawky face with beauty, as she gripped a pint of cider in a dark pub. One more loss from the past.

I take a moment, but not long. It's been twenty years since I last saw Jessica. And we were never close. In fact, I'm not sure either of us really liked the other. We just happened to move in the same circles for a few brief years. I'm very sorry for her friends, her poor parents, but I don't feel like I did when I heard about Mickey. That pain is raw. Fresh. Happening now. And it is ongoing. Jessica may have known about my tattoo, but she can't be the one behind this – so she is off the list.

Which leaves...

This can't be right. It just can't. There has to be another explanation? Perhaps Tobi should be on the list, but no, I discounted him. This is just coincidence. Horrible awful coincidence. I force my arm to move, to circle the names that fit all three criteria: those who know I have an angel wings tattoo, those who know where I work, and those who know where I live. Four names are left ringed in angry, shaky red:

Matt.
Rob.
Danny.
Zayn.

My four suspects.

Of course, people I love know those three things about me. Danny and Zayn are the closest to me. They know everything

I have allowed them to know. Did they find out about Lily? The incident? *Slut. Liar. Dripping red spray paint.* The thought is horrifying, still now. It must be coincidence they are on this list. It can't be them actually doing this. My pen hangs over their names, ready to cross them out. But then images, memories come to mind. Since the incident I've survived by sensing danger – did I ignore my own instincts?

Hellie stepping away from Danny. The rage in Danny's eyes when he looks at me. Rob intensely watching me across the office. Zayn looking away when answering a question, his voice strained. The face of the shadowy figure emerging from the alleyway flicks between Zayn, Danny, Rob.

I turn the list face-down.

This is a process of elimination. A scientific exercise. I just have to prove what I already know: that it's not any of the people I care for most. A hole empties in my chest. That's all. Then this feeling will stop. Danny stood behind Wade. Rob's eyes narrowing as he stares at Wade's back. Zayn's hands thrusting forwards. I just have to prove it can't be any of them.

I take out four fresh sheets of paper. In clear capitals I write one name on each of the pieces of paper. In the lounge I take down our framed poster from the David Hockney exhibition, resting it against the wall. In its place I Blu Tack, equally spaced, the names of my four suspects. Or, the names of the four people it could be. I print out and add photos. One for each. On another piece of paper, I write the three things I know they all have knowledge of to date, in large writing, and pin that up as well. To the other side I add the notes that have been sent to me.

Pushing the coffee table back, I create room to pace and stare at everything I know. It's just a set of un-emotive facts I need to turn into a story. That I need to piece together into a recognisable whole. Like I do at work. Find the hook among the tangled weeds.

Matt from Unity is a stranger. This all started happening after I met him. He knows where I work. He knows where I live. He knows about my tattoo. He has to be the one doing this. Has to be. Because I can't bear the alternative. One of the notes detaches from the wall and drifts down. If only I hadn't written that stupid journal. If only I'd destroyed it years ago. I stare at the name of my husband scratched in red biro. If Danny had disposed of it properly, I wouldn't have to be doing this. I wouldn't be staring at his name, at Zayn's, at Rob's, on our bloody living room wall. Four people wouldn't have been killed.

My phone rings. I don't want to think about why Danny didn't answer before, about what he may have been doing.

I snap it on. 'Where are you?'

'I was about to ask you the same question,' Rob's cool voice slices me like a knife. I glance at his name.

'I thought you were Danny.' I look at the clock. How has it got so late?

'Apparently not for the first time,' his voice sounds cruel, cold. Business-mode.

Guilt crawls over me. I told him I had no feelings for him. Now I have him on a list as a possible suspected serial killer? 'Rob, I—'

'Beth, is there a reason you are over two hours late into work?'

My insides twisted. He sounds distant. Is that normal? Yes, he's always been able to compartmentalise. I haven't got time for his alpha male bullshit today, though. Not on top of this. 'I – something has happened.'

'Something has happened to Beth? Well why didn't you say? That makes it all fine then.' I blink at the sarcasm in his voice.

I messed with his one true love: his work. I push my hair back off my face. Perhaps I should tell him about this? I glance at his name on the wall. 'I thought you were out with clients today?'

'Things change. I'm sure you understand,' he says bluntly.

I can't deal with this right now. I massage my temples with my fingers. 'Okay. I'll be there—'

'You will be here when I tell you to be here, because I pay you,' he snaps.

'Because you pay me?' Like a prostitute. Heat swarms up my neck.

'I don't care what has happened between us – I will not allow you to make a fool of me like this.'

Make a fool of me? What the hell? 'I am not—'

'You are my employee, Beth. You are under contract. You have contracted hours. You will be here when I say you will be here.'

'When you say?!' How dare he. After everything. There's silence on the other end. 'Rob?' He's hung up! The childish bastard. I try to slow my breathing. I've had enough of the men in my life failing me. Where's the guy who kissed me? Who touched me? Held me? I feel the horribly familiar sweep of nausea as I stare at his name on the wall.

He was like a stranger.

BETH

'What the hell do you mean – hanging up on me?'

Rob looks startled as I slam into his office. I feel the chatter of the rest of the company flinch, before they crane to no doubt hear what the hell is going on.

The shock on his face dissolves into his preferred sanguine look. He rises, walks towards me, and for a moment I think he's going to touch me, push me, hurt me in some way. The face looming out of the shadows. I move aside, wrapping my arms round myself. But he simply side steps me, and closes the glass door to his office. Sealing off the rest of the world. I don't relax. Anger powered me here. Anger and fear, a curdled smoothie I can still taste on my tongue.

Rob returns to his desk. 'Won't you sit down, Bethy?' Here we go with the *Bethy* crap again. He signals at the chair opposite him.

I ignore him. 'Is this some kind of punishment, because of us . . .' I glance across the office, but everyone seems to have returned their attention back to work. Probably dismissing my actions as only to be expected in what feels like, and almost certainly looks like, increasingly erratic behaviour. 'Because I told you no?' Was it really only twenty-five days ago I heard about Mickey? Only two weeks since I was sat at my desk reeling with shock from Kareem's death? With each new blow the life Beth created grows more precarious. I hate making a scene like this. The pieces of my life are swirling round me like confetti, impossible to grab hold of. Impossible to put back together. It reminds me of those last awful days of Lily. Back in Sevenoaks there was nowhere to hide from the horror. The words printed in the newspaper;

the slurs uttered in the street. The graffiti on Mum's house, drenched in recriminatory red. *Killer. Slut.* They destroyed me for an accident. I've already been hounded out of one life, and now it's happening again.

'This has nothing to do with *us*.' Rob's snidely amused tone drags me back to the present.

Could he have found out about Lily? About the festering core that has infected my every moment? I sit. I let my handbag slide to the floor. A huge wave of tiredness hits me, and I'm dully aware this is the aftermath of shock. Adrenaline draining away. Cortisol waning. My limbs burn as if I've been in the gym. But there's no post-workout buzz. I feel sore, heavy. I want to lie down, let myself drain away into the ground.

'Are you all right?' Rob is up out his chair. I'm dimly aware I must look terrible. I'm shaking. When did I start shaking? I watch my hands vibrate with fascination, as if they are not part of me.

'Christ,' Rob continues. 'Bethy, what's wrong? Talk to me? I shouldn't have spoken to you like that, I'm sorry. Do you need water?' He opens the door. 'Chloe, get me a jug of water. And tea. Have we got any biscuits?'

His words absurdly making me think of picnics and green outside spaces – a tea party in the sunshine. Whoever has that journal knows. They know it all. The ugly teenage truths. The inner doubts. The fears. The dreams. What Lily did. It's as if someone has peeled me open and looked inside my mind. I am horribly exposed. I'd written about everything. Everything. My knees lock tightly together. I feel my toes claw at the bottom of my shoes. I want to roll in on myself. Someone has read that. How could I have been so stupid? I'd just left it out where anyone could find it, because I was too busy to dispose of my own secrets. I invited the monster back in. I make bad things happen. I am dangerous to be around.

Rob closes the blinds, so the rest of the office can't see in. 'Bethy?' He says softly, kneeling in front of me, stilling my shaking hands. 'What's happened? Is it Danny, did you tell him? Has he hurt you?'

I can't tell Danny, because he doesn't know the truth. Can't tell him he married a liar. Can't pull the rug from under our teetering marriage. From under Oscar's world.

'If he's hurt you, I'll kill him,' Rob says.

I shake my head.

'Look, you can move in with me,' Rob says. 'We can go get your stuff now. Or just buy you new things. I'll sort this out.'

His words reach me through the vibrations. Their meaning dripping into rigid stalactites in my sore body. 'Someone is killing my ex-boyfriends.'

'What?' Rob's eyebrows pinch together.

'My exes. My ex-lovers. People I've slept with. Someone is killing them,' I pull my hands away from his, stand up, start to pace. I have to walk and talk.

'What?'

'There's a diary. A journal. Something I used to keep. One of those things women's magazines tell you to do – write about your relationships, to help you understand them. You know, like that bit in *Mamma Mia!* where she finds her mum's old diary and tries to work out which of the three men her mum slept with is her father. The dot, dot, dot bit?'

Rob looks like I'm insane.

Of course, he hasn't seen *Mamma Mia!*. 'That's not important. But I only just figured it out. That someone has this journal – my journal – cause they are sending me letters cut from it. Look,' I pull the notes from my handbag, their cut words and letters from my journal rustle like leaves stuck to the pavement.

There's a gong of a knock on the glass door from Chloe. 'Here you go,' she says, pushing the door open with her hip. Her hands full with a tray of water and biscuits on a plate. She looks curiously at me.

'Thanks,' I manage.

'Yes,' Rob says, as if he's only just noticed her. 'Thank you, Beth has had a—'

'Bit of a cough.' I cut him off. I'd like to take a glass of water to prove my point, but I don't trust my treacherous hands. 'Water is great. Just what I needed.' I keep the notes down at my side, but Chloe still looks towards them. I turn as if I'm reading something important laid out on Rob's desk.

'Yes, yes,' says Rob. 'Thank you, Chloe. I'll take it from here.' He takes the clinking tray from her, and ushers her back out the door.

It feels good to say it. Getting the words out there makes it clearer in my mind. I keep a journal of all my sexual experiences. Or I used to. I stopped years ago. Before Danny and I got married. And like an idiot I posted a photo of that journal saying I was going to throw it out. Then someone took it. It's the only thing that makes sense. No one else knows precisely who I have slept with. Or how many people. And the notes – cut from the same journal – just prove it. That is why the lined paper felt familiar. It was. Someone has this and they are using it against me. They are finding and killing all the people I have slept with. 'I should have shredded it.'

'Beth,' Rob's voice is soft, but this time there is real anxiety there. I see it etched on his face: the same look of trepidation my mum had, as I stepped from the back of the police car, in my custody tracksuit, clutching the belongings they'd let me keep in a plastic evidence bag. *What have you done?* 'I shouldn't have shouted at you Bethy, that wasn't fair of me. It's obviously upset you—'

'I don't care about that. I know it sounds crazy.' A half-laugh rises to my lips and I wonder if this is what hysteria feels like? 'It is crazy. But look – I have proof.' I place the notes out on his desk.

Cautiously he joins me, peering at the collage of letters and words cut from my own hand.

'These have been arriving over the last few weeks.' It feels both like an age since the first note arrived, and also mere moments since it decimated my life. That pinprick sharp point in time where I assumed it was a direct marketing campaign to be recycled, and when I read the first words. Only a week after I posted the photo of the journal online. How could past me have been so foolish? But I know the answer: I was distracted. Hellie's knickers in the car, the stupid drunken revenge snog with Rob. It was like I wanted to exert control over my life again, put a positive spin on it all: I posted the picture as proof of my own productivity. *Look at me, I have cleaned out my house, I have the perfect, tidy, minimalist life!* I wanted the validation of praise. I needed people to like the woman I'd made myself into, to reinforce that choice.

'They're messages, see?' I rearrange the two halves into the 'dead man walking' notes for Rob. 'This half came after Mickey, my first boyfriend, was killed. And the second half after Kareem, my next boyfriend, was knocked down in a hit-and-run.'

'But these are just scraps of paper, sweetheart? Just random words, even if they are in your handwriting. Surely this is just some strange joke, or some weirdo who is sending them to you?' Rob fingers one of the pages.

'Four of my exes have died in the last three weeks.' Rob stiffens beside me. 'The first four people I ever slept with.' I pause, thinking of Wade. Not wanting to verbalise it. 'Including a one-night stand that virtually no one knew about. In the same order I slept with them. And this one.' I pushed the final web address note forwards. 'This one is a link to the news story about Wade. The final one. He was the guy who was pushed under the Tube train last night. Minutes after I spoke to him.' I don't draw attention to the mention of the tattoo. My skin prickles. Rob's name is on my suspect list. But I need his help. I can't do this alone.

'That was an accident,' Rob said.

'You don't know that. The CCTV footage makes it look like he was pushed,' I say. 'I think he was murdered. None of these deaths have been solved – two stabbings, a hit-and-run, and now a body under a train.' The enormity of it all bubbles like acid inside me. They are all dead because of me. I need to stop this. I need him to help me.

The colour drains from Rob's face. 'Murder? CCTV footage? Secret notes? Do you know what you sound like? This is insane. You can't possibly think—'

'I didn't, I couldn't, but now I do. I know someone is doing this. They are targeting people I've slept with. People who I wrote about in that journal. I don't know who and I don't know why, but I'm sure.' My voice cracked. 'Horribly sure.'

'There must be some other . . . ' I can see him grappling with what I'm saying. My paltry evidence. I think of the police after the incident, how they wouldn't listen to me, wouldn't believe what I was saying. Of my own fear that somehow this is all in my head. But these notes are real. Tangible things I did not create. They were sent to me. 'Rob,' I try to sound decisive. I have to make him listen. He could be the one doing this. He could help me. 'Robbie – there's only one more person on the list to go before he reaches Danny. Tobi Weinstrasse, and he lives abroad. I think Danny could be next. I can't let anything happen to him – to Oscar's dad.'

BETH

'You have to go to the police.' Rob stares at the CCTV clip on the news site in front of him.

The moment I did they'd see Lily, not Beth. 'They'd never believe me. I don't have anything concrete – nothing that actually ties all these men to me. They would think – like you did – that I'm crazy.'

Rob rubs a hand up and over his face. 'I didn't . . . ' He trails off. 'But this is . . . Do you really think Danny's in danger?' He looks straight at me. And I picture each of the men I've slept with looking at me. Pleading for answers, asking me why? And I don't know what to say. I don't know what to tell them. It's my fault.

'Yes,' I say simply.

'I could go to the police for you?' he says. 'I mean, I'm a successful business owner, they would have to listen to me,' he reasons.

Because he's a man, and I'm just a delusional woman? Perhaps there's truth in that. But the moment they make the connection to Lily, their focus will shift: they will think I've been doing this. 'All I have are the notes,' I say.

'They could fingerprint them? Find out who's doing this.'

'This isn't an episode of CSI. And that would still rely on them taking this seriously. It's still just my word that I slept with all these people. That there's something going on.' He looks at me, and I can't read the expression on his face anymore. 'I mean some people would know – or they'd have a fairly good idea. Mickey and I dated for nearly two years, but others? Who could they ask? The men who have been killed have gone. There's no proof these are my exes. No proof that I slept with them in that order. And these notes – they are all in my handwriting.' The impossibility of it all presses down on me again, a firm pain on my solar plexus.

'We have to try. For Oscar,' Rob already looks different, his stance, his gestures, as if the threat has already altered his molecular structure. Something primal, protective has been triggered. For the first time since this started I don't feel completely alone. But that doesn't change the stark facts.

'I can't. When I was younger – before you knew me – I had some trouble, with the police,' the spectre of Lily fills the room. I've spoken her name for the first time in years, to Wade, to Tobi. It's as if I've called her forth. Let her into the world now.

Rob is staring at me, as if I'm speaking a foreign language. His eyes big, lost like Oscar's after a night terror. Lily hovers there . . . but I can't, even now, even after all this I don't want him to know about her. About me. *Slut. Killer. Liar.* To look at me with disgust. 'I need more – something they can't ignore.' I won't sit by and do nothing any longer. I'm over that. The shock and the tears, and all the reacting. It's not me. I'm going to take control. I've done it before. Lily smiles. 'I'm going to find whoever is doing this, and I'm going to stop them,' I look Rob directly in the eye.

His face looks lined in the dimmed light in here, as if it's aged in the last twenty minutes. The burble of the office, the rest of the world getting on with life, as if everything is fine, just the other side of the glass. 'How?'

'I'm going to fight back.' And as I say it, I feel the renewed sense of purpose. I feel the blizzard of confetti still, and drift to the floor. Now all I need to do is work out how to piece this all together, so that I can see the truth. 'And you can help. There's CCTV cameras in the office,' I say.

'Now wait a second, Beth,' he says.

This is the only way. My only lead. 'There's one in reception – he came to the office to deliver that note. Chloe told me. I can't believe I didn't think of it before.' My excitement makes me pace. This is how I get him. Matt. Whoever it is. This is how I get this all to stop. 'He'll be on camera.' All we have to do is watch the tape. And then this nightmare will be over.

BETH

'This isn't a client pitch, Beth,' Rob sounds exasperated.

'No, it's not,' I snap. 'Someone is doing this to me. To people I care about. And I've had enough of just taking it.' The words are strong, calm. Far from the threatened hysteria of before. They form solid shapes in my mind. Ideas. Plans. 'I'm going to fight.'

'Fight?!' He looks at me as if I've totally lost it now. 'Beth, you're a PR from London, not some superhero. What the hell do you think you can do?'

But I'm not Beth, I'm Lily. I lost everything once and I was strong enough to survive. I can do it again. 'There's some things I could try. I've been thinking about it. Whoever is doing this doesn't know I'm on to them.'

'On to them? Listen to yourself!' He looks aghast. 'This isn't a game. Jesus – if you're right people are dying – you can't just—'

'I'm not imagining this,' I bark. He stares at me as if he can't believe I interrupted him.

'Look, Bethy,' he says, gesturing with his hands, as if talking to an upset child. 'I'm not saying that these people haven't died.'

'Whoever is doing this murdered them.' I cut him off. 'The third note was left in reception. You've seen the others. That's proof.' He raises his eyes as if to say *'Oh yeah, proof'*.

I grab my glass of water. Sip it belligerently, daring him to say more.

Has he always thought of me this way – under-estimated me? Suddenly he doesn't look like the hot guy I first snogged fourteen years ago. He looks old, and a little foolish in his try-hard man child clothes. I can't believe I kissed him. What is wrong with me?

I sit on the chair furthest away. 'If we look at the film on the day that note was left, we'll see who left it. We'll know who is doing this.' He has to see this is the only way forward?

'What did Danny say?' Rob speaks as if he hasn't heard me. 'I notice he's not here.'

'He can't know,' I say quickly. He looks at me, something flickers behind his eyes. I'm glad I didn't confess to Rob about Lily. I've lied to Danny from the start. If I told him this now, if it all came out, after Hellie, after everything I've already sacrificed, it'd be the final straw. Destroy our family. And I can't do that to any of us.

'Surely he's noticed a load of your ex-boyfriends have died over the last two weeks?' Rob sounds incredulous.

I can't confess I haven't told Danny anything, that my own husband doesn't even know who he has really married. 'He only knows about the first one – and that someone else from my school year died.' The lie prickles over my tongue.

Rob whistles. 'And he hasn't realised anyway?'

'I've sent him away. With Oscar. And our nanny. I want them safe. Rob, if I could just look at that CCTV – all this could be over.'

Rob leans forward. 'Bethy, I don't want to upset you,' I stare at him. Not now with the sickly nickname. 'More, I mean. It's just . . . ' His eyes are wide. 'Danny could be involved in this.'

My heart starts thumping. The glass feels brittle in my tightening grip. 'What?'

Rob speeds up, warming to his theme. 'You said the diary thing, your journal – that you threw it out?'

'Recycled it,' I say. The word mundanely cool on my lips in the rising heat of the conversation.

'Whatever – that you got rid of it. Well, surely Danny saw that?'

Danny carried it all out for the bin men. It was on top. Just resting there. 'Anyone could have seen it – I posted a photo of it, and other stuff, on Instagram.' Like an idiot. Inviting this into my life.

'Yes, but don't you see that's a bit of a reach that someone would just happen to identify the journal from a photo online – that they would know what was in it?' He looks at me expectantly.

'Maybe they didn't know. Maybe they took it and just got lucky.' The thought makes me feel sick.

'Maybe,' Rob pushes on. 'But isn't it more likely that someone closer to home, someone you live with, would have known what it was?'

I'm fairly certain I never wrote Lily's name in it, or Beth's. I don't think. I didn't address myself on the page, but I did use Iain's, others. If Danny had opened it, googled those names he could discover Lily within seconds. But I would know if that happened, surely? 'I hadn't used it for years. He wouldn't have even looked twice at it.' I drop my eyes from his, study the knots in the artificial wood floor. 'It was more a thing I did when I was younger.' Though I was still writing in it when I met Danny, when we fell in love. Using it to process my feelings. Doing what was expected of me – journal your thoughts: it's like free therapy. Except therapy is confidential. Why hadn't I burned it?!

'Bethy, you know he has the best motive?'

I jump up, iced water spilling over my fingers. 'Don't be stupid. Danny would never hurt a fly.' I think of the disappointment and hatred burning in Danny's eyes. His name on the wall. Guilt that I would suspect my own husband making me sound defensive. 'You don't know him.' I think of Hellie. Of the distance between us over the last few months. The anger at me that bubbles up during rows. The way he looks at me as if I am to blame for everything. Could he have found out? Does he know? Has he been lying to me all this time, like I've been lying to him? 'He's a good man.'

'It's usually the husband,' Rob says knowingly.

'He's about as far from a murderer as you can get,' my hand shakes as I put the glass down. 'He's kind, loving—'

'So why did you kiss me?' Rob sounds triumphant.

I grab my handbag. Start shoving the notes into it. Try to control my breathing. The air suddenly close, oppressive. 'I'm going to work from home – given everything.'

'Sweetheart,' Rob jumps up, as I wrench open the door. 'Err – Beth?' His voice changing to that of boss, as people outside glance up. 'I'll give you a call later about – err – this project.'

'Let me know if you change your mind about what we discussed?' I don't keep the bitterness from my voice. He could stop this all now.

Chloe smiles at me, looking expectant, but I don't slow. Outside, gusts whip litter along the pavement, defiling the pristine fronts of the flawless corporate offices. I don't stop until I reach the end of the road, and duck down a side alley full of industrial bins. I take big gulps of rancid air. It doesn't matter what I've said. Or what I haven't said. Whoever has that journal knows the truth. And it could be anyone. Rob is right: Danny and Zayn can't be ruled out. And neither can he. They are all on the list.

It could be any one of them.

HIM

I'll admit I'm surprised. I stare at the door, willing her to come back. Slide a finger down my shirt collar, try and loosen it. I did not expect this after last night. I don't think anyone would expect this. Absurdly the *Monty Python* sketch pops into my head: they'd never expect the Spanish Inquisition! I pinch myself. No, not dreaming. This is real. And I didn't have to even play my trump card: Danny's bit of skirt. She's just let him waltz off with her. Right under her nose. It's like leading a lamb to slaughter. I smile. But he'll get what's coming to him.

I cross the room, lift her glass and take a sip of the cool water, pressing my lips carefully against where she rested hers. Then check to remove any lipstick. But she wasn't wearing any today. That rankles. Is she no longer trying for me? No, it is the shock of it all. This nonsense about the journal. But this is it. My chance to get rid of Danny once and for all. Fate has played her right into my hands. It was meant to be. I always land on my feet.

I imagine this is what young soldiers felt before they left for the trenches. A chance to lock down the deal. Because when faced with danger, people realise what is truly important, don't they? I will let her calm down, see sense. And then it will be easy from there. I'll play along with this, keep up the pretence, and then, when she's come to rely on me, it will be easy to move her into mine. Make sure she feels safe.

I lift the receiver, then opt for a text instead. Give her space to see reason. This has rattled her. I will help her calm in the storm. I am her knight in shining armour. I am her saviour. The only one she can really rely on. Victory is so close I can taste it on my lips. Play this right, and I can get the prize. I can have my Bethy.

BETH

Outside, my phone beeps. Danny. Crap. I'd forgotten about the voicemail I left him. I open the message:

> *You're asking about recycling? That's what you want to talk about?*

No kiss. I feel like I did when I was a little girl caught doing something naughty. A hollow sickly feel in my stomach. And I want to fix it. I press call straight away. It rings. And rings. And goes to voicemail. He's only just sent the message. I know he's there. I press call again. Of course I was panicked when I realised we'd – *I'd* – put my personal journal out on the street, advertised its presence to the whole of Instagram. But Danny doesn't know that. Doesn't know it's a literal matter of life and death. And I can't tell him. It rings out again. Dammit. And Hellie is there.

I type out a message:

> *Please pick up – I'm sorry. I love you xx*

It shows as delivered straight away. The little dots appear on the screen showing he's typing a response. Still typing. Then they disappear. Nothing happens. No message. Did he delete it? Change his mind? What was he going to say? I press call again. Come on, just pick up. It goes through to voicemail, I cut it off, try again. If I can just get him to speak to me.

The new message tone bleeps in my ear. Shit.

I need some time to think.

What does that mean? He's away on a bloody holiday with his mistress, that I'm paying for. What more does he need?

But I sent him there. I sent him away for Oscar's sake. To keep him safe. My nose prickles, tears forming in my eyes.

I want to talk to Oscar xx

The dots appear again. And this time the message does arrive:

Hellie will organise a FaceTime.

Hellie?! I could call her and ask her to hand over the phone to Danny, but I can't face the humiliation. How can Danny be so cruel? Oscar's my baby. I should be able to talk to him whenever I want. Everything is spinning out of control. I swipe angrily at my face. Is this it? Is this the end of our marriage? I feel my insides wrench hard. This isn't what I want. This was never what I wanted. I should have confronted Danny when I found out. I should have sacked Hellie. But I'm an expert at looking the other way, pretending everything is fine. Beth's whole creation, my whole life, is a conjuring trick designed to distract people from the ugly truth of Lily. I thought if I just got on with it, Danny would get it out of his system. Every marriage has its challenges. We've been married for ten years. You can't be with the same person for all that time and not expect there to be moments. I thought Hellie was just a moment. And if I acted like I didn't know what was happening, Danny would come back to me. He would see what we have. Had. We're a family. I fought so hard to get here. We're supposed to be together.

But it left me feeling ugly, old, rejected. It left me open to Rob. Just one time. That's what I told myself. I deserved it. Danny had done it so why couldn't I? But as Rob had pulled me onto his lap and I'd felt him stiffen, I freaked out. Pulled away. Made my excuses. I didn't want him, I wanted Danny. I couldn't go through with it. So why am I the one who feels guilty? Why am I the one who feels terrible?

A woman in a raincoat, headphones on, nearly clips me. I'm almost at Liverpool Street. People moving all around me, past me, leaving me behind. Carrying on with their lives while mine dissolves in the rain.

I squeeze the bag on my shoulder, the notes inside. Is that what this is? Me falling apart? Is this some crazy manifestation of my own guilt? Calling forth the universe to punish me for all the lies I've told. I deserve it. I deserve it all. I lied to Danny. I lied to Oscar. I lied to everyone. Is this vengeance for what I did to Lily? What I did to Anna?

My phone beeps, and I scrabble quickly in case it's Danny. Instead, I see a message from Rob:

I'll get a copy of the CCTV.

He's going to help. We're going to find out who is doing this. Proof I can take to the police to show I didn't send these notes myself. That they are tangible threats linked to four deaths. That I'm no longer Lily. They will listen to Beth, to me, they'll have to. It's finally going to be over.

Then I think of the four names pinned to the wall at home: Matt, Rob, Zayn, Danny. My suspects. Am I ready for the truth?

BETH – TWO DAYS AFTER THE PARTY

The balls of my feet sting as they slap against the wet ground. Run. I glance back. He's there. I tug at my insufficient T-shirt, trying to hold the hem down over my knickers, the material flimsy against my naked breasts. I should have slept in my clothes. I glance again. He's closer. Hood up, face covered. Branches grab at me. I twist. Stumble. Run. Where's my phone? Lost. Gone. I try to call for help but my voice has been strangled from me. Must get to a crowded area. Must get help. I can see shapes up ahead. People! The muscles in my legs howl. I try to shout again. Nothing. I must reach them. Why won't they turn? Why won't they help? Their backs face me in rejection. Please. I desperately reach for the shoulder of a woman, to alert her. The sex doll swings on its hook to face me, the fake flesh like cold play dough in my hand. Its mouth a grotesque scream of pleasure. They aren't people – they're all dolls. Hanging in the trees. Naked breasts. Legs bent back. Gaping genitalia. Dead glass eyes. It's a trap. And finally, my scream comes . . .

The shrill doorbell tears into my dream, wrenching me awake by an angry beating heart. Is it him? I reach next to me for Danny before remembering he's not here. *And not talking to me.* But at least he's safe. I hope. My heart thumping, still stuck in my nightmare, I untangle myself from the duvet. It's damp to the touch. I pull yesterday's jeans from the floor, dragging them over my feet, the zip scratching at my leg. My phone plugged in is devoid of messages. No one has called in the night. No one has tried to contact me since Rob sent that text saying he'd help.

I need to see who delivers the note to the office on the CCTV. But as I hurry into a jumper the same thoughts run through my mind. Is it a ploy? Is it Rob? He was at my house. At work. My mind spins, whirls, thinks of the papers downstairs pinned to the wall. The names. My suspects. The doorbell sounds again. Insistent. *The Postman Always Rings Twice.* The title of the film comes to my mind, almost comically – and then I remember the plot. About an affair. And murder. And fate getting her revenge.

I run down the stairs; the dark shape of a man visible through the frosted glass panel in the front door. I grab the heavy bottomed vase from the hallway table, weighing it in my hand. My heart still drumming the warning from my dream. The bare skin of my feet soaking in the cold from the hallway tiles. He knows where I live. He's killing everyone I've ever cared about. Wiping out my past one piece at a time. The chain is still on the door from last night, I don't remove it before opening the door a crack. Ready to push it closed if he tries to force it.

It's an Amazon delivery driver. A huge box in his hands. What I ordered last night. The second part of my plan. Relief washes over me, leaving me foolish. I have to unhook the chain. 'Hang on!' I call. Closing the door and sliding it across. I reopen it and take the box. It's heavy, reassuring. I go to smile but he's already on his way. I'm pretty sure they're paid by the number of items they distribute. An endless racing Hermes who can never deliver all his warnings in time.

I lock the door carefully behind me and carry my treasure into the kitchen. I grab a penknife from the drawer and slice through the black tape. Inside are multiple boxes. From under the stairs I grab our set of screwdrivers, and a drill. Both are dusty. Danny is not very practically minded when it comes to DIY, and I haven't got the time. It's easier to hire a handyman to come in and do the odd jobs. But this won't wait. And I don't want anyone else to know what I'm up to.

The FaceTime ringtone on my phone sounds over the drill. Hellie calling – connect? My heart leaps into my mouth. Oscar. I pick up the phone, and move quickly away from the window, and into the hall. Nothing incriminating in the background. Press accept.

Oscar's face fills the screen.

'Darling! You okay?'

'Hi Mummy!' he calls, the camera zooming towards his mouth and nose.

I can't help but laugh. It feels alien in my body.

'What you up to, gorgeous boy?' I sit on the bottom of the stairs, cradling the phone.

'So, guess what?' he starts with his favourite phrase at the moment. My whole body aches for him. 'We went to the pond on the common. And the ponies were there. The grey one is the best. But you can't stroke them. And we didn't bring my Christmas book,' his face appears fully on the screen and he looks away, as if the Blyton book he got for Christmas might appear.

'Oh, that's a shame, but I can bring it with me when I join you guys.' Is that still going to happen? I engineered this whole trip to keep Danny and Oscar safe, but also to help save our marriage, our family. But it feels like that's got further away, not closer. But I have to believe there's still hope. That we can find our way back from this place. I force myself to smile as I say, 'Then we can read it together. How's that?'

This isn't fair on Oscar. This isn't fair on me. My family are hours away. Am I only getting what I deserve? Regardless of everything else, all the lies, me and Danny, all of it: Oscar is an innocent.

Oscar starts to pick at something on the bottom of his trainer, talking in little words to himself, and mostly giving me a perfect view of his ear. My heart aches afresh at the attention span of six year olds. Soon he won't need me at all.

'Is Daddy there?' I ask tentatively. Guilt washing over me straight away. Who uses their child to reach their husband who is ignoring them? When did things get so grubby?

'Daddy's not here,' says Oscar without ceasing his excavation of his shoe.

'What?'

I hear Hellie's voice in the background. The rustle of a hand over the microphone, as the camera tips and spins in a sickening blur. Snatches of Oscar's voice. A pair of socked feet walking across the stone floor of the cottage we had such a wonderful holiday in. Then the camera steadies, as Hellie's face appears, as she balances the phone on the kitchen side. The top of her wholesome green cable knit jumper visible. No Oscar.

I hate her at this moment. With her flawless twenty-something skin and her out-of-bed casual bun. With her fresh-faced beauty that doesn't require expensive haircuts, or make-up, or fillers. With her slender waist. She has my little boy. My husband. She is in one of our special places. Even though I sent them there. Even though there was no choice.

'Beth?'

'Hi Hellie,' I manage.

I can't believe Danny would use our child's nanny rather than speak to me directly.

'Erm,' she looks over her shoulder, drops her voice. 'Danny's not here,' she says.

He's gone out rather than talk to me. I imagine him sitting in another room, out of sight, laughing at how stupid I've been. 'Look, when he gets back, can you get him to call me?' I say coldly.

'No, I mean he's not staying here.' She looks down, unable to make eye contact, even through the screen.

'What?' Ice trickles over my skin. 'What do you mean he's not staying there?'

She clears her throat. 'He said he needed some time alone. So, he dropped me and Oscar here, and then . . . Well he went to stay somewhere else.'

Shame squeezes me like a sponge. This young girl who... Our nanny.... This young girl is telling me where my husband is. 'Where is he?'

'I don't know.' She looks miserable. 'I didn't know if I should tell you.'

'Of course you should,' I snap. How could Danny just go off like this, and not tell me? He just left Oscar without saying anything.

'I'm sorry,' Hellie says miserably. 'I really am, Beth.' Her voice waivers, like she's close to crying.

'Right. Okay. Well don't get upset.' I will kill him. 'You and Oscar are there, that's good. Did he leave you the car? What about food?'

Hellie makes a visible effort to pull herself together. 'No. But it's okay, we can walk to the village shop.'

'And he didn't say when he'd be back?' Is he coming here? I think of the tools laid out in the kitchen.

'No,' she says.

'Okay. Have you got enough money? Do you need me to send you some?' How could he abandon our child?

'No, it's okay,' she says.

'Alright,' I rub at my tired eyes. 'Keep all the receipts and I'll reimburse you when you get back.'

She nods.

I swallow, my pride sharp as it goes down. 'And let me know if he reappears. Or you hear from him.' If he calls you first, before me, before his wife.

Hellie nods.

'Thanks for letting Oscar call,' I manage.

'Course. Any time,' she says.

We say awkward goodbyes and cut off. I text Danny straight away:

Where the hell are you?

I can see the message is delivered. He must be somewhere with signal. Does that mean he left the Black Mountains completely? We can only ever use Wi-Fi up there. I can't believe he's abandoned Oscar. That I drove him to this. The thought that he knows the truth, that whoever is doing this has told him about Lily takes my breath away so sharply I flinch. That hasn't happened: I would know if I'd been outed. I am ahead of this still, just. After an hour I give up expecting an answer from Danny. Wherever he is, he has no intention of telling me. I reassure myself he's merely sulking. And I get back to work.

Two hours later and everything is in place. I've fitted a new motion-activated doorbell camera that broadcasts straight to my phone. And I've hidden nanny cam cameras throughout the house. God bless Amazon Prime. If another note is delivered here – if anyone comes into the house – I will catch them in the act. And then I will have them. Now to lay a trap.

Picking up the kitchen scissors I start to cut.

BETH

I arrange to meet Rob at a cafe I selected on Google. Somewhere I've not been before. I need to vary my route and routine. I travel the same way to work every day. It's Saturday lunchtime, and I'd usually be at e5 Bakehouse with Oscar. It's too easy to work out where I will be. And where I won't be. Too easy to let someone find me. That changes now. They don't know it yet, but the rules have changed: I know what they are doing. I know they will be on CCTV at my office. I know they have my journal. For once, the balance has tipped in my favour.

My phone buzzes. A message from Zayn flashes up:

> Hey you, Soz I've been incommunicado – had to dash to Dublin office for pointless meeting (!!). Nate said you were here before the party? Drinkies? xx

I swipe it off my home screen. I want to talk to Zayn. To hear his voice. But I can't. Right now, the fewer people I share things with, the better. My fingers wrap round the edges of my phone, itching to post the photo: to start the ball rolling. For the first time in weeks I feel a modicum of control. And it is intoxicating. It reminds me of those first weeks of Beth. After I changed my name. A totally fresh start: a new life. Phase two. If I can make them think everything is as it was, not let them realise I'm on to something, then I can get them. But part of that is not being caught. I had to involve Rob, but no one else can know I'm viewing the office's CCTV. Hence meeting here.

The Anniversary Party

It's more of a greasy spoon than a cafe. A last gasp on a parade of shops that moves from well lit, freshly painted gentrified knick-knack store, through chicken takeaways, to this 99p-for-a-cuppa leftover. Perfect. I'm early so I can choose my spot. Inside fulfils the promise of the grimy window and faulty light up 'Open' sign. It's all chipped laminate tables and sticky sugar pourers. They even have what look like original aubergine plastic napkin dispensers on the tables. The kind that would be sold for an ironic fortune in the knick-knack store up the street.

The kitchen area is open, allowing a clear view of a fat man with a grubby white T-shirt, and a waist apron stood over two small hobs. He's frying bacon and eggs, presumably for the table of paint-splattered decorators sat in the corner playing clips out loud on their phones and laughing. Eighties pop classics boom from a tinny radio. They don't look at me. An advantage of being nearly forty. I might answer back. I allow myself a little smile.

Directly behind the counter waits a young girl, in her late teens, early twenties at the most. She has the same tiny frame as Chloe, the receptionist at work, but it doesn't look right on her. Like she's undernourished against her will. Her dark hair is pulled back into a ponytail, and she's buttering slices of white bread. She looks up and smiles, her whole face illuminating in an instant. 'Hi, what can I get you?' She says, her accent somewhere Eastern European.

'Tea, please,' I say. I'm guessing there's no point asking for green or camomile.

'I'll bring it over,' she says, nodding at the empty tables behind me.

I select one in the corner by the window. There's enough wall that I'm not visible through the window, and I can see the whole cafe. It's also the furthest away from everyone else. I don't want to be overheard. I check my watch. Rob should be here any minute. I untuck my red hair from under my baker boy cap, and scan the street outside. I'm fairly confident no one followed me. As well as ordering my home cameras, I spent yesterday watching YouTube videos on how to work out if someone is stalking you. They all started with the disclaimer that this could happen to anyone. And then proceed to show lots of clip art of scared looking women, and shadowy male figures. Despite the more pressing concerns, I still felt my feminist hackles rise. Then realised I had assumed it was a man doing this to my exes. But perhaps it isn't? Could a woman have overpowered everyone to date? I know we can be dangerous. Mickey was stabbed. A knife definitely gives an advantage to the wielder. Kareem was killed in a hit-and-run. Phil was stabbed outside a pub. Could that have been a woman? And Wade was pushed. I blink away the remembered grainy image of his body flying towards the tracks, as the table of decorators explode into more raucous laughter. It could be a woman. It is possible. But there are no women on my list. No women that are alive and know about my tattoo. Only four men.

Are you being followed? Check behind you every thirty seconds. Stay alert. Focused. Notice anything out of the ordinary. Analyse the situation. Listen to your instinct.

In the first months of Beth I did that, waiting for someone to out me as Lily. But when it never happened, I got sloppy. Wandering around caught up in my own world. It would have been easy to follow me. I check my watch again. Panic tugs at my diaphragm. What if they've got to Rob? If they know somehow that I've spoken to him? Could they be listening to my phone? No. Rob knows to be careful. I warned him to be safe. I sent him YouTube links last night – advice.

If safe, stop and look at something in a shop window, or fix your hair in a car window – this may give you the opportunity to see your stalker's reflection. Memorise their appearance. Cross the street. Change direction. Do it again. Stay in public places. Call your friends or family to come meet you. If you can't get hold of someone scream. Shout. Make as much noise as possible. Contact the police.

I am almost there. This will be the evidence I can take to the police. *Memories of how the officers looked at me, shouted at me, the smell of the cell come rushing back.* The thread comes away in my fingers, the cuff stitching unravelling. Whoever is doing this knows about Lily. But I have to maintain the lie to Rob. He would never agree to help if he knew who I really am.

What to do if you are attacked. Use anything you can as a weapon: a heavy bag, a book, keys. Kick them in the groin. Poke them in the eyes. Scratch them.

I've watched enough CSI style shows to know that forensic evidence found under victims' nails can identify a killer. Do they advise scratching for that reason? It may not stop the attacker, but it could catch them if you die. Presumably there was no DNA found on Mickey, or any of the others. Or none that is recorded. I also learnt last night that there are over 6 million people on the UK National DNA Database, from crime scenes and arrests. If there was DNA at any of the crime scenes, it must mean it doesn't match anyone on the system. That it's someone who doesn't have a record. Danny has never been arrested. Neither has Zayn. Their whole lives have been untainted by crime. I don't know about Rob or Matt. Or if there is any way to find out? I should have been up on this stuff. Paid more attention to what was going on around me. Been more cynical. I bear the cost of not staying alert.

If all else fails – run. But don't turn down any blind alleyways . . .

The door rattles as it opens. Rob! Thank God. He is wearing his own baseball cap, and has his leather rucksack over the shoulder of his dark jumper and jeans. Tom Cruise does spy wear. His eyebrows rise as he takes in the cafe. 'I thought I had the wrong place.' He pulls up a chair. 'Or rather I hoped I had.' he indicates the china mug I'm holding. 'Why do I feel like I might be about to go down with food poisoning?'

'Did you bring it?' I reach for his bag.

He hugs it to him. 'All in good time.'

'We don't have time,' I hiss.

'I know,' he leans forward. 'But I thought you wouldn't want to watch this in front of the staff?' He looks up with a beaming smile as the young girl from behind the counter reaches us. He takes his cap off, running his hands through his floppy hair, the picture of casual calm. 'Good morning,' he says, a hint of flirtation as he clearly takes in her slender hips.

For the love of God. I stare at his bag. This is it. I will see the footage and I will know who is doing this. I can finally have something to show to the police. They'll have to listen then. It won't be about me.

'Hey – what can I get you?' She turns to a fresh page on her notepad.

'A mug of that delicious-looking tea should hit the spot,' says Rob.

'Anything else?' The waitress smiles back, one foot turning in towards him.

'I'm sure you could tempt me,' he gives a little wink. 'How about a bacon sandwich?'

'Coming up.' Her face remains impassive. I hide my smirk.

'What happened to food poisoning?' I watch her go, making sure she can't hear us.

'Jealous?' he says with a grin, his entitlement shielding him from the young girl's indifference. I think of Chloe in the office. Hardworking, eager to learn, smart. Does Rob see any of that, or just a pretty face?

He's obviously chilled out overnight about the murderer making their way through my list. 'You know this isn't a game, right?' I stare at him.

'Thing is, Beth. All this – the threat – it's made me realise what's important. How we should live in the moment,' he reaches for my hand.

I pull back. 'Let's just watch it, yeah?'

'Okay,' a grim twist appears at the corners of his mouth. He opens up the bag, pulls out his laptop. 'I had to order this,' he says, taking out an external disc drive. 'Seriously, when was the last time you saw one of these?' He glints the CD in the light.

I want to say, '*It's your outdated security system*,' but I don't.

'It only just arrived before I left,' he says.

It feels like the machine takes an age to turn on. Rob plugs in the external disc drive and loads the disc, with a nails down a blackboard scrape. 'It was a cheap one,' he shrugs. 'Quickest they could do.' Amazon are making hay from this situation.

I realise I'm gripping the table, pressing into the laminate like I'm giving fingerprints.

Rob turns the computer so we can both see. A rectangle is open on the screen, over the innocuous work folders on Rob's desktop. One says Unity. I think of Matt and his *Treasure*, about my dream last night. Does my subconscious know something I don't? *Listen to your instinct*. In the frozen rectangle is an image, from above of our reception. The camera is angled down, about forty-five degrees, towards the door, only a slither of the receptionist's desk visible. You can't see whoever is behind it. I guess Rob feared the outside only, not misdeeds by in-house staff. I can only make out a few things on it. The edge of the phone. A pad. No envelope, I don't think. But you can't see anything closer to Chloe's chair.

Rob glances at the counter, but the young girl is collecting plates from the lads in the corner. 'This should be from 10 a.m. You said I sent Chloe out to collect my suit?'

How can he not remember? I feel like every second of the last few weeks is scored into my flesh. I nod.

He presses play.

The image moves, tiny light variations as people walk past outside. Like a time lapse. There's no sound.

A blonde figure comes from the side, pulling on her trench coat, untucking her hair that's caught down the back of her collar. Pulling on her bag. 'There. That's Chloe going out for your dry cleaning.' I recognise her jumpsuit from that day.

We watch as the figure pushes through the doors, and out of sight.

Rob's breathing grows quicker. The scent of his aftershave stronger as we both lean towards the screen. My fingers ache against the sticky table, but I daren't let go.

'Maybe we didn't get him?' Rob says.

'Shush,' I say. Though there's nothing to talk over. The pixelated light from outside our office flickers across the empty atrium floor.

'Perhaps we got the wrong day?' Rob says.

'No. Her jumpsuit. It's right,' I say. It has to be. It has to be on here.

I turn the laptop towards me, as the waitress brings Rob's sandwich and tea. Let him talk to her. Block everything else out. He has to be there. There's no other way into the building. Unless they were inside already? I feel a cold chill run up over my skin. There were only four people in the office that day. If they were inside already it could only be one person. Rob's teeth tear through the flesh in his sandwich. Does he already know no one will be caught on camera because it is him doing this?

BETH

Ketchup rests on Rob's lip like congealed blood. The walls of the cafe close in on me. The braying decorators in the corner rise with a painful scrape of chairs on the floor. The beat from the radio pulses with loud angry static. It's him. Rob did this. I picture him in his baseball cap, collar of his coat turned up, outside my house, stooping to pick up the journal before quickly walking away. I see him cutting the pages, rearranging the letters. I see him placing the note in my bag, on the reception desk. I see him stepping out the shadows of Hyde Park and confronting Mickey. I can't breathe. A small noise is forced out of my nose.

'There!' says Rob, jamming a breadcrumbed finger towards the laptop. I jolt backwards, my chair legs squeaking with a horrible judder against the floor.

Stay calm. Don't show him you know.

'There,' Rob repeats, more excitedly, a piece of bacon fat dangling dangerously from the bread in his grasp. 'It's him.'

'What?' I look at the video on screen. A figure. A man is entering our office. Tall. Broad shoulders, under a dark padded jacket. And a dark beanie hat pulled down obscuring his hair. Dipped forwards so we can't see his face.

'It's him,' Rob repeats.

'I don't know – wait.' The man on the screen takes something from his pocket with a gloved hand. An envelope. 'That's it! That's the note that was left for me – it has to be.'

'Do you recognise him?' says Rob. 'Who is it?'

'I don't know.' There is something familiar about his walk, but it could be any number of men that I know. 'It's not clear enough. I can't see.' If he would just look up. *Look up. Look up.*

We watch as the man looks from side to side, behind him. I hold my breath. But he still doesn't look up. He walks towards the reception desk and reaches forward, his hand out of sight, as he places the envelope down. Then heads back towards the door.

My heart is racing. 'Look up, dammit!' I say.

Rob is silent. We are both transfixed to the screen.

Look up! Then he's pushing open the door, daylight turning the ground at his feet lighter. And he's gone.

'There has to be more,' I say. 'What about other cameras?'

'It's the only one we have,' says Rob.

I grab the laptop, sliding the cursor along. Perhaps he comes back. There's a shape. I stop fast forwarding. Chloe re-enters with a cellophane wrapped bag draped over her arm.

'That's it,' says Rob.

'It can't be,' I say, desperate. 'What about other people's cameras? Other offices on the street?'

'We should go to the police,' he says.

I laugh. 'With what? A man on CCTV visiting our office.'

'You must have recognised something about him,' Rob is still staring at the screen. 'Watch it again.' He rewinds the tape. The same figure appears.

'I don't. Perhaps Chloe saw something – she might remember him?' I know she doesn't. I asked her. I accosted her on the street. The man on the screen walks calmly towards the desk again, the hateful note in his hand. I can't even see his skin tone. He must have known there was a camera.

'She arrives fifteen minutes later,' says Rob. 'He's long gone.'

'What about you?' There were three guys in the office. Christoph and Geoff work with noise-cancelling headphones on, their backs to reception, but Rob doesn't. He likes to walk around. Take in the atmosphere.

'Me?' Rob's eyes open in surprise.

'You were there when he came in – do you remember anything?'

'I was probably in my office—'

'Probably? You need to think.' He has to remember. 'Concentrate. Did you come out at all? Did you go into reception? Near it? Did you see anything?'

Rob runs his hand through his hair, his Patek Philippe watch glinting in the strip lighting. 'I didn't – I can't. It was three weeks ago.'

'Try harder,' I snap.

'What about you?' he says sharply. 'If anyone is going to recognise him it's you. You must recognise something?'

'No,' I say, staring at the screen. But it's a lie. I can see something. I just don't want to face it.

'Look,' Rob says, his voice softening. 'I think you should take some time off, till we get this sorted, yeah? Work from home next week.'

I nod, but I'm not really listening to his words. It's a man in the video. For sure. That gait, the way he walks. He's tall, you can tell by the shadow. Broad under his jacket. Strong in his movements. I run through the images on my wall at home. It could be Unity's Matt, the angle not clear enough to reveal if there were the wisps of a sickly beard there. But it could also be Zayn, or Danny. Even Rob. He could have left his office by the fire exit, come back in the front. He would know where the cameras were better than anyone. They all fit the build.

Instead of ruling any of them out – I've simply confirmed it could still be any one of them.

BETH – THREE DAYS AFTER THE PARTY

I didn't know until I tried to order some online, that pepper spray is illegal in the UK. It counts as an offensive weapon. It's illegal to own or carry it. Which does not make me feel safe. Self-defence spray in the UK is dye. Just dye. That you spray at your attacker, and it dyes their skin and clothes red for a number of days. Great, so if Mickey had had this with him, for example, he'd still be dead, but the guy doing this would look like a bad postbox costume. But I'd rather survive this. I'd rather everyone survived. My heart twists each time I think of anything happening to Danny. But I ordered a dye spray anyway. And a 140-decibel rape alarm. It's the best we have to offer over here. For someone who's always been anti-guns, and thinks the US system is insane, I'm surprised at how quickly I want one to protect myself now I feel truly under threat. From the latest box from Amazon I take out the plastic sealed kitchen knife. My scissors struggle noisily to cut through the packing. The blade is sharp to the touch, but I run it a few more times through my block sharpener to be sure. Weigh it in my hand, the handle metal, balanced, smooth. I try standing with my feet hip width apart, my weight equally distributed, soft knees, like I've seen online. *How to overpower someone bigger than you. Fatal stabbing wounds.* I thrust the knife forwards into the air. I don't feel reassured, I just feel sick.

The CCTV was inconclusive. The professionalism of that word makes me feel better. It's the kind of thing they say on those twenty-four-hour police custody shows. I've been watching those at speed on YouTube. Taking notes on how to trace people.

I don't have any forensics, or a police database at my disposal, but I have checked the CCTV. *Inconclusive.* So, I moved to my next stage of the strategy. My trap.

The sound of footsteps behind me make me jump. I swiftly drop the knife back into the main box with the red spray and the rape alarm, folding the lid to.

'All done, love,' says the locksmith, wiping his hands on a rag from his belt.

'Bolts on all the windows?' I cross to my handbag.

'Yup, and on the back here,' he shows me how a shiny silver bolt slides straight up through the door frame and into the wall above the backdoor. And how its twin slides straight down into the ground in its newly drilled hole. Tiny shavings of white painted plaster gathered round it like petals. 'You twist the key to lock it in place,' he says as he turns the little key that dangles from the lock over every bolt. 'And I've changed the locks on the front. Got you a bank quality Yale. No one will be getting through that – unless they're invited!' He grins as he takes me through the various new keys.

'Thanks – this makes me feel a lot better,' I smile, alluding to the made-up attempted break in I've used to justify this.

I sign the paperwork, pay him (extra because it's a Sunday), and get him out the house as soon as possible. Double locking and bolting my new precautions after him. And exhale. No one can get in.

Including Danny.

I will deal with that when I need to. For now, he need not know. I just need to feel secure. And I need to be able to control my environment for what I have planned.

I return to my box, and gently lift it up. Underneath lie new notes. Their letters cut from my handwriting; their words arranged on lined paper. But these weren't sent to me. These I made all by myself.

BETH

I line my phone up over the photo and shoot. The remnants of dissected words litter the rest of the table. I crop the image into a perfect square. An edge of wood from my kitchen table borders the lined piece of paper. It's not exactly the same as that in my journal, but it's as close as I could find in the house. I've even gone to the effort of using different pens to write out the various words I snipped. I want them to know this is no accident. No quirky coincidence. I sharpen the image so it is crystal clear, and then press post. No comment. Just what is on the screen.

As is Instagram's way, the image at first disappears from my screen, and is replaced by my feed. Photos of contacts, colleagues enjoying their lives, seascapes and sunsets flow through my fingers. I still imagine what Carmen would be doing, sharing now. Wonder if she ever thinks of me? That intense female friendship closeness of our twenties contrasting with the empty relationships I have with the people I follow now. My life is bereft of a close female friend. And I wonder if I have unconsciously avoided bonding with other women? Did I think I didn't deserve to have that after I betrayed one of us? Broke the girl code. Or was I scared that they would see through the same facade men are so willing to take at face value? I sacrificed my friendship with Carmen when I walked away from Lily, and it still wasn't enough to stop my past coming for me. But I re-wrote my story once, now I'm doing it again.

I click onto my home page, and there it is. The most recent image on a grid otherwise made up of the best of me, and Danny, and Oscar. The pattern of pictorial displays of Beth's success interrupted by this latest image. I click onto the photo, and it fills the screen. The words clear, and cut from my own hand:

I know who you are.

Excitement, nerves, anxiety, I'm not sure what, takes its seat in the pit of my stomach. Already people are hearting the image. I click through to see names I vaguely recognise. A florist I once worked with on a project, Chloe the receptionist. I didn't realise she followed me? What does she think? What do they all think? That this is some insightful Insta-quote about seeing the real you? Ha! You couldn't make it up.

Instead it's bait. I've learned from my online research, that sometimes you need to prompt action. Force a suspect to break their pattern. Act out. And in doing so they might reveal themselves. I want to force him into the open.

How long until I post the next message? What will happen? Will they message me? Have they already liked it? I think about Chloe. Could it actually be her? No, of course not. It was definitely a man on the office CCTV. Besides, I've only known her a few weeks. And at twenty-one, or whatever she is, she wasn't even born when I slept with Mickey.

I think about that idea, turn it over in my hands, inspect it from all sides. My belief that this is something to do with the past. With Lily. Why start with Mickey if that's not what this is about? But then I think of creepy sex dolls Matt, and that doesn't make sense. I've only known him for a number of months, but he is the right gender, the right build, the right fit. He feels right. As in he feels very wrong.

I need to stay focused. I have logically eliminated people from my suspect list. I know who is on it. One of them must be doing this. I flick back to my Instagram grid, past smiling photos of me and Danny, me and Zayn messing about. One of them must have done it.

My phone jumps in my hand – a message from Zayn. A shiver runs down my spine. It's a WhatsApp message, not Instagram. It could just be coincidence. It could be nothing. I swipe it open:

Hey babes, You feeling better? I could pop over tonight – found some hash brownies Nate baked?

Feeling better? Oh yeah – I told him I had cystitis yesterday to buy me some time. He knows I suffer with it, and it's best to rest up, and stay well away from the booze. Also, it's something that's not visible from the outside should he bump into me. The timing is odd. Has he seen my Instagram post? My finger hovers over my screen. Should I reply or wait? Should I post the next message? I can't bear this much longer. I have to know who is doing this. It has to stop.

I sweep the first note aside, and straighten the second. Repeat the process from before. Shoot. Crop. Sharpen. Post. Nervous anticipation drags a chair across the floor of my stomach, to join the others already gathered there. I look at my notes from the police documentaries I watched. If I can get *them* to act out, to alter their behaviour. I could make them reveal themselves. And then I can stop this. I take the knife from the Amazon box, laying it on the table. Then next to it I add the spray, the rape alarm. Then I sit with my phone in my palm, and wait. On the screen, I read, and reread, the same words cut from my own hands. Hearts start appearing beneath the image. The words clear, in multi-coloured pens, a tiny slither of wood bordering them:

Let's talk.

This is the turning point. I am rewriting my narrative. It's no longer just going to be happening around me, to me. I'm changing it. Altering its path. It's like a public relations campaign, when you take bad news, and you spin it into something positive.

You change the story's trajectory. That's what I'm doing. But this time it's not Lily's tale of woe, its Beth's. Beth will make them show themselves. Beth will take the evidence to the police. This time they will believe me.

I don't know what I expect, but nothing happens. Apart from me jumping every time I feel the vibrations of a bus passing outside. There are no coded messages under my posts. No texts. Before I know it, I'm cycling through all my platforms. Waiting. And then it comes. An email from Rob. Every message, every communication feels like a potential bomb. I sat opposite Rob, I looked him in the eye, I showed him the list. Was I too scared to acknowledge there was something off in his reactions? A band tightens round my gut. Is this confirmation it's him? Does this email confirm the killer is Rob? I have to open it.

BETH

Fear fixes me to the sofa. My fingers won't do what I tell them, some primal instinct in my body knows this is dangerous. There's an attachment. I can see the usually innocent paperclip symbol. What's he sent me? A photo of a note? A photo of something else? Images flash through my mind. Mickey's shocked face as the knife goes in. Kareem flying through the air before he slams into the ground. Phil clutching his stomach, blood pouring through his fingers. The oncoming tube lights.

A shout from outside makes me jump. A man is barking into his phone, as he marches past the window. I force my attention back to my screen. Hype myself up to turn and face the monster.

Open the email.

Open the attachment.

Do it.

I click open, half looking away in case it's bad. It's a screenshot of a news article online. From the BerliNews.

EXPAT MAN DIES ON U-BAHN TRAIN TRACKS

The man who died at U-Bahn Alexanderplatz in the early hours of Saturday morning, has been named as British national Tobi Weinstrasse . . .

The band round my gut slips upwards fast and hard, clutching round my chest. I scan the email. *Horrific accident . . . . Popular Sustainability Start-Up Founder . . . Berlin resident . . . Community in shock . . .*

I can't get air past the tightening band. Rob has written underneath:

This guy was on your list right??? This is mad.

Google confirms it. *Tobi Weinstrasse died when he was pushed in front of a train at Berlin's Alexanderplatz, a Metro station popular with late-night partygoers.* I spoke to him Thursday, he must have been killed less than thirty-six hours later. The same M.O. as Wade. This must be proof? But it's in a different country. It's not enough. But I know he's been killed. Murdered, like the others. If only he'd listened to me – anger floods through my veins. If the stupid man had just listened! If he'd just done as I'd asked instead of insulting me. I can't tell which is stronger, my anger that someone is doing this, or that Tobi didn't listen to me. He was yet another person hearing what they wanted to. Twisting me, my words. If Tobi had not been so arrogant, not automatically assumed this was about him, then maybe he would still be alive? Because it isn't about any of them, is it? Mickey, Kareem, Phil, Wade and now Tobi. It's about me. And I was too late. My message was too late.

I didn't really think Tobi would be targeted. He lives – lived – in another country. So, whoever did this travelled. They got on a plane and flew there and pushed him under a train. When? Friday? The day I left Rob in the office – he'd have had all afternoon and evening to catch a flight. And now he's sent this to me – is he taunting me? Does it mean it is him? Zayn said he was away at his Dublin office Friday – he only texted Saturday morning. But that message could've been sent from anywhere in the world. Matt's voicemail also said he was away. Was his phone turned off so there'd be no international dial tone? So he couldn't be traced? And Danny is somewhere he's told neither me nor Hellie about. Berlin? I stare at the names on the wall. It's under two hours to fly to Berlin from London. There are over twelve flights a day. Any one of them could have flown out there, and back, and I'd never know. Commuting to commit murder. How can I monitor where they all are? Know where they've all been? And then I know what I have to do. What I should have done as soon as I had four names.

I have to have them followed.

HIM

The window opens on my laptop as soon as I insert the disc. Their footage is sharper than the camera in ours, the entrance of our building clear in the background. If I had to share my footage with any of the other offices around here, I'd be embarrassed. I'll get Chloe onto the company to come overhaul the system. That will play well with Bethy as well. Show I'm really doing all I can.

When I was approached to join the Neighbourhood Watch style scheme for local businesses, I'd done it for the cheaper insurance premium. There's a shared pool of security resources, which means I can access the company opposite's surveillance footage. No questions, no cops, and no need for anyone else to find out I've viewed it.

It's a resource I should have utilised before. A great way to covertly monitor the staff. I already read everyone's emails. That's responsible business ownership. I don't bother looking at my employees' emails to clients – they're all bound by non-compete clauses. No, I look at the stuff they send to each other, to their partners, to their friends. I know Christoph's husband has asked for an open marriage, and that Christoph is really not happy about it. His drug use has increased since then. Geoff pretends to be friends with everyone in the office, while slagging them all off to each other. Chloe is mostly 'SO BORED!!!' And, embarrassingly, she finds me hot. And I have read everything Bethy has ever sent to her friend Zayn, or to that idiot husband of hers. I don't just dip into her correspondence, I study it. I see what mistakes he's made, how I can capitalise on his lack. She tells that Zayn guy a lot. Too much, really. You shouldn't share certain things, but it's useful for me. She tells him what she wants, what she misses in her life. I see the lies she tells herself when she says she loves Danny. I know I can give her what she really wants. This is the perfect opportunity.

I click on the video window and check the date stamp, fast forward through the frames to the right time. Being a lateral thinker really gives me an advantage. It's strength of character, an act of ongoing determination. I've worked hard all my life. Given it all to everything I've done. I've earned everything I have. That's why Bethy will come around to my thinking in the end.

A black-clad figure in a baseball cap flits onto screen from the left, innocuous among the other fast-moving office workers, and then disappears into our building. I stop, rewind and press play again. I watch the figure enter the shot from the left, approach our entrance. The head down, a dark shape elongated by the baseball cap's peak. The figure reaches for our door handle. I rewind again. Click to zoom in. There is a slight drop in quality, but you can still see a large amount of detail. The figure walks towards the building again, and: there! Just as he reaches for the door handle, he looks over his right-hand shoulder. Checking whether anyone is behind him. Whether anyone is following him. And I can see it, very clearly. Nose, eyes, lips, all visible. His face frozen on the screen.

I sit back in my chair, fingertips resting lightly together, looking at the image. I take a photo with my phone.

And then I wipe the disc.

BETH

How do you pick a private investigator? You google. Like you do everything else. You rule out those with spelling mistakes on their websites. Or those with cheesy stock photos lifted from eighties US thrillers about taking a bullet for the president. And any that display casual misogyny about 'proving she's a gold digger'. You whittle it down to those whose call line is manned on a Sunday. You look at reviews. There are reviews for everything, even Matt's sex dolls. Everyone is keen to share their special critical insight. Their curated picks. Yes, picking a private investigator is easy. Calling them, that is another matter.

I have always been the kind of person to pick up the phone and brazenly cold-call people. But the last few weeks have dragged me back to Lily. I'm wandering round the muddy trenches of my mixed past, as gunfire whistles overhead. I can't see who's attacking me, but they are relentless, and I am getting starved, worn down, depleted from the constant death. The disastrous call with Tobi still makes me feel sick. My shaking mess at Anna's. I remind myself cold-calling, whether it's to journalists, or to private investigators, is all about jumping straight back in after a bad one. Hiding in the cold wet mud only delays the inevitable. I need to rally my troops. But how do you recover from the type of conversation I had with Wade? Or with Tobi? When your world has tilted once more? I don't know how much more of this I can take. But I have to. Because that is what humans do. We persevere. The accident, what followed could have destroyed me, but I chose to survive. What other option is there?

I dial the number.

'Hello?' It's a male voice, and I can't help thinking of Raymond Chandler and the hardboiled private eyes of noir films. Except this man sounds nothing like that. He sounds quite softly spoken really, the slight edge of Estuary English soaking his inflections.

'Hi, is this, err, Detective Investigations London?' I grip the phone tighter. Stare at the names on my wall. Glance at the bolt that is slid across the lounge sash window. If there was a fire would I undo them in time? What about Oscar? But he doesn't – can't – live here at the moment.

'Yes, that's us, how can I help?' I imagine him putting down his coffee, closing the Sunday papers he was reading.

I swallow. This whole thing is mad. 'I was wondering how much it would cost to have someone followed?'

'Where do they live and work?' says the PI. 'Which area?'

'London,' I say. I don't actually know where Matt from Unity lives. He has the advantage of me there. I glance at the bolt on the window again, as if it might have moved in the last few minutes. As if there might be a face pressed against the glass.

'We would normally recommend two to three operatives to tail one person. It's easier for operatives to stay unnoticed if they pose as a couple, in a car, or cafe for example. And you need to keep rotation up, so the same people or cars aren't noticed.'

Christ, that sounds expensive.

'Depending on your aim, we may also recommend twenty-four hour surveillance.'

'Okay,' I swallow.

He's still working his way through his usual spiel, barely pausing for a response. 'Our basic surveillance operatives are charged at £65 per hour, with an increase for a specialisation, or unsocial hours.'

I quickly scribble the numbers on a pad in front of me. Say I allowed for two operatives, for twenty-four hours, at £65 per hour each . . . That would be £3,120 just to follow one of my suspects for one day. I'd need to do the same four times over. Just one day would cost £12,480. I haven't got that kind of money just lying around. Who does? And I'd have to have them followed until I knew that they weren't responsible for this. Until another note was delivered. Or until someone else dies. My stomach lurches. 'Thank you,' I manage. 'I err will talk it over with my business partner and get back to you if we decide to go ahead.' In my mind I've built a backstory that these guys are being watched for possible employment.

I hang up and drop my head into my hands. I could sell the car? But that would likely only raise £10k if I was lucky. And how would I explain it to Danny? I can't tell him, because he would be one of the people I would be following.

I feel queasy. I thought I could just farm this problem out, like I would a leaky tap. That if I threw money at it like I have with the locks, and the cameras and knife, I would feel better. I would find a solution. But there's a difference between a few hundred pounds and thousands. I just haven't got the resources. I suddenly feel completely helpless. I'm all alone trying to navigate the trenches of this nightmare. It's just me and the enemy.

My phone buzzes threateningly in my hand. A text from Rob. Air catches in my throat:

Let's talk.

My flesh creeps with goosebumps, it's the same phrase I used in my Instagram bait. It's him, it's Rob. He's made himself known, visible above the parapet. Oh God, he was here, in my home, near Danny, Oscar. My phone buzzes with more:

This afternoon, 5 p.m. The office. Come alone.

A Sunday evening, it'll be deserted. Can I take this to the police? No, it's still not proof. They won't believe me, they won't stop this, they won't save Danny. Only I can do that. I'm ready. The whistle has been blown. I'm going over.

HIM

He sits in the corner chair, half a smile on his cocky face. Waiting for me to speak. Thinking he's so clever. Well, you've been outmanoeuvred, son. 'It took me a minute; I'll give you that. To recognise you. Coffee, or something stronger? Ever tried Japanese whisky?'

He waves away the offer. Suit yourself.

I open my drinks cabinet, taking a moment so he can admire the marquetry. 'Bit too *Mad Men*?' I laugh. 'I couldn't resist.' Reach for a bottle. I need it myself. Excitement ripples over my skin. I feel alive. Buzzing. The goal is in sight. Everything lining up perfectly. Nothing beats the high of winning.

Chloe's only half filled my ice bucket from the cooler in the kitchen. I will have to remind her again. I load my glass, swill the amber liquid.

Sit back down. Take him in. Yes, a surprise, I'll give him that. But not an unpleasant one. I sip. 'Thank you for coming in today.' I indicate the printed image from the CCTV on the table. *Not that you had a choice*. He shifts in the chair, frowning. *Let me show you how a pro does it*. 'It seemed about time you and I had a little chat.' I take my time, savouring his discomfort like my whisky. I rest the glass next to the printouts. The honey sweet flavour of victory. 'I've been in business for many years. This is my third firm. The first two I founded and sold. That's how I operate: start things up, get them going, and then sell to the highest bidder. You understand?'

He barely responds. God, is there anything behind those eyes at all? I'm going to have to spell it out.

'I have a large number of assets I can call upon,' I glance at the two bags by the door. Allow myself a smile, as he follows my line of sight. 'Now, I don't know why you've been doing whatever you want to call this situation with Beth. And I don't care.' I hold up a hand to stop him interrupting. 'But it strikes me that you are a man who understands process. You've been going through her ex-partners one after another,' I hold my hand up again. 'Don't bother denying it. I know about the notes. I have you on camera delivering one. And let me assure you I have no interest in going to the police.' I let that sink in a second. Show him I'm on his side. 'I have to admit, it really is quite ingenious, the way you've done it. I mean no one on the outside would expect any of these "incidents" as being linked.' *Bit of flattery*. 'And I admire that. Which is why I have a proposition for you.' I lean back. This is just another transaction. Just another piece of the puzzle to be turned to my favour. I adjust the cuffs of my shirt from under my blazer, so the embroidered monogram is visible.

He raises an eyebrow in question. An indication to go on. Close the deal.

'One of those bags,' I indicate with a nod to the door. 'Is full of cash. Unmarked, non-sequential bills.' This is fun now; I feel like the Godfather. Powerful. *The man*. Whatever this guy was up to, it's no match for me. You don't just avoid a situation; you turn it to your advantage. You bring it home. 'And I want to gift that to you.' I smile, enjoy the look on his face. 'But don't worry, I don't want you to miss out on your fun, or whatever you get from this. I want you to go ahead and kill Danny, her husband. I assume that was always the plan?'

Everyone has a price. That's what business has taught me. You can bend anyone to your will if you find the right number. And this is a huge number. I've emptied the Swiss account. Power flashes through my veins. When I think of that chump's face, his hands on my Bethy. And he has the audacity to cheat on her with some slutty little nanny. No. She is better off without him. Then she can be happy. Happy with me.

He walks over to the bags. Prods one with his boot. *Got him.*

'That one is mine. It contains my clothes. I intend to take Bethy away from all this. I intend to look after her. The money will set you up for life. Take it abroad, spend it on getting a new identity. I don't need to know the details. I don't need to know anything. I just need to know we have a deal?' I rise, stride towards him, hold out my hand. One shake and I get everything I want. My Bethy gets the life she really deserves. And all this, this becomes nothing but the faded tawdry past.

He turns to look at me. The ice in the bucket cracks and resettles. A muscle in his cheek flexes. 'Beth and you are—?' He tips his chin up in a curiously old-fashioned way.

'Oh yes,' I smile. 'We've been close for years. It was only a matter of time before we rekindled the old flame, and all that.' *Well, we will do, once that piss-poor excuse of a man she calls her husband is removed.*

His eyes glitter. Nostrils flare. His whole body an accelerating wall towards me. It's so fast. The flash of silver. A knife. In the split second before it lands, time stretches just enough for me to realise: I made a serious miscalculation.

Then there is only white-hot searing pain.

BETH

I haven't sat still. Why make me wait? Why make me come to the office? Does he think he can explain? Why has he done this? Rob, the first man I let kiss me after Iain. Beth was new, I was still developing a feel for her. Constantly worried someone would see straight through me. I had to stay away from Mum (until she had safely moved, and things had settled down). I stayed away from everyone and everything from before. I was lonely. I just wanted, needed, physical comfort. The warm touch of someone else. And to cleanse myself of Iain. But when it came down to it I couldn't go through with it. I wasn't ready to sleep with someone else. Has he been harbouring this, like an obsession all this time?

I met Rob at a networking event. There was instant attraction. He was impressive, driven, one company already under his belt. Broad shoulders. Tanned skin. He was always a player. And then years later, when I found Hellie's knickers in Danny's car, I was desperate for reassurance. Desperate to feel wanted. But I knew the moment his hands touched me it was a mistake. I stopped it. Is this all punishment for rejecting him not once, but twice? These thoughts rave through my mind. *Rob did this.* All the times he was 'at meetings', or in his office with the blinds down. There's the fire exit. He could come and go, completely unobserved. Did he follow me when I went to see Wade? Was he watching? I've known, somewhere deep inside, before all this, something wasn't right. He felt too intense, too close after the stupid kiss. I thought I saw him a few times, his eyes through the blinds in the office. Once on the street, following me, watching. But you tell yourself you're imagining it. He's a nice guy. But the night of the anniversary party he was at my house, he left the note, he threatened to tell Danny. No wonder he couldn't give me a straight answer when I asked him where he was when the one was delivered to our office: that was him in the CCTV image. And Tobi? Oh God. He must have already done it when we met at that cafe. Fresh off a flight back to London, that's why it needed to be lunchtime. Not because he was waiting for an Amazon package. He suggested I take time off work this week. He wants me out the way.

Well no more. I grip the handle of the knife inside my handbag as I walk towards our office. The softening daylight casting shadows across the empty pavements. A last flash of sun unreachable along the building tops.

My phone buzzes, making me jump. *Rob (Trench PR) calling.*

I release the knife, hearing it clang against my laptop. I have everything with me. I'm going to make him confess, record it. Something the police cannot ignore.

'Hello?' I swallow. There's the sound of rustling, movement, like fabric on the other end. Is this some kind of trick? 'Rob? Hello?'

Nothing. He must have called me by accident. Unease drops a heavy anchor in my stomach. I'm about to hang up when I hear it. Something else. I strain my ears. Not fabric. A wheeze. A wet wheeze. Like someone is fighting for breath. Danny? Rob? Something is wrong. I start to run. 'Rob? Rob is that you? Say something.'

There's a cough, a horrible wet splutter. *It's not Rob.* Because he sounds like . . . oh God, I was wrong. He's not the killer. I'm halfway down the road to the office. 'Are you at the office? I'm almost there. I'm coming. Rob?' My voice comes in pants.

The road is virtually empty, it's Sunday. This is an area full of offices. The usual weekday bustle of people is gone. I look around desperate, there must be someone to help.

A wet wheeze comes from the phone.

'Rob? Rob? Can you hear me? Hang on. I'm here. Where are you?' The door to the office is locked. I scrabble for my keys in my bag, all the time keeping my phone pinned to my ear. 'Rob? Are you here? Are you inside?'

Rob coughs, splutters, and I hear him struggle.

'Rob! Hang on.' I can't find the keys. Where are they? I empty the bag out in desperation. The clang of metal onto concrete. I grab it all, my laptop, the knife, sharp against my hand. Do I need a weapon? Is whoever did this still in there?

'Him,' wheezes Rob through the phone.

The sound, so unlike his usual voice stills me for a second. *The horror.* I scrabble with my keys, fight to find the right one. Force it into the lock. Find the next, then force that into the top lock. My arm screaming as I turn it. Is he here? Is he still here? 'I'm calling the police,' I say as tears roll down my cheeks. 'I'll call you back.'

Rob makes a strangled noise. A desperate attempt at no. He doesn't want me to hang up. 'Okay – hang on. I'm at the door.' I kick at the bottom where it sticks, as it flies back with a glass clang.

'Rob!' I scream. I run into the office. Everything looks normal. I tear towards his door. 'Rob!'

I push the door to his office open.

Red.

Blood.

Rob on the floor.

My bag, the laptop, the knife thud to the ground.

'Oh my God. Oh my God – Rob!' I rush towards him, slipping in the blood. So much blood. Fall to my knees. Cradle his head. His eyes are wide, fearful. He looks at me. Tries to speak. Blood bubbles out of his mouth. 'Rob! Don't die! Rob – stay with me. Hold on – I'm going to get help. Help!' I scream. Where's my phone? In my hand. I hang up. Rob's phone lying next to him on the floor lights up as the call disconnects.

I stab at mine. 999.

'Help me! You've got to help me!' I scream into it. 'My boss.' Rob's eyes fix onto mine, he tries to move his fingers, but instead of gripping my top they make a wretched dance in mid-air.

'Don't move, Rob, don't move. Help's coming,' I say. Then into the phone. 'My friend, my poor Rob – he's been attacked. Please you've got to come quick. There's blood. Lots of blood.'

Rob's fingers flex again, desperate, grasping, pathetic. They point towards the upturned table, a glass, papers strewn across the floor. Work files. 'What is it? What do you want?' His fingers twitch. Stretch for my T-shirt. I cup his face, stroke his cheek, try to wipe the blood away, my tears fall onto him. He tries to speak. Blood burbles up out of his mouth and nose. Oh God. 'Don't die,' I cry.

He tries again, pulling me closer. My whole body shakes as I put my ear next to his mouth.

He takes a great wracking wet breath. The blood and words bubble up out of him. 'My Bethy . . . Sorry,' he breathes.

And then I feel him go.

BETH

I'm cold. Sweating. Cold and sweating. There are flashing blue lights in my peripheral vision. And paramedics in dark green. Police in flashes of neon yellow. They seem far away. And someone takes Rob from me. And hands are on me. Those hands covered in blood. And a mouth is moving but I can't hear. I'm going to be sick. I have to lie down. I'm going to be sick. And a silver blanket is wrapped round me. A face, concerned, peers over at me. Rob? No, not Rob's. Never Rob's again. They kneel over Rob. And I want to tell them it's too late but I can't form any words. And I close my eyes.

And then there are more hands. Kind hands. Gentle hands. And they move me, guide me. And there are faces. Faces that talk. And it's all noise. And faces. And mouths that move. But I don't hear. And people in white forensic suits process me. They pluck Rob's hairs from me. Little hairs, slick with blood. His blood. And they take fibres, and scrape under my nails, and take my fingerprints. I'm moved gently, as if you would a small child. Turned, guided, supported. Helped out of my clothes. Someone gives me a coverall. The plastic bag they put my jumper in. Another for my jeans. And it's like before. Are they going to lock me up? Are they going to take me away? Do they know? Shock is an overfamiliar old friend. It tightens over me like Rob's blood drying on my skin. A coating I can never wash off. People move around me. They tell me to wait. I don't know what for. More questions. More prodding.

I watch as a woman, police, puts her card into my wallet. Hands it back to me. And I just want this to be over. Tears splash onto my fingers, I open my phone and text Danny.

Please come home. I'm sorry. I need you.

I want Danny and Oscar. I want to hold them close. I want Danny to curl himself round me on our bed, to stay there, safe, warm, protected. But there are more goldfish faces pushed into mine. More questions. Nodding makes my brain wobble. I close my eyes.

'Are you taking birth control?' says a paramedic. His face is square, like Lego.

I shake my head.

'I'm going to give you something for the shock.' He rolls my sleeve up. 'Help you sleep tonight.' The Lego head smiles.

I don't know how long I have been here. The spinning slows. The camera zooms out. Images. Words. They break through. It's dark outside; the sun has gone. It is like cold water waking me. My silver blanket rustles in the breeze. I am in the back of a police car. Like before. Lily has been here, and I want to tell them I know – I know what they have to do. My limbs heavy. My eyes keep closing. My head nodding. The dark streets of London are light filled outside the window. But there is no light for me. No light ever again. That is for the others now. I will never be one of them. I will never smile in the same way. I will never laugh in the same way. I will never feel like this again. All the lights outside are sharp and dangerous now. I will close my eyes and stay there forever.

The car slows outside my alien house. The cop gets out and opens the door for me. 'Got your wallet, keys, phone?' she asks. They are in my hands. I don't remember holding them, but there are no pockets in the plastic coverall they gave me. I nod. 'Do you want us to accompany you inside, ma'am?' Her face is a blank thumbprint to me.

'No thank you,' says my voice. I imagine dropping my weighted body into a freezing lake. Letting the water swallow me. This coverall dissolving. I could float. The street outside my house is an unknown.

'Is there someone who can keep an eye on you?' the female cop says.

'Yes,' I nod. I just want to be alone. I want to be away from them.

I hear the engine start up as I slide my key into the lock. They will wait till I'm inside. I unlock my hidden fortress. I can't hide from the smell. The smell of home. Familiarity. What was, and what will never be the same again. I want to rip this coverall from me. I blink and I'm in the utility, pulling it off me, pulling on fresh clean jeans and jumper. I inhale the fabric conditioner. This will make it better. The tears come in a painful sob. My chest sore. My throat sore. I realise I have already been crying. A sound like the one I made when Oscar came. A part of me is ripping out of my body. And I'm so tired. I just want to close my eyes. Curl up on the clean towels. Make it all stop. I grip my phone, close my eyes, underwater again, slow mo. I'm in the hallway. Can I make it up the stairs? They stretch away like a never-ending mountain. Then I see it. Focus.

An envelope sticking out from under the hallway table.

Somewhere far away, I register the note must have slid when it dropped through the letterbox. Or I kicked it when I came in. I force my bag of water feet towards it. Open. Look. My jelly hand snatches it, anger, hatred, fear, threaten to break through my heavy blinking eyes. The paramedic gave me something. His Lego head said I would sleep. *Not now*. I slide along the wall into the lounge, the sofa catching me. Pull at the blanket. *Must stay awake*. My soupy eyes watch my hands pull at the envelope. *Must read it.* Must stay awake. The same lined piece of paper. The familiar letters, cut, but not neat this time. Jagged torn scraps, the same words over and over, like torrential rain in front of my nodding eyes:

Liar. Liar. Liar. I'm coming for you whore.

BETH – FOUR DAYS AFTER THE PARTY

The sound of the key in the lock makes me sit bolt upright. Ouch. The note in my hand. My wallet in my jeans pocket, pushing against my hip. I fell asleep. My phone's plugged in; I don't remember doing that. I throw the blanket off, snatch my mobile up. My stomach falls away as I see the messages. Hundreds of them. Unknown number. All one word. Over and over.

> WHORE.
> WHORE.
> WHORE.

It rains down on me like hail. *Rob. The bubble of blood. The note.* I shouldn't have let them give me that sedative. There's a scraping sound. Metallic. A thud. Someone is shouldering the front door. Oh my God. He's here. He's come for me. My spray, my alarm, they're in my handbag – where is that? I must have left it in Rob's office. *The bubble of blood.* A knife? Miles away in the kitchen. The scraping sound intensifies. Then another thud. I'll never make it. I grab a weighty coffee table book. There's the long drawn out ring of someone leaning on the doorbell. My phone! I scrabble to open up the camera on the front door. My heart pounding. There's another thud. It sounds like the kick of a foot. He's coming. He's coming. It's Matt.

My hands are shaking so much I open the wrong app on my phone. Internally I'm screaming to call the police, but there's no time. I swipe again at the app. And my heart stops. It's not Matt standing there. It's not Matt trying to get into the house. It's Danny. And in his arms is Oscar. My Oscar.

Danny's face, fish eye in the camera, peers in confusion. 'Beth? You there? What the hell is going on?'

I'm unbolting the front door before I remember about my text to him. It's like a drunken flashback. A dirty slap from Rob's office. The blood and the smell leave their angry palm print on my memory. I pull open the door.

Danny looks pissed. Oscar delighted. 'Mummy!'

'My baby!' I dive for him. He's in his sleeping onesie, bare feet poking out. They obviously set off early. The last of the Monday morning commuters pass on the other side of the road, their normality jarring.

'What the hell, Beth – you changed the locks and you didn't tell me?'

'I counted twenty-seven green cars. Green is my new favourite. There were only two purple,' Oscar talks over his dad. I pull him into me, bury my head in his hair. His scent. So clean. So pure.

'Oh, my baby, my baby. I missed you so much.' His tiny warm strong body in my arms. 'You feel bigger – have you grown?' I laugh, pulling back to look at him.

'We brought you a present! I found it on the beach,' he says.

'The beach?' I look at Danny, who is staring at the camera doorbell. They should have been nowhere near the beach.

He looks up. Gives me a sheepish smile. 'I took him. Just the two of us.'

Just the two of us.

Danny pulls Oscar away from me. it feels like a loss. He plants him down. 'Right, little man. Rucksack into your bedroom, please.' He pushes him gently into the house. We both watch him scamper up the stairs, bumping the bag beside him.

'It's over,' he says quietly.

Over? *Blood bubbling out of Rob's mouth.*

'It was months ago.' He shifts next to me.

I think of Hellie and him the night of our party. She's been here. I sent them away together. 'Hellie?' I turn to look at him.

'It was a mistake.' A muscle in his cheek flickers. He stares straight ahead. 'We both know that. Hellie had been seeing this guy and he'd ghosted her. And you and I, well . . . ' He turns to look at me, his eyes searching, desperate. He takes my hands.

I'm dimly aware we're standing on the street saying this, but I don't care. I don't care about anything but Danny and me right now.

'She's got a new job. I gave her a reference. She'll be gone in a few weeks. Give us time to sort out something else . . . ' He trails off. His eyes pleading. 'Beth, I know things haven't been good with us for a while.'

'Rob,' I manage. My voice shaky. Raw.

He flinches, looks down at my hands in his. 'I thought there was something.' Pain and anger tinge his words.

'We kissed. Only once . . . and then I stopped it. I thought I was losing you.' The force of the realisation breaks over me. Oh, poor Rob, he didn't deserve this.

Danny looks relieved, 'I thought I was losing you.'

'I never wanted that,' the thought of no Danny is too much. I fold against his warm chest, his strong arms wrap round me, and he rests his cheek against my head. It's the first time I've felt safe for weeks. I've missed talking to him, talking things over, snuggling into his side at night. And I know I have to tell him the truth. The lie has grown too big, I let the darkness that swirled around Lily infect the good that we had here.

'I think we should get help. See someone, a therapist,' Danny says into my hair.

I nod and blink back tears. We will need that, more than he knows. Just let me have a few more seconds of this peace, of this warmth. I need to believe we are still strong enough to survive this. I clutch his T-shirt. The enormity of it all is unmanageable. Do I start with Rob? Why did they kill him? And then I realise:

Danny was with Oscar. They drove back this morning. There was no way Danny could have killed Rob. He isn't the one doing this. Elation flushes any lingering doubt from my mind. *It was not the husband.* Danny didn't do it.

'Right,' Danny says, half-laughing, half-sniffing back his own tears. 'Shall we take this indoors? I need to get these unloaded.' He bends to pick up the cases from the pavement, leaves me with the gift of knowing he's innocent. How could I have ever thought the man I love was capable of this horror? Danny carries the cases past me, his smile meeting his eyes. A smile, a look, I haven't seen for weeks. Just for us. *Danny didn't do it.* But that means he is in danger. *The bubble of blood.* He is next on the list. The list! Oh my God.

'Danny, wait!' I rush inside. The suitcases are in the hallway, the lounge door open. I'm too late. The window of opportunity for us slams shut. The monster inside laughs with Lily's voice. I destroy everything.

Danny is staring at the wall. Our Hockney canvas on the floor. And the photos and names of all my exes pinned up there. Any residual tiredness from the drugs is ripped away from me. Everything is crisp, horribly in focus. Mickey's smiling blue eyes. Wade's photo printed from the news, his fiancée and daughter cropped out. There are the details of where, when and how they died written underneath each photo. Stabbed. Pushed. Hyde Park. Sevenoaks. Brighton. Holborn. Berlin. And the four names written in red capitals: Rob. Zayn. Matt. Danny. It's all there. I want to pull Danny away, stop him from looking.

'Danny, please. I can explain.'

He turns to me, his mouth open in distress. 'Beth – what is this?'

'Knock, knock!' Comes Hellie's voice from the front hall.

I hear her pushing the front door to. I hear her coming down the hallway. I have to stop her, I have to get to the lounge door.

'I thought I'd come over and help with the unpacking,' she says.

I take two massive strides but it's too late.

'The door was open,' Hellie's voice cuts off as she takes in the lounge wall. Her face a look of confusion.

'Beth,' Danny sounds scared. 'What is this?'

'I . . . ' I stare at the faces of the men I've slept with. The faces of the men who have died because of me. Rob's rasping breath. His panicked eyes. Bubbles of blood. All the men I've lied to Danny about. And Lily. All the death and horror I tried to shield him from. I was trying to protect him. Us. Me. I stare at Rob's name in red letters. I blink and the pen ink turns to dripping blood. How could I have suspected Danny? There are only two names left now: Zayn and Matt. And it's so clear, it's Matt. This all started after he entered my life. He was the one who did this.

'Beth?' Danny sounds small, like Oscar.

Not Beth. I can't bring myself to look at him. He wasn't supposed to find out like this. How can I explain I suspected him of being a killer? That our trust was so worthless. But then our trust, our whole relationship, is built on the shifting sands of my lies. The falsehoods I've projected. Danny was right when he said I never wanted to talk. That I could never accept something was wrong. That I was too focused on everything looking perfect. Because that's how you fool them. I constantly pretended everything was okay, because I thought that was how you made it okay. But I was wrong. And now it's too late to talk. 'I can explain . . . ' But I can't. What can I say? Lily bubbles up inside me like the blood.

'Who are these men?' Danny points at Mickey's photo. Turns back to look at me. 'Why did you change the locks?'

Hellie is stepping towards the wall. I wish she would go, if I could just talk to Danny. But my mural of lies is pulling her in too. 'That's the man in the newspaper – the one who was pushed under the Tube. I recognise his photo,' she looks at me with something like concern, and something like fear.

And I slept with him. He slept with me. He raped me. And I never told my husband. I never told him about any of this. I never even told him my real name. And I see something awful click behind Danny's eyes. Some semblance of recognition. Has he always felt the darkness deep inside? 'Beth – who are these people?' Danny sounds desperate.

And I want to make it better. I want to make it all okay. I try to speak but I feel like a chastised schoolgirl. I feel like Mum has just screamed at me for embarrassing the family. Like I can't get anything right. There is no way to fix this. The sand has shifted, and we are all tumbling down. *Slut. Killer. Liar.*

Hellie looks scared, she keeps glancing from me to Danny. But he won't meet her eye. He's just staring at me as if he's seeing me for the first time. From upstairs I hear Oscar bouncing around in his room. He sounds so happy to be home. I can hear him talking to his teddies. And my heart aches, he doesn't deserve this nightmare. Oscar starts playing a YouTube video, and I have the vague sense I've forgotten something else? But then everything is displaced. Like someone's come into my house without my knowledge, and moved everything by a few centimetres. It looks the same, but everything is very, very wrong.

'I think we should get a doctor, or someone,' Hellie says quietly. She's not talking to me.

Danny turns back to the wall. 'I'm taking these down,' he sounds scared, angry. *Say something. Tell him.* 'My son lives here,' his words make my heart break.

'I'd like you not to do that, please, sir,' the assertive male voice startles us all.

In the doorway stands a solid looking twenty-something brown-haired man, and the older police detective who put her card in my wallet last night.

BETH

My first instinct is alarm. Hellie only pushed the door to; anyone could have come in? I glance up as a reassuring noise comes from Oscar's room. He's okay.

'The door was open,' the detective has her dark hair pulled back into a ponytail, her almond face coming into focus sharper than in my trauma blurred vision last night. The front of a grey blazer is open over her black T-shirt and matching grey trousers. *In charge. Knowing.* 'I'm Detective Inspector Shah, and we have a warrant to search these premises, sir,' she holds out a piece of paper at Danny.

'Now hang on – what is this?' says Danny.

Hellie looks truly terrified now.

'I'm Trainee Detective Constable Tatchell,' the younger man produces a warrant card from inside his black coat, showing a glimpse of red tie and white shirt underneath. His eyes widen as he takes in the wall of photos behind Danny and Hellie. 'We're going to need to get CSI down here.'

'Ms. Taylor,' DI Shah says, her gaze fixed on me. 'We met last night?' She sounds sympathetic. It's a trap. It's happening again.

I face Danny's bewilderment, but instead of forming words, my hands jerk. How can I explain? What can I say?

'What's happening?' repeats Danny, in his desperation.

'Sir, if I could perhaps ask you two to step outside, please,' DI Shah calmly stands aside for them to pass. Her casual grouping of Danny and Hellie together stings. I'm going to lose everything I care about.

'This is my house,' Danny seems to puff himself up. 'You can't just come in here and, and – don't you need a warrant or something?'

'We have one,' DI Shah says, and the tiny relaxation of her stance seems to accept Danny and Hellie won't move, that what will happen next is inevitable. I feel the floor rush out from under me.

The male cop has his notepad out, and is reading, speaking. 'We recovered a laptop from the scene last night, which we initially thought belonged to the murder victim.'

'Murder? Who's been murdered? What is this?' Danny's voice is high-pitched, indignant. *We are not the type of people to be involved in murder.* And I see in that moment he does it too. We enable each other, we create the perfect facade. Were we drawn to each other? Or did I train him?

'Oh my God,' Hellie whispers, her pale long fingers to her mouth.

DI Shah is still watching me, her dark eyes intent, unrelenting. *Can she see it? Can she see her?*

The guy, the trainee, clears his throat, continues from his notes. 'But when our tech team opened it up, they found the laptop was actually yours.'

Oh my God. That's what I forgot. My laptop. I left it at Rob's office. *Blood bubbling up. The sound Rob made before he died.* I reach for the sofa arm to tether myself. *My laptop.*

'And they found some pretty interesting search history,' the male cop adds.

My research. It's like Lily and Beth have broken apart and are fighting inside me: they've pushed me out of my body. I'm watching all this happen and I can't stop it.

'And when we ran your fingerprints through our database, imagine our surprise when they pinged against another name?' The guy can't hide the delight in his voice.

I try to speak, to stop them, I shake my head: *no. Please don't.* DI Shah's head sharply tips, like a predator sensing prey. She mirrors my look to Danny. *She knows he doesn't know. She's watching.*

'You haven't always been known as Beth Taylor, have you? You used to go by Lily Burnell,' the pages rustle in the cop's hand.

'What?' Danny says.

The male cop gives a half a smile, an ugly thing. 'When we worked out you changed it after you were arrested and questioned in connection with a serious accident that befell a woman who was romantically linked to your boyfriend at the time, things started to fall into place.'

No, it wasn't like that. I can explain. But the words won't come.

'You've made a mistake! Tell them they've made a mistake!' Danny looks at me pleadingly.

I'm losing him and there's nothing I can do. Nothing I can say. It's happening again. *I'm so sorry.*

Hellie's face quivers, she puts a hand on Danny's arm.

DI Shah's voice is practised, placating; the only option. 'You may be more comfortable having this conversation at the station?'

The shouts of the prisoners. The smell of urine, vomit, bleach. The sound of the metal door clanging shut. I screw my eyes shut against the memories. 'No, please . . .'

The male cop is eager to push on. 'You've spent hours and hours searching for, some might say tracking, a number of men over the last few months. Men who had links to Lily Burnell,' he reads again: *my own damning list*. 'Michael Armsmith, Kareem Farah, Phillip Brown, Wade Ellison, Tobias Weinstrasse. And now like Robert Trenchard yesterday, all those men are dead.'

It feels like a hand has clamped round my windpipe. *You've got it wrong.*

Hellie gasps. DI Shah's voice is steady, almost neutral: 'In the transcript of the 999 call you made yesterday, you referred to Mr Trenchard as "*my* poor Rob". Which is odd, because when I spoke to you, and when I checked with my officers, no one can remember you calling him anything but your boss?'

I hear Danny's breath quicken. I can't look at him.

The male cop goes in for the kill. 'I took a look at your movements over the last few weeks. And do you know what I found? You contacted Phillip Brown's office the night before he was killed. Our Brighton colleagues had all his messages on file, and there is one from a woman claiming to have worked with him in WHSmith in Sevenoaks – which it turns out Lily Burnell did. Saying: "It's a matter of life and death". Now that sounds like a threat to me?'

'What are you saying?' Danny sounds like he's far away.

The male cop ignores him, his shoulders pulse with pent up excitement. 'And Wade Ellison, the man who was pushed under the Tube at Chancery Lane?'

A small noise escapes from Hellie. Danny looks dumbfounded.

'That investigation team have been trying to trace the mystery woman who was seen having coffee with him minutes before he was pushed to his death – you may have seen the television appeals? And do you know what? Here is a description of her: a white, redhead female, thirties or forties, with a distinctive orange coat – I couldn't help but notice that in your hall you have an orange coat hanging up. And don't you think that sounds like you? Because I do. I think it sounds exactly like you.'

I shake my head, no, they've got it all wrong.

DI Shah speaks, her tone a false flag of neutrality. 'Tobias Weinstrasse requested your calls and emails be blocked thirty-one hours before his death. Before he too was pushed to his death in front of a train. Why do you think he did that? Our German counterparts are keen to talk to you about that.'

My nails sink into the sofa. Their words, faces, looks, spin in front of me. *Killer. Liar. I didn't. I couldn't . . . They can't think.* 'No,' I whisper.

DI Shah steps towards me, her voice hardening. 'On Friday fifteenth of March you ordered an 8-inch kitchen knife – which was recovered at the scene of Robert Trenchard's murder. And we believe is similar to the one used in the attack.'

'Beth?' Danny's voice sounds desperate.

The constable jumps in again. 'That's Robert Trenchard's name up on your wall there – and that paper looks faded, like it's been up a while? Like he was always part of the plan, yeah?'

'No,' I shake my head. Try to shake off the words.

DI Shah pulls her own small notepad from her jacket pocket, flips through. 'The day you ordered the knife, and the day after, you spent a lot of time online researching – and I quote: "How to disarm someone who is stronger than you. How to overpower someone who is stronger *than you*." And "How to incapacitate someone who is stronger than you".'

No. No. No.

The DI shifts her stance as she closes her notebook. 'The time is 10:03 a.m. Beth Taylor, you are under arrest on suspicion of the murder of Michael Armsmith, Kareem Farah, Phillip Brown, Wade Ellison, Tobias Weinstrasse, and Robert Trenchard.'

My legs give way, and I stagger sideways into the sofa arm.

'You do not have to say anything, but it may harm your defence if you do not mention when questioned something which you later rely on in court. Anything you do say may be given in evidence. Do you have anything on you that may hurt me or my colleagues?'

I didn't . . . I couldn't . . . I shake my head. Danny's face is white with shock. Hellie is gripping his arm. I try to tell him I didn't do this. *I'm not Lily. I'm not a monster.* But nothing comes out. *Slut. Killer. Liar.*

'Ms. Taylor, or Lily, if you prefer?' The male cop puts a calloused hand round my elbow, forcing me to my feet. 'You need to come with us now.'

BETH

Instinct makes me try the back door as the male cop walks round to the driver's side. Locked. They wouldn't trust criminals not to just open the door and get out, would they? Criminal. That's what they think I am. A serial killer. It's a small mercy they didn't cuff me. I stare at my hands. This is really happening. I can see DI Shah talking to Danny through our open doorway, she has her own car keys in her hand, ready to follow us. To charge me for multiple murder. Danny looks ashen. I've never really appreciated what that word means, but I see it now. It's like all the colour has filtered out of him. His familiar features brushed from clumps of grey dust. My fingers reflexively try the handle again. It's like child locks. *Oh Oscar*. I can hear my breath and heartbeat loud, panicked, almost drowning out the crackle of the radio in the front of the car. They think I did this. If only I'd gone to the police earlier. But no, that's how I ended up here. I gave them my name. I led them to me. And all the stuff I looked at online, all the things I bought – the weapons – it makes it look worse. It makes it look like I did this. A flash of panic in Rob's eyes. His grasping hand, blood burbling out of his mouth. A perfect bubble of blood. Before it burst.

I pinch my thigh, the skin sore under my jeans. Is there – could there be any way they are right? Did I do this? Hellie suggested I needed a doctor. Has something happened to my mind, my sanity, could I have done all this and not known? A thought chills me: have I been sending myself the notes? Lily staking her claim on the life she got denied. They are in my own handwriting after all. No. That's not what's happening. I'm not mad. I haven't done this. Someone has done this to me. Was it all a trap? Did he – Matt's face flashes through my mind – do this to me? Was this always his plan? Bile hikes up my throat.

The front door opens and the cop slides in, the car rocking slightly as he lowers into his seat. The vibrations from the starting engine plucking at each of my taut nerves.

'I didn't do it!' I need him to understand. 'Someone is framing me!'

'That's what they all say.' He doesn't turn, merely signals and turns the car to drive away. To take me to prison. Then there's a noise from our house.

The front door smashes against the outside wall, and Oscar comes running out in his onesie and bare feet. 'Mum!' He screams. He must have heard. Seen. A sob grabs my throat.

'My baby!' I twist to look back, hands against the window as if I might touch him. His tearstained uncomprehending face breaks my heart.

'Oscar – no!' Danny appears just behind him. The DI's alarmed face. And my heart stops. No! All noise falls away. I watch as in slow motion Danny makes a grab for Oscar. But our boy is fast, he dodges between the bins. Danny careers into them, knocking them flying. The DI right behind him. Her face, grim, seeing what's going to happen before it does.

'Oscar!' I scream. Hellie is at the door running for him, her arm outstretched. But she's too late. Oscar, crying, scared, weaves left and right, dashing straight into the road in front of us.

'Stop!'

There's a scream of brakes, the car yanks hard left. My face smashes into the back of the passenger seat.

'Shit!' says the cop.

My baby! I yank on the locked back door. Smash my hand against the window.

Hellie is screaming. Danny's face is frozen in horror. The DI has a restraining hand on his shoulder, holding him back. The male cop is out of the car, leaving the door, slipping, running to . . .

Oh my God. Oh my God. My baby. My darling baby.

Oscar is standing stock still, tears pouring down his little face, the bumper of the car pressed up against his onesie. His chest heaving up and down.

'Baby? My love! Are you okay? Is he okay?' I slam my palm against the headrest in front.

'Alright there, son,' the cop is saying. 'Did I hurt you?'

Hellie and Danny are upon him in seconds, scooping him up, turning him, checking him, covering him in hugs and kisses. He's okay. He's okay. Thank God, he's okay. It's a miracle. If the cop hadn't braked. If he hadn't swerved. Tears are streaming down my face. The DI is murmuring, her notepad out.

If I hadn't been arrested this would never have happened. This is my fault. No, this is his fault. Anger rips up through me. He did this. He put me in this position. He put Oscar in danger. Nothing can happen to him. Nothing can happen to Danny. I won't allow it. And suddenly I know what I have to do. It's all so clear. Whoever is doing this wants me. That's what going to make this stop. Danny is crying, hugging Oscar to him and rocking. The cop has his hand on his little shoulder. I know what I need to do to keep the people I love safe. I have to give *him* what he wants.

I stand, as much as the car ceiling allows. One foot on the floor, and stretch forward through the gap in the front two seats as far as I can. I reckon I have seconds if this is going to work. All eyes are on my little boy. My heart calls to him, I want to go to him. But I can't. I have to stop anything else bad happening. If they take me away no one will be standing in the killer's way. My son and my husband would be unprotected. Pulling myself over with my two hands, I half climb, half fall into the front seats, the handbrake jabs into my leg, my bruised face scrapes down the fabric of the chair. I have to go. I don't turn, I push myself forward, out the open door. My back leg gets caught in the footwell, and I crash down onto one knee. My palms sharp with grit from the road.

I can hear Oscar sobbing, the cop still talking to him. 'Well you gave me quite a fright there, son, I can tell you.'

'He's a good boy,' Danny says. Over and over. Like it might be in dispute. Like near misses only happen to naughty children. It's the shock, I recognise that. I've been through it multiple times over the last few weeks, so much that my body knows what to do with the flood of adrenaline now. I can marshal it. Freeze, fight or flight. Lily chose wrong in the past. I won't do that now. I push up off the ground and sprint hard.

I'm across the road before I hear the shout behind me. 'Oi!' yells the cop. 'No!' A grunt. The pound of steps. 'This is zero-three-four-tango – India, in pursuit of suspect. Suspect heading down . . . ' He's barking instructions into his radio. Bringing in reinforcements.

The words fade as I dodge down the side alley of the house opposite. It's a mirror of ours. One foot onto their green recycling box, two on the top of their bin – thank God it's landfill waste day. Two hands on their back fence. And I vault. The evergreen laurel bush beneath a burst of sharp jabs and fragrant sap as I snap branches in my fall. I roll off the bush, pulling at my snagged jumper. *Get up. Keep running.*

If there's anyone in the house in front of me they're not visible. The double glass doors into the kitchen, and two windows above are empty of faces. I cross the garden in seconds, and take the side gate into the alley that runs between this house and the next. And then I'm out onto the main road. With each pounding stride I hear the words in those texts over and over: *whore, whore, whore*. There's no notes now. No pretence. He has my number. And he's coming for me. Or I'm coming for him. The road opens up into a dual carriageway; shops, bridges, alleys in all directions. I have to get away. I see a bus at the stop opposite. I zigzag across the lanes. Angry beeps from black cabs. Squeals of brakes from cars. Shouts. Gestures at windows. *Keep going*. I reach the bus just as the doors are closing.

'Please! Wait!' I hammer on the glass.

And thank God for a kind driver. The bus exhales as he brakes, and opens the doors.

'Thank you!' I pant, stoop so I can see past the driver. Watching the various alleyways, waiting. Any second now the police will appear. We need to go. I tap my Oyster card. We need to go now. The doors close. The bus lurches like my stomach. I drop into the nearest seat and sink down low. I daren't look over the edge to see if they're there. If I can just get away unseen, they won't necessarily know which way I've gone. I think of my Oyster card. How quickly can they track that? I need just a little time. They would've taken everything off me at the station, I know from before. The bus turns right. Just enough time. I take out my phone. Thank god I still have it. The messages are still flooding in. Still the same unknown number. It must be a pay-as-you-go. *A burner phone.* I remember this is what stalkers use from my earlier research. I almost laugh. My research? I was only playing at investigating, far out of my depth. I wasn't tracking this man down; I was playing into his hands. The DI said all the evidence pointed to me. The more I struggled, the tighter the web wound round me. *Slut. Killer. Liar.* The messages change. A near hysterical laugh escapes me like helium from a balloon valve. A little old lady in a green mac turns to look at me. After all this, I finally have something the police would take seriously. In my palm the phone flashes like a warning light as a stream of new messages preview on my screen. They all say the same thing.

I'm going to kill you.

BETH

The police believe I did this. Danny's face as he stared at me. Oscar crying out my name. Everything has been obliterated. Ripped into pieces like my words from my journal. Maybe it always had to end like this. A wiping out of everyone, of everything. The final note from last night is still in my pocket, the words still accusatory. *Liar. Liar. Liar.* All the lies I've told, the names omitted. It's like he was trying to make me face the truth in the most brutal way. Those names on the wall, those faces, that's who I am.

But as I stared at the mess of it all on that wall, saw it through other's eyes, as my world crumbled, something clicked into place. In Rob's dying moments he reached for papers in his office. He was trying to tell me who did this.

The tube whines as it turns another corner: I take my phone off airplane mode. Quick. I've kept moving, but I don't want the police to find me before I do this. One bar of signal. It's the only choice left. The only way to protect my baby, to protect my Danny. I think again of his face. The confusion, the horror, and then something so close to despair it can only be love. I have to make this stop.

I send the first message. Then I type the next. My finger hovering over it. Am I really going to do this? I think of Rob stretching towards the papers on his office floor. His blood all over me. Too many people have died. The lies stop now. It's not Danny – he has an alibi. It's not Rob, God rest his soul. And now I know it's not Zayn. Among those work papers was a brochure for Unity. Rob died trying to tell me it was Matt.

That intense stare. The flowers. The appearing at the office. This all started after I started work with Unity. He's a psycho. He must have come for Rob. An ambush. A tear falls onto my phone screen. No one else can get hurt. No one else can die. I press send:

I will be at Unity warehouse.

It was always going to come to this. Just me and him.

BETH

The clouds have drawn down, darkening the sky as I arrive at the warehouse. As if a lid is pressing firmly down on the day. The very world itself closing in. The car park is as eerily empty as it was the first time I came here. Is this where he planned it all from? Is this where everything unfolded? Damp gravel squelches under my feet, my breath is visible in little gasps of mist. I want to run. There have been no more messages from the unknown number. Is he on his way, or is he here already? I force my feet on. I'm doing this for Mickey, Kareem, Phil, Wade, Tobi, Rob, for everyone who shouldn't have died. For Danny and Oscar. For me. For answers.

The front door's locked, and I can't see any lights on in the office. I walk round the side of the building, to the back, where they unload the deliveries. My phone is gripped in my hand. I know from my research – the very research that convinced the police I'm guilty – that phones make good weapons. Especially if you bring one down hard on someone's nose. And I've nothing else. I can't stroll into a shop and buy something lethal when I'm wanted by the police. I've no keys to slide between my fingers. No knife. I think of it clanging to the ground as I reached the office yesterday. *The bubble of blood.*

I edge along the building as the first spots of rain fall, sharp and cold like flecks of ice. The back door, which rolls across to let trucks drive in, is ajar. Has he left it for me? I check behind me once more, grip my phone tighter, make sure there is as much edge protruding as possible. *Ready.* I steal in.

It's dark inside and my eyes struggle to adjust to the gloom. My breath catches as I make out a shape. But no. It's a doll, hanging on a hook. I step towards her. There are more behind her. Their hair glossy and long. The closest one to me swings gently round so her serviceable holes are all screaming at me. Her round glassy eyes dead, watch me in their reflection. Just swinging gently. Swinging? None of the others are moving – someone must have knocked her.

In the moment the thought comes, so does the movement. Behind me. I throw my arm up to bring my elbow down like the YouTube video advised. But it meets solid muscle, my phone flung from my hand smashes down onto the ground. I scream. A hand grabs me, turns, holds. And there's a knife.

'Shut up,' says a voice.

I feel the blade press against my chin. The hot bulk of solid flesh immovable behind me. Feel myself freeze.

It's the wrong voice.

He starts to walk, and I'm forced to do the same in front of him. His knees bucking into the back of mine, the knife pressing into my flesh. *It's the wrong voice. It's not Matt.* My mind scrabbles to catch up. A sharp sting on my chin as the edge breaks the skin. I feel liquid, blood, run down my neck. I'm shaking now, my teeth chattering against themselves.

'Keep moving,' he barks.

But I know it. I know that voice. How? No? This is all wrong. This can't be happening.

And we're alongside the hanging dolls now. Their naked silicon flesh shining in the gloom. For a second I think one has been taken down, is sat, half-falling, unnatural against the far wall. But then I see the clothes, jeans, T-shirt, the hands bound tight behind his back with tape. The same metallic duct tape that's round his ankles, forcing him onto his knees, tipped forward, shoulder against the wall. The dull glint of the tape obscuring his mouth and eyes. It's Matt. His hair is stuck, wet to his head. Blood. Is he alive? He's innocent – it's not him. I did this. I brought this on him. Another innocent on the altar of my lies. My feet catch at the floor, as if they alone don't want to keep moving. But my body can feel the knife. Where did my phone go? If I shout will I be heard? *The car park was empty. The road deserted. There's no one here. No one to help.*

'Turn around,' he says.

I don't want to. I don't want to see.

'Turn!' He jabs the tip of the blade into my back.

Tears start. I don't want to cry. I don't.

I turn. It is him. 'I don't understand.'

He reaches up and pulls down one of the metal hooks that hang from the ceiling.

He's going to hang me like one of the dolls. 'No!' I scream. *Run.*

His hand smashes into my jaw. Goes through it. Through me. No air. The floor goes from under my feet.

I slam into the ground. Grit and concrete puncture my skin. Matt's unnaturally bent body swims in and out of focus. I'm going to die. *Oh Oscar. My darling Oscar, I'm sorry. Danny, my love.*

He yanks a G-string from a nearby doll, sending the air above into a frenzy of legs and arms. Wraps it round the hook. Grabs my shoulder. The pain makes everything blur. My hands are yanked up, wrists bound, and then hooked above. He pulls the chain, so my toes skate the floor. I feel the tissue in my shoulder rip, as if it's unzipping round the triangular scapula. My scream comes out in a gasp. Swinging. The black dots slow. He's standing there. Standing there smiling.

'With the other cumbuckets, where you belong. This was a good choice to meet here. Freaky place,' he laughs.

'Why?' I spit the words with gristle and blood. 'Why are you doing this, Nate?'

BETH

He drags a chair over from the side, the metal legs shrieking against the floor. I try to twist to see my phone, but pain sears up my body, presses down on my ribs from above so I can't breathe. Nate. Zayn's flatmate, Nate. How? Why? It's not supposed to be him?

'Let's talk,' he says, stopping the chair in front of me. 'That's what your little online display said, didn't it?'

'Why?' I repeat. My head spinning with pain, confusion.

He pinches and hikes the material of his jogging bottoms to sit. Leans forward, casual, rests his elbows on his knees, his hands loosely together. Broad in his black zip-up hoodie, he could be waiting for the bench press to come free at the gym, were it not for the wet knife on the ground next to him. 'You know you're the first to ask that,' he says. 'Though none of the others said much at all. Not much time for chit-chat if you're pushed onto a tube track,' he smiles as if he's just delivered a joke, not confessed to murder.

'You pushed Wade?' The floor skitters under my feet. My eyes have adjusted to the gloom in the edges of the warehouse. Along from the crumpled body of Matt is Nate's recognisable holdall. Has he been carrying round a knife, duct tape, all this time? Is that the knife that killed Rob?

'Easy to find him and *Tobias*,' Nate makes quotation marks in the air. 'Idiot posh boy names: typical Chads peacocking all over the internet.'

Chads? Manosphere slang for alpha males who get all the girls. I think about Tobi's Instagram account full of him with bikini clad women – is that what this is? Jealousy? 'You killed Tobi, in Berlin?' I can't make the pieces fit in my head.

Nate shrugs. 'Thought you might have seen me do the Holborn one – brought my flight forward after you came to the Soy Boy's place,' he grimaces. He means Zayn. He sounds like an angry teen, not a grown man.

'Don't call him that. He was nice to you – we were nice to you. What have you done?' My mind is whirling through the last few weeks, seeing every horror from a fresh angle.

'The accountant was the only one that posed anything close to a challenge. Got him through a regional WHSmith manager in the end – little phishing scam got me his National Insurance number. After that it was easy to trace him.' He looks at me as if I should be impressed.

'I don't understand – why did you do this?' Since he's been talking, Nate has been focused on me. Is Matt still alive behind him? Could he get help if I distract Nate?

Irritation darkens Nate's face. 'Yeah, well you really did a number on me, Lily.'

Ice runs through my veins. *Lily*. He knows? Shock obviously shows on my face.

Nate smiles that ugly dead-eyed smile again. 'I would've thought someone with your transformation skills would recognise a fellow master?' I blink, trying to find the meaning in his words. Is this because of what Lily did? Is Nate linked to Anna? No, that doesn't fit. 'Mickey didn't recognise me either,' Nate says, seeming to read my thoughts. 'Tried to give me his wallet, actually landed a punch. I had to wear long sleeves for a week after.' Nate twists his face into a tragedy mask. *"Please, no. P-p . . . please help me".*' Then laughs.

The tears sting as they run over the cut on my neck. It was Nate on the CCTV. Tall, broad shouldered, dark. Nate who took my journal. Nate who sent the notes. Nate who traced every man I'd ever slept with, and then killed them all. 'Mickey was a good guy. He was my . . . ' Grotesque images violate my brain.

'Your first love,' Nate sneers. 'You think he might have said your name at the end?'

'He came to see me. That day. We . . . ' We had something. I was someone to him. And it cost him his life.

Nate laughs. The sound echoing round the space, slapping back against me. Matt still hasn't moved. 'It was me who came to see you. I just gave your fat neighbour his name.'

Everything I thought is wrong. 'Why did you do this?'

His tone drops, he stares at me with cold malevolent eyes. 'Because you fooled me.'

'Because of Lily?' I say. I had no choice. 'I had to get rid of her. Beth was new, a chance to start over.' The confession pours out of me. I should have said this to Danny. I should have shown him my true self, trusted that he would still want me, still love me. Instead, I built lie upon lie: I never gave us a chance. Pain shoots up my back, black dots swarm across my vision. I'm going to die here and I'll never get to tell Danny I'm sorry.

Nate stands, the chair squeaks, I flinch. He starts to pace back and forth, hunching in on himself. The pressure on my shoulder as I twist to keep him in sight makes me feel sick. I try to breathe deep.

Then he's in my face. I can smell metal on his breath. 'I believed you,' he says, spittle hitting my cheek. I blink and the room blurs. No, don't pass out . . .

'I never lied to you – I don't know you!' The force of my words makes the hook above me creak, the fabric binding my wrists cuts deeper into my flesh.

Nate's face is so close to mine I can see the pores round his nose. 'Do you remember the first time we met?'

'What?' I try to clear my head. 'At Zayn's. After you'd moved in.'

He laughs softly, turns away. 'Oh no, we'd met many times before that,' he bends down and picks up the knife. *He's going to kill me.* I try to twist my hands free but it only sears pain down my side. Nate is still facing away, his voice calm, turning the knife over in his hand. 'We first met the night my father died. Twenty-three years ago. This week. It's the anniversary,' he gives a sad smile.

He's insane. This is some kind of fixation.

'I was out with Jessica, and I saw you. Saw you first, then got to speak to you.'

My mind catches on the words. Tries to make sense of them. 'Jessica? From school?'

'Yes,' he says dismissively. 'When you were Lily, and I was Jonny.

'Jonny?'

He indicates his body. 'Before I maxed up, switched my game. Which I did for you!' he says accusatorily.

He's lanky Jonny, with the long dyed black hair and glasses, that Jessica dated? The cool guy standing in the background of the photo taken by the swings? And then I catch it, around the eyes, the nose. He's worked out, got contacts, cut his hair, but it's him. Jonny. How did I never see it before? Just like me he reinvented himself. But Nate's an attractive successful man – I thought he was gay? 'I don't understand?'

Nate is pacing again, the knife bouncing in his loose grip, as he walks in an agitated circle. I can no longer tell if he's talking to me or himself. 'I was so naive with Jessica. She just used me for what she could get – my car, my money, my ID.'

This is madness, he's unwell. And from somewhere I know I need to keep him talking. Keep him from making his next move. My breathing sounds more laboured, my head's so heavy. *Try.* 'Tell me what she did?'

'She was actually proud she got you to defile yourself with that tattoo,' he points the knife at me. Saliva pools in my mouth.

Only those with angel wings can fly. The note, the threat. Someone else did know about my tattoo. But I only met Jonny a handful of times. The floor quivers, I can hear my heart beat loud in my ears. My mind tries to reason out the logic: there must be a mistake. But my body knows there's a threat. *Don't startle the predator. Fawn. Smile. Be nice.* I'm an expert at this; Beth is an entire construct of people-pleasing. I work in PR. And now I'm selling it for my life. I will myself to make a comforting noise.

Nate continues: 'You can't trust women because they lie, and they cheat, and they fuck anything that walks. You have to find a pure one, that's what my father told me. And there you were: like a gift direct from him. Jessica thought she was belittling you, saying you wouldn't sleep with Mickey. That you were uptight. But I saw the truth. You were good. You were pure. You told me that night how much you loved him, how he was the perfect man, and I saw your perfection reflected back. The perfect couple. I was so jealous. So consumed with jealousy that he'd found you first. But I knew that you two would be together forever. I thought you would be together forever. And I let you go. I got rid of Jessica shortly afterwards, washed away that stain.'

The words swim and swing in front of me. *Got rid of Jessica? The car crash I read about. She died. There was another passenger – a twenty-two-year-old male.* 'You were in the car? When she crashed?'

'No, I crashed it. Undid her seatbelt just before we hit the tree,' he waves his hand dismissively again. The knife shimmering in the air.

This can't be happening. This doesn't make any sense. Jessica. Jonny. Twenty-three years ago.

'I mourned you,' Nate says solemnly. 'But you were taken. Gone. You would marry Mickey and that was clearly how it was meant to be. I met Isla at work, and I found hope again. Until she stopped me looking at her phone. Started hiding things from me. They all reveal themselves at the end. Open their legs and show themselves. Everyone, except you,' he grabs my chin, pulls me angrily towards him.

My body screams. I scream. Everything burns.

'When I went looking for you and realised Lily had been disappeared. When I saw what they'd done to you, I actually felt sorry for you. Court records, the investigation, it was easy to find that monster Iain – he wasn't drummed out of his own life.'

Iain's name feels like it's been torn from a part of me. Nate's – Jonny's – face swims in and out of focus, twisting ugly with sneers.

'I was angry at him for denying you me. I expunged him from your record – that's what showed me the way.'

I try to hold on to the meaning of the words – Nate killed Iain? When? Nate's voice shifts again, his fingers rough on my chin, holding my head up, making me see. Behind him swathes of hair from the dolls waft between vines and snakes in my vision. How long have I been here? His words come back into focus.

'. . . Your mother's name was the same on the land registry – then it was just a matter of time. You're a good girl, wholesome,' he makes the words sound angry, dirty. 'I knew you'd come home eventually.'

I try to make my tongue move, my lips, I'm shaking. What he's saying is ripping through my life – everything I thought was backwards. Wrong.

'There you were – Beth Taylor,' he says. 'Married with a kid. That man took what should have been mine. I mourned the loss, but I couldn't look away. I kept an eye on you. One of the rare good ones.'

Snapshot memories flood my mind – the feeling of someone watching. A turned head in a packed bar. The sense of someone too close behind me on the Tube at rush hour. A shiver in the darkness, as I walked home from the station in the cold grey gloom of winter. My keys between my fingers, my phone in my hand, crossing the street to get away. I thought they were strangers, a random dodgy man, or tricks of my imagination. For years. It's just part of life as a woman. I was being paranoid. Except I wasn't – he was always there. He lives with

Zayn. I have slept under the same roof. He could have hurt me anytime he wanted.

'I forgave you,' Nate's anger drags me back to the present. Matt's body crumpled against the wall, the shiny perfect eyes of the dolls seeing who we really are. 'Even when I read that filth you'd written.'

My journal. It wasn't the start of this; this is so much darker, buried, festering for years. *I didn't even remember Jonny till I saw that photo shared on Mickey's screen.* 'I don't remember you,' the words twist out of me.

Nate half laughs, an ugly thing. 'I did all this for you, for innocent pure Lily. I saw I could eradicate these stains from your record like that monster who drove you from your life. Reset your body count. Give you the life you should have had. Make you that unspoiled gift my father gave to me all those years ago.'

'No,' I try to shake my head. I don't want this. Mickey, Kareem, Phil, Wade, Tobi, Iain, Rob, no matter what they did, no matter how they treated me, no matter how I treated them, I didn't want this.

Nate's grip tightens on my neck. Blood pulses out. How much have I lost? 'Look at me,' he shakes my head. 'Your marriage, your family, your life was perfect: you said so. You had everything I wanted, and I was happy for you.' My protestations to Zayn. My Instagram posts. The anniversary party. The perfect couple. I needed it to be true to save me from Lily. My life is a lie.

'No, no,' I try to shake him off. The floor swims up, away. I don't want this.

'No, because all the time you were fucking your boss,' he is pure rage. His teeth clenched, like an animal about to attack. He squeezes hold of my chin, hard, harder. Black dots swarm.

It's not true. I wasn't. None of this is true. 'You don't know me.'

'No,' he spits. His breath on my face. 'I see you clearly. You're a deceitful whore. A lying slut.'

And I know it then: he's going to kill me. I'm never getting away.

And I remember the videos. The articles. What to do if you're being stalked. What to do if someone attacks you. And I think of Mickey's smiling blue eyes. Kareem taking my hand. Phil's long fingers. Tobi's lashes. Iain's sad smile. Rob's laugh. And Danny, my beautiful, kind, caring Danny who I pushed away through fear. And our Oscar. Our love made our perfect smiling child. I just wanted to be the best I could. The best me for everyone I cared about.

I pull down on the hook, hear my shoulders rip. And bring my knees up hard. My head down fast. I feel my knee connect with his groin. The ooft firing out of him, as my second knee hits his nose, as my forearms force him down.

He staggers back howling, grabbing his balls. 'You fucking bitch!' He half falls.

'Help!' I scream. 'Help!' And I remember what they say to do if you're attacked. 'Fire! Fire! Fire!'

Behind us Matt stirs – I scream louder.

Nate scrabbles for the knife, his eyes wild. 'You fucking bitch!' The blade flashes in the air, swings down. I close my eyes.

I'm so sorry, Oscar. Mummy is so, so sorry.

BETH - TEN WEEKS LATER

'I do ask, where possible, that both partners are honest. About what has happened, about their actions, and how they feel. Recovery, especially after a betrayal, is always harder if lies are told early on.' The marriage counsellor, Sue, a padded woman of fifty with no-nonsense glasses, smiles at us both.

I clear my throat. 'Our circumstances are quite unique.'

'I've worked with a wide range of couples and issues – those who are married, living separately, bi and pansexual, polyamorous. Don't worry, I've heard most of it before,' she gives a little chuckle.

'An obsessive stalker from Beth's past tracked down and killed seven of her ex-boyfriends. Then he tried to kill her.' Danny reaches across from his armchair to take my hand. The left, as my right is still in a sling. He gives me a little smile.

Sue pauses, looks at me. Is that recognition? It's been in all the news. *Crazed Serial Killer Incel Murders Woman's Ex-Lovers One by One*. Nate had released a pre-recorded 'manifesto' on multiple social media platforms at the time he attacked me. In it, he made confused references to incel culture – aligning his actions to the sexist belief system in which he was an involuntarily celibate man, denied sexual and relationship access to the women he believed he was entitled to. I girded myself to watch it, fearing it would make me feel more sadness and guilt for those he killed. But his rants about physically attractive 'Chad' males, and nonsense about women being 'femoids' felt closer to someone talking about Unity's AI sex dolls than real people. I would have discounted him as a conspiracy theorist, were it not for his lionisation of those responsible for misogynistic terror attacks in 2014 and 2018. And knowing the terrible things he's done.

After the manifesto aired, it didn't take journalists long to uncover Lily's story, but it's been different this time. Anna taught me it's better to face adversity head on; ignoring or hiding things never works. And I wrote to each of the families of the men Nate killed, and to Jessica's parents. I can't undo or explain why Nate did what he did, but I can express my sorrow and share my memories of their loved ones.

We've been staying in an Airbnb booked in Zayn's name to avoid the press. Zayn confessed he always knew why I'd ditched Lily, and he never really cared. 'It's not like your core values were different, babe. But it was your choice,' he'd shrugged over McDonalds' milkshakes he'd smuggled into my hospital room. It was heartbreaking to see Zayn realise Nate had engineered becoming his flatmate to keep tabs on me. Forensics found spyware he'd installed on Zayn's laptop and phone. Nate recorded all the conversations we'd ever had. He had my journal, other items of mine. A coat, a bag I thought had been stolen, a hairbrush, a scarf I thought I'd lost. And, most chillingly, a lock of my hair. He must have clipped it off the bottom of my ponytail, and I never noticed.

Zayn and I have cried in each other's arms more than once as our comprehension of Nate's deception came to light. The police located two properties belonging to him. One from proceeds of Nate's father's house, and the other from Nate's genuine software skills at writing popular security programmes. Hidden at one was the car that had struck Kareem on his bike.

But Zayn's not responsible for what Nate did, and I could never think he was. I keep telling him that. And he keeps telling me the same thing back.

For years I'd feared Lily and the lies I told would be discovered, it became my normal to be in survival mode. I was so hyperalert to being seen, I didn't see someone else lying to me and everyone else around us. Deep down I know my reaction to the smears against me after Anna's accident, wiping out Lily's existence, was driven by a desperate desire not to be abandoned again. But when I was actually outed, the horror of everything Nate did eclipsed everything else. It took me losing everything to realise the normal I'd made as Beth wasn't ever safe. I've started to process it with my own counsellor, vocalising that what Nate did was not my fault. Just as he'd warped our first encounter in the grief of his father's death, twenty years ago, I too had tried to reinvent myself after a trauma. The psychologists call it splitting; it's a defence mechanism where you see situations, yourself, or others, in all or nothing terms. In order to survive what happened with Anna, I saw Lily as all bad in my mind and built my external reality around that. By default, Beth had to be all good. Nate projected his own sense of reality onto me, but I was just a vessel. No different than Unity's sex dolls being a fantasy that vaguely resembles a real human woman. (I have written to Matt at Unity briefly too. I'm relieved he's fine, with no long-term injuries from where he was attacked, but after being in that warehouse I cannot face those dolls ever again).

I squeeze Danny's hand, and he strokes my palm with his thumb. When it came down to it, he didn't care about Lily at all. He only cared that I hadn't trusted him with the truth about myself and my past. I feared he might be a killer, and, in those hours after he saw my wall, he feared I might be a killer too. We both betrayed each other, but we both came so close to violently losing the other, we couldn't bear the pain. We love each other more than anything. Oscar, Danny and me: our family.

'We have a lot we need to work through,' I say, meeting Sue's gaze with a small smile. 'But we want to try.'

'Both of us,' says Danny, tears at the edge of his voice.

The Anniversary Party

If Sue recognises us, me, our story from the newspapers, she doesn't let it show. 'That is a good place to start from,' she says. She makes notes, her pen dancing over the page in a reassuringly rhythmic way. The sides of her mouth turn slightly down, and her eyebrows knit as she looks at us. Perhaps considering what we have been through. What it means about us that we are both here. Can we find the gold to meld our broken pottery pieces into something more beautiful than before? Permanent scars that enhance and glitter like kintsugi.

After DI Shah received my text telling her I was innocent and I was going after the real killer at Unity Sex Dolls, she and her response team raced to the warehouse. They arrived just as Nate – I still can't think of him as Jonny – swung the knife at me. That's the moment I always reach in my dreams. When I wake up crying in Danny's arms that they didn't reach me in time, that I'm sorry.

Nate has been charged with the murder of Mickey, Kareem, Phil, Wade, Tobi and Rob. The attempted murder of me. Of grievous bodily harm with intent to kill Matt. And, after I gave my evidence in the days of interviews that took place in the hospital, DI Shah is trying to find proof to connect him with Jessica and Iain's deaths too. It turns out Nate's old girlfriend, the one called Isla, had filed – and withdrawn – domestic abuse complaints against him. She's been a missing person for a number of years, and the police fear he may also have killed her. But he only wants to talk about what he thinks I deceived him into doing. How this was all part of the incel rebellion to overthrow the 'normies'. The Crown Prosecution Service are confident he'll plead guilty, so none of us will have to relive this in court.

The soft scratch of Sue's pen on her pad reminds me of my journal. Of working my emotions into the pages. How Nate tore them out and rearranged my life into how he wanted it to be. The true extent of his actions so extreme I know I didn't cause them. This wasn't my fault. Nate doesn't get to dictate who I am, just like Iain didn't, nor Wade, nor Rob, nor judgemental strangers, the press, my mum, nor even Danny and Oscar. For too long I gave my power to others while I tried to bend into what I thought they wanted, mistakenly believing it would save me from future pain. I thought it was selfless to be what my husband, my boss, my clients, what society wanted, but it was just a way of manipulating those around me. I was lying to everyone, but most of all myself.

Outside Sue's window a tumble of dusky pink roses offers their hearts up to the late May sun. London has been enjoying a heatwave, and soon we'll slide into June, the lengthening daylight hours obliterating the last of the cold dark shadows. Oscar will be outside running around in P.E. today. We have managed to keep the worst of this away from him, and he's been delighted his temporary bedroom has a flat screen TV. He will come out of this the most unscathed.

'Are you receiving trauma counselling?' Sue looks at me.

'Yes,' I reply, returning my eyes to the rose painted room. Though, it's nothing like the colour of the real thing. An imitation of perfection is always a failure. 'I intend to continue throughout the trial.' Until justice is served, and after, for me and my family.

Sue nods, satisfied. Makes a further note in her pad. 'And you, Danny, are you seeing anyone separately?'

'Yes. I have been for a while.' He gives me a sheepish look, though he already admitted this when I was in hospital. 'I told Beth I was working late.' The times my darkest doubts led me to suspect he was the killer, Danny was seeing a therapist to try and work out how to navigate what he'd done with Hellie, what he could do to reach me.

Together we have started to dig out the myriad spiny secrets we've stuck under our skin. I already feel lighter.

'Okay,' Sue's voice is comforting. 'So, if you are both happy, then we can proceed?'

Danny nods, his eyes glassy. I smile at him, blinking away the tears that have gathered in mine too. I no longer have any hesitations or doubts. Beth subsumed Lily, became one. Beth has loved and lost, and cried, and laughed. Beth is a mother, a partner, a friend, a fighter. Take me or leave me. I look directly at Sue. 'Yes,' I answer.

I am finally ready to be myself.

ACKNOWLEDGEMENTS

A book reaches publication with the help of many clever and insightful people. Thank you to my editor Cara Chimirri at Hodder, (and Jo Dickinson and Ruth Tross, for earlier incarnations). To copy editor Laura Gerrard, marketing Charlea Charlton, cover designer Aaron Munday, production Inayah Sheikh Thomas, and all the wider team at Hodder. Thank you to Guy Herbert at Marjacq Scripts Ltd, David H Headley and Elena Berry, and all at DHH Literary Agency Ltd. Thank you to my TV & Film agent Jonathan Kinnersley, Tia Armstrong and all at The Agency. And extra special thanks - with a cherry on top - for my supportive (and patient) literary agent Diana Beaumont at DHH Literary Agency Ltd.

A book is often woven from many moments of generously shared knowledge, research, professional and emotional support, and this book more so than any I've written before. From first word to publication, work on The Anniversary Party has spanned six particularly tumultuous years of my life. I am not the same person, nor the same writer, as I was when I started this story. Readers, friends, family, loved ones, both past and present, helped pick me up, keep me going, and got me to a final complete manuscript, in ways they may not even have comprehended. I cannot list just how much everyone I've encountered has supported me to this point, but please know I am, and always will be, grateful. Thank you.

To Mum and Dad, love you xx

Don't miss this gripping and twisty thriller from Angela Clarke.

Framed. Imprisoned. Pregnant.

Jenna thought she had the perfect life: a loving fiancé, a great job, a beautiful home. Then she finds her stepdaughter murdered; her partner missing.
And the police think she did it . . .
Locked up to await trial, surrounded by prisoners who'd hurt her if they knew what she's accused of, certain someone close to her has framed her,
Jenna knows what she needs to do:
**Clear her name. Save her baby. Find the killer.
But can she do it in time?**

RAISING READERS
Books Build Bright Futures

Dear Reader,

We'd love your attention for one more page to tell you about the crisis in children's reading, and what we can all do.

Studies have shown that reading for fun is the **single biggest predictor of a child's future life chances** – more than family circumstance, parents' educational background or income. It improves academic results, mental health, wealth, communication skills, ambition and happiness.[1]

The number of children reading for fun is in rapid decline. Young people have a lot of competition for their time. In 2024, 1 in 10 children and young people in the UK aged 5 to 18 did not own a single book at home.[2]

Hachette works extensively with schools, libraries and literacy charities, but here are some ways we can all raise more readers:

- Reading to children for just 10 minutes a day makes a difference
- Don't give up if children aren't regular readers – there will be books for them!
- Visit bookshops and libraries to get recommendations
- Encourage them to listen to audiobooks
- Support school libraries
- Give books as gifts

There's a lot more information about how to encourage children to read on our website: **www.RaisingReaders.co.uk**

Thank you for reading.

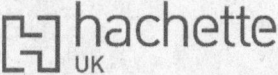

---

[1] OECD, '21st-Century Readers: Developing Literacy Skills in a Digital World', 2021, https://www.oecd.org/en/publications/21st-century-readers_a83d84cb-en.html

[2] National Literacy Trust, 'Book Ownership in 2024', November 2024, https://literacytrust.org.uk/research-services/research-reports/book-ownership-in-2024